The Omnipotent Child

The Omnipotent Child

How to Mold, Strengthen and Perfect the Developing Child

Om-nip-o-tent...
unlimited in power,
ability, or authority.

THOMAS P. MILLAR

MD CM FRCP (C)

Second Edition
1989

The Omnipotent Child:
How to Mold, Strengthen and Perfect the Developing Child

© Thomas P. Millar 1983, 1989

Canadian Cataloguing in Publication Data

Millar, Thomas P. (Thomas Palmer), 1923–
The omnipotent child

Includes index.
ISBN 0-9693271-2-9

1. Child rearing. 2. Problem children. I. Title.
HQ773.M44 1989   649'.153   C89-091045-6

Published by:
Palmer Press
#23 - 659 Clyde Avenue
West Vancouver, B.C.
Canada V7T 1C8

Typeset by The Typeworks, Vancouver, B.C.
Printed by Hignell Printing Limited

International Standard Book Number 0-9693271-2-9

Printed in Canada

This book is dedicated to my children, Bruce, Greg, Laura, and Doug.

ACKNOWLEDGEMENT

I would like to acknowledge the editorial assistance of Laura M. Coles who, despite her filial loyalty, most ably insisted that this book conform to reasonable literary standards.

CONTENTS

Preface to the Second Edition

Since the first publication of this book in 1983, the term 'omnipotent' has become a household word, at least in Canada. Many parents tell me that my description of Dewey is a description of their child. At a recent conference of primary grade teachers I asked the assembly how many 'omnipotent' children were showing up in their classrooms these days, suggesting perhaps two or three per class. Five was the consensus. It would appear the syndrome is epidemic in the land.

And not just in America. The Omnipotent Child has surfaced in Japan in sufficient numbers to warrant a name. He is called *ochi benki* (angel lion) which, I am told, is because his behavior, tyrannical at home, is angelic in school, a pattern often seen in Canada too. In China where the one-child family has been prescribed by law, overvalued and minimally disciplined children are now so common they too have acquired a title: they are called *little emperors*. If, as many believe, the fabric of American society was irretrievably altered by the advent of the Big Chill generation, imagine the havoc a million adolescent Deweys will someday bring to life in the commune. Is this the way the world ends, not with a bang but with an unreared generation?

The characters that I have used to illustrate parent-child situations in *The Omnipotent Child* first surfaced in a stage play entitled *Don't Shoot, I'm Your Mother.** It tells the story of a mother, Lydia, trying desperately to

*To date *Don't Shoot, I'm Your Mother* (Vancouver: Palmer Press, December 1988) has failed to attract a producer, but now that it has been published perhaps that situation will change.

deal with her willful child, Dewey, not only for his sake but also to save her marriage and salvage her self-respect.

In the course of speaking to many parent groups I find few still buy the 'love is all' approach to child rearing. Parents today recognize that discipline is as important as love in child rearing. What they need is help with setting the limits and expectations that generate adaptive growth.

I have had much clinical feedback from parents who have read my book, many of whom tell me how things have changed in their family as a result of implementing various measures described in *The Omnipotent Child*. It has been instructive to see how different people take different things from the book. For example, parents whose natural tendency has been to slip into ineffective overcontrol see in the book advice to back off, to limit their training to a few crucial areas and to deal with these without hassling their child. On the other hand, uncertain parents, those whose inclination is to do nothing and hope the problem will go away, often report that the book has given them "permission to be firm."

Through such feedback, I have come to realize that there are passages in the book where my meaning is not stated as completely as it needed to be. For example, one day I overheard a six-year-old boy chatting to another child in my waiting room. "We have a new rule around our house," he told the other. "You only get to hit your sister twice a day."

Now this was not the message his mother and I had intended to send him with our "Hit Your Sister Program." Because he was in the habit of elbowing, jabbing or otherwise clobbering his younger sister whenever she came in range, Mother and I had decided to have a Hit Your Sister jar. Every time he hit his sister Mother was to drop a chip into his jar. When he had three chips be would get a punishment. Then the jar was to be emptied, and the chip accumulation would begin again. But somehow our program had sent him a different message than we had intended.

Since Mother was waiting in my consulting room I joined her. She told me that the program had been working well, that most days he was getting two chips in his jar, then cleaning up his act for the rest of the day.

That was when I discovered that Mother was in the habit of beginning each day afresh, that is with an empty jar. Children learn exactly what parents teach, and in this case that meant you get to hit your sister two times a day for free.

The remedy was obvious. Change the program such that, if he ended Tuesday with two chips in the jar, he began Wednesday with two chips in the jar. As I expected, when Mother communicated the change of plan to him, he hit the roof. To his mind she had moved the goalposts. However, she stuck to her guns and soon it was taking him two days to get his third Hit Your Sister chip and a punishment card.

If it had been a 'swear' jar, perhaps it wouldn't have mattered so much. If the child utters two unacceptable words by ten a.m. and then bites his tongue for the rest of the day, we are getting more restraint than indulgence and training is proceeding. However, hitting your sister is a more serious misdemeanor, and sending a message that tolerates any hitting is probably inappropriate.

It is such feedback as this which has shown me where my specific parenting measures need to be refined or communicated more clearly.

I believe specific parenting measures are the way to go. It is no good telling parents to be firm. Parents need to learn *how* to be firm. This learning is forwarded by my spelling out specific programs, parents writing them down, posting them on the fridge and following my recipe until the purpose of each ingredient becomes clear.

Further, I believe there are principles of discipline that must be heeded if the limit-setting is to work. Whenever I spell out a program of discipline, I do so in terms of these principles. While this may seem repetitious at times, my hope is that this approach will teach parents how to design their own disciplinary programs

To punish the child when the principles require this is truly the hardest segment of the disciplinary process. It is so very easy to overshoot, undershoot or, guilty and despairing, decline to shoot at all. Parents need all the help they can get to punish in a reasonable way. As I dealt with this problem repeatedly I developed a method which I call Punishment Cards. I communicated the method to my medical colleagues through a short paper entitled "A Card a Day Keeps the Social Worker Away." I have incorporated that program in this second edition of *The Omnipotent Child*.

Another expansion included in this second edition has to do with preventive parenting. Dewey is nine years old. He is already in difficulty with his adaptive growth. So it was I entitled my chapter on management measures "A Little Remedial Parenting." However many normal three- and four-year-old children are still very much embedded in the omnipotent illusion. Dealing with the omnipotence illusion in such children is not remedial parenting; it is *normal* parenting. It involves measures which promote the adaptive growth of the child and *prevent* his one day becoming a Dewey. Some of these measures, such as getting the three year old to go to bed and stay there, have been included in a new chapter entitled "A Little Preventive Parenting."

The Omnipotent Child was not written for teachers. The material on schools was intended to help parents understand how such school-based problems as finishing classwork were related to adaptive maturity, and how they at home could better prepare the child to cope with the educational environment. However, teachers see many omnipotent children in

their classrooms, and many educators recognize the validity of my adaptive training model. Some have shown considerable ingenuity in adapting
my parenting measures for use in the classroom.

While the teachers might wish for a book dealing with the omnipotent
child in the classroom, this is thorny ground for a health professional to
venture upon. Even when the communication remains professional in
tone, significant differences of opinion exist. For example, some educators
feel that therapy of disturbed children is a school responsibility. I do not.
Furthermore many educators would have the teacher become a surrogate
parent to the child. In my view, teachers are not in a position to do the
parents' job for them.

Another difference that surfaces is that many educators disagree with
the disciplinary thrust of my adaptive training model. One principal expressed the view that I lacked compassion for children. One professor of
education took me to task for recommending that children be kept after
school to finish their work. In her opinion this constituted a violation of
the Canadian Bill of Rights which issue, she informed me, would soon be
tested in the courts. Clearly, the 'love is all it takes' model still flourishes in
some educational circles.

I am unwilling to tackle these problems in a book intended for parents.
However I cannot ignore them, so I have explored the mutual ground between home and school in Chapter Nine, entitled "Parents, Teachers and
The Omnipotent Child." Further, since I have already written extensively
on educational issues in the psychiatric and lay literature, I have attached a
bibliography of these writings so that interested parties may explore them
at their leisure.

Some have criticized The Omnipotent Child for the space taken to place
the Western family in an historical and philosophical context. I am not
sure if it is the space they are concerned about or the philosophy enunciated. Perhaps they are just cookbook enthusiasts. In any case I think they
are wrong. Parents need more than recipes. They need an understanding
of parenthood that will allow them to write their own recipes. This involves an historical perspective on the task and an understanding of its social significance. So my version of these matters remains. However, as a
concession to the pragmatists, specific management programs have been
highlighted and an index added.

Now that the omnipotent child is being identified in a variety of cultures, perhaps my view of him as the product of accelerated cultural
change will interest the social historians. They had better be quick, because I believe we have touched bottom. I am persuaded from my work
with parents that the omnipotent child has almost had his day. With the
return of discipline to parenting, times are changing in America.

Each generation of parents reconstructs the society by the way in which it rears its children. If three generations can ruin a society, three generations can build a new one. There is a widespread disgust with moral decay surfacing in America. People have had enough of pornography and recreational sex, violence and contempt for life. An ethical rebirth is in the late stages of gestation.

As young people rise against these things, they will parent their children in accordance with their emerging values. I hear echoes of this quiet ethical revolution among the young people who come to me for help these days. Asked the goals of their child rearing, few now answer in terms of equipping the child for personal advantage in a minimally moral society; more see their task as guiding the child to the realization of his humanity: teaching him to live as part of society not as a guerrilla in an alien environment. And I see hope that this stumbling Western world may, in the next decade or two, become healthy again. When this has happened the Omnipotent Child will disappear and become but a memory of a time when the world had lost its way.

1

The Dewey Syndrome

"As for my people, children are their oppressors... "

ISAIAH CH.3 V.12

An unusual child has been growing up in America these last twenty years, a child so different from what his parents are, or wished him to be that they sometimes wonder how they could have produced him, wonder what they did wrong, how they failed.

Over many years it has been my privilege as a child psychiatrist to sit in the eye of this particular hurricane. I have looked long and deeply at how these parents have tried to rear their particular child, have spent many hours in my playroom encountering these children in all their provocative glory. As the years passed I began to perceive a pattern to these children. Furthermore, I began to realize that this outcome was related to specific kinds of difficulties in parenting. For reasons that will become clear as we proceed, I have elected to call this picture the Omnipotent Child Syndrome.

The Syndrome

Let me begin with a capsule of the circumstances that usually precede the decision of parents to seek professional help. The story runs something like this.

Dewey is nine years old and in the fourth grade at Brookside School. His teacher, Miss Grant, called Dewey's mother one afternoon in early December:

"He never finishes his seat work," Miss Grant said. "He starts, but the first little stumbling block he encounters, a number fact he can't remember or an unfamiliar reading word, and he grinds to a halt, looks at the wall as though he hopes to find the answer blazoned there. Then off he goes, daydreaming. Then first thing you know, he's whispering, or throwing spitballs. Lately it seems a day doesn't pass but he's disrupting the class."

"I had no idea," Mother declared . . . after all this is December and the first time Miss Grant has called.

"I don't like to alarm the parents unnecessarily," Miss Grant said. "But I can't stand over him all day, you know. I mean he is in fourth grade. He should be able to do a little seat work without constant supervision. I do have other children, you know. Some of them a good deal less bright than Dewey."

"Oh! I understand, Miss Grant," Mother said. "And I really do appreciate the extra effort you've been putting in." As it happens Mother had been hoping things would be better this year, and as time passed with no word from the school, she had allowed herself to believe that they were. Her disappointment was acute.

"I don't mind individualizing my approach," Miss Grant said. "And I have. But things have not improved one iota. He's still not finishing half the assignments."

"Perhaps if you kept him after school," Mother offered, not really thinking this will work, but responding to the fact that Miss Grant seemed to expect her to suggest something.

"I have," Miss Grant said grimly, "but that doesn't do any good either. Unless I stand right over him, he just sits there till the time's up. We are only allowed to keep them half an hour, you know."

Mother nodded to the telephone; she gets the same thing at home about taking out the garbage or cleaning his room. Unless she stands right over him nothing gets done.

"He just doesn't seem to feel any obligation to do the school work," Miss Grant said. "Lots of children his age worry if an assignment's late, but not him. I don't think he cares."

Miss Grant, remembering the incident that made her decide to call, went on. "Today, I told him I was not going to let him get away without finishing his math assignment. He just gave me *that* look—so I told him, 'Dewey, if you haven't finished that page of math by recess, then I'm keeping you in, but if I have to, you're going to be sorry.'"

"He didn't finish it?"

"He certainly did not. He did nothing. Deliberately. So I kept him in." Miss Grant paused a moment. "If looks could kill I'd have been dead a million times over. That's when I told him."

"Told him?"

" 'Dewey,' I said, 'life has obligations and life has privileges. If you don't meet your obligations you don't get your privileges.'" Miss Grant paused rhetorically, and Mother murmured agreement. Miss Grant continued. "'Since you did not meet your obligation, then you are going to lose a privilege.'" Miss Grant paused again.

"Of course," Mother agreed. Even so, she was sure that kind of talk wouldn't impress Dewey.

"You know what he did then?" Miss Grant asked. "He yawned. Right in my face."

"Oh dear!" Mother said apologetically. "Perhaps he was just tired and didn't mean to be rude?"

"Rude! In a moment you'll hear rude." Miss Grant picked up the thread of her story. "So I said to him, 'Dewey, it's your job to do all your assignments. And on time. You didn't do your math so you are not going on tomorrow's field trip with the rest of the class.'"

Mother flinched. She knew how Dewey reacted to that kind of thing.

Miss Grant continued. " 'But it's dumb math,' Dewey said. So I told him, 'Dewey, the math isn't dumb. What you mean is you don't like doing it. But you still have to do it. There are other kids who don't like it, but still they do it. And life's like that, sometimes we have to do things we don't like. We all have to. Besides, sometimes when you do things you don't like, you start getting interested in them. The first thing you know they are your favorite subjects.'"

Miss Grant transferred the telephone to her other ear and carried on. "Well, I don't think he bought that, but he said 'O.K.! O.K.! I'll do the dumb math. Tomorrow, when we get back from the field trip.'" Miss Grant snorted. "No way. Once we were back from the trip fat chance I'd have of getting that math out of him. 'No Dewey,' I said, 'you can do the work while we are on the field trip because you are not going.'"

Now, Mother told herself, comes the rude bit.

"You should have heard him. I mean whatever came into his mind came out of his mouth. 'You can't keep me from going on that field trip. You're not the boss of me. I don't have to do what you say. Kids got rights.' He pulled out all the stops." Miss Grant, who had waxed progressively more indignant as her account proceeded, snapped. "He ended by calling me a bossy old bitch, and gave me the Nazi salute. I don't have to take that kind of thing, you know."

Mother tried to apologize for Dewey, but Miss Grant was not in a mood to listen to apologies.

"I yelled at him, I admit it. And I don't believe in yelling at children, but Migawd, it would take a saint." Miss Grant paused a moment. "You have to understand I had a class of children watching this performance. I couldn't let him get away with that kind of thing, not and retain control of my class from then on." Miss Grant barely stopped for breath. "Not that he's got a friend in the class, he's so bossy. Every recess you can hear him out on the playground giving everybody orders."

A little stung by the vivid picture Miss Grant was painting Mother said, "I wish you'd called me earlier in the year. Dewey's father and I don't believe he ought to act like that."

"I just wanted you to know," Miss Grant said, "that he'll be coming home, and God knows what his version will be."

"Thank you for alerting me," Mother replied.

"He spent the day in the principal's office," Miss Grant said. "His last words to me were not to expect him to come to my dumb old school again." Miss Grant laughed weakly. "I wouldn't be too surprised if he had a stomach ache tomorrow."

And he did.

Often, it isn't until some such crisis in the school or community erupts that parents realize their child isn't just going through a difficult phase which he will outgrow in time. It is not easy to face up to the realization that one's child is not making it, that somehow the parenting hasn't quite done the job it is supposed to do. It takes many parents quite a while to make the decision to seek professional help. Eventually, however, Dewey and his parents will find their way to the child psychiatrist's consulting room.

When they did to mine, I set out to assemble a picture of their family and Dewey by obtaining a history from the parents, interviewing the child, and finally, as the situation warrants, contacting other persons with knowledge of the problem or arranging for special examinations such as psychological or neurological tests when indicated. Let me recount such a sequence now.

History

It is my practice to ask both parents to attend the initial visit. Although the mother could probably give an accurate history on her own, it is helpful to have the father there too, not only because one gets a chance to observe the relationship of the parents to one another, but also because doing so involves both parents in seeking the solution to the problem.

Mothers usually begin while fathers hang back, not too sure they approve of the whole enterprise. I find that in general women are less threatened asking for help than men are. However, if the advice given does not conform to the woman's prejudgments about the situation, she is much more liable to dismiss it out of hand than is a man.

So Dewey's mother Lydia, nervously mangling her gloves but putting on a brave front, told me about the school crisis, and passed from this to an account of her own concerns about Dewey.

"He dawdles getting dressed in the morning. It's just like Miss Grant says, he doesn't do anything unless you're standing right there, keeping him keep moving. He'd never do his teeth if I didn't supervise." Mother moved back from the edge of her chair. "As for cleaning his room, forget it."

"He simply refuses to do things?" I asked.

"Most of the time it's 'inna minute, Ma.' But his minutes tend to stretch."

"And stretch and stretch," Frank, the father, muttered.

"It takes at least two reminders to get him started," Lydia continued.

"Six tellings and a yelling," Frank corrected.

Mother ignored his intervention. "He soon slows to a halt. Five minutes later when I go in I find him day dreaming at the window or making faces at himself in the mirror."

"Going to bed's the same," Frank said. "Until you threaten him he doesn't think you mean business."

"But we shouldn't have to threaten him to get him to do things, should we?" Lydia asked.

Recognizing a loaded question when I hear one, I looked at the father.

"Threatening is no worse than nagging," Frank said.

They both looked at me. "I gather you've both tried hard to get him to meet his responsibilities, but nothing seems to work?" I countered.

Lydia nodded a vehement agreement. "It's his job to take out the garbage. I remind him. He always says he's going to, after the next commercial, but he always forgets."

"You should just turn off the T.V.," Frank said. "And don't turn it back on until he has finished the job."

"I've tried that," Lydia complained. "We always end up in a battle-of-wills. 'I'm not taking out the garbage until you turn that T.V. back on.' 'I'm not turning that T.V. back on until you take out that garbage.'" Lydia shrugged helplessly.

"And it's never Dewey who weakens first," Frank observed.

"Frank thinks I'm too easy on Dewey."

"Well! Aren't you?"

"If I am," Lydia replied, smiling with her teeth, "it's to make up for your strictness, dear."

"Oh no!" Frank protested. "You've got it backwards. If I'm strict, it's to make up for your being too easy."

"If you were home with him all day," Lydia said, shaking her head, "you'd find yourself giving in too. Sometimes it's easier to do it yourself than yell at him."

"It certainly sounds as if Dewey hasn't much patience when it comes to doing things he doesn't enjoy," I interjected. I address my remark to the father. I could see the mother is getting upset and, since I don't want them traumatizing each other too badly at this juncture, I decided to give her a rest.

Frank nodded in vigorous agreement. "He has no patience at all. If he can't get out of some tedious duty then he does the absolute minimum. Everything has to be now. He can't wait for dessert. If he's playing a game he can't wait for his turn. And if he's losing you can be sure we're all going to be accused of cheating, and soon he'll quit."

Frank's directness was making Lydia uncomfortable and though Frank knew it, he continued anyway.

"Just two nights ago, I left him doing a page of math. I came back later to check. Such a mess, numbers not in columns, crossing out, half-erased scribbles. More than half the answers were wrong. I mean, I ended up wondering if near the end he hadn't just started putting down any number at all, just to make it look as if he had done the work."

"Math isn't his favorite subject," Lydia offered nervously.

"Work isn't his favorite subject," Frank snapped. "If it isn't fun, Dewey doesn't think it's fair to put it on him."

"Apparently he hasn't developed much tolerance for the tedium of work," I intervened. "How does he handle other unpleasures? Say some disappointment? Supposing some pleasure he had been counting on didn't work out, how does he handle that?"

"Terribly!" Frank shook his head. "Although he's nine, he's liable to cry like a three year old."

"Now Frank," Lydia protested. "Be fair."

What she means is be loyal. It is a real problem for parents to report their children's symptoms. It seems somehow disloyal to do so, and they often have to preface each complaint with some extenuating remark.

But at this moment, Frank was not so inhibited. "I *am* being fair," he said, not about to have his serve broken. "In fact, just the other night I took him and his friend Kenny to a movie. When we got there, there was a big line. I could see we weren't going to make it when the picture changed so I suggested we go to the corner for a milk shake before going home. No way. He insisted on waiting. Well, we didn't get in, and guess who started crying." Frank shook his head. "Right there in front of the theater."

"He'd been looking forward to that movie for a whole week," Lydia said in extenuation.

"On the way home," Frank continued, "he got really mad, and I mean mad. He wanted to sue the theater owner for false advertising or child abuse, anything at all, just to get even. The least he was going to settle for was a letter to the editor. I wouldn't be surprised if he writes one; he's like that. If anybody crosses him, look out."

"Oh Frank!" Lydia exclaimed as she administered the *coup de grâce* to her mangled gloves.

"But Lydia, you know he's like that."

"If he is," Lydia said, close to tears, "we did it to him."

If he is, we did it to him.

There, expressed in a phrase, stands one of the most serious impediments to child rearing extant these days: the notion that, whatever the child is, the parent did to him. It's as though the child brought nothing to the relationship at all, as though all children were equally easy to rear, and if this one isn't doing well then it must be the parents' fault.

What we are dealing with here is guilt, naked and unadorned. There is a strong pull on the psychiatrist to respond to this with some reassurance, but it would be premature to do so at this time.

Often a simple, "why don't we leave deciding *how* you've got where you are with Dewey until we have the whole picture and can give some thought to what we can do about it," is sufficient to keep the history taking from bogging down in a morass of mea culpas and mutual blamings.

It is often wise, when tensions are high like this, to move the discussion into some less loaded area, perhaps to earlier times when mothering was more joyful and the things to be reported about Dewey less critical. So I asked Lydia, "tell me, what was he like as a newborn?"

Dewey turned out to have been an amiable, responsive infant, lively but not overactive, fairly intense in his reactive style, quite easily distracted, certainly not one of your can-entertain-himself-for-hours babies. However he was regular, the product of a normal pregnancy and an uneventful birth. It is clear, he may have been a bit challenging to rear, especially for a first-time mother, but there is nothing really pathological or even far out about his temperament.

Of course, children's temperaments vary, which makes some of them harder to rear than others, especially for some mothers. And there is such a thing as a temperamental match. If some sweet southern lady, raised in the gentle tradition, and unlikely to say damn if a hammer fell on her toe, has a placid, sunny and accommodating little girl, things are liable to go swimmingly. But give her a high energy, intense, moody boy, and tensions may mount. Then, because she is as "civilized" as she is, the madder Mother gets the more protective she becomes, and soon the child-rearing *fat* is in the ambivalent *fire*.

Since temperamental characteristics are inherited, reasonable parent-child matches tend to occur quite often. With adopted children, of course, such inherited matching cannot occur, which may well be an important reason so many adopted children seem to get into psychological growing-up difficulties.

In any case, it is important to try to get a picture of what the child brings to the parent-child interaction, to determine what kind of a baby this particular mother was given to rear.

I am also interested in the mother's circumstances when she began parenting. Dewey's mother was surprised to find herself pregnant and, like most women in that situation, soon became enthusiastic about the enterprise. Neither parent had any serious health, family or personal problems to complicate things in these last few years. Dewey's father changed his job not long after the baby was born, but there were no serious problems. Like most young people they didn't have money to waste, but neither have they had serious financial worries to absorb their energies.

In fact things had gone swimmingly until Dewey was two years old. "I just never believed the terrible twos could be that terrible," Lydia said. "Suddenly he was so cranky and demanding. Wouldn't let me out of his sight. He seemed to expect me to entertain him all day long."

"If he said 'jump,'" Frank interjected, "we were supposed to come to attention, salute, and ask, 'how high dear?' Which we did more than was good for him or us."

"He sounds as though he's still a bit that way," I commented.

"He may not issue orders as bluntly as he used to," Frank said, "but no way will he accept that we have a right to set limits on him."

"Everything turns into a battle-of-wills," Lydia said. "I don't know how to avoid it. I mean I try to be fair, but sometimes I get the feeling he wants to argue, that he's looking for something to argue about."

"Make a good lawyer," Frank muttered.

"We tell him bedtime in ten minutes," Lydia said, "and he pleads, 'just until this show is over.' Well, if that's maybe fifteen minutes, I say 'O.K., but get in your pajamas during the commercial.'"

"Which he doesn't," Frank said.

"Even though he promised," Lydia agrees. "And then he gives me an argument: 'why do I have to go to bed, you're staying up.' I try to tell him that's because we're the adults."

"He doesn't buy it," Frank said. "He thinks he should have all the prerogatives of an adult."

"Do you make him go to bed then?"

"Oh yes. He doesn't get to stay up. Well, I mean not as late as us." She shook her head. "Sometimes, I get tired of arguing, and let him have one more show. I know it's wrong, but after a day of Dewey, it's hard to stay firm."

"Do you ever punish him for not getting to bed on time?"

"I've tried. It never does any good. If you take away some T.V. time he just says he wasn't going to watch anyway. You can't punish him, because nothing bothers him."

"He always finds something else to do," Frank agreed. "And makes damn sure we know he isn't suffering."

"I don't like to punish," Lydia said. "I don't think child rearing should be parents ordering and kids obeying. Nowadays it should be more a democratic relationship of equals, shouldn't it?"

I know the book she's checking me out on, but I'm not about to let the history-taking deteriorate into a philosophical discussion on parenting. However, before I had to field the question, Frank jumped in.

"Dewey would never settle for just being equal. He wants to be in charge. His idea of fair is what suits Dewey. He has no idea that fair for him might be unfair for somebody else."

"He's a bit self-centered at times," Lydia acknowledged. "But then he's only nine years old."

"A little self-centered! You ought to hear him playing in the yard," Frank said. "He's Attila the Hun, organizing the troops. No wonder they go home."

Lydia sighed. "It's getting so he plays with younger children a lot of the time."

"They'll do what he tells them to," Frank explained.

"These battles-of-wills," I asked, "are they over important things?"

"Often it's some little thing," Lydia replied. "Once he gets his back up he's got to win. Even if it means settling for one little concession, 'just three minutes more, Mom.'"

"That's winning," Frank said. "That's what's really going on. Winning! Only three more minutes maybe, but then he won."

"Three more minutes doesn't hurt," Lydia muttered.

"Not getting it sure hurts him," Frank argued.

"It sounds as though getting that little concession has become a matter of pride to him."

"Exactly," Frank said. "If he goes to bed when we say, he acknowledges our authority. To him that's a put down, and no way will he accept that."

"We aren't trying to put him down," Lydia said. "He just sees everything that way. I think it hurts his self-esteem."

"Other kids go to bed when they are told, and it doesn't seem to hurt their self-esteem," Frank objected.

There is a pause. They seem a little spent having covered so much painful ground.

"Do you think his self-esteem is a little down?" I asked Lydia.

"Oh yes."

"He may sound arrogant," Frank agreed. "But he really isn't that sure about himself. It shows."

"But you said . . . " Lydia begins.

"That going to bed oughtn't to be such a put down to him," Frank interrupted. "But I know it is. And I'm sure it's got something to do with his self-esteem."

"Sometimes he says it right out," Lydia said. " 'I'm dumb. Nobody likes me. I can't do anything right.' "

"But he's not dumb," Frank said. "Already he reads *Time*." He grins. "If that counts. And he understands numbers, even if it's like pulling teeth to get him to do times tables."

"And he has to be perfect," Lydia added. "He can't lose a game. He can't even accept that his father and I can bowl better than he. He seems to feel that if he doesn't come first, he's no good at all. He never seems to make allowances for himself as a child."

"He doesn't think he is," Frank explained. "He expects a full voice in adult affairs. And often gets it. Somehow or other we always end up doing things his way."

"Not always, Frank."

"Well, maybe not always," Frank conceded, "but who always chooses the restaurant when we go out for dinner?"

"But Frank, you like Chinese," Lydia protested.

"That's not the point. I also like Italian."

"And Armenian. And Mexican, and . . . " Lydia smiled. It was the first time she had done so since the session began and it was a pleasant sight.

"I'll tell you one area in which Dewey reigns supreme," Frank said. "Vacations. No way are we allowed to go on vacations without him."

"You haven't been away from him at all?"

"Not since he was four, and your mother came for two weeks," Frank said to Lydia, who seemed about to protest.

"But we do go out in the evenings."

"To a chorus of 'where are you going? When will you be back? Why can't I go? Will you call me when you get there? Be sure and leave the number so I can reach you if I need you,' " Frank declared.

"Sounds like he has a little trouble with separation," I commented.

"Sometimes," Lydia acknowledged.

"At night?" I ask.

"Has to have the hall light on and door open," Frank said. "Wants someone to lie down with him. He'd come into our bed if I didn't draw the line. I think he is a little too attached to his mother."

"He's just a child, Frank."

"Does he worry about you then?" I asked Lydia.

"Oh yes. A little."

"Lydia! If you're ten minutes late getting home from somewhere he's checking out the window every two minutes. And he's always after you to quit smoking." Frank turned to me. "Doesn't want her to get cancer."

I can see Dewey's concern pleases his mother a little, and I haven't the heart to tell her that what he is probably worried about is not *her* but who will look after *him* if she isn't around.

"Then you and Frank haven't really been away from Dewey for... almost six years I guess?"

"Has it really been that long?" Frank asked the wall.

"Don't forget, we went to Seattle that weekend," Lydia said.

Frank reached over and placed his hand on hers. "And you spent the whole weekend wondering whether Dewey was surviving."

"Not the whole weekend."

Gradually I pieced together a picture of Dewey's style. He is an avoider. If he is to participate in some new activity like Little League or swimming lessons, he's all gung-ho until the time nears, then he's not so sure, and it takes quite a bit of encouragement to get him there. He's O.K. for a time or two, but soon it's "Aw, baseball is dumb."

"He expects to be Mickey Mantle first time out," Frank said, "and when that doesn't happen, he loses interest."

I discover that Dewey hasn't many friends. He tends to run through friendships quickly, alienating the kids with his bossiness and insistence that things focus around him. Now he plays with younger children and with one boy who's a lot like him.

"I guess they have to settle for each other," Frank said.

While Dewey talks big, he is really quite timid. He's beginning to isolate himself a little, to spend more time watching T.V. than playing outside. His favorite show is the *Six Million Dollar Man,* but the cartoon super heroes come a close second.

Despite all these negatives, Dewey has no really grave symptoms. He may want to avoid school a bit, but it doesn't amount to a real phobia. He's difficult, but he isn't really malicious or destructive. Despite his poor work habits, he's learning what he needs to know, and I'm sure he's up to grade level in achievement. He has no habit disorders, doesn't wet or soil, doesn't steal, and while he sometimes shades the truth in his favor a bit, he isn't a blatant liar.

"He doesn't seem to be maturing properly," Frank said. "If he doesn't get over some of these ways of his, he's going to have real problems when he's older."

"How do you think he's going to feel about coming in to see me?" I asked them. Many parents worry about this, and Dewey's are no exception. I helped them with how to tell Dewey. "No matter how you present it, chances are he's going to be negative, but don't worry about that. Most kids are pretty uncertain about this kind of situation. My main concern is that he doesn't arrive at my office under the impression he's going to get his eyes checked. It's best to select one unequivocal symptom, one he cannot possibly deny, and focus on that."

Since they seem uncertain I do it for them. "Present it to him like this," I say. " 'Dewey, we get crosswise you and I. I want you to do something you don't want to do. The first thing you know we're yelling at each other. You don't like it, and I don't like it, but it keeps happening. We don't seem to be able to find our way out of it. Dr. Millar is a doctor for that kind of problem. We've been to see him and told him about the problem in our family. Now he wants to meet you, and see what kind of person you are, and learn how you feel about the situation.'"

"He's not going to like it," Lydia said uncertainly.

"I can just hear him. 'I'm not crazy, I'm not going to any shrink,'" Frank added. "Oh! Sorry!"

"Don't be. If being called mild names like that upsets a man, he oughtn't to be in child psychiatry. In fact just the other day one of my child customers who was a little annoyed that I was slipping his mother out from under his thumb said to me, 'You're old, you know. You're gonna die soon.'"

"He did!" Lydia said.

I nodded. "Just tell Dewey when the appointment is, that you're driving him, and not to worry, nobody thinks he's crazy. Whatever you do don't let him seduce you into arguing with him."

Frank looked at Lydia and grinned. "Lots of luck," he said.

"If you ignore him," I continued, "he'll bluster a bit. At first it will be 'I'm not going so don't think I am,' but if you just don't answer soon the story will change. It will become, 'O.K. I'll go, but I'm not talking, I just won't say one word.'"

"But what good will seeing him do if he doesn't talk?" Lydia asked.

"He'll talk," I reply. "Almost always, with up-front kids like Dewey, I'm lucky to get a word in edgewise."

"I hope he doesn't just refuse to get out of the car," Lydia said, much doubt in her voice and manner.

I can see her uncertainty about bringing him might well encourage Dewey to stronger resistance, so I suggested, "maybe his father should bring him. It doesn't matter who brings him. I'm just going to be seeing Dewey."

"Could it be on a Saturday?" Frank asked. "I have trouble getting away week days."

So we set it up for Saturday next when Frank can bring him. Lydia seemed surprised and a little pleased that Frank is willing to handle this part of things.

"Can you make it eleven o'clock," Frank said. "He might forgive you for being what you are, but you make him miss Spiderman and you're done for."

I laugh. Now that it's Frank's problem he's not quite so nonchalant about getting him here. However, I am not really concerned about what Dewey missing Spiderman will do to the interview to come. And if by chance he refuses to get out of the car, I'll come down and interview him there. In fact, for school phobia kids I've even made home visits. So we arrange the appointment for eleven the following Saturday.

The Interview

Dewey arrived at eleven the next Saturday. By the time I came out to the waiting room to get him, he was immersed in a Charlie Brown book. He looked up briefly when I come in, avoided my gaze, and returned to his book. I can see he's nervous but cool.

I waved goodbye to my previous patient, an equally cool nine-year-old girl, who surveyed Dewey with a practiced eye. She gave me a wave. "So long, Frog," she said, flouncing out the door. Her mother shrugged, looked at me over her glasses, and minced after her daughter. Being a child psychiatrist is really a lot of fun; every kid is a fresh adventure.

I noticed that Dewey wasn't really reading; he was watching things. When he looked up at me to catch my reaction to being called "frog," I caught his eye. He frowned and raised the book until it hid his face.

"This must be Dewey," I said to Frank. Dewey didn't look up. "Come on into my playroom Dewey." I turned to Frank "We'll be at least forty-five minutes. Why don't you go get a cup of coffee?"

Father gave me an 'I've done my share' look, said "see ya later, Dewey," and stood up. I waved him out. Dewey lowered his book and uncertainly watched him go.

"Come on," I said, and led the way into the playroom. I did not look back. I knew he wasn't right behind me, but it's a rare kid who can, starting dead cold, defy that early in the game. I was reasonably sure he'd follow. And if he didn't I'd handle the situation somehow.

As I went I chattered a bit, as though assuming he was right behind me. I entered the playroom and turned. As I did so he arrived in the playroom door.

Dewey is an open-faced, nice-looking boy with dark eyes and chestnut brown hair. He was wearing blue cords, colorful Adidas runners and a Star Wars T-shirt. Within him curiosity was warring with cool; I could see he was interested in the models and toys on my shelves, but since it was his game plan to be uncooperative he was in a bind. Perhaps he decided that was my fault too, for he gave me a sullen look and stood there turning his head slowly from side to side, like El Toro taking in the sunlit plaza.

With a sweep of an imaginary cape I indicated the far chair, the one facing the door—they always feel better if the escape route is visible—and declaimed, "have a seat."

Dewey looked at me. I detected a hint of uncertainty in that casual armor of his. He sauntered over to the chair, slid into it, and started fingering a plastic dinosaur handy on the play table.

"My name is Dr. Millar," I sat down opposite him. I took out my pad and wrote his name. "And you're Dewey. How old are you Dewey?"

I know how old he is, but when kids are a bit anxious, it helps to start with a really easy question.

He looked at me as though considering whether answering one question was violating the oath of silence he had taken with respect to our interview. I smiled as though ignorant of his contrary status.

"Nine," he said.

"Nineteen," I repeated, and wrote down that number.

"Nine," Dewey said emphatically as though humoring the deaf.

"You sure don't look nineteen," I shook my head.

"I'm nine, I said!"

"Oh, nine. That's better. You'd never pass for nineteen you know." I scratched out my nineteen I'd written.

"You knew," Dewey said, giving me a suspicious look. "My Mom told you."

"Yeah!" I smiled. "She said you go to Brookside School and times tables is your favorite subject."

"I hate times tables," Dewey said. "She didn't tell you that."

"As a matter of fact," I said with a grin, "she said you don't like them at all; in fact she said you hate them."

"Times tables are stupid. Kids shouldn't have to learn them," Dewey challenged. "Every kid should just be given a calculator and never mind stupid times tables."

I know a couple of school principals who would agree with him, but that wasn't relevant at that moment so I asked Dewey, "what's two times two?"

He looks at me with contempt. "Four."

"Mathematical genius," I said aloud and wrote that down in my notes.

Dewey almost laughed but caught himself in time. He settled back in his chair. "How come you got all those models?"

"Kids make them."

"How come they don't take them home?"

"They're not finished. Some of the boys who see me every week like to build models. When they finish them they take them home."

"I'm not coming every week," Dewey announced.

"And you didn't want to come today either," I said.

"They made me."

"I know exactly what you said to your Dad on the way over here."

Dewey thought that over a moment, then challenged me. "Oh yeah! What?"

"You said, 'O.K., I'll come, but I'm not talking. I'm not saying one word.'"

"How'd you know that?" Dewey asked. Suspicion shone in his eyes.

"I can read minds."

"Oh yeah!" Dewey scoffed.

"I can. As a matter of fact I can tell you what you are thinking this very minute."

He looked at me uncertainly.

"You're thinking, 'this guy can't read minds.'"

Dewey looked startled for a moment, then grinned. "Aw, that's just what anybody would think. You can't read minds."

I shrugged as though to say, I guess this kid is just too smart for me.

"I saw a guy on T.V. once that could bend real coins with his mind," Dewey said. "But they musta faked it. When the camera was turned away they coulda bent it with pliers."

I could see that Dewey is not overly trusting when it comes to the adult world.

He looked around the room and asked, "how come kids paint their models?"

"So they look more real. I help them."

He walks over to the shelves. "I bet I could paint a model as good as that." He picked up one of the models.

I walked over and gently took the model from him. "The boy has been working hard on that and they break easily, so I think we'd better not handle it too much."

Dewey shrugged, "I could build better 'n that."

Being on his feet, he started wandering about, following wherever his eye led him. He flitted, getting the surface information, then drifting on to the next attractive color or interesting shape. Spoken to, he did not reply. Even if I asked him a question, unless the subject interested him, he let it dangle. His unresponsiveness now had more the quality of indifference than resistance. I played a few games with it, and it soon became clear that Dewey was minimally aware of any social obligation to respond even with a closing "I don't know." He is still too egocentric to perceive the social dilemma of his auditor left dangling when not answered.

I went back to my chair and watched him for a while, commenting occasionally, but content for the moment to see what he might produce spontaneously, now that I had defused his initial contrariness.

The initial phase of many first interviews goes much like this. The child, uncertain or contrary or a mixture of both, needs to be helped over his apprehension or negativism. I find it best to ignore these, to fool around with a little nonsense, show him enough of my style to amuse and reassure him.

Of course there are some children who refuse to come in from the waiting room. Rather than separate the child from the parent I usually detach the parent and see the child in the waiting room for the first few minutes. However, if a battle-of-wills becomes necessary, I have it. After all, such are frequently part of the problem, and the sooner the behavior appears in the office, the sooner we can go to work understanding and dealing with it.

Rarely do children remain sullen and uncommunicative throughout the entire interview, particularly not those suffering from the Omnipotent Child Syndrome; they have neither the patience nor the self-control to sustain such a pattern.

Even so, one has to work at communicating with children. It is not possible to interview them in the passive mode Sigmund Freud prescribed for adults. One has to set up communicative interaction, not just by asking questions but also by expressing provocative opinions or generating imaginative exchanges. Each situation is different, and the child psychiatrist needs to acquire a repertoire of methods and develop ingenuity in utilizing these to involve the child.

The purpose of the diagnostic interview is not simply to obtain information about the child's inner life. While that data is useful, the child psychiatrist is primarily concerned with appraising the child's coping style. How does he deal with the world and himself? Does he cope, or is his one of the myriad non-coping or life avoidant styles? How does he handle his feelings? How much self-control has he? How fragile is that control? How tuned in is he? How perceptive? How obtuse? Is he open or closed? Naive or suspicious? Burnt or trusting? Can he laugh? How sensitive is he to limitations placed upon his autonomy?

Children are neither able nor willing to answer questions about these things. Children don't come to the psychiatrist for help; they come because their parent has made them come. They aren't motivated to reveal themselves. In many cases they have an opposite feeling, that the psychiatrist is sticking his nose in their business without invitation. Unlike the adult patient, if time passes without communication it doesn't usually bother the child as much as it does the psychiatrist.

However, I recall one loquacious seven-year-old who, after the usual initial resistance and fifteen minutes of increasingly informative banter, said, "hey Doc, we've been fooling around long enough. We got to get down to talking about my problem."

"O.K," I said. "What is your problem?"

"My problem," he replied, "is my mother. She won't do what I say."

Returning to the interview at hand, I decided the time had come to get Dewey back into direct communication with me, time to activate his coping style in order to get a better look at it.

The best way to activate a coping style is to give it something with which to cope. I could of course precipitate an authoritative encounter; the history makes it clear such would undoubtedly produce interesting reactions. However, I prefer this kind of thing not take place too early in the interview. There are reasons for this. In the first place, once you get into a battle-of-wills, even a trivial one, the rest of the child's pattern tends to become obscured, and the child can come out looking a whole lot more willful and contrary than he really is. In the second place, if most of the interview has been fairly non-threatening, one is better set up for a return visit should a treatment plan emerge from the evaluation. So I watch for an opportunity to intrude myself on Dewey.

At that moment Dewey sat down at the table. He had found a bottle of split-shot fishing weights which I use to weigh down the nose wheel on model airplanes. "What are these for?" he asked.

"Let me see," I said, holding out my hand. Dewey handed them over to me. I poured some out on the table. I picked one up and started examining it.

"These are turn-to-animal pills," I said. "If I give you the right one, I can turn you into any animal you want to be."

Dewey gave me a here-we-go-again look and sat back in his chair. "Those are fishing weights."

"They look like fishing weights," I admitted, "but they are really pills. Of course they only work for a week, but it's nice having a holiday from being a person for a week. . . birds don't have to go to school, you know."

"But they get shot at by hunters," Dewey said, spilling out some more weights. He began arranging them in rows. "I wouldn't want to be a bird."

"What would be the most fun to be?"

Dewey gave me a suspicious look. "Nothing. It wouldn't be fun to be nothing."

"O.K.," I replied, deciding to come in the back door. "What would be the worst animal to have to be?"

Dewey thought a moment. "A dinosaur. They're extinct." He looked up from arranging weights. "But if I was, I'd be the only one in the world.

Everybody would want to come and see me."

"And you'd be the most powerful creature in the world," I pointed out.

A wicked look came into Dewey's eye. "I could go over to Brookside School and stomp a few classrooms I know."

I shook my head. "Dinosaurs on the monkey bars!"

"Old Grant would throw a spazz," Dewey chuckled.

"Probably wouldn't be too pleased," I agreed.

"I'd be a Tyrannosaurus Rex. A huge one, with big teeth. A Tyrannosaurus Rex could throw a whole elementary school clear across the road you know."

"Then they couldn't have school," I objected. "That'd be terrible."

Dewey snorted derisively. "School is the dumbest place going."

He then went on to give me a four-minute dissertation on the evils of education, a dissertation that ranged from his opinion of the curriculum—old fashioned and irrelevant in this age of calculators—through recesses—too short—to the teaching staff—assembled, he was sure, for the purpose of ruining kids' days with their bossy and demanding ways. Somehow he ended on the subject of field trips.

"Kids got rights you know. Like recess. And going home on time. I could call the social worker, you know; they've got a hot line for kids. Teachers can't take away kids' rights to go on field trips."

"I heard Miss Grant wouldn't let you go because you didn't finish your math."

"My mom told you that, didn't she?" Dewey said with narrowed eyes; clearly Mother was going to hear more about this betrayal of his privacy.

"Actually I read her mind."

"She told you," Dewey declared.

"You're right. She told me," I confessed. "She and your dad told me all about the ways things are at school as well as home. About the problems like finishing your school work and getting dressed in the mornings. They told me about things because they're worried about you."

"They don't need to worry about me," Dewey said. "There's nothing wrong with me. When can I go home? Isn't the time up yet?" He looked at the door as though considering bolting.

I showed him my watch. "Our appointment is for forty-five minutes. We've got twenty-five left."

"TWENTY-FIVE MINUTES!" Dewey shouted. "Maybe your watch has stopped!" He looked at the door again.

Hoping to deflect our battle-of-wills for a little longer I decide to see if I can change the subject. "I see you're right-handed," I said. "Are you right-eyed too?"

"Boy! This is borrrring!" Dewey said.

"Most people are right-eyed."

"What ya mean right-eyed? I don't write with my eye."

"People see best with their right or left eye." I said. "I'm right-eyed."

"Whoop de do!"

"You're probably right-eyed too."

"Oh yeah! How can you tell?"

I rolled a sheet of paper into a tube. "Look at my nose through this tele-scope and you'll see which you are."

Uncertainly, he took the paper and sighted it on my nose. He was hold-ing the tube to his right eye.

"See," I said, "you used your right eye."

"I could have used the left if I'd wanted to."

"Try! It'll be a lot harder." I could see he was cooling down again. I watched him fumble the tube to his left eye and then close his right eye with his free hand. "At least seven out of every eight kids in your class are right-eyed. Did you know that?"

"Big deal," Dewey said.

"Here," I handed him my pencil and the pad with the notes on it. "Try writing with your left hand. When I do, it comes out looking Chinese."

He took a stab at writing with his left hand but he couldn't do much. By now he'd become pretty cool so I asked him, "tell me, Dewey, what are the kids like at Brookside?"

"Aw, you know. Some finks. The girls are yukky. I'm third toughest in my grade."

"Who's first?"

"Trevor. You know Trevor?"

"Never heard of him." Even if I had, I would never have told Dewey. I don't want my patients teasing each other about going to the shrink.

Dewey looked disappointed. He was probably hoping to get something on Trevor.

"If this ruler," I said, picking it up from the table top, "was your class, and on this end was smart, and on this end was dumb, and all the kids in your class were on the ruler, where would you come?"

Dewey indicated a spot about one inch from the smart end. "Cathy is the smartest. But she does the dumb work," he added, as though this con-stituted some kind of cheating. "I don't do dumb stuff."

"What about popular?" I asked. "If this end was the kid everybody liked most and this end was the worst, where'd you come?"

"That would be old Pampers down there," Dewey said pointing to the worst end. "Her name is Pam, but she acts like a baby so we call her Pampers. She doesn't like it. Sometimes she cries. What a baby!" Dewey's disgust was boundless.

"And where do you come?" I asked again.

"Oh, about the middle," Dewey said.

"They got a nickname for you, Dewey?"

"Everybody's got a nickname."

"What's yours?"

"It's just because it rhymes."

Since he was beginning to look a little uncomfortable I decided not to pursue the matter further. However Dewey chose to.

"Some of the kids call me Screwy, but that's just because it rhymes. I don't care. That Trevor's the really screwy one; he thinks he's tough. When the teacher leaves the room he takes over and bosses everybody."

Gradually a picture of his peer relationships emerged. While he wasn't a scapegoat he was certainly taking some teasing, and he had begun, as so many of these children do, to expect things to go sour so, preferring to be the rejecter rather than the rejectee, he was starting his days bristling in anticipation.

"Every class has a Trevor," I said. "And a Pampers. And a smart girl like Cathy."

"I don't mind Cathy," Dewey protested. "She's O.K. For a girl."

"Would you like me to turn you into a girl, Dewey?"

"No way!"

"Just think, you could have Barbies and everything. "I said with a grin.

"Yuuk!"

Now that Dewey had become a little sunny it became apparent how negative his usual style had grown to be. All things being equal, any conversation with Dewey was liable, at the turn of a phrase, to fall into a push-pull kind of interaction. All that was needed was for you to take a stand. If you said black, Dewey would say white. The closest to agreement you could ever expect from Dewey would be dark gray.

I managed to get him talking about his interests and found he was filled with grandiose fantasies involving the Six Million Dollar Man. His accounts were shot through with the theme of naked and overwhelming power.

I drew pictures for him of people whose faces I filled in to his specifications.

"Make him mad," he said. "He's mad because they made him go to bed and his favorite show was just coming on." He then elaborated on the ways that the kid is going to get even and became quite heated as he warmed to his subject.

"They try to do that to me, but I sneak out and watch from the door. I don't see why kids have to go to bed; grownups get to stay up."

I gave him some felt pens and as he talked he drew me a picture, a poster advocating Kid Power.

Distantly I heard the waiting room door close. Since it was undoubtedly Dewey's father returning, I carried on. "Tell me, Dewey, have you thought what you want to be when you grow up?"

"I'm going to be in the army and drive a tank," Dewey said. "Or maybe fly a jet." He stood up. "I think that was my father."

I nodded. "I think so."

"I'll go check," Dewey said.

"No need, Dewey. I told him forty-five minutes. He knows to wait."

"I'll just tell him," Dewey said, standing up.

"That isn't necessary, Dewey," I said, indicating for him to sit down.

"Why can't I go now?" Dewey demanded, not sitting down.

"Because we're not finished. It'll only be a few minutes more." It was clear that Dewey was determined to set up a battle but I tried to deflect him.

"Come on now Dewey, sit down and tell me about your grandfather. Your mother says he sometimes takes you fishing."

"I'm not sitting down," Dewey said, sidling towards the door.

I stood up and moved my chair into the path toward the door. "I guess you don't have to sit down if you don't want to."

Dewey looked at me uncertainly. "How much longer did you say?"

I checked my watch. "About four minutes."

"You let me go in two, and I'll sit down," he offered.

As his father said, all Dewey wants to do is win. But would it be good for him? Already I know I am going to suggest treatment to the family, so sooner or later Dewey and I are going to have to sort out what adults decide and what kids decide. Part of growing him up is going to be confronting his omnipotence illusion. If I compromise now, the next round will be that much harder.

"You don't have to sit down if you'd rather stand."

"But what about my two minutes? You didn't answer me about that," Dewey said, walking toward the toy shelves.

"The time you leave is not your decision. It's mine. It's only a few minutes now and then you can go. What are you going to do when you leave?"

"None of your damn business," Dewey snapped.

"Dam business? I don't have any business with dams. I'm not a water man."

"Funny!"

Clearly Dewey was caught up in the power struggle, and it didn't look as if my efforts to help him save face were going to be effective.

"I'm never coming back you know," Dewey said. "This is a dumb place. You're a dumb doctor."

I decided any words from me now would just aggravate the situation so I remained silent.

"How much longer now?" Dewey asked loudly.

I checked my watch. "Two minutes."

Dewey grabbed a model from the shelf and held it over his head. "You'd better let me go," he shouted.

I stood up. "Dewey! Don't you break that model!"

Dewey dropped the model on the shelf and ran across the room. "If you hit me I'm telling."

"I'm not going to hit you, Dewey," I said, picking up the model and checking it. "But neither am I going to let you leave until the time is up. There are some things you decide and some I decide, and when the appointment is over is a thing I decide, so just cool it."

Dewey turned his back to me and stared out the window. He remained there saying nothing until I opened the door for him and told him he could leave. He disappeared through it like a scalded cat and rocketed through the waiting room waving at his father to follow.

As I entered the waiting room Frank stood and looked at me enquiringly.

I shrugged. "We ended in a little battle-of-wills."

"I heard." Frank said. "Sorry."

"Don't worry," I grinned. "It's the nature of my business. He was a little feisty at the end but we'll both survive."

Additional Information

The next day, after getting the parents' permission to do so, I called Miss Grant. I was relieved to discover she was happy to talk to me. By and large she confirmed the picture of Dewey the parents had given me.

It was my impression that Miss Grant had been quite patient, not particularly indulgent of Dewey, and that she had varied her approach considerably in an effort to find some way to deal with his recalcitrance, but that nothing had worked. At this point she seemed strongly motivated to prove how impossible a child Dewey was, more as a defense of her teaching than as a rejection of the child. Sometimes teachers can get into continuing power struggles with kids like Dewey and become part of the problem, but this was not the case here.

Since there was no indication of any real disability for learning, I did not feel psychological testing was necessary to clarify the diagnosis. Nor was there reason to suspect a neurological component so such a consultation was not necessary.

Diagnostic Formulation

These data then are the main facts from which the child psychiatrist must formulate his understanding: what he learns from and of the parents; what he learns from direct contact with the child; what he learns from others having significant contact with the child. To be sure, when circumstances warrant, it may be necessary to undertake special medical studies, such as a neurological examination, a brain wave test, or psychological studies. However, in the usual case, the history and the direct examination of the child provide the significant findings.

From these data then let me offer a brief explanation of what is going on with Dewey. It will take the book to complete the job, but it would be inappropriate to leave the case history without giving some preliminary indication of the relationship of its elements one to another.

Dewey has a lot of symptoms. He avoids duties and responsibilities both at home and at school. He can't get along with kids, and he isn't easy to live with at home either. He's willful, contrary and sometimes rude. He has poor self-control for a nine year old, as his tears and tantrums show. His bragging covers an uncertain sense of his own worth. If he trusted his parents more he wouldn't still be plagued with anxiety whenever they separate from him.

These symptoms and qualities are best understood in terms of that pattern of adaptive immaturity I call the Omnipotent Child Syndrome. There are four central or cardinal characteristics of the syndrome.

Cardinal Characteristics
The Omnipotent Child Syndrome

1. The Omnipotence Illusion
2. Egocentricity
3. Intolerance for Unpleasure
4. Impaired Self-Esteem

Dewey has not found a way to accept his childhood, to give up his *illusion of omnipotence* for a belief in his parents' power and good will towards him. He struggles to deny his real child weakness, which leads him into willfulness and the conviction that authority is there to demean, not to protect and nurture him.

Dewey is *self-centered* to the point that he regularly misreads his environment in terms of self. His insensitivity is such that he offends and doesn't realize what he has done to generate offense. He is not so much selfish as imperceptive. Like the four year old, he believes that when he closes his eyes, it's night for the rest of the world.

Dewey has but *limited ability to tolerate the normal unpleasures* of life. He wants it now. If it's no fun, take it away. Minimal anxiety fells him. Disappointment overwhelms. Anger erupts. There is no restraint in Dewey. He has not developed the capacity to contain unpleasure.

Finally Dewey has little sense of worth. *His self-esteem is fragile,* and a good deal of his unacceptable behavior results because he is trying to force others to endorse a worth he does not feel within himself.

Dewey's adaptive growth has faltered. He is trying to cope with a nine year old's world with the adaptive equipment of a four year old. If he is unhappy, it is because such incompetence leads to repeated failures. His emotional conflict is a result of his condition, not its cause.

Why has Dewey's adaptive growth not proceeded well? When we look into the history we do not see parents who have withheld affection and concern; instead we see parents who have not found a way to train their child. They have *nurtured* adequately, but they have *disciplined* poorly.

At this point my clinical task is to meet with the parents and explain Dewey's condition to them. Then we must make a plan to catch up the lost ground, to set Dewey's growth in motion again. We must devise ways to deal with each aspect of Dewey's adaptive growth failure: his residual omnipotence, his egocentricity, his impatience, and his defective self-esteem.

The next four chapters will be devoted to examining each of these characteristics individually. Each chapter will begin with a clinical description of the particular characteristic in action. Then the other ways in which that particular characteristic commonly manifests itself will be recounted.

From the clinical picture we shall then move to a developmental perspective, first describing the process of normal psychological development with respect to the given cardinal characteristic. How does infantile omnipotence normally give way to the comfortable acceptance of rational authority? How does the egocentric toddler become a reasonably perceptive and accommodative child? How do patience and persistence develop? How is self-esteem constructed?

This leads us naturally into a discussion of parenting techniques aimed at promoting (or, when the syndrome has already developed, remediating) each element of adaptive growth. Each chapter will end with a detailed program of management of the clinical problem with which we began the chapter.

Let us turn now to our first such chapter, a discussion of infantile omnipotence.

2

The Omnipotence Illusion

"... You're not the boss of me. I don't have to do what you say."

EVERY CHILD AT SOME TIME OR ANOTHER

The Cardinal Characteristic

The three year old was sitting in her high chair feeding herself. She dug her spoon into the cooked cereal, stirred it about a moment, grinned at her mother, then conveyed an unstable load to the approximate vicinity of her mouth. After managing to insert a little less than fifty percent of the porridge into her mouth, she leaned her head against the chair back, chubby arm along the tray, spoon at parade rest, and surveyed her kingdom. Her eyes seemed almost calculating as she munched and cogitated.

Suddenly she raised her spoon to the vicinity of her right ear and threw it to the floor. "Pick it up," she ordered her startled mother.

"That wasn't nice, Pammy," Mother said as she retrieved the spoon, wiped and returned it.

Pammy looked at the spoon. She looked at her mother a moment, then once more raised the spoon to the vicinity of her ear and gracefully lobbed it across the room. "Pick it up," she ordered loudly.

At this point most mothers might have tried to amuse or distract Pammy from her provocative agenda, but Pammy's mother didn't. She retrieved the spoon once more, wiped it on her apron, and returned it with a warning. "Throw it again, and I won't pick it up."

Pammy inspected the spoon a moment, glanced at her mother in a sidelong fashion, then raised the spoon in the vicinity of her right ear once more. She paused a moment, looking at her mother, who said nothing. Pammy frowned and hurled the spoon across the room. "PICK IT UP!" she shouted.

"No way." Mother, who had been through the "battle-of-wills" bit before, got up from her chair and walked over to the kitchen counter where she busied herself putting things away.

Pammy threw a tantrum. She shoved her cereal bowl off the end of her tray, slid down in her chair, arms above her head, until the retaining strap halted her. There she stuck, yelling loudly and angrily.

After a few seconds Mother took Pammy from her chair and carried her, struggling, to her room and deposited her in her crib. Then, closing the bedroom door, Mother left Pammy to holler.

Pammy yelled constantly for four minutes. At first she shouted commands that her mother attend her majestic presence immediately. When these were ignored her tone became more complaining that imperious. Soon she was uttering intermittent yelps, which gradually became woebegone in tone.

Mother went to Pammy's room and picked her up from her crib. She ignored the brief resurgence of vocal indignation and carried Pammy back to her high chair. Then she did something many mothers would hesitate to do: she gave Pammy another bowl of porridge and her spoon.

She challenged her.

Pammy looked at the porridge. She looked at her mother. She picked up the spoon. She looked at her mother again. Mother returned her gaze calmly, saying nothing. Pammy raised the spoon to the vicinity of her right ear. Still Mother said nothing. Then, deciding her head was itchy, and the spoon was an ideal implement for the job, Pammy began scratching behind her right ear.

What we have here is a typical battle-of-wills which three years olds are famous for. The only atypical thing is that Mother won so handily, but then this was her fourth child and she had been around this mulberry bush before.

Battles-of-wills are normal events in early childhood, inevitable once the parent starts to intrude upon the infant's self-appointed agenda. The toddler struggles to preserve the omnipotence illusion which has been the principal source of his security. But the magnitude of his realistic helplessness cannot be denied much longer. He battles to preserve the illusion, but it is a struggle he must lose if he is to develop trust and overcome his separation anxiety—if he is to give up "magic" for realistic coping skills.

The happiest way to traverse the pre-adolescent years is to for the child to come to feel secure in the shelter of his parents' authority, to give up his omnipotence illusion for a belief in his parents' unlimited power, to believe that they are on his side, and to experience their limits and expectations not as put-downs or denigrations but as protection, as evidence of their concern for his well-being.

It does not seem this way to the child in the throes of surrendering the throne. To him the situation seems desperate. To him it seems you are either a king or a slave; either you give the orders or you can expect to be ordered about as insensitively as he has been ordering them. There is no place in the child's understanding for autonomy, the notion that he has a right to a degree of self-determination appropriate to his maturity.

In order for the child to give up his omnipotence illusion, his parents need to set effective limits in a few crucial areas. For his sake the parents need to win a few battles-of-wills. They do not need to overwhelm the child with their authority. They need to leave room for him to make a few choices. "You may wear the red socks or the green, but you cannot go without socks." "You may wash first and dress second, if you wish, but you have to do both before you come down."

If parents err on the side of indulgence, the child will retain his omnipotence illusion, because it is possible to do so. If they come down on the side of overcontrol, he will struggle harder, for his fear that he is about to be inducted into slavery will seem well-founded. Planful firmness about a few items, coupled with leaving him a few choices, treads the middle ground and works better.

These days, more parents seem to err on the side of permissiveness than overcontrol, and the result of this is evident everywhere. Indeed, one has only to keep one's eye open to observe even adults engaged in interpersonal encounters which have the characteristic of throwing their spoon on the floor.

If parents have trouble setting limits and communicating expectations, their child is liable to have trouble navigating the omnipotence-devaluation phase of adaptive growth. When this happens, the struggle continues and surfaces in the child psychiatrist's office in a variety of ways.

Manifestations of Retained Omnipotence

Parents complain that their eight-year-old child does not obey: "he won't do what he is supposed to do"; "he just ignores you when you ask him to do something"; "he won't do his homework, and I can't get him to do it." Duties, chores, anything the child experiences as tedious, the child won't do unless he is constantly supervised, and when one undertakes such supervision, battles-of-wills ensue.

Of course no child likes to do tedious things, but there is a difference between the child who is simply avoiding unpleasure and the child who feels his right to be totally self-determining is being threatened. The avoidant child, when pressed, grumbles but complies. He accepts that his parent or teacher has the "right" to expect things of him.

Not so the omnipotent child. He reacts to increased pressure with less compliance rather than more. "The more you press him, the more he gets his back up," mothers report. Such pressure, it seems, changes the subject. The issue is no longer "I don't want to do that because it's no fun." It now becomes, "who do you think you are telling me what to do?" or "you're not the boss of me, I don't have to do what you say." In such cases a battle-of-wills develops.

Some mothers report, "I've learned the best way to get him to do something is to make him think it is his idea," which of course is to defer to his omnipotence illusion.

With such a child, the disobedience often escalates to defiance and, if the mother is particularly uncertain or paralyzed by guilt, she may find herself the principal subject of an omnipotent tyrant.

The fact is the child does not accept that the parent has the right to require something of him. Such children feel there is no special prerogative of parenthood and often they say so. "You and Dad get to stay up late, so why can't I?" Explanations that involve any differences in the rights of parent and child are rejected out of hand.

Some children are fiercely omnipotent. They seek to rule their families, most particularly their mothers, and they react violently to obstruction. One mother described her eleven year old as follows: "He wants to rule, everything has to be his way. He bosses us all. If I try to be firm and make him do what he is supposed to do he has a tantrum. He abuses me. He calls me stupid. He sometimes even spits in my face. He insists on doing what he wants. He won't go to bed at night. He never brushes his teeth, and once when I tried to insist, he ran out of the house and didn't come back until after supper. If there's something at school he doesn't want to face, like a test, he just refuses to go, and he's too big for me to carry to the car."

Another mother described her nine year old's behavior as follows: "He's a tyrant, he tells me what to do and if I don't do it that very minute he screams and yells at me. He won't let me talk on the telephone. He insists I hang up, and he screams until I do. I'm his slave," she concluded morosely.

Another mother described similar overbearing and demanding behavior from her ten-year-old daughter. "If I don't do what she wants she threatens to kill herself, to put her finger into the light socket, or to run out in front of a truck. Twice now she's taken a knife from the kitchen drawer and threatened to stick it in herself. What can I do? She's just wild enough to do it when she gets like that."

Sometimes similar manifestations at school are the reason for referral to my office. One child refused to remain in his seat when the teacher told him to, and when she tried to put him out in the hall, he climbed out on to the second story window sill and threatened to jump. This same child revealed the pervasiveness of his omnipotence illusion on another occasion when the teacher announced she had compiled a list of children who were to remain after school and finish their work. Although the child's name was not on the list, he was so offended by the teacher's assumption of authority that he took the list from her desk, tore it up, and deposited it in the waste basket. When he was finally escorted to the principal's office he reacted by "firing" the principal.

Amusing as some of this behavior may seem, these children are in earnest. They cherish their omnipotence illusion, and when it is challenged they defend it.

Dramatic examples make the omnipotence illusion obvious, but sometimes it is less openly expressed. One child, for example, would not start his classwork without several reminders. Eventually after much pressure he wrote his name but nothing else. When further pressed he completed the worksheet but left out all the capital letters on the words. What he was doing was refusing the teacher's authority in his own fashion. Though he complied superficially, he maintaining the reservation that by making changes in the work he was not really doing it; he did not do what *the teacher* asked, he did what *he decided* to do.

Maintaining the omnipotence illusion requires not only that others not expect the child to obey them but also that they obey the child. So it is that the omnipotent child sets out to run the household. If he had his way, and some try mightily to do so, every morning he would hand each family member his or her agenda for the day.

The omnipotent child seeks to dominate playtime and often alienates his peers with his bossiness. When this leads to rejection, omnipotent children often end up playing with younger children who will let them lead or with a passive child on the social fringe who has to take what he can get. When they do play games they are the teacher, the general, the chief. When they cannot be, they storm, threaten, and if this does not work they withdraw from the game and go home and watch T.V.

Attempts to boss outside adults meet with less success, but the child often achieves a surprising degree of control over his family. He is frequently deferred to to a remarkable extent. "It's easier than fighting with him," his mother says with a shrug. So he sends back his dinner and

Mother makes him a sandwich. Or she fishes his favorite shirt out of the laundry and irons it at the last minute in time for school.

One frequent manifestation of the omnipotence illusion occurs in a form of interpersonal interaction I call *role swapping*. In order to deny his mother's parental prerogative, the child reacts to her expression of it by assuming the identical prerogative himself. Mother says, "I'll punish you," and the child responds, "no, I'll punish you." The teacher prepares an assignment for the children, and the child prepares an assignment of his own, assuming the prerogatives of the teacher.

In my playroom I run into the same thing. A seven-year-old girl of the imperious persuasion attended my playroom recently. Late in the interview she observed my notes from my previous interview with her parents and she asked what those were.

"Those are my notes," I replied. "Your mom and dad were in telling me about your family, and I wrote some of it down so I wouldn't forget."

"About me?" Suzy asked suspiciously.

"Some about you," I replied.

"Let me see!"

"They're not typed yet. You couldn't read my writing."

She looked into the file and decided I was right, as I knew she would. (Even I can't read my writing if I leave the matter over three days.) She picked up a pencil and a piece of paper and said. "I'll keep notes about you. Did you have an unhappy childhood, Dr. Millar?"

During the last fifteen minutes of our time she offered me several variations on this role-swapping gambit. When it was time to go I got up, went to the playroom door and called back to her. "It's time to go, Suzy." She looked up from her notes, shook her head and, with a little grin, said, "send in the next patient."

Implicit in role swapping is the rejection of the difference in prerogatives between the child-parent, child-teacher, child-doctor, which is, of course, a manifestation of the retained omnipotence illusion.

Some omnipotent children state their views about the distribution of power quite openly, as the following common quotes illustrate:

"You're not the boss of me. I don't have to do what you say."

"It's my room, I'll keep it dirty if I want."

"No second grade teacher is going to boss me about."

"I'm not your maid, you know."

"Kids should be the bosses."

"I don't have to take this, I can go live by myself, you know."

Many children accuse the limit setter of being mean and authoritarian, and many a parent has been the recipient of the "Hitler" epithet. Some children threaten dire consequences if the adult persists in his or her "unfair" assumption of "boss" power.

They utter threats such as, "when I grow up I'm going to shoot you." Or, if the offending boss be a teacher, "I'll bring dynamite and blow up the school."

More sophisticated children generate more subtle anti-authoritarian gambits. "I'm bringing a tape recorder to class and I'm going to hide it in my desk and make a record of how Old Crow yells at the kids, and then I'm taking it to the school board." These maneuvers have a way of keeping up with the times; these days I hear a lot of talk from children about calling the child abuse line. This threat is supposed to generate instant adult deferment, and sometimes it does.

The refusal of these children to accept adult authority is evident in other behaviors too. One seven-year-old child was out in the car driving with his father when they passed the state capital. "That's where they make the laws," his father said. The child averted his eyes and would not look. Later, the child made it clear to me that he felt laws were unfair and he didn't want to acknowledge the impressive presence of a whole building devoted to their creation.

Some children openly reject the notion of God's power, once again seeing this as an affront to their right to be wholly self-determining. However, they are not above invoking this power to put others in their place. "You're not the boss of this office," one seven year old told me when I had indicated to him throwing toys was not acceptable. "God is."

The play of these children is often dominated by "power" themes. When I wrote the first edition of this book television had climbed on this bandwagon through such continuing series as *The Bionic Man*, *Superman*, *Spiderman*, and *The Six Million Dollar Man*. Today the basic theme is the same, but the actors have changed. *Iceman*, *The Incredible Hulk*, *Aquaman*, and *Robocop* now carry on the omnipotent tradition. Indeed, there was a day when Jack and the Beanstalk catered to the same childhood preoccupation.

Some children become obsessed with a particular cartoon hero. One child would spend his entire play day enacting the role of the Six Million Dollar Man. Of course he was Steve Austin and the other children were either villains or menial henchmen. Furthermore, he would insist hotly that bionic power was real.*

---

*Listen to Hitler's insistence on his own omnipotence: "One word I never recognized... in my battle for power: capitulation. That word I do not know and I will never know... that word is again capitulation, that is the surrender of will to another person. Never! Never!" Domarus Reden, as cited in Robert G. Waite, *The Psychopathic God* (Scarborough, Ontario: Signet, 1975).

These omnipotent children are determined to have their own way, and if they cannot bully their parents they learn to manipulate them. For example, most, sooner or later, learn that the phrase "you don't love me any more" is magically effective in dealing with resistant parents. They learn also that threats to injure themselves are similarly effective. "I'm going to run out on the road and get hit by a car. I don't care what happens to me," is a maneuver that quickly turns an irate parent to solicitous mush.

One articulate eleven year old in a single-parent situation spelled this out for me. "If you run away, your mother will be so glad when you return you can do anything you want with her. The thing to do is to scare her." He went on to confide in me, "mothers do what children want because it gives them a feeling of security, especially if they are the only parent."

As one sees child after child caught up in this strong need to deny the reality of his childhood dependency and the limitations in his power, one soon recognizes that the omnipotence illusion is desperately important to these children. Why?

It is not just that they want to avoid tedious duties, although this is part of their motivation. No! To them to accept their parents' authority is to acknowledge the realistic differences in the power of children and adults. This is simply more than they can bear. So they struggle valiantly to preserve the omnipotence illusion. In time it becomes clear: *they seem to feel that it is only by controlling the world that they can be safe in it.* It is growing beyond this notion that is so difficult for them.

In order to understand and ultimately to deal with this, let us now examine the normal course of the omnipotence-devaluation phase of psychological growth.

The Omnipotence-Devaluation Phase of Adaptive Growth

Although the newborn is wholly dependent upon others for his survival, he has no knowledge that this is his true state. The infant lives in a sea of feelings and ill-defined perceptions, and he cannot yet separate one from another. His state is, to quote St. Augustine, "a blooming, buzzing confusion." He feels cold and hunger. He sees light and hears noise, but he has as yet no well-defined self to tell him which sensation comes from within and which from without.

Hungry, he cries, and, somewhere from out of that vague sea, satisfaction in the form of food arrives. Once this happens a few times he begins to differentiate inner (hunger) from outer (satisfaction).

His first notion of power has to be one of omnipotence. He knows nothing of such factors as cows and milkmen, of stoves and mother love. All he knows is that he hollers, the bottle comes, and the sequence keeps happening.

However, in time he comes to identify his mother as a particular configuration in that external sea, a looming moon with two blue craters and a red lined cavity that makes cooing noises and is somehow associated with a variety of satisfactions. Even though he begins to realize she is not part of himself, he still believes she is subject to his will. He cries and she comes; it must be because he cried. He is too immersed in self to conceive his mother as a separate individual with a choice in the matter.

He is possessed of the omnipotence illusion. It is an inevitable state of infancy. It protects the child from an appreciation of how truly helpless and vulnerable he is. If the child knew how simply his care could be abandoned, how utterly dependent he was, he would be flooded with anxiety. But that realization is acquired slowly, and as it is acquired he is also equipped with competencies that take some of the sting out of the reality.

Once the child is on his feet, his disillusionment proceeds apace. He runs into natural laws such as the law of gravity. He tries to fly from a chair and thumps his forehead a good one. He scolds the floor, tells the rotten world what he thinks of it, but he doesn't try to fly again. Furthermore, he begins to learns something about the true distribution of power in the world.

Infants enjoy tweaking the nose of gravity. The denial of its power seems sometimes to motivate their play. If you hold an eighteen-month-old child on your shoulder and let him swing a heavy door with his hand he is delighted to move that enormous object by his force alone. He will play the game as along as you are prepared to hold him there. Similarly, I believe balloons are appealing to small children because they are large things that can move. It is play that seems, for the moment, to deny their powerless state.

But there are more large things they can't move than large they can, so, despite balloons and other such things, disillusionment proceeds. Provided of course that his mother allows such learning to proceed. I recall one mother telling me about her three year old who was immensely offended when the sofa wouldn't remove itself from his path when he ordered it to do so. He shoved it to no avail. He fell to the floor, kicking and banging in a temper tantrum. It took him fifteen minutes to get over his outrage. His mother, a sensitive caring woman who did not wish to see her child so traumatized, took to keeping an eye on his living room excursions, and when he approached the sofa she would crouch behind it so that when he pushed, she pulled, and the sofa did move, thus sparing her the trauma of witnessing his distress but doing nothing to disillusion his omnipotence.*

*Sometimes I wonder about Mohammed ordering the mountain to come to him. I mean, at his age! Do you suppose his mother was in the habit of crouching down behind whatever served for a sofa in those days? And Canute, ordering the ocean to retreat; whatever happened to his omnipotence-devaluation phase?

At the same time as his omnipotence is gradually being disillusioned, the child's awareness of the boundaries of self is increasing. Soon he separates his identity from that of his mother. Since she is the principal satisfier of his needs, the more separate he perceives her, the more necessary it is for him to assure himself she is subservient to his will.*

Eventually he comes to recognizes her operant power, that she can move the world in ways that he cannot, but he does not recognize the independence of her will. He begins to see himself as the executive. It is as though she were a robot and the buttons were his to push as he wished. One articulate three year old expressed this most succinctly when he announced, "she's my mother. She *has* to do what I say."

As long as the child wins the battle-of-wills he is reassured. He *is* omnipotent. She does *have* to do what he says. The world is under his control, and all is well.

But, as we have seen, Mother gradually and naturally becomes less willing to defer to the child's demands. For one thing the demands are escalating, both in frequency and magnitude. Since the child is no longer just sleeping and eating, he intrudes upon her time to a much greater extent than before. Many children would have their mothers constantly at their side entertaining them. If Mother does not start denying him occasionally, her life will no longer be her own. Whether or not it results in a battle-of-wills, Mother is going to have to say no sometimes.

Furthermore, Mother is beginning to realize that she has another job to do besides simply nurturing the child. As she watches her tiny emperor cruising his kingdom, she realizes that others are not going to be willing to reorganize their lives for his benefit, that as soon as he ventures outside of the protection of home, he is going to have to do a little accommodating to others. And if she doesn't train him for this, nobody else is going to.**

THE PROCESS OF DISILLUSIONMENT

So Mother begins the process of omnipotence disillusionment. She does not fetch his bottle so promptly as before. "It won't hurt him to wait while

*The child in the womb is a part of his mother. With birth he becomes physically separate. However it will be some months yet before the psychological anschluss will dissolve for either party.

**There is evidence to suggest that Adolph Hitler's mother was not up to this child-rearing task. "Worries about Adolph's health helped produce the excessive maternal solicitude which Klara showered on her son until she died... several of the neighbors found the mother's love for the child verged on the pathological." (Waite, *The Psychopathic God*.)

I heat it," she thinks. So she ignores his protests a little longer than she has heretofore been wont to do.

"Where's the damn bottle?" her child thinks. Well, maybe he doesn't swear; but only because he hasn't yet learned the words, not because he doesn't feel like it. He begins to get worried. "Wow," he thinks. "If she does not come when I call, who will feed and look after me?"

He has received a hint of his powerless condition and he rejects the input. "No way!" he declares. "She *has* to come when I call, and I'll just prove it." He hollers! She comes! "That's more like it," he assures himself, as that uneasy feeling settles in his breast.

What uneasy feeling? When he's older he'll recognize it as anxiety. For the moment let's call it the vague presentiment that his omnipotence might not be quite so absolute as he thought. He has received a hint of the truth of his situation, that he is *wholly* unable to fend for himself, that he is *totally* dependent upon his mother's care, which *she might just withhold if she chose to.*

But tomorrow, when the whole sequence happens again, and the next day too, he begins to suspect that somewhere there is a leak in the boat of his omnipotence. To the omnipotent child this is bad news indeed; he needs her to fetch and carry! Holy diapers, Batman, what if she doesn't come at all? Who will feed me? Where is she? *So it is that as omnipotence is challenged, separation anxiety arises.*

The normal two year old does not take this kind of thing lying down. He fights back. And this is what the *terrible twos* are all about.

Not every mother experiences a terrible twos with her toddler. Some children are so mild tempered, and the situation so low key, that omnipotence devaluation proceeds without much ruffling of the surface waters.

Sometimes, if this is Mother's first child and she has nothing else to do but serve him, she continues to obey her child's orders. Sometimes she is just too soft and caring to grasp the nettle. Sometimes, just a child herself, like Hitler's mother, it is beyond her limited capacity to cope with this most difficult aspect of parenting.

However, in most families, when the heretofore sunny two year old becomes provocative and demanding, Mother recognizes the need to fight back. It's not easy. When he says "I don't want Wheaties, I want Corn Flakes" and Mother brings Corn Flakes, now it's Rice Krispies he wants. Then back to Wheaties again. There is no satisfying him. Why? Because his agenda is to set up a battle-of-wills, win it, and preserve his endangered omnipotence illusion.

That may be his agenda, but it cannot be his parents', for the child's adaptive growth depends upon surrendering the omnipotence illusion and learning to trust. Mother cannot pander; she must sometimes confront. Where does this take her? Into a battle-of-wills.

In lively, up-front children, battles-of-wills escalate into temper tantrums. Dealt with properly the adaptive sequence I call omnipotence disillusionment is soon worked through. However, if it not dealt with properly, the terrible twos can persist and become the terrible threes, fours, fives or even forties.

With pre-school children omnipotence-devaluation is a normal developmental process, much easier to handle then than it will be later. This is preventive parenting. With the eight year old we are into remedial parenting which, while not impossible, takes longer and is harder.

NAVIGATING THE NORMAL OMNIPOTENCE-DEVALUATION PHASE

The central event of the omnipotence-devaluation phase is the battle-of-wills. To be sure these may sometimes be avoided by finding a way to make the child think the solution you seek was really his idea. "Wouldn't it be fun to play in the bath now?" Or the child may seduced into compliance. "I'll race you to the table." But these measures are like Chamberlain settling for 'peace in our time.' They simply defer the inevitable until a time when battles-of-wills may be much harder to deal with.

It is part of normal growing up for the child beginning to suspect he is not omnipotent to seek to prove he is. This is of course is why maternal expectations now precipitate a battle-of-wills. When a child really wants— really needs—to have a battle-of-wills, it's very hard not to end obliging him.

One day a five-year-old child was brought to me by his mother. I led him into my playroom. He glowered at me. Clearly, he did not want to be there.

"You can play with anything you want," I said, waving at my toy shelf.

"I wanna play with the blocks," he demanded.

I brought him the blocks.

"No!" he said pushing the blocks aside. "I wanna play with the cars."

So I brought him the cars.

"Nope!" He shook his head. "I wanna play with the puppets."

I took away the cars and brought him the puppets. By now I was curious to see how long he would keep this up, so I just smiled and fetched. We went though a couple of more items, fetched and refused. Each time his face had grown darker and more angry.

Finally, terminally exasperated, he looked at me and shouted, "I wanna play with sumpin' you haven't got."

Battles-of-wills, inevitable or not, may be won or lost. Each outcome has a very different impact on the child's adaptive development. Here are the scenarios of both winning and of losing as I believe small children probably perceive these events.

Scenario A: The Child Wins

1. I am all powerful. I know because my mother always obeys me.
2. She's not obeying me. Does that mean I'm not all powerful?
3. No way! I am all powerful and I will prove it. Here we go! Into battle.
4. It worked. She obeyed me. I am all powerful.
5. In fact I'm pretty hot stuff, and don't you forget it.

Obviously the child who wins a battle-of-wills has had his omnipotence illusion confirmed and so makes no adaptive progress. What of the other case?

Scenario B: The Adult Wins

1. I am all powerful. I know because my mother always obeys me.
2. She's not obeying me. Does that mean I'm not all powerful?
3. No way! I am all powerful and I will prove it. Here we go! Into battle!
4. It didn't work. She didn't obey me. Maybe I'm not all powerful?
5. I'm nothing. I'm powerless. I'm weak and worthless. I cannot control my mother. She could abandon me. Then who will feed and look after me? I'm doomed.

This is a sad state of being and it is not surprising that the child struggles against it with vim and vigor. But it is an unreal appreciation of his situation. True he is weak and powerless and he cannot control his mother, but in the normal family he is valued, indeed of great worth in his parents' eyes. He will be fed and looked after. Perhaps not so promptly as he demands, but with care and concern. Most important of all, Mother doesn't leave him. She is there in the morning when he wakes.

There is no way for the child to appreciate this reality except by experiencing it. The child who loses a battle-of-wills and discovers that his needs are met anyway begins to realize that his apprehensions are groundless. This reduces the magnitude of his separation anxiety. It also disillusions his omnipotence. "Maybe she doesn't fetch the moment I call," he tells himself, "but she comes eventually." Soon this becomes "maybe I can't *make* Mother do what I want but I can *count on* her doing what I need."

When the child surrenders his omnipotence illusion, he exchanges it for another illusion, a belief in his parents' omnipotence. Mother is all power-ful. She can heal hurts with a kiss or a laying on of hands. She can tame teachers, intimidate principals, and fire governors if necessary. Father is the strongest father on the block. He can lift cars by the bumper if he wants to. Just as the child once overvalued his power, now he overvalues his parents' power. And will do so until adolescence upsets this particular apple-cart.

The child has found a new equation for security. *Perhaps he is no longer the king, but he is a close friend of the king, and he is going to be all right.*

There is no happier way to traverse middle childhood than secure in the knowledge of your parents' power to protect you. To live in the shadow of the king frees the child. No longer does he have power worries, his energies are freed for growth. He can spend his days acquiring adaptive strength and building his persona while others take care of his security.

The mother who continues to defer to her child when she should be standing up to him is not only perpetuating his illusion with respect to the distribution of power but is also robbing her child of the chance to learn to trust, condemning him to a life in which he must control his world to feel safe in it.

Let us consider now how successful navigation of the omnipotence-devaluation phase leads to the capacity for trust.

TRUST

.As every suspicious husband knows, you don't have to trust those whom you can control. So it is not until the child recognizes that he can-not control his mother that her continued care of him can generate trust. It is the conventional wisdom that all that is necessary for a child to learn to trust the world is that he receive regular and loving care. This is not so. Over the years I have seen many, many concerned and caring parents whose children have developed very little trust. The problem in these cases has not been a lack of love and caring from the parents but a failure to disillusion the child's omnipotence such that he comes to realize his parents care for him because they love him, not because they are sub-ject to his omnipotent will.

It is not possible to overestimate the importance of this consequence of the successful disillusionment of infantile omnipotence. People who must live their lives devoid of trust in their fellow man surely tread the lowest byways of this vale of tears.

How then is trust related to omnipotence devaluation? The sequence goes like this. When the child loses a battle-of-wills, he finds he cannot control his mother. But his security has always depended upon the illusion that the world was his to command. He becomes insecure. "If I can't control her, what if she doesn't feed and care for me? She could leave. I could starve. Where is she?"

So it that the first effect of omnipotence disillusionment is that it leads to anxiety, most particularly a form that has come to be known as separation anxiety. But what happens? The child is still fed and looked after. Perhaps not so promptly as he orders but still looked after. What does this tell the child? His anxiety has proven groundless. "Maybe I can't make her do what I want," he realizes, "but I can count on her doing what I need." So is trust born. So long as the child believes he is king, he cannot come to trust. It isn't until he accepts that he cannot control his mother that he can learn to trust her.

Here, in summary form, is a brief recapitulation of this crucial sequence.

The Genesis of Trust

Stage I
1. Loss of omnipotent illusion
2. Child realizes his dependent situation
3. Anxiety develops

Stage II
1. Mother meets needs
2. Anxiety proves groundless
3. Trust develops

The Fate of the Omnipotence Illusion

The child who works through the devaluation of his omnipotence comes to believe that while he is not omnipotent, his parents are, and he is safe in their care. He proceeds through middle childhood in a protected state, at least until adolescence generates another disillusioning experience.

With adolescence the illusion of *parental* omnipotence bites the dust. As the child matures, particularly in his capacity to think in more complex ways, he begins to see his parents not as the king and queen but as members of a group of persons variously called adults and parents. He begins to see his mother as a mother, and perhaps not necessarily the most competent one on the block. When this insight arrives, the child is forced to re-examine his working comprehension of power.

Many adolescents are disturbed by the knowledge that their parents are not all powerful. It has both attractive and upsetting aspects. It is attractive because it seems to suggest to them that they are going to be free now to run their own lives, and their striving for independence is heartened by this knowledge. However, it is upsetting because it leaves them without a protective power base. "If my mother and father are not omnipotent, then my faith in their power to succor me under all circumstances was misplaced. What if something terrible happens? Who now will rescue me?"

To be aware of one's parents' fallibility is to be vulnerable once more. This is one reason adolescents seem so impossibly contrary at times.

If a fifteen-year-old girl asks her mother, "what shall I wear to the dance?" believe me, there is no right answer.

If Mother says, "why don't you wear the pink dress?" the child will say, "oh, you're always telling me what to do."

If Mother says, "I'm sure whatever you choose will look nice," the child will complain, "why is it you never help me?"

This is the power confusion all adolescents experience. One moment they want to be told what to do, and the next no way will they permit that kind of ordering about.

There was a time, in the history of the world, when the adolescent solved this problem by transferring omnipotence from his parents to God, who was then seen as a benign and potent protector. I believe that the phenomenon of adolescent religiosity used to arise, at least in part, out of this psychological sequence.

It is unlikely in Western society that many children do this anymore. There is not a widespread personal faith of this dimension among young people today, and so this route to security is not open to most of them.

What then happens to these children? I believe that in most cases something like this goes on. If the child has had good parenting, that is to say reasonable expectations, well enforced, he will have coped with most of the things that come his way. Coping brings confidence. With each growing up task mastered the child feels more competent. Eventually he comes to feel "I have coped with most things that have come my way, and so I can probably cope with those yet to come."

So it is that the reasonably mature adolescent ventures into the world a bit apprehensive perhaps, but not overwhelmed by his new independence.

However, the child who has not worked through earlier phases of his growth is unlikely to have succeeded enough to build this kind of confidence. He may well find the world overwhelming, and sometimes he may search for some omnipotent being to attach himself to.

These days gurus and messiahs abound, ever ready to absorb new followers, to make their decisions for them, to pander to their needs, be these for the disparagement of the establishment or the assertion of their right to continued and unremitting pleasure. Is this not what Charles Manson had to sell? Self-indulgence *sans* guilt? If one reads the story of the Manson family, how like omnipotent children are these middle-class hedons, these egocentric defiers of conventional morality?

What of the person who reaches adult years and has not worked through his omnipotence devaluation? Do such persons exist? Indeed they do. A successful outcome of omnipotence devaluation is not inevitable, and some persons grow to adulthood having constructed an adaptive pattern that still contains the omnipotence illusion. While this is most often a crippled state of psychological being, it is not incompatible with some kinds of success, for example high achievement in such power-tinged occupations as governing people and directing plays. Indeed unrestrained omnipotence may be a mental set favorable to certain kinds of creativity, for to believe in one's omnipotence is to be freed from those mental constraints which may hem in a humbler man, impressed as he is with the greats who have gone before him.

Sigmund Freud was, I believe, a man like this. Listen to this fragment of his childhood. When Sigmund was ten years old, and his sister eight, their mother "who was very musical, got her to practice the piano, but though it was at a certain distance from the cabinet, the sound disturbed the young Freud so much that he insisted on the piano being removed, and removed it was. So none of the family received any musical education, any more than Freud's children did later."

Psychoanalyst Eric Fromm, commenting on this incident, says, "it is not hard to visualize the position the ten-year-old boy had acquired with his mother when he could prevent the musical education of his family because he did not like the noise of the music."

This smells mighty like an unresolved omnipotence-devaluation phase to me, as do some other aspects of Dr. Freud's personality.

Not all persons work through the omnipotence-devaluation phase of adaptive growth successfully. Some spend their lives fighting the same battle over and over again. Because they have not learned to trust, their security continues to depend on control, control of the persons and events that touch their lives. They battle endlessly to dominate those persons, to determine the course of those events. Their marriages tend to reflect their omnipotence psychopathology. Some such persons move the battleground into the community. They fight the boss or the police. Many criminals have prominent omnipotent child characteristics.

The fact is, though retained omnipotence may enhance creativity, it tends to lead to a troubled and joyless existence which may, at least for the suffering individual, not be worth the candle.

In the normal case too, man's appreciation of the nature and locus of power in his affairs continues to grow throughout his lifetime. Recognizing the facts of power and his own helplessness proceeds at different rates for different persons, but eventually the reality imposes itself on us all. The knowledge of the inevitability of one's own death is a powerful stimulant to this growth.

Death of course is the ultimate humbling, and fear of it for some persons is more a fear of loss of power than of pain, for to accept one's own death is to acknowledge one's ultimate helplessness.

For the Christian, of course, this acknowledgment is the beginning. The believer is told he must "come as a child," that is "acknowledging his powerless state," if he is to experience his salvation. And others, commenting from a philosophical rather than a religious base, have said similar things. Henri Frederick Amiel tells us that "humanity only begins for man with self-surrender." Many who have come close to the reality of their own death report that the experience illuminates their lives from then on.

So the journey toward a realistic appreciation of the nature of power ends when one comes to grips with and accepts his own mortality. How many reach that goal is in doubt, for the journey requires that a man be brave and honest with himself and others. To face up to this he will need the best adaptive equipment his parents can give him. A successful working through of the omnipotence-devaluation phase of psychological growth is the first and most crucial step towards acquiring that equipment.

The Need for Discipline

It seems obvious that Mother must win some of the battles-of-wills if she is to lead her child through the omnipotence-devaluation phase. She does not have to win them all, but to go on allowing her child to think everything is his idea or charming him into compliance is simply to postpone the inevitable.

Even so many modern mothers don't see it this way. They have, up to now, been caring for an infant. It is natural for a mother to defer to her infant's demands. It is not only a rational act in view of his helplessness, but also it is an instinctive maternal response. But once the child is on his feet and talking a bit, it begins to become clear that Mother has another duty to her child besides simply nurturing him. That duty is training him, and that training involves discipline, that is setting limits and expecting things of him.

Maternal awareness of this new need arises naturally. The toddler now begins to intrude upon his mother's day. Since he is not napping so much and is on his feet and can follow her around demanding that she play with him, Mother has to begin denying him occasionally. If not, she will become his slave. Self-respecting women are not prepared to do this.

Mother begins to feel he is too big to whine and be so demanding. She begins to recognize that if he continues in his way, others won't make the same allowances for him she is prepared to make. In this natural way, mothers move from simply *nurturing* the child to *training* him. They do not need to read a book to see the need for this transition. Indeed, it might be better if they did not, for many modern child-rearing books over-emphasize the nurturant aspects of child rearing. Indeed, some claim that all that is necessary to rear children is unstinting love; the training will take care of itself. Furthermore, by the liberal use of negative examples involving deprived, abandoned, and neglected children, they scare mothers away from their natural recognition of the need for discipline and training.

Some mothers become militant in their condemnation of discipline. One such mother, who happened to be dealing with an unusually articulate three year old, was determined to be the best mother this world has ever seen. So, when her three year old questioned every limit and expectation offered, Mother answered her questions, repetitious as these often were.

When I pointed out to her that the child was not really seeking information, she was simply delaying compliance, Mother protested, "surely the child is entitled to an explanation of why the thing is required of her." I pointed out to her that the child had had the explanation several times already. I advised Mother thus. "Tell her, 'I told you why yesterday, and we don't need to explain again. Let's get started.'"

Mother told me that her child would simply not accept this, that she would want a further explanation of Mother's refusal to explain, which she, the mother, would then feel compelled to offer, and so further delay would occur.

"You are the mother," I told her. "You aren't required to answer every question your child puts to you. Just tell her to do it and if she asks why then say, because I am telling you to do it. Now, no more stalling."*

Mother was appalled. No way would she ever tell her child to do something simply because "Mother said so." To her mind this was hopelessly authoritarian. That, of course, was the end of me. She went home and returned to her 'child rearing is a relationship of equals' manual.

If parents are to disillusion the child's infantile omnipotence, they must appreciate the true situation between the parent and the pre-school child. *In no respect, except in his rights as a human being, is the child equal to the parent.* He has almost no knowledge, experience or judgment and is largely

*An incident similar to this occurs in the movie *The Big Chill*. See Appendix B.

unable to understand the real world in which he lives. He cannot deal with his feelings and will follow them straight into serious difficulty if someone doesn't set limits for him. To allow him an equal voice in affairs concerning him, simply because he demands it, is an abdication of the parents' responsibility to be the parents.

Disillusioning the omnipotence of the pre-school child depends upon such a comprehension of parenthood. The fact is the parent is in charge of the bulk of the child's life. While the parent does not have to be mean or overbearing, she should make no bones about saying to the child, "no, you can't climb on the window ledge" and take the child down despite his protests.

All children occasionally protest when they can't have their way. Sometimes these difficulties can be minimized with a little tact and wise management. For example, warning the child of an impending change of direction is often helpful. "In five minutes we're going to have supper." The child screams "No!" But you leave and say nothing. During that five minutes the notion of supper drifts about his mind, and when the five minutes is up and you come for him, he might well jump up to accompany you and ask, "what are we having?"

The important thing is that the child ends up doing what he is supposed to do when he is supposed to do it. Children learn more from events than they do from words, and if the child regularly does what he should at the time he should, eventually he comes to accept the parents' right to set limits on him. So it is his omnipotence illusion is gradually dispelled.

But what of the child who, despite reasonable tact and consideration, still will not do as he is told and, if one insists, initiates a battle-of-wills and ends having a temper tantrum? How is Mother to deal with him?

A Temper Tantrum Control Program

Many parents come to me with pre-school children who are having temper tantrums whenever they cannot have their way. Though many of the mothers are sure there is something terribly wrong, what it usually comes down to is a high energy child in a vibrant but normal omnipotence-devaluation phase which Mother doesn't how to handle.

Oftimes, before I can outline a program for the control of tantrums, I have to deal with some common misunderstandings. Some persons feel that if the child is having a lot of temper tantrums he *must* be horribly discontent, and the problem is therefore one of nurturance. They feel the child is angry because he is not receiving an adequate amount of affection, that is, that Mother does not love him enough. Most often this is not the case. To be sure neglected or rejected children will be discontent because of their lack of nurturance, and may express themselves through temper tantrums when things are expected of them. Even so it is more often the case that such children become sullen and passively contrary. These children need more than better discipline. First they need better nurturance.

Most children having temper tantrums are not, in my experience, in trouble with nurturance. To be sure the mother and child aren't presently experiencing much joy in each other's company, but that is the result of the temper tantrums, not the cause of them. Most such cases in my practice come down to an energetic, intense child by temperament, reacting to the psychological pain of omnipotence devaluation with the same vigor he brings to the rest of living.

So having ascertained that there is no other cause for the tantrums, I set up a program with the mother for their control. Let me illustrate this program with a case. Let's call our willful little three year old Terry.

"He has temper tantrums all the time," the young mother complained. "He throws himself down and he yells and kicks, and he keeps it up until he's hoarse, red in the face and sweating. I try to comfort him, but no way. Once he's started there's no talking to him; I don't think he hears what's being said."

"Have you any idea what triggers these?" I asked her.

"Anything! Any refusal! Cross him in any way and he starts yelling and demanding. I can't always give in to him," the mother said, shaking her head in despair, "but it seems the only way to keep peace. I had no idea the terrible twos could be so terrible; he was such a sunny child up until six months ago."

I reviewed the family situation with her. There was no indication of any serious family situation which might have affected her ability to nurture the child.

Terry had always been an energetic and lively child, but a sunny one who was affectionate, approachable and doing fine in his physical and mental development. He walked at a year, he had a few words then, and seemed to have his bowel training almost under control. But shortly after he turned two, Terry had become very demanding, a little clingy, and the temper outbursts had begun.

For the last four or five months he had been having multiple temper tantrums. Their frequency had increased to the point he was now having as many as ten outbursts in a day. There might have been more if it was not for the fact that Mother "walked on eggs" when she was dealing with him.

As is so often the case, Terry had become more clinging of late and settling him at night has become a problem. "Lie down until I go to sleep" had become his demand, and since he would have a tantrum if he didn't get his way in this, Mother had taken to lying with him until he went to sleep.

I explained to the mother that Terry's tantrums were not caused by emotional deprivation or conflict but were his intense way of reacting to a normal phase of growth. I then explained the omnipotence-devaluation sequence to her.

"The trick is to find a reasonable way to manage the tantrums so that we can bring Terry through this adaptive phase," I said. "Here's my program for dealing with temper tantrums."

Temper Tantrum Control Program

> The Signal
> The Silent Seven
> The Removal
> The Timing
> Persisting

THE SIGNAL

"When Terry begins to yell and scream, stand back, point your finger at him, and say, 'you're having a tantrum.' Then cross your arms and look at him."

Mother is to point her finger for two reasons. The first is that small children, like express trains on tracks, need simple signals if they are to grasp the essential information, en passant as it were. The second is that the yelling child is often making so much noise he may not hear the accompanying word.

The word doesn't have to be 'temper tantrum.' It could be 'fuss,' or 'whoop de doo.' It doesn't matter so long as it always the same word. One Vancouver mother said "you're Stanley Parking." This was because one day when she and her husband had taken the boy to Stanley Park, he threw such a wing ding that they had to take him home again. Now, when she says 'Stanley Parking,' her child understands exactly what she is talking about.

The signal is just that, a signal. In time it should register with the child and indicate that *Program A is up and running.*

THE SILENT SEVEN

Once the initiating signal has been sent Mother crosses her arms, looks down at her child, and counts to seven. In her head! This is why I call it the 'silent seven.' Soon the child realizes that when Mother's arms are crossed some kind of a timing process is underway.

One four year old whose mother began to use my temper tantrum control program was really impressed with the silent seven, particularly its arm-crossing component. As soon as Mother crossed her arms and began the silent seven he would stop yelling and complain to his mother, "don't cross your arms." Then he would wander off, tantrum terminated, muttering to himself about weird mothers who were forever crossing their arms.

The purpose of the silent seven is to give the child time to stop his tantrum before removal takes place. Though this will not happen for a while, as the program begins to work, it will become apparent how essential to the training process the silent seven is. Without it there would be no opportunity for the child to improve.

THE REMOVAL

"In the beginning," I told his mother, "Terry will not stop fussing during the silent seven and it will necessary to remove him." The best way to accomplish removal is to escort, propel or carry the child to the room one plans to use for containment. Since most children will come right back out again, it is necessary to secure the door. I think it best if the door is secured ajar with a long and sturdy hook and eye. This contains the child but it does not separate him to the degree a closed door does. Furthermore it allows one to place the containment timer outside the door, on the floor, where the child can see it but not reach it. The removal is intended to deal with the tantrum. One cannot stop the child yelling, but one can terminate its communicative import by putting the child in his room.

If other methods of removal will suffice, then they may be used instead. But beware, they might not be effective. For example, one mother said she would prefer to have him go to a corner of the kitchen and sit in the chair for four minutes.

"If he will stay," I agreed.

"I think he will," she said and she was right, but what he did was sit there and harass her for the four minutes. I would have preferred that he got the message "if you are going to whoop and holler then you can't be out here with me."

Some mothers are concerned about locking the child in his room. In part, I agree. But only in part. Omnipotent children are concerned about separation and putting them in a closed room might generate some separation concern. This is why I prefer the door ajar. But separating the child is better than restraining him physically. Restraint remains acutely interpersonal and can quickly accelerate to physical contact. It is better if the child goes to his room and both parent and child have a chance to cool off.

THE TIMING

There needs to be a containment timer; one of those portable egg timers that ding when the time is up works well. I usually instruct Mother to place it on the floor out of the child's reach but within sight through the door jamb. I recommend it be set for four minutes.

There are two reasons I like to use the visible timer. In the first place he can't con a timer. It won't go faster because he is woebegone or because he is screaming. But a mother will; her heart softens or her resolve weakens and she may let him out. This says to the child that *he* can control his egress, which does nothing to disillusion his omnipotence.

The second reason I like to use the timer is because it soon tells the child there is an end to the detention. To put a child in his room for an indefinite period is much more liable to lead to destructive behavior. The child is like a prisoner with a life sentence; why shouldn't he tear the place apart?

"Four minutes is an awfully short time," some mothers say.

"But it is enough to make the action communication that we want to make," I reply. "It says to the child, 'you can't do this, and if you do I will give you a consequence.' On a deeper level it says to the child, 'you are the child and I am the parent. Some things I decide, and this is one of them.'"

I usually take the opportunity to point out to the parent that it isn't the magnitude of the consequence that effects the child's behavior, it is the consistency and inevitability of the response that carries the action communication. "Four minutes regularly applied is enough to do that. Furthermore, since you may have to do it seven or eight times the first day or two, four minutes is long enough. If you make it longer you won't be able to keep it up."

So when Terry has a tantrum, he is taken to his room, kicking and screaming, and is deposited, door latched ajar, with the timer going for four minutes. Of course his indignation knows no bounds.

When the dinger sounds, Mother opens the door. "Your time's up. You can come out now."

Terry does. Like the bull entering the arena. Soon his tantrum is in full flower again.

Mother points her finger at him and says "you're having a tantrum." Then she gives him the silent seven, returns him to his room, fixes the latch, sets the timer and retreats to the kitchen. When the four minutes are up, she lets him out. The whole thing begins again, and she will have to return him again. Once more, though, she follows the routine, giving him the signal and the silent seven before removal.

The fourth time Mother lets him out, gives him the signal and starts the silent seven, Terry will stop yelling.

While I don't know for sure what is going on in such a child's mind, I think something like this is happening. "Migawd! She's doing that bit with the finger and arms again. I know what comes next." So he falls silent and walks off muttering about mean mums and crossed arms.

PERSISTING

In the usual case the child will go through the whole performance again later the same day. This is all right, for as long as Mother goes through her routine exactly as designed, she is giving Terry his second, third or fourth lesson, and it is through repetition that children learn. The more frequent the repetition the quicker the learning. The important thing is that each lesson send exactly the same message.

In the usual case it takes two or three days of this kind of training before its effectiveness begins to show. Soon the response is of this order. When Mother takes a step back, points and says in a quiet voice, "Terry, you're having a tantrum," fifty percent of the time he will stop during the silent seven, and fifty percent he will have to go to his room. But only for one trip. In a couple of weeks the signal is all that is necessary to stop the tantrum.

This program is very sensitive to its details. Never, for example, repeat the signal before following through. This tells him you don't always mean it. Don't let him con you into letting him out before the time is up. And guard your timer. Once the child realizes "it's that timer I can't con" it may disappear into the garbage. Also, don't let him define tantrum. "I was only kicking not yelling, that's not a tantrum." You're the mother. You decide what is a tantrum and what isn't.

With Terry it took three heavy days before Mother became convinced the program was going to work. When I saw her the next week she was feeling much better about things. "He still has occasional tantrums," she said, "but most times when I back off, point the finger and give him my spiel, he stops fussing before he has to go to his room."

Terry still wants his way, still wants to do what was in his mind to do, but he has learned that when the finger points and the word 'tantrum' is heard in the land, unless he cools it immediately, he will find himself in his room. Seeing no option, Terry now usually complies with the limit or expectation that triggered his resistance. He comes to supper or gives up on the idea of going to the park "this very minute."

The psychologically crucial event, of course, is that Terry has begun to accept his mother's discipline. He is obeying her and finding that doing so, while sometimes inconvenient, has not the tragic consequence he feared. While he cannot control his mother as he once imagined he could, she still gives him what he needs. And obedience, however generated, is still obedience, and is incompatible with the omnipotence illusion. Terry's adaptive growth has been well served by this program to control his tantrums.

Such parenting success has a useful effect on mothers too, and often after a program of this kind, one hears mothers say something like the following: "I don't know what got into me, letting that child bully me. I mean, I *am* the parent, and he *is* the child."

Having grasped the nettle of discipline, done the hard thing and found it to be within her capacity, Mother develops respect for herself both as a parent and a person. Furthermore, often to her surprise, she discovers her child is not angry with her for being strict; in fact he seems sunnier, and they have begun again to enjoy being together.*

When the child is a pre-schooler, a program like this is often all it takes to get adaptive growth in motion again. However, if Mother had not found a way to deal with Terry's tantrums and he had continued on his willful and demanding course, in a few years he would have been well into the omnipotent child syndrome. Then the task would become much more difficult. And once children are into adolescence it becomes almost impossible for parents to alter an inadequate coping style.

So much then for the omnipotence-devaluation component of adaptive growth. It is time now to discuss the second cardinal characteristic of the syndrome, the child's continuing egocentric perception of the world, so that we can see how its opposite, the capacity to read and accommodate to the needs and rights of others, can be nurtured in the child.

---

*There is a question that never fails to arise whenever I speak to a group of mothers. Some person always carps "that tantrum program is all very well, but what am I to do when my child throws one in the supermarket?"

The purpose of the program is to *train* the child. With a three year old, you keep him home until when you give him the signal he regularly stops his tantrum. Then you take him to supermarket with you. Chances are when you give him the signal he will stop his tantrum even though you haven't a way to remove him. If he doesn't, when you get home you put him in his room for the four minutes he couldn't serve earlier. Then, next time you go to the supermarket you make a production out of not taking him.

"But I won't fuss," he'll say.

"You might. We'll just skip a time for you."

The time after that you try him again. A couple of those, coupled with effective home training and soon when you start the silent seven in the grocery store, he will cool it in the same way he has learned to do at home.

3

Egocentricity

"*The disease we all have and that we have to fight against all our lives is, of course, the disease of self.*"

SHERWOOD ANDERSON

The Cardinal Characteristic

"Johnny! It's nearly time for supper. Better go wash your hands," Mother called from the living room door.

Eight-year-old Johnny, slumped in the big chair, his eyes fixed upon upon the television, gave no indication of having heard.

"Johnny! In five minutes supper will be served." Mother wiped her hands on her apron and took a step into the room.

Johnny did not flicker an eyelid.

It was nearly time to take the potatoes off the burner. Mother considered leaving him there. But darn it, this was the fourth time that day Johnny had left her dangling when she spoke to him. Mother came part way across the room, raised her voice a decibel or two and called, "JOHNNY! . . . Did you hear me? I said wash your hands for supper."

Johnny frowned and brushed at his ear as though a fly were buzzing somewhere in the distance.

Mother clomped over. "Johnny! Did you or did you not hear me tell you to wash you hands?" A frown of annoyance crossed Johnny's brow, then melted away.

Mother placed a heavy hand on Johnny's head, turned his face toward her and snapped, "Johnny Williams. You look at me when I speak to you."

Though Johnny's face now pointed in her direction, his eyes had swiveled to keep the television screen in focus.

Mother turned the chair.

Johnny looked up at her and, shaking his head in exasperation, said, "do you have to bug me all the time? I heard ya. I was going to do it. Inna minute, inna minute! Gee whiz! Bug! Bug! Bug!"

Mother turned off the television and, over his protests, pointed him toward the downstairs washroom, then retreated to the kitchen. "I suppose I do bug him," she muttered to herself. "But if he'd just answer, I wouldn't have to. And if I don't bug he won't do it. He'd never have washed his hands. He'd have sat there until I fetched him. 'Inna minute, inna minute!' Him and his inna minutes!"

That night after supper, Mother discussed the incident with her husband. "It's almost as though he doesn't hear. *Maybe we should get his hearing checked?*"

You'd be surprised how many parents who eventually arrive in my office have first had their child's hearing checked. With negative results. Johnny's problem is not hearing, it's attending. In their hearts, the parents knew it. As Johnny's father said later, "whisper something about going to McDonald's for a milkshake, and he hears from thirty feet away."

The problem has nothing to do with the eardrum or any other part of the acoustic chain. The problem has to do with egocentricity. Much of the time Johnny is immersed in self. Like the normal three year old, Johnny comprehends the world as though he were the sun and all others planets orbiting around his being.*

Johnny is too egocentric to recognize his obligation to respond to others when they speak to him. If he ends up missing some goody because of his inattention, he will be indignant for he feels that his parent has let him down. In his view, it is Mother's job to make sure he gets the message, not his to make sure he receives it.

All small children are egocentric. They need to be trained out of their immersion in self. Without realizing it, Johnny's mother has been fostering Johnny's egocentricity by accommodating to him when she should have been requiring him to accommodate to her. Unwittingly she has taught him something she did not wish him to learn.

Johnny has learned that when Mother calls from the living room door with a message, one of two sequences will follow. Either she will call him two or three times then go away, or she will call him three times and not go away. In the second case she will intrude upon him, place her hand on his head, swivel his chair, whatever it takes to make sure he gets the mes-

*Jean Piaget, the famous psychologist, has concerned himself with this aspect of the child's development. He uses the term egocentrism. He describes the egocentric young child as "the unwitting center of his universe" and documents the many ways in which the child is "unaware that there are points of view, of which his is only one."

sage. In the second case, she will probably also give him a little static.

It has become so that, when such a communication situation arises, Johnny knows there's a better than even chance Mother will give up and go away. So why break your concentration? Why disturb your T.V. viewing when, with a little bit of luck, you may not have to. Maybe you lose a few, but the worst that happens is that you get yelled at.

Under these circumstances, how is Johnny ever going to learn to give up his egocentric immersion in self?

For Johnny, the situation is very convenient. Mother has become his social secretary, screening out the *you-can-get-away-with-it* calls from the *you-must* calls.

So long as the parent accommodates to the child in such a fashion, the child will not leave his egocentric cocoon. He will retain that pervasive self-orientation so characteristic of the omnipotent child.

Manifestations of Egocentricity

Retained egocentricity manifests itself as symptoms in family life; in the community, particularly with peers; and in the moral development of the child.

IN HOME LIFE

Parents complain, "everything has to go his way. If we plan something as a family and he doesn't want to go, he makes a terrible fuss. We can't seem to make him see that others have rights too; that his brother, for example, is really looking forward to going to the park to see the whales. There is no convincing him that perhaps next time the family will be doing something he wants."

All that is in the egocentric child's mind is how his plans are being disrupted by the contemplated action. He is unable to place himself in the point of view of others and see how by doing his thing he will interfere with their doing theirs. Furthermore, if the family insists upon him accommodating, as they must do if they are ever going to disillusion his egocentric comprehension of the world, he is resentful. And he let's them know it. Oftimes in ways that disrupt.

"The trouble," Mother says, "is this. If we don't go to see the whales, it's not fair to the rest of us, but if we do, he finds some way to spoil it for everybody. He'll whine or sulk. Perhaps even some such thing as throwing a wing ding in Stanley Park."

One mother told of an incident which illustrates how self-centered and imperceptive these children can be. "We were watching T.V., my husband, myself, and the two younger ones. At about seven-fifteen p.m. Chip came barreling in from play. Well, he just marched straight across the family room, nearly stepping on his little sister in transit and, without so much as a by your leave, changed the channel."

" 'We were all watching that, Chip!' the kids and I protested. My husband took action. He changed the channel right back again. You should have heard Chip's howls of outrage," Mother continued.

" 'But I'll miss my show,' he yelled. And he kept yelling. Until my husband marched him upstairs nobody heard a word from the T.V. Eventually he came back down, but he sulked the rest of the night. And you know, he *still* believes he was the injured party. He just doesn't seem to recognize that the rest of the family have rights too."

Now I'm sure most families have an occasional episode like this; egocentricity is dispelled only gradually. Children need to be taught to accommodate. They learn by experiencing such disappointments as missing their program because a clash of rights has arisen. After losing a few such clashes they start to notice the situation of others before imposing their desires on the group. When they fail to show such growth and persist in egocentric behavior, we know their adaptive growth is not proceeding.

Egocentricity manifests itself in other ways. Consider these common parental complaints.

"You can't discuss anything with him. He hears only himself."

"He never stops to think. I could be standing, burning my fingers on a casserole, and he'll stand right in front of me, demanding that I fix his stuck zipper this minute."

"When he plays games, he never notices how the others are doing. The only turn he's interested in is his own. And he's great for changing the rules when it suits him."

"He has no sense of property. If he wants to use something that belongs to somebody else, he just takes it without asking—but take something of his and see what happens!"

"He's very outspoken. He says whatever comes into his head and never seems to think how his words might offend others. My daughter, who's three years younger, knows better than he does in matters like that."

"He has a fierce sense of justice, but it's one-way justice. All he cares about is what's fair for him, not for others."

All of these behaviors make for tension in family life and, by the time parents come to my office, life at home has often deteriorated to the point that there is very little good will remaining between parent and child.

IN THE CHILD'S COMMUNITY

As one might imagine, the child's egocentricity serves him even more poorly outside of his home than in it. Parents may not like his behavior but they do not reject him because of it. Children are less tolerant and peer problems are common.

The usual story is that he plays poorly, is bossy and doesn't accommodate to the group or its ways. He is happy to play baseball when he's at bat, but when it's his turn to be in the field, he goes home or wants to change the rules. This behavior alienates his peers who, as everybody knows, can be very direct with their critical labelling. They call him names, ridicule him for his immaturity, and before long he is very much on the edge of the group.

Since the child does not understand how he offends and is hurt by the rejection he experiences, he reacts. He may become belligerent and quarrelsome. Soon he is starting each day with a chip on his shoulder and quickly generates the rejection he had anticipated. Sooner or later most such children start withdrawing from their peers. They begin staying by themselves, going to the library at lunch time or recess rather then remaining on the playground.

A common pattern is for the egocentric child to start playing with younger children, those a grade below who, flattered by the attention of the older child, will let him organize the play his way. Besides he is bigger and stronger and can dominate.

Sometimes egocentric children begin playing with one child, often one with social difficulties of his own who also has to take whomever he can get. Their play of these two egocentrics is often painful to behold as each insensitively seeks to impose his agenda on the other.

If a child is to be accepted by his peers, he needs to make some effort to fit in. He needs to stand back a moment, read the action going on, its rules and goals, take into account the social nuances, such as who's leading and who's following. Then he must find a way to join the group, to insinuate himself into the social exchange and gain acceptance. For the normally maturing child it isn't really as complicated as it sounds, but it does take a some perceptivity, some capacity to consider the point of view of others.

The egocentric child has little of either of these things. He reads only his own desires. If the group is playing a game, he's liable to barrel in and take over the action he finds most attractive—picking up the bat, for example, in a game of scrub baseball. Of course this transgresses the social contract, and he is rejected for his imperceptivity. Since he truly doesn't know what he did wrong, he goes away convinced they are rotten kids who don't like him for no good reason at all.

There are other ways in which the defective social judgment of the egocentric child manifests itself. For example, a three- or four-year-old child may throw a stone. Though we scold him for it, we understand that he means no serious harm, he just isn't yet able to comprehend the possible consequences of his action. On the other hand, we feel the ten year old who throws a stone ought to know better. But if the particular ten year old has remained egocentric, he probably doesn't. Such children know only their own anger and are imperceptive about the possible consequence to their victim.

As children grow older, they grow capable of *social decentering,* that is become increasingly able to move their locus of perception from themselves to the point of view of another. This temporary shift into the victim's mind would have enabled the child, in the stone-throwing instance, to imagine how it might feel to be the recipient of the stone, such that, when he returned to his own point of view, he might decide to name call instead of throw the stone.

As peer problems continue, the egocentric child usual makes some kind of a patch-up social adaptation. Certain of these patch-up adaptations lead to further psychological damage.

For example, some of these children become *scapegoats*: they develop a special role in the group, that of the victim. If one watches them in action it soon becomes clear that they have become as much generators of the role as recipients of it.

Other children develop what I call a *negative identity.* They give up trying to be accepted as a worthwhile person and settle for another role, that of the bad guy, the cut-up, the daring kid who daily goes to the principal's office. They seem to have decided it is better to be notorious than despised.

So peer problems are commonly manifestations of continuing egocentricity. To be sure, other factors may play a part in this, but if the child is to be successful with his peers he is going to have to become tuned in, perceptive, aware of other person's rights and needs: in short, less egocentric. The failure to accomplish this leads to social ineptitude which itself leads to progressive isolation and unhappiness. This is not what parents want for their children.

MORAL DEVELOPMENT

A most serious manifestation of continuing egocentricity has to do with the moral development of the child. As children grow older and become more aware and communicative, parents naturally begin to expect them to accommodate to others. They see the child doing things that offend their standards, and they correct him.

"No, Timmy, you have to share your candy."
"That's Sally's toy. Give it back to her."
"That's no way to talk to your grandmother."

In each of these instances it is another person's right that the child is being led to consider. Indirectly, he's being taught not to be so self-centered, to note the impact of his actions on others and modify them.

It is by intruding on the child's egocentricity that parents lead children to become aware that others have rights. While morality may begin with rules, it is perfected by developing such awareness. Let me explain. If I ask the average five year old who comes to my office, "why shouldn't you steal?" the conversation that follows will run something like this:

"Because it's bad," he responds.

"Why is it bad?"

"Because your mother will get mad."

"Any other reason it's bad?"

" 'Cause the police'll get you." He starts losing interest in the conversation. However I carry on.

"Why does your mother get mad?"

" 'Cause it's bad," he says, looking at me as though I were a little dense.

This is all you'll get out of a normal five year old: stealing is bad because Mother disapproves. This is what I call a *rules morality*: behavior is bad because it is against the rules. It is an essential first stage of moral development.

If I ask an eight year old whose adaptive development is proceeding well, "why shouldn't you steal?" I get a very different answer. What I usually hear is some variant of: "if you take it, they lose it." This morality is not based upon rules but arises from an appreciation of the victim's situation. It is what I call a *social morality*.

Clearly, the core adaptive capacity involved in replacing the small child's rules morality with the older child's social morality has to do with becoming less egocentric. The four or five year old has but a vague notion of how his actions affect others; the eight year old is much more capable of social decentering, mentally putting himself in the place of another person and arriving at some comprehension of that person's role in the social interaction.

When this growth lags, moral development lags also. For example, there was a thirteen-year-old boy in my community who had on several occasions 'borrowed' other children's bicycles without their permission. Eventually the police became involved and made it clear to the boy that this was stealing, which slowed the behavior but did not terminate it.

Then one day this boy arrived at the police station on his own. However, on this occasion he came in the capacity of aggrieved citizen; someone had stolen *his* bicycle. He was most indignant that he should be victimized in this way.

The police found it hard to share his outrage. In fact they were amused, which infuriated the boy. 'What kind of community was this where the police so blithely neglected their clear duty?'

This boy was an egocentric child. He was unable to decenter, that is to shift identity from perpetrator to victim and back again. A more mature child would probably have been embarrassed to seek the help of the police after his prior contacts with them. Not this child; for him the role of perpetrator and victim were totally unrelated life experiences.

Leading the child out of his egocentric posture is crucial to the development of conscience. To be sure, moral training begins with *rules,* for the child is still too immature to comprehend and appreciate the rights of others. But the goal is that the child become capable of *moral understanding,* not merely obedience. He must come to feel a sense of *ought, not merely must, or else.*

To illustrate how parents may begin and further this process, let's take the case of a mother who has decided it is time Dierdre learns to share. Dierdre has some candy, so Mother says, "Dierdre dear, I think you should share your candy with Jane."

Chances are Dierdre won't agree. So Mother will say, "how do you suppose Jane feels watching you eat that candy? Don't you think she must want some?"

Dierdre, who is a normal three year old, hasn't much idea how Jane feels, and she really doesn't much care. But she is concerned with her own pleasure, so she'll probably respond by clutching her candy to her chest, turning her back and, between hasty mouthfuls, saying, "it's *my* candy."

What Mother does now is going to have a profound impact on Dierdre's moral development.

A very common error mothers make is to repeat their verbal attempts to have Dierdre come to an understanding of Jane's state of being. "Can't you see Jane wishes she had some candy?" They do not realize that Dierdre is still minimally capable of the social decentering they are expecting of her.

Some mothers will now try to put a guilt trip on a child as yet incapable of feeling guilty. "Not sharing isn't nice, Dierdre." Or "you are being selfish."

Though they may scold and disapprove, *they allow Dierdre to eat all her candy herself.* They disapprove of her not sharing but they don't *make* her share.

The first step in moral training is to *make* the right behavior happen. In this case, Mother should have taken Dierdre's candy from her, broken off a piece, given it to Jane, and said "in our house, we share."

Dierdre will be outraged and probably won't hear Mother's explanation of the right and wrongs of the situation. It doesn't hurt to offer such explanations for eventually they will have an impact. However the crucial things is to make the sharing behavior happen.

To be sure, the next time Dierdre has candy she may sneak into her room so that she will not have to share it, but even this is a gain, for it means she is aware of her mother's standard, even if she is doing her best to avoid having to comply with it.

If Dierdre is made to share regularly, in time she will come to accept this as a rule of the household. The piece she offers may be small, but she will make the offer. Then one day she will come home from Betty's house and tell her mother, "you know what happened? Betty had some candy and she didn't share! Isn't that awful?" Dierdre's rules morality has come to include the sharing value.

Later, when time and training has led Dierdre into becoming a less egocentric person, she will be able to convert her rules morality into a social morality. She will be able to perceive Jane's suffering and salivation, intuit her pain, and share out of a dawning sense of humanity rather than fear of consequence.

Rules morality must precede social morality. Unless the rule is enforced, the social morality cannot develop. Many perfectly moral parents seem not to understand this, and they lecture their children on the wrongness of their acts, but they are too kindly to take the candy from the protesting child and give some to the friend. In such cases, moral development lags.

Similarly with such parents, when the child steals, they are reluctant to confiscate the loot, so they allow the child to keep the item and pay for it later, out of their allowance. Any bank robber would be happy to have a deal like that waiting for him, should he be so unfortunate as to be caught.

When a child small child steals the parent must do three things:

Training the Child Not to Steal

1. *Do not allow the child to profit from the theft.*
   The child doesn't keep the item and pay for it later; this is profiting.
2. *Make him return the item to the victim.*
   This emphasizes the social implication of the stealing behavior by confronting the victim.
3. *Punish the child for stealing.*
   Just not profiting is not punishment, nor is the embarrassment of returning the item.

If the parent is on the alert for light-fingered behavior and invokes this routine on every such occasion, in time the child will realize the inevitability of Mother's response and learn to forsake the behavior.

The same principles may be applied to the problem of lying. Five year olds discover lying as readily as they discover mud puddles. Even so, they need to encounter a rule about it, if they are ever to succeed to an appreciation of its social content. For a program to manage such incipient imaginative communication in the young child see Appendix D.

We have seen how egocentricity and morality are at war one with another. The parent who would train his or her child to live a moral life must understand that while rules are the essential beginning, it is leading the child out of his normal egocentricity that completes the job.

All children grow *older* and *bigger* but they do not all grow *up*. As a consequence there are many egocentric adults rattling about this troubled society. In these latter times we have seen the emergence of the 'me' generation, a pattern of wholly self-oriented young people; that prince of egocentrics, the psychopath, with his hedonistic amorality, has been multiplying at a geometric rate.

In order to arm ourselves to prevent such outcomes, let's now examine is some detail the normal developmental process that leads the egocentric infant moves from his total "me-ness" to that sensitivity to the needs and rights of others which allows him to accommodate to the world.

Normal Development of the Capacity for Social Decentering

The infant is born wholly egocentric. Since he cannot yet understand where his body ends and the world begins there is no way for him to comprehend himself as a person in an environment of other persons. Technically it will be some time before he can truly be described as self-centered, for he has first to establish a steady sense of self. But when he finally does, it will be as the unwitting center of his universe.

Parents tolerate the normal egocentricity of the infant. He is just a baby and one does not expect him to fit into the family; instead one fits the family to him. When he cries Mother tends to his need. The baby cannot explain his problem, but then most mothers don't need an explanation. They can read his cries. These may all sound the same to the father, but most mothers can say with assurance, "he's just hungry," or "he's wet," or "he's just mad, but it's nap time; he'll settle down."

It is not clear to me whether mothers learn to do this or whether they are, in some mysterious way, psychologically attuned to the child. Sometimes I think the latter. It seems to me that mothers live with the baby for nine months before he has any true reality to others. When he is born he is abruptly separated physically from the mother and she from him, but the psychological separation may be much less dramatic. I suspect there may remain some degree of psychological union for some time. So there is a question in my mind as to how truly separate from her the infant has become. Is she able to feel his feelings, sense his state through psychological processes that began in their shared biology and are not yet wholly terminated? Having observed many mothers for many years I think this may be the case.

In any case, mothers are sensitive to their infant's needs and they respond to them. When the baby cries the mother comes and feeds, comforts or changes him. In time these *needs-arise-and-satisfactions-come* sequences teach the baby to discriminate between those unpleasant feelings that are relieved by food and those that respond to some peculiar operation involving cloths and pins. Furthermore the repetition of these sequences reinforces the child's awareness of the inner feelings that led to his cry and which were alleviated by Mother's response.

However, what if Mother does not immediately respond? What if she does not immediately feed the hungry baby? Perhaps he has to wait while she heats the bottle, or perhaps Mother feels it is time he ate more, and less frequently, so she is going to hold off feeding him for twenty minutes. How does this sequence of need felt, expressed, but then satisfaction delayed affect the child?

It tends to diminish his awareness of his inner distress and increase his awareness of his environment. Let me explain. At first he will protest vigorously, but when satisfaction is not immediately forthcoming his attention tends to turn away from his inner distress to the environment from whence satisfaction comes. So he looks about himself, at first randomly perhaps, but soon he is trying to locate that large, mobile form he has come to associate with warm bottles and dry behinds. He may listen for those sounds of approach whose significance as footfalls is yet beyond his comprehension. If the bottle arrives immediately, this process of delay, frustration and search is not initiated.

So it is that frustration and delay tend to increase the child's awareness of his environment, whereas prompt satisfaction of need merely reinforces his awareness of his inner self.

It is clear then that, from the very beginning, leading a child away from his natural egocentricity, his normal infantile immersion in self, depends upon "intruding" upon him, that is, not accommodating to him in that total fashion appropriate to the care of the newborn.

Mothers have to come to this. It is their natural inclination to respond to the baby's need with prompt satisfaction. When baby cries, Mother jumps. Some mothers are very prompt about this.

I recall a particularly energetic baby who, when his satisfaction was even briefly delayed, let Mother know in terms that roused the neighborhood.

His mother, a gentle and sensitive woman, was particularly pained by his distress. She took to heating his bottle and sitting beside his bed when he was about to wake, ready to pop it into his mouth the moment he first peeped. When this child grows up, I venture to guess that he will be in good touch with his inner feelings, but his egocentricity is unlikely to have dissipated much. And, for that matter, there's a good chance his omnipotence illusion will have remained intact too.

What of the opposite case? What of the child who is raised by the book, fed because it is seven-thirty whether he is hungry or not, or not fed because it isn't seven-thirty yet, regardless of his protests? Let me illustrate this other outcome with a somewhat extreme example.

There is a condition in children called Anorexia Nervosa, a condition in which the child will not eat, seems not to experience hunger, and in some strange way has an unrealistic and intense investment in being slim. Some of these children starve themselves to death.

I had occasion to treat one such child in hospital, a twelve-year-old girl who was a talented television actress. It was necessary to hospitalize her to maintain a level of nutrition compatible with life. In hospital, as at home, she struggled valiantly to avoid food intake and to dissipate calories.

She came to me one day shortly after she'd arrived on the ward. She said to me. "You're going to make me hungry at five o'clock."

"How can that be?" I asked her.

"Because that's when you serve supper," she answered.

I was mystified. One is not hungry at five o'clock because five o'clock is supper time; one is hungry because one feels hungry. It is an inner sensation, and if its arrival happens to coincides with supper time, hooray!

Once I got to know the girl better I realized she did not really know what the feeling "hunger" was. Somehow she had suppressed her inner awareness, not only of the sensation we call hunger but also of a lot of other areas of feeling, including her anger.

When I finally put together a picture of her infant care, I saw that her mother, a very egocentric and rigid person, had raised her infant in accordance with an inflexible schedule which was almost totally unresponsive to signs of distress from her child. If the first mother accommodated too promptly to her infant by sitting beside his crib with the heated bottle, this mother accommodated not at all.

When this little girl cried for her bottle she did so because she was feeling hungry. The bottle's eventual arrival bore no relationship to the extent or magnitude of that hunger. Since they were irrelevant to satisfaction, in time the child learned to ignore her feelings of hunger. When an internal feeling is responded to, one's awareness of that feeling increases, but when it is not responded to, one gradually extinguishes that awareness. Since the child's other feelings had also been ignored by her egocentric and insensitive mother the child gradually learned to suppress awareness of them too. By the time she came into my care, she was so out of touch with her feelings that she could accuse me of generating hunger by serving supper at a given time on the clock.

It follows that, if the infant's egocentricity is to be successfully dissipated, he needs to experience a balance between gratification of his needs from an environment reasonably responsive to him and demands from that environment that he begin to read and respond to it.

Given such infant care, it is still the case that the normal two year old sees the world as his oyster.* However his mother is beginning to recognize the need to change this state of affairs. The balance of parenting begins to shift away from total gratification to the expectation that now and again he do some of the accommodating.

Now events conspire to force the issue. Since the child no longer naps mornings and afternoons and is on his feet and can follow her around, he is much more into her world. If she is to get anything done, she is going to have to start saying, "no, Johnny, I can't play with you now, I have things to do."

Furthermore, Mother may now have another infant, another egocentric sun about which she is required to orbit. I do not believe the astronomers have yet discovered a planet that succeeds in orbiting about two suns simultaneously, so if Mother is not to fly apart, one of these suns is going to have to become a planet.

Johnny does not like becoming a planet. He prefers being the sun, and he protests his demotion. He may even come up with a solution to the problem. "Let's send the baby back."

Even if a baby isn't involved, the child will still protest his demotion from sun to planet. If he happens to be a particularly intense and energetic child, his protest will be vigorous. If his mother tends to lack assertiveness and has read a lot of 'love is all' child-rearing literature, she may have some difficulty dealing with her insistent toddler.

The more demanding the child becomes, the harder it is to feel loving towards him. Before long Mother begins to feel a little guilty. She begins to wonder if the reason he is cranky is because she is not giving him enough love. In an effort to correct this she accedes to his demands; she stops what

---

*Even three! When my three year old used to join us playing hide and seek, he would stand in the corner, cover his eyes, and giggle merrily, firmly of the belief that if he could not see us, we could not see him.

she is doing and plays with him. This of course only teaches Johnny that if he just yells loudly and long enough, Mother will go back to treating him like the sun. It is from such beginnings that problems with continuing egocentricity usually arise.

On the other hand, if Mother is a self-respecting individual she is able to say to herself, "I'm a person too; it won't kill him to wait a little. It's time he learned." So she tells Johnny, "no, I'll play with you later." She sticks to her guns, if necessary putting him in his room if he has a tantrum.

When this happens, Johnny is made to accommodate to her. He has taken the first step on the long journey that will eventually leads him out of normal egocentricity into an increasing awareness of others and their rights.

This is a slow journey. Its stages might best be illustrated by describing how children gradually become able to play cooperatively with one another.

When parents play with children they come more than half way in the interaction. The child grunts and Mother, from long experience, interprets the grunt. Other children cannot. Similarly, in the play, Mother has no agenda but to cooperate. She isn't building a road in the sandbox which comes into conflict with his road. She fits to his plan. Other children do not. So peer relations sometimes give a clearer picture of how far the child has come out of his egocentricity than does his interaction with his parents or other adults.

When children first come together their play tends to be solitary in character. The child is interested only in what he is doing, and he ignores others except perhaps to appropriate something of theirs if he needs it. The bulk of the two year old's play is like this.

Three year olds begin watching each other play. They begin to notice what the other is doing, even if they don't participate with him. Soon they get involved in parallel forms of play, not truly interactive, but aware of each other. Since the child isn't yet able to decenter, seeing what the other child is doing from that child's perspective, he is not yet ready to do any true accommodating.

By the end of the third year, most children begin to make true interpersonal contact. "You can drive on my road, but only this part." This interaction may be brief in duration but it is a step past playing parallel.

As children begin to interact in a more sustained way, they have to share, take turns, or else retreat from the interaction. They tend to do each at various times as they still have only a limited capacity for give and take.

If a four year old has been learning to be less egocentric at home, because his parents are no longer willing to accommodate to him all the time, he may take this skill with him to nursery school. Now one begins to see play in which the children cooperate with one another from time to time. However, each does tend to put his own interests first. "You have to play my game 'cause it's my house," the child says or, if he is a sophisticated child and the roles are reversed, "I'm the guest, so we have to play what I want."

Most five year olds are able to play cooperatively, at least part of the time, but still they occasionally retreat to looking or to intermittent contact types of play. However, once the ability to play cooperatively is seen one knows that the growth process is under way.

Truly cooperative play, that is play in which the children recognize each has his own point of view, is of course a strong indication of developing social maturity.

Until the child is able to recognize that others have their rights and needs, that their intentions may be different from his own, he will misunderstand events. Some children thinks their parents discipline them because parents enjoy the process. The child who turns dressing in the morning into a chasing game is often convinced his mother is having as much fun as he is. It is not until the child has become less egocentric that he can understand his parents' behavior in consistently realistic terms.

I once saw an eleven-year-old girl who told me "my mother cries to make me feel bad." While some mothers will do this, I happen to know that this mother cried because she was genuinely despairing about her relationship to her daughter. However, her egocentric child interpreted all the world's actions in terms of their effects upon her. "If it makes me feel bad, that must be the reason she did it." This child is still too egocentric to appreciate her mother's mental state. To ask her to behave to please her mother is to demand a function of her of which she is not yet able.

When the child, aware of his parents' feelings, behaves to please the parent instead of to avoid a consequence, child rearing becomes a much more pleasant process. Unfortunately, behaving to please does not become a significant mode of action until a considerable amount of psychological growth has already been achieved. That growth has largely to do with egocentricity.

For the child to be willing to modify his behavior to please his parent, two things are necessary. First, the child must be able to perceive how *the parent feels,* whether he is pleased or displeased. Then the child must be able to see *a connection* between that parental feeling and his behavior.

The very young child, or an older one who has remained egocentric, does not appreciate how his parent feels. All that fills his mind is how *he* feels. He is being asked to do something he doesn't want to do, or not do something he wants, and *his* distress at this frustration dominates his awareness. The child who is insensitive to his parents' state of feeling will certainly not be moved to modify his behavior on account of it.

Even if the child does detect that his parent is displeased or unhappy, he must see a connection between that parent's state of feeling and his behavior. But egocentric children tend to see the world from their own point of view exclusively and so interpret events in terms of how they affect them, not others.

So it is that one must begin with rules, approaches that intrude upon the small child's normal egocentricity until he begins to suspect there are others in the world with other points of view, other desires than those which fill him. Now is the door opening to training techniques that are less action oriented, more interpersonal and rational. Now approval-disapproval comes to have sufficient meaning for the child to become an instrument of his further training. (This is discussed further in Chapter Six.)

A Remedial Program for the Mother-Deaf Child

Let's return now to consider how parents might by their parenting intrude upon the egocentricity of the child. Let me use the example with which I opened this chapter. You remember Johnny who did not hear his mother when she called him for supper?

Egocentricity is what is involved here. And it's probably showing up in a lot of other places too. He's immersed in self. He's doing his thing. He does not want to be intruded upon. "Inna minute . . . inna minute" he says, whether the instruction be "come for supper," "hang up your coat," or "come in the house." Mother can't find a way to move him short of six tellings and a yelling, and she is certainly tired of that. Here is my program for dealing with the six tellings and a yelling situation.

THE SECOND TELLING JAR

The Program

Mother gets a glass jar and three 'counters': chips, buttons, pearls, whatever's handy in her household. Then, even though what she says probably won't get past the eardrum, to be fair, she explains the program to the child.

"You don't like me nagging and yelling at you whenever I want you to do something, and believe me, I don't like doing it either. So! No more six tellings and a yelling! Here's the new deal. When I want you to, say, come to supper, I'm going to call out to you: 'Johnny, come to supper, and it's four minutes to second telling.'"

"Four minutes to what?"

"Second telling! And in four minutes I'm going to call to you again: 'Second telling.' That means you have ten seconds to show up on my horizon. If you don't show I'll come fetch you, turn off the T.V., lead you to the table. Whatever it takes. But if I have to fetch you, then you will get a chip in your second telling jar."

No answer! The subject does not enthrall him.

"And when you get three chips, you'll get a punishment, like maybe losing one of your T.V. programs or your bike for a day. Then I remove the chips and we start over."

By now his eyes are glazing over; he's heard this kind of thing before. Never mind. After nine chips and three punishments he'll have figured out how the program works.

The Course

The following is the way things usually go. When he doesn't come to supper, or go take out the garbage, or get started on his homework, Mother goes through her routine. Of course the second telling doesn't yet get him moving and Mother has to fetch him to the task. She gives him a chip. He shrugs. Or perhaps he has a tantrum, which she manages with her tantrum control program. She then returns to the subject at hand, the second telling program.

Soon he has earned his third chip and his first punishment. "I don't care. I wasn't planning to ride my bike after school today anyway." This maneuver is called the 'sweet lemon'; all children come into the world equipped to use it.*

Soon Johnny has earned another three chips and another punishment. He may have moved on the second telling once or perhaps even twice, but by no means is the problem solved. Even so, now that six tellings and a yelling have stopped, both the household tension and the decibels have reduced significantly.

Next thing you know he's responding to the second telling call with the cry of "No sweat. I've only got one chip in the jar." Which means, of course, that he's beginning to keep count. Soon when you call second telling, he comes slumping to the task. "O.K.! O.K.! I heard you."

The indicator of progress is that it's now taking him two days to get three chips, whereas the first week he was getting nine chips and three punishments a day.

The second telling program is among the most popular of the specific measures I recommend to parents in trouble promoting the adaptive growth of their child. This is because Mother no longer has to escalate to

*For a detailed explanation of the 'sweet lemon' see pages 94, 122.

yelling to get him moving. It's the quiet she finds so refreshing.*

Why is the second telling program so effective? Because it is constructed from the elements of sound discipline. While these will be dealt with at more length at a later point in this book it is not amiss to introduce them at this point. So let's examine those elements one by one.

The Elements *of sound discipline.*

THE EXPECTATION   The parent is now giving the child a clear expectation. Nothing vague or advisory such as "I wish you would take the garbage out now and again, Michael," which of course is as much complaint as expectation. Furthermore, since Mother is now programming her behavior to follow through she moves away from harassing him with trivia and sticks to a few main and reasonable expectations.

THE TIME LIMIT   If one does not set time limits, one ends nagging. "Four minutes to second telling" is a time limit. Not only does this take the place of nagging but it also gives the child transition time. Nobody wants to drop what he or she is doing this instant and come to supper or go hang up his coat. The four minutes gives the child time to adjust his mind to the task to come, time to accept the expectation. Soon 'second telling' becomes a magic phrase which moves the child. Indeed it is often the case he soon comes to beat the clock, arriving in the kitchen before Mother has got around to calling out 'second telling' and asking, "hey, Mom, what's for supper?"

THE SUPERVISION   Johnny must come to the task or he is not accommodating to Mother's agenda; she is tolerating his. This of course panders to his egocentricity and so generates no growth. If he does not come on second telling, he is fetched.

THE PUNISHMENT   The chips are a method of punishment. If you set up a regular program of getting dressed in the morning and the child does not make it on time you can give him a punishment such as lose half an hour prime time T.V. or no bike after school that day.** The most this can lead to is one punishment a day. If you gave him a punishment for every second telling he would soon have no privileges left. So the first advantage

---

*Even so, not all 'experts' approve of my second telling program. One editor of a woman's magazine declared it was silly and unnecessary. All Mother had to say to the child was "come to supper or you won't get any." But if the 'six tellings and a yelling' problem is this easy to manage, why are so many mothers having trouble with it?

**In choosing punishments, one never takes away the child rights, such as his right to food and shelter. To do this is to go past punishment into punitiveness. For more information on this, see pages 118–24.

of the chip jar is that it offers a way to respond consistently to a frequently occurring, minor behavioral failure without swamping the child.

It is important that children come to connect the imposed consequence with the behavior that led to it if they are to change the behavior. The chip is something to give the child now that establishes that connection, even though the final consequence does not actually happen until later.

Chips are much more than a gimmick. They are a valuable action-communication device. Those who derogate them as childish probably haven't had much experience communicating with children.

These then are the four principles of discipline involved in the second telling program. When each is given proper weight in the design of discipline, growth results. Overlook any one of them and the intended program will fail.

Finally, through the device of 'second telling,' we have intruded upon Johnny's egocentricity. We have invested the outer world with psychological significance—chips—that Johnny quickly learns not to ignore. Thus have we directed his gaze outwards and altered his egocentric posture a modicum.

Effective discipline always intrudes upon the child's egocentricity. Furthermore, whenever we require the child to accommodate to us, we also make an action statement about power, letting Johnny know that he is not the boss of the world, that he has, in some things, to defer to his parents' choices.

It is also that case that this same disciplinary technique influences the development of the third adaptive competency we are interested in, "tolerance for normal unpleasure," the subject of our next chapter.

4

Patience and Self-Control

"Art thou the victorious one, the self subduer... ?"

FRIEDRICH NIETZSCHE, *THUS SPOKE ZARATHUSTRA*

The infant is a 'now' creature. When the baby is hungry he wants the bottle... now! When he's frightened he wants to be made safe by Mother's instant arrival on the scene. When the toddler sees his dessert, no more meat and potatoes for him. Cleaning his room is a mountain of expectation to the seven year old.

The infant has little or no tolerance for tedium. This capacity must be developed through practice, that is the regular experience of degrees of the unpleasure, not so little as not to stretch the child's capacity, not so much as to overwhelm it. The omnipotent child has not experienced this steady training and he continues unable to cope with degrees of anxiety, anger, disappointment or tedium normal to his age. Let's begin our description of this cardinal characteristic with an example.

The Cardinal Characteristic

Here is a common clinical scenario I call Toast and Tears. It involves getting dressed in the morning, a common problem for immature nine year olds.

"It's twenty to eight, Bryan," Mother calls from his doorway, an ear cocked toward the stairwell listening for signs of disaster from the kitchen. "I've got to go back downstairs to look after your little brother. You get dressed now. NO DAWDLING. Remember what happened yesterday?"

Bryan's eyes are open, but there is reasonable doubt that his optical cortex is actually registering visual impressions. He does not answer.

"Bryan!"

He turns his head in the general direction of the sound.

"Bryan? Did you hear me?"

Bryan nods.

"Say something so I know you're awake."

Bryan grunts.

"No dawdling." Mother whirls and departs, the aroma of burnt toast lending wings to her feet.

Bryan picks up a sock, slowly rolls it, and places the open end over the toes of his left foot. He grabs either side of the sock band and starts pulling. The sock slides over his foot until it reaches the heel. It stops. Bryan gives it a tug. The sock resists. He gives it a dirty look and a mighty tug. The sock does not move from the heel. Bryan's inertia collapses him backwards across the bed. He lies there, defeated.

As he rests Bryan stares at the water mark on the ceiling. "Looks a bit like Darth Vader." He cocks his head to one side, "or maybe Jaws, coming in for the kill." He drifts into a fantasy, a mental state infinitely preferable to battling uncooperative socks.

Ten minutes later Mother arrives on the scene. She finds Bryan flat on his back one sock half on but otherwise as undressed as when she left.

"Bryan! You haven't even started dressing."

Bryan raises his foot in denial. "The sock stuck."

"All you have to do is give it a hard tug." Mother pulls him from his lying position on the bed.

"I did."

"Some pairs are a little tight; they stick at the heel. You have to pull really hard." Mother drops to her knees and starts pulling the sock over Bryan's heel.

"I can't pull that hard," Bryan complains.

"If it was after school and you were going over to Jimmy's to play, you'd be able to pull hard enough." Mother shoves the sock up his calf.

Bryan says nothing. The fact is he wouldn't have worn socks if he was going out to play. She only checks in the morning.

Mom finishes the job and gets to her feet. "Now get dressed. And hurry or you'll be late for school."

"I wasn't yesterday," Bryan mutters.

"Because I drove you," Mother snaps, getting to her feet. "No way am I driving you today. Finish dressing. No more dawdling." She stomps down the stairs, feet thumping her displeasure.

Bryan starts in bravely, but the shirt buttons manage to get into holes one step removed from where they ought to be. The thought of undoing each and doing it up again is a mountain of tedium. Bryan turns from that dread prospect and drifts to the window to see what the birds are up to. Nothing much. Soon he's flat on the bed again, sliding off into outer space. That is where his mother finds him ten minutes later when she returns to check on his progress.

"Migawd Bryan. You're not dressed. What's the trouble now?"

"The buttons got in the wrong holes."

"Well, take them out and put them in the right holes." Mother again drops to her knees and starts doing it for him. All the while she is lecturing him of the subjects of childhood independence and task persistence. "Now," she says as she finishes, "no more dawdling. There's barely time for breakfast as it is." And she leaves.

Bryan returns to dressing. Does pretty well too until he can't find his other shoe. He looks under the bed. It isn't there. Since he happens to be near the bed, and a little discouraged, he drops down for a wee rest, and that is where Mother finds him seven minutes later.

Now, you must understand, Mother has read all the child-rearing books. She's been through the natural consequences bit. Even though she knows yelling is not an approved form of parent-child communication, she yells. She knows empty threats undermine her authority, but she makes them anyway.

She yells and she threatens. What's more, it works. Bryan scurries about, an eye over his shoulder observing the storm front. Somehow he finds the energy to wash his face, brush his teeth, and comb his hair. It is her standing there emitting thunder and lightning that keeps him on task.

All the time Mother is letting him know she is not pleased. In fact she is using some terminology she is going to regret later. Bryan ends in tears. There is no time for breakfast so it's out the door with a cold piece of toast in his hand and tears on his cheek.

As she stands behind the window curtain watching him go, Mother is filled with pain and remorse. "Every morning—nagging and tears." She shakes her head in despair. "What a way to start a school day!" She slumps for the kitchen, despairing of her motherhood, ready to turn in her apron and take the night flight to Peru.*

That afternoon, after flagellating herself all morning, she bakes him a cake to make it up to him. Which he eats happily. However, the next morning when the sock sticks, guess what happens all over again?

---

*For a further elucidation of the Night Flight to Peru Syndrome the reader is referred to my play *Don't Shoot, I'm Your Mother*.

THE UNPLEASURE OF TEDIUM

This morning scenario appears in my practice over and over again. The problem is that Bryan has very little tolerance for tedium, in this case that of getting dressed in the morning. Sure the sock sticks, but that is a little fence to climb. Even so, unless he's got a heavy deadline or a wild satisfaction imminent, Bryan just can't climb those little fences. It's the same with his school work; the first number fact he can't remember he's staring into space. Send him to the basement to get a jar of preserves, and fifteen minutes later he's standing by the work bench having forgotten why he went downstairs.

Bryan's mind is like a car with a worn-out gearbox. The first time it encounters even the most gentle of uphill grades it slips into Pleasurable Idle so smoothly that even Bryan doesn't realize forward movement has ceased. So unless he's constantly supervised even the routine tasks don't get done.

Bryan automatically and unwittingly avoids *unpleasure*. Any activity he does not find continuously pleasing he labels *borrrring* and turns away from it. There is another side to this coin. Bryan is addicted to *pleasure*. He thinks life should always be providing some.

So it is that such children are chronically discontent. They feel that unless life is presently joyful they are being short changed. And, if the mother involved is one of those who believe childhood should be nothing but golden every moment of every day, she will take the blame for her failure to make it so.

Because such children are not trained to tolerate tedium, they want everything now, not later. Bryan has remained a 'now' child. Books take too long to get to the good parts, so he reads the comics. He decides he wants to play the guitar, but when he isn't a rock star in two weeks, he quits. It's the same with baseball and hockey; whenever he encounters the need for some practice, needs to tolerate a little present tedium for some future pleasure, he isn't up to the task, and he packs it in with face-saving contempt. "Aw! Baseball's dumb."

There are other forms of unpleasure for which children need to develop tolerance: the unpleasure of disappointment, of anger, of fear or anxiety. The omnipotent child is usually no better at coping with these unpleasures than he is at coping with tedium.

THE UNPLEASURE OF ANXIETY

There are those who feel that childhood ought to be a time free from anxiety. This cannot be. Childhood is a time of steadily widening horizons. Life continuously presents new challenges to the growing child. Each of these is an occasion for anxiety as well as an occasion for growth.

All children have to make a first visit to the barber, to the dentist, to the doctor for a shot. They all have to take their first trip down the playground slide or into the swimming pool. Each mastery increases the capacity for future coping with anxiety. Eventually the child can try out for baseball, stand up to a bully, or make a speech in front of the class.

It is important that children be led to cope with such normal fears. The protective parent who shelters the child too much robs him of such mastery and delays the process of adaptive growth. In most cases this has happened to the omnipotent child, and he is often much more anxious than his omnipotent demeanor suggests he is.

Since the sheltered child does not learn to cope with anxiety, he develops techniques for avoiding it. Faced with some new expectation he projects an image of "woebegone dismay," and the sensitive parent, not wanting to cause him pain, withdraws the expectation. "All right. I'll stay with you one more day." Or, if the child cannot generate parental extenuation that way, he develops stomach complaints, headaches, or other symptoms which imply he cannot be expected to cope in his weakened condition. In time such children learn to *avoid* rather than *cope* with the expectations of life.

To avoid all conditions that generate anxiety is to avoid life itself. It is estimated that there are thousands upon thousands of "agoraphobics" populating our cities. These persons, afraid to venture from the safety of their homes into streets and department stores, are imprisoned in their childhood dependency. These avoidant adults cannot be analyzed out of their phobias; they need to be taken by the hand and led through the coping they should have experienced as children, the coping that would have led to mastery and self-confidence.*

THE UNPLEASURE OF DISAPPOINTMENT

Childhood contains another unpleasure the child needs to master, the unpleasure of *disappointment or loss*. The six year old, happily anticipating

---

*There is a form of anxiety which bears a special relationship to omnipotence devaluation. This is called separation anxiety and it is often first observed in relation to this phase of adaptive growth. Early normal manifestations occur at bedtime, when the three year old wants Mother to lay down with him until he goes to sleep, or cries when the sitter comes or when he has to be left at nursery school. The child is still fearful of functioning out of the protection of home and parents. It is my view that school phobia and agoraphobia are symptoms which grow out of the failure to work through normal separation anxiety when it first arises during the omnipotence-devaluation phase of adaptive growth.

a trip to the zoo, is dismayed when the car comes up with a flat tire. He cries. When he is more mature he manages his disappointment better. Not so the omnipotent child. He comes apart when the stress is minimal. "You promised," he wails. "You gotta keep your promise. You just go get that flat fixed this minute." And when Mother cannot, or will not, he may go on to a full-scale temper tantrum.

Of course, parents should keep their promises whenever possible, but there are always times of disappointment. The child grows from disappointments experienced and mastered. He gradually comes to handle such with ever increasing self-control. However, the child will not learn to handle disappointment if he is forever protected from it.

Some parents go to great lengths to protect their child from life's little blows. If he loses his dollar, Dad gives him another one. If Mother buys a sweater for Jane, because she needs one and they are on sale, she feels compelled to buy something for Johnny too, so he won't be disappointed. If Bryan's T.V. plans conflict with his mother's, guess who gives up her show? For mothers to defer to small children is as natural as to bear them. Less natural, but equally important, is for Mother to recognize when to move away from her infant-centered existence to one in which the child is required to wait a little, to do a mite of accommodating. As she does so coping begins to take precedence over indulgence, training over nurturance.

There is a particular situation in which parents commonly try to preserve children from disappointment. It has to do with losing pets. If one lives in the city and has a dog or cat, there is a statistical probability the pet will be killed in an accident. Sad, but reality. This is a blow to the child. Understandably, parents try to protect their child from this 'trauma.'

What they do is rush out and replace the pet with another. This is the wrong thing to do. Not only does it fail to replace the lost pet, but also it confuses the child. Sometimes it generates conflicts involving loyalty to the old pet and attraction to the new. Most importantly, it interferes with the normal psychological process involved in accepting and coping with loss. The child who loses his pet experiences loss and that kind of unhappiness associated with loss which we call sadness.

Of course the child cries, and the parent comforts him as best she or he can. As time passes the loss is felt less keenly . . . the hurt heals. This is the normal psychological process involved in dealing with loss, the same adults go through when they lose something precious to them. The child is capable of going through that process, and when he succeeds in doing so, an important thing happens: the child experiences loss and masters it.

To master unpleasure is to increase one's tolerance for the it. Five inches of tedium today seems unbearable, but tomorrow a foot is child's play.

Three ounces of anxiety today amounts to terror, but one pound tomorrow is experienced as moderate nervousness. Disappointment that seems unbearable today is barely cause for a "that's life" shrug tomorrow. Like weight lifting, each repetition strengthens the psychological muscle. So it is, as the child experiences his disappointment, he gradually recovers from his sense of loss and is happy again.

The child who loses his cat learns, in the only way such learning takes place, that loss is not inconsolable, that a day will come when he will feel better again. So he is braver, more willing to invest of himself, to care and not fear losing that for which he has learned to care.

There are people who live narrow lives because they are fearful of losing. They will not invest of themselves. But the child who has lost something important while yet a child, and has survived that loss, is stronger and perhaps more willing to brave such future risks than he might have been.

THE UNPLEASURE OF ANGER

There is a fourth unpleasure we all have to master, the unpleasure of *anger*. Anger is an unpleasant feeling, not only for the object of the anger but also for the angry person. It upsets; it jangles; it lingers. But anger is inevitable, not only in the life of the adult, but also in the life of the child.

The frustrated infant experiences rage. If he had the power to express that rage, it is unlikely any mother would survive the first year of child rearing. He cannot kill, so he screams his rage. However, rage experienced eventually becomes rage mastered. By degrees the child comes to endure his rage and eventually to master and control it.

It is characteristic of the omnipotent child that he cannot handle his anger in a fashion appropriate to his years. He is explosive; he has temper tantrums. He goes too far. He says "I'll kill you" when he is merely unhappy with your behavior. He is abusive when he is simply at odds with your point of view. He threatens. He over-reacts in a way that raises the hackles. He is arrogant and overbearing when disagreement is all the situation calls for. When frustrated, he may hit or throw things or become destructive. It isn't that his frustration is any more acute than other children's but that he cannot modulate his expression of feelings.

It is evident that the temper tantrum control program outlined in Chapter Two, as well as disillusioning the omnipotence of the child, also serves to stretch the child's tolerance for the unpleasure of anger. In order to illustrate this process further let me describe another technique for managing a lesser manifestation of anger parents often complain about. The behavior in this instance is rudeness.

I hear complaints of this nature. "When he gets mad, he calls me

Dumbo," one mother said. "If he gets mad enough he tells me to shut up," another says. "The other day he gave me the finger," a third reports. Such gems as "ya gonna make me," or "nyah, nyah, I don't have to do as you say," raise the hackles of other parents.

My program for this problem is the Rude Jar. This is simply a jar which Mother so labels. She then shows it to him and explains, "Johnny, you are rude. You say things like 'shut up' or 'make me' and sometimes you put your finger up like that. Well, I don't want you doing that anymore, and I'm going to train you not to. Here's how it works. Whenever when you say or do something rude, I'm going to say 'that's rude' and put a chip in the jar."

"Big deal," Johnny snorts. "Chips in the jar!"

"And when you get three chips, you get a punishment."

"What punishment?"

"I'll see. Something like no *Cosby Show* tomorrow night, or grounding your bike for a day. One of your punishment cards."*

Johnny shrugs and departs. "Another dumb program. It won't last a week," he thinks.

Johnny will probably get three chips full a couple of times the first day, a total of six chips which translates to two punishments. Maybe if he's an enthusiastic practitioner of the rude art he'll get nine. That means he gets three punishments. He'll be a bit surprised when Mother follows through the third time but he'll pretend he doesn't care.

The next morning Johnny will get three chips by noon. "What's all this chip Mickey Mouse?" he will protest, but that afternoon, after two more chips have found their way into his jar, he will clean up his act, maybe even get through the day with nothing more than the occasional inaudible mutter passing his lips.

The next morning he gets a fast chip, a punishment, and then two more not quite so fast chips. A few hours of verbal restraint then follow. In a few days, he is down to three chips a day and we are getting restraint on fifty percent of the occasions that, in the past, would have resulted in rude behavior. That amount of restraint is enough to generate some growth in self-control. This, of course, was our purpose in initiating the program, training him to limit his expressions of anger and annoyance to a vocabulary acceptable for his age and situation.

But more than getting rid of rudeness has been accomplished. By teaching him to curb his tongue Mother has stretched his tolerance for the unpleasure of anger. And it is often the case that when the child learns to tolerate more anger without giving way to its expression, he also shows a

*For an explanation of punishment cards see Appendix A.

little more patience, better self-control, a little more persistence. Tolerance for unpleasure is a general capacity and what stretches it in one area, stretches it in another. Though the measure might seem small, the adaptive consequence for the passage to adulthood may be large.

We have seen that the normal child who receives effective training gradually masters the unpleasures of tedium, anxiety, disappointment and anger. The omnipotent child lags in this aspect of adaptive growth as well as the others. He is in danger of becoming an pleasure-bound, pain-avoidant adult.

There are many adults these days who are adaptively immature when it comes to dealing with life's unpleasures. I speak of impulsive, short-tempered persons, who marry in haste but cannot sustain the giving required in the mutuality of marriage. Such persons take the cash and let the credit go; they end up not paying their taxes or get in trouble with their credit card. Since they cannot work well, they resent the boss's authority and are unrestrained in their expression of this resentment. They tend to drift from job to job. As adults they have grown big, but they haven't grown up. Lacking the self-control to cope with society, they fail to realize much of their human potential, and at worst they end imprisoned to protect society from them.

The pleasure-bound child becomes the reckless adult, a creature of impulse and whim. It was such youth who became known as the 'now' generation of the sixties. The evidence suggests that many of these persons, though now well into their forties, continue to play a terrible price for their failed adaptive growth. (For an analysis of these people, see Appendix B.)

The question becomes, how can parents best train the child to cope with life's normal unpleasures? How can the parent lead the child to master his anger, to tolerate tedium, to accept disappointment, to be brave about his uncertainties?

Developing Patience and Persistence in the Child

The first thing in grasping this nettle is to recognize that training the child is as important a part of being his parent as loving him. Not all parents understand this. I see many parents who seem to feel that if they simply love their child and, in their own behavior, demonstrate self-control, concern for others, and acceptance of rational authority, then the child will somehow incorporate those capacities in his being, that some process of osmosis will carry the needed capacities into the child.

This is not so. To be sure, some children seem not to require as much training. It is a well-known observation that some children are a whole lot harder to train to patience, persistence and self-control than others.

This is a matter of temperament. Some children are intense and energetic. Such children require very determined parenting to lead them to patience and self-control. Other more placid children respond well to average parental determination.

Two aspects of temperament seem particularly relevant here. These are *activity level* and *intensity*.

Activity Level: Some infants are so squirmy they need two hands and a foot on their chest to change their diapers, and bathing them is a liquid adventure for both participants. Other less energetic children don't disturb their bed covers when they sleep, lie quietly in their bath, and move slowly about the house. Obviously, these less active children will require a lot less parental input to train them than the overly active child.

Intensity: Some infants react intensely to life; whether that reaction be a negative or a positive one, it is intense. When such a child is hungry he screams and becomes so distressed that he cannot be distracted by holding or playing with him. Other infants are much more placid. If they are hungry they whimper, and they don't spit out food they don't like; they just hold it in their mouths and won't swallow.

Obviously the child who experiences each frustration intensely is going to have a harder time learning to tolerate unpleasure than the child for whom such events, while unpleasant perhaps, do not seem so overwhelming.

So the energetic and intense child needs much more determined parenting input than the low-energy, placid child needs, and when children do not acquire tolerance for unpleasure at a normal rate, it is reasonable to ask just what *kind* of child was this mother given to rear.

Even so, each child, regardless of his temperament, must acquire a reasonable degree of tolerance for unpleasure if he is to cope with life. If he's energetic and intense then his mother is simply going to have to try harder.

The process of such training begins with the infant in his crib. He wakes hungry, and he cries. His mother puts the bottle on to heat. He must wait while the bottle heats. He must, for a few minutes, tolerate hunger and waiting. When he does, he practices waiting. And, eventually, the bottle arrives. His unpleasure goes away. And the process is repeated regularly.

What happens to the child immersed as he is in this process? He practices waiting, and with practice waiting gets easier. As well, he learns that the bottle eventually arrives. At first he thought, "this feeling is awful and, who knows, it may never go away." But he finds it does. Regularly! Another thought arises, "the bottle arrived before; it·will probably arrive again." He becomes optimistic; now it is easier to wait.

This training for coping with unpleasure continues and increases. Once the child gets on his feet, his mother *must* deny him sometimes or she will become his slave. So she says, "no, I can't play with you now, I have things on the stove."

When the next child is born, attending him takes more and more of Mother's time, and even more limits have to be set on the first. Each limit set, each expectancy communicated, requires the child to cope with a little unpleasure and stretches his tolerance a degree.

If Mother continues to serve the child excessively—"O.K., I'll pick up your toys, but just this once"—not only does she fail to stretch the child's tolerance for unpleasure, but she also teaches him that Mother can be had. So it is that mothers passing from the nurturance to the training phase of parenting must harden their hearts a little and stop doing everything for the child.

This passage ushers in the omnipotence-devaluation phase of adaptive growth. But the child is a whole creature, and at the same time as he is working out his omnipotence devaluation, he is experiencing unpleasure. The mastery of such unpleasure generates patience and persistence, courage and self-control.

Let me close this chapter with a program designed to deal with a problem in which intolerance for unpleasure is a major component.

Getting Dressed in the Morning: A Remedial Parenting Program

Let's go back now to the anecdote with which we opened this chapter, the trouble Bryan's mother was having getting him dressed in the morning. In the context of how she might manage this more successfully, perhaps we can demonstrate how effective discipline develops tolerance for one of life's unpleasures—tedium—but also serves to disillusion infantile omnipotence and diminish egocentricity.

Remember our scenario? Mother had dispatched Bryan to school, a cold piece of toast in his hand and tears in his eyes. And we knew that next morning it was just going to be more of the same.

What is Mother doing wrong? Is there some way she can manage the situation more effectively? Let's deal with the first question first.

Mother has slipped into a very common mode of poor discipline which I call *ineffective overcontrol*. It is *ineffective* because it doesn't work. Oh, it does get Bryan dressed in the morning, but tomorrow when the sock sticks it will be more of the same. And tomorrow. And tomorrow. And tomorrow. It is *overcontrol* because Mother is always there standing over the child, supervising, cajoling, assisting, nagging, and eventually, thundering and lightning at him.

Bryan hates ineffective overcontrol, and so does his mother, but she feels she has no choice. "If I didn't stand over him, he'd be late for school every morning, and he'd never get any breakfast."

Mother, doing what she feels she must, has slipped into a vicious cycle. In the morning nagging and tears, followed by a miserable day for Mother ruminating over her morning anger such that she ends telling herself, "tomorrow morning, no matter what happens, I am not going to raise my voice to that child."

No! Tomorrow she is going to be kind and firm and not get angry, no matter what.

The next morning comes and when the sock sticks, guess who ends up flat on his back, elaborating fantasies about that stain on the ceiling? Mother grits her teeth and controls her anger. She ends up dressing him but the worst that escapes her lips is a mildly intoned: "do you think... dear... that tomorrow morning... you might try... just the tiniest bit harder to dress yourself without Mother standing over you?" "Sure thing, Mom," Bryan replies, but Wednesday morning it's more of the same. This time Mother barely manages to keep her cool. It costs but, God bless her, she really tries.

Thursday morning she labors but she simply cannot stand it any longer. She erupts. The whole schmear, thunder, lightning, name calling, threats. In fact, as he is going out the door she is telling him of her plan to take the afternoon plane to Peru and don't expect to find her there when he comes home.

By the time Bryan gets to school he has forgotten her threat, he's heard that kind of thing before. But at home the guilt is incredible. The day is a flagellation worthy of the most masochistic of holy orders. By nightfall she is a resolutely reformed character. However, next morning the vicious cycle starts all over again.

What is Bryan learning from all this? You can be sure he is learning something, even if it isn't what Mother intended to teach him. Well, I've interviewed a lot of Bryans in my playroom and they usually perceive this situation thus.

"Why did your mother get so mad at you Thursday morning?" I ask.

"Thursday morning?" Bryan looks puzzled a moment and it is clear he doesn't immediately remember. Clearly he found the whole thing a lot less troubling than his mother did. "Oh yeah, she threw a real spazz."

"What made her so mad?" I ask again.

"Aw, she was just in a bad mood. She gets that way." He rolls his eyeballs and shrugs his shoulders.

"She told me the reason she got mad was because you didn't get dressed on time," I say.

"Nope," Bryan shakes his head. "Couldn't be that. I didn't get dressed on time Tuesday and she didn't get mad. I didn't get dressed on time Wednesday and she didn't get mad. All she did was ask me to hurry up a whole lot of times. Naw, she was just in a bad mood." He gives me a knowing look. "You know how women are."

Bryan has learned something about this woman. He has learned that if you don't get dressed on time in the morning, three times out of four the worst that will happen is that Mother will get a little antsy. With those kinds of odds going for you, why worry? Further, he has learned you don't have to do what Mother says until the thunder and lightning starts.

Mother doesn't want to have to lose her temper just to get Bryan to move. Even so, that is what she has taught him.

More important still is what Bryan has *not* learned. He has not learned how to persist when the going gets a little tough. He has not learned to accommodate to others, not learned that his mother is a person with rights, towards whom he ought to be occasionally considerate. He has not accepted her rational authority and learned that to obey is not necessarily disgraceful or demeaning. In short, his adaptive growth has lagged.

What ought to be happening? What if when Mother called Bryan in the morning he leaped from bed, brushed his teeth, combed his hair and got dressed by eight o'clock without having to be reminded, threatened, or punished. How much better for Mother's nerves would this be!

When things go well with discipline, this is where one expects to be with a nine year old. But getting there is a staged process. One expects to take the five year old through the dressing process step by step. "Put on your shorts, now your shirt. Here, I'll help you with the buttons. What a big boy you're getting, able to dress yourself." Later, it's laying out the clothes and leaving the child to do the main parts himself, and still later it becomes "be done by eight o'clock and don't forget to brush your teeth."

As the child grows older and more able, Mother moves back on her supervision, leaving more to the child. Eventually a little praise and encouragement when he succeeds and a little disapproval when he dawdles is enough to keep things in motion.

But things do not always proceed this easily; some children need more training input than that. Furthermore, some mothers are not consistent enough, and, running late, will dress the child when he is well able to do the job himself. Some mothers are not clear enough about their expectations, or not firm enough, not determined enough to persist in the face of his reluctance. "Perhaps he's not ready to do it himself," they wonder, and they end dressing him.

For a variety of reasons, mothers can slip into standing over a nine year old and saying, "put on your shirt. Put on your shorts. Pull on your socks." Step by step they supervise him. But this is treating the nine year old as though he were four or five. This may get him dressed, but it will not lead him to do the job himself, nor will it promote his adaptive growth. Still mothers feel they have no choice. "If I did not stand over him, he'd be late for school every day."

If Mother and Bryan were my regular patients, and I had decided this was a good place to begin a little remedial parenting, I would ask Mother, "can Bryan dress himself?"

"Of course he can," she would undoubtedly reply. "If he's in a hurry to go to his friend's house, he can dress in a flash."

"Then expecting him to dress in the morning isn't an unreasonable expectation?"

"Of course not. Other children do it all the time without their mothers standing over them."

"Then let's insist upon it. Let's say to Bryan, 'it's your job to get dressed in the morning. . . WITHOUT SUPERVISION . . . and I expect you to do it from now on. Furthermore, getting dressed means: underwear; two socks, matching, one on each foot; shirt buttoned; shoes on and tied; and don't forget your belt.'"

Mother smiles. She recognizes that there is a tendency among nine year olds to regard socks and belts as optional attire.

"You have to spell it out," I tell her, "or sure as shooting he's gonna say, 'you didn't say I had to wear socks,' or possibly, 'shoes tied wasn't part of the deal.'"

At this point most mothers bring up other morning duties such as washing his face, brushing his teeth, combing his hair, making his bed, putting his dirty clothes in the hamper and pajamas away. After some discussion we agree that for now we will only *program* one thing, getting dressed, agreeing that if we try to correct all of his shortcomings at once, we would overwhelm him and probably fail. We can come back to those other things later.

"Now we have made it clear what he is to do, we need to set a time limit on it being done."

"Time limit?" Mother queries.

"Yes, a time limit. Unless you'd prefer to nag?"

Mother shakes her head vigorously.

After some discussion we decide the job should be finished by eight o'clock which gives him plenty of time to dress, get his breakfast, and be out the door so as not to be late for school. It also allows a little extra time to supervise if we have to.

Now we have to make sure he has a way of knowing how much time he has left. With a nine year old that's easy, you just put a clock in his room. With other children you may have to use a radio, saying "when the news comes on you've three minutes left." With even younger children you put a timer in the room. "When the buzzer goes off you've got three more minutes to be dressed.""

What you must not do is remind him of the time yourself. "Bryan, it's seven minutes to eight. Bryan it's five minutes to eight. Bryan it's four minutes to eight." That's nagging, and it's what you are trying to get out of doing.

NOW HE KNOWS PRECISELY WHAT HE IS TO DO AND WHEN IT IS TO BE DONE BY.

Now Mother is to leave him to it. Mother is not to call, remind, come up, ask, peek, or send up his little brother to see how things are going. She is to leave him alone to do the job because that is our goal—to have him dress himself without supervision.

"He won't dress, you know," Mother says.

"I think you are right." I reply. I use the word "think" because some children, when warned about the planned program, do an overnight turn-about, but most don't, and she is probably right, he won't dress.

"So what am I supposed to do, let him be late for school?" Mother asks.

"No sir! It's his duty to go to school and yours to make sure he gets there. So, at eight o'clock you go up and supervise. You'll probably find him flat on his back, one sock stuck at the heel, lost in space. Don't yell. Don't scold. Take a seat. Get comfortable and supervise. 'Put on your shorts, put on your pants.' Item by item, step by step you supervise him, just as though he were five years old."

"How will that grow him up?"

"Supervision doesn't, but you have no choice, so you are doing what you are forced to do as quickly and conveniently as possible. So long as you stay in the room there with him he'll keep going and in another six or seven minutes he'll be dressed."

"Then what?" Mother asks.

"Then you say to him, 'Bryan, It isn't my job to stand over you and get you dressed, not at your age. Furthermore, I have a lot of other things to do. Even so I've had to come up here and supervise you, which is not fair to me. So, every morning at eight o'clock when I come up, if you are not dressed, I'll supervise you, but that will cost you.'"

" 'You mean you are going to charge me for supervision?' Bryan will reply, astounded at the idea."

"Explain to him, 'Bryan, by charge, I mean there will be a consequence. You will lose half an hour of a selected privilege, and I select the privilege. And that is the way it is going to be every morning until you've learned to get dressed on time.'"

" 'What privilege are you gonna select?' Bryan will ask, a calculating look in his eye. You don't have to answer him, and often it's best not to, at least not right then. Give him a stall. Tell him 'I'll let you know later.'"

The punishment, or consequence for those who feel more comfortable with a euphemism, is given because he required supervision to complete his task. For the sake of illustration, let's suppose we decided to penalize him half an hour T.V. time after supper on days he doesn't get dressed on time without supervision. This is what I call the *reinforcer*. It is action communication which, speaking louder than words, underlines the parent's determination.

So now we have:

1. Made the expectation clear and specific.
2. Set the time limit.
3. Accepted the need to supervise.
4. Arranged for a consequence if supervision is required.
5. Explained all this to Bryan.

At this point I usually tell mothers the probable course of events. I do this because it almost always happens exactly this way, which reassures the mother and makes her more responsive to my future directions. This is what I tell mothers:

"The first morning when you arrive at eight o'clock he will be lying flat on his back on the bed, one sock half over his heel. You will have to supervise him step by step but you will keep your cool. It's a lot more nervous-making to stand in the kitchen wondering if he is getting dressed and going up every ten minutes to see than it is to tell yourself, 'well, whether he is or not I've got a plan. At eight o'clock I'm going to take care of it. Till then I'm not gonna fret.' And when eight o'clock comes you've organized the ten minutes so you aren't frantic about the baby or the burnt toast."

"Now you supervise him, and you'll manage not to yell. Furthermore, he will be dressed by eight-ten, which leaves ample time to get him off to school. He may not have dressed himself, but he does get out the door without shouts and tears, which is a big step to cooling some of the tensions."

"That night, when it comes time to lose his half hour T.V., he will look at you nonchalantly and say, with studied poise, 'as a matter of fact, I didn't intend to watch T.V. tonight. I had other plans.' And he'll go in his room and read, or play with the dog, or find something else reasonably interesting to do."

This tends to infuriate and dismay parents and indeed leads many of them to utter that famous lament of terminally frustrated grown-ups. "It's no use punishing, because nothing bothers him." I warn them about this sweet lemon technique and tell them neither to escalate the punishment nor to give up on it.

"Stick to the plan," I tell mothers. "In time he'll change his tune."

The second morning when Mother arrives in his room at eight o'clock, he will again be flat on his back, checking out the stain on the roof, the sock barely over his toes. But again, Mother is to keep her cool and supervise him, and he will make it out the door without tears. That night when punished he will say, "as a matter of fact I wasn't planning to watch T.V. tonight." Then he will find a comic book, bring it out to the kitchen and, while Mother is washing dishes, walk up and down turning pages and laughing uproariously at the comic strips.

The third morning when Mother arrives the sock may be on, but he won't be finished. Some other stumbling block will have felled him. Probably he will utter some eloquent excuse. "I couldn't find another shirt; and the one you laid out I can't wear because every time I do I get bad marks in spelling."

Mothers should ignore such gambits, stay cool and supervise, perhaps wish him better luck tomorrow morning.

"That's not fair," he will protest. "I was half dressed. I should only get half a punishment."

Mothers should tell him it was a nice try, but no way. He has but one simple duty to accomplish and lots of time. Since he didn't make he gets the whole punishment, and that's that. He may complain a little but chances are that, for a change, breakfast will be a relatively amicable occasion.

That night, when it comes time to punish him, Mother won't hear the "I wasn't going to watch T.V." spiel. This time he will get mad. "You've no right to take away my T.V. That's my favorite show. Every kid on the street is watching that show. As a matter of fact my teacher assigned it for homework."

If he can't bully his mother out of the punishment he may try another tack. "Tell you what, Mom, you let me watch that program tonight and I absolutely guarantee you I will get dressed on time tomorrow."

Mothers who buy this con end with egg on their faces. The right answer is this: "Tell you what, son. You be dressed tomorrow morning on time, and you'll be watching T.V. this time tomorrow night."

The fourth morning when Mother goes up he will be dressed. She won't have to supervise him and that night she won't have to punish him.

The fifth morning, as Mother mounts the stairs, he will call, "walk slow,

I'm almost finished." The next morning, the sixth, when Mother arrives in his room she will find him flat on his back on the bed, sock stuck at the heel, lost in space again.*

Why did we lose it? Because he hasn't been punished for two days. The consequence, having not been recently suffered, if not completely faded from memory, has lost its urgency. So he lapses.

At this point Mother must do exactly what the program calls for. That is, she must supervise without scolding and offer the usual punishment that evening. She must not give him another chance, must not say to him, "I am not going to punish you tonight because you did so well for a couple of days, but I am counting on you getting dressed properly tomorrow morning. You will, won't you dear?"

It is essential that the same behavior always results in the same consequence if the training message is to embed itself in his developing persona.

It usually takes three weeks before the program is working most of the time. By the fifth week the child is making it five days out of six without supervision or punishment, which is normal for nine year olds.

Remember, getting dressed in the morning was not the primary agenda; it was the vehicle to lead us to our real goal. Our goal was to grow him up, to promote his adaptive growth in the area of coping with tedium.

When we began, pulling his sock over his heel was more unpleasure than Bryan could master, but now he is doing it most of the time. *We have stretched his tolerance for tedium just a trifle.*

Other things have happened too. When Mother charged him for having to supervise him she sent him an action message. That message said, "I am a person with rights. You must come to recognize that and accommodate to me sometimes." He did so accommodate and in doing so *became a little less egocentric than he had been.*

Furthermore, by setting a clear limit and finding a way to make him meet it, or be punished, Mother exercised her reasonable parental authority. She was not overbearing. Neither was she capricious, weak or inconsistent. It is such steady authority which most successfully *disillusions a child's omnipotence.*

Capricious or overbearing authority is hard to accept; it has too much of the "I'll show you who's boss" tone, and children are bound to resist it.

---

*The sixth morning, if the program started on a Monday, will be Saturday morning, and he doesn't have to go to school Saturday and Sunday, so shouldn't we forget the program until Monday? No way! Two days is too long a gap in an initial training program. It O.K. to change the ready time to nine o'clock because it's the weekend, but the rest of the program should remain the same.

Weak or inconsistent authority does not have to be accepted; it can be evaded.

In this instance, Mother has been planfully firm. She has succeeded in demonstrating the difference between an adult's and a child's prerogatives. Giving her child an experience of rational authority, she has led him a step down the road to giving up his omnipotent illusion and accepting his childhood.

And when, after a couple of months getting dressed in the morning is not a problem, the program will no longer be necessary. Then, one morning her child will say, with pride in his voice, "hey, Mom, you notice how I always get dressed on time in the mornings now?" *This, as we shall now learn, is a brick of self-esteem settling in place.*

This is the subject of our next chapter: the fourth cardinal characteristic of the omnipotent child, his sadly deficient self-esteem.

5

The Wounding of Pride

"Pride works from within; it is the direct appreciation of self. Vanity is the desire to arrive at that appreciation from without."

ARTHUR SCHOPENHAUER

The Cardinal Characteristic

Seven-year-old Peter was giving me an account of all the adult things he deemed himself capable of doing.

"I could beat my father at bowling if I really tried," he declared, nodding his head affirmatively. "I could shoot a real gun. I could drive a car if I had to. I know how to steer. I know where the brakes are . . . and the gas."

He paused, anticipating contradiction I suppose. Receiving none and having exhausted all examples of estimable power that came to mind, he summed up his position in this pithy way, "I can do anything adults can do," he frowned, "except adultery."

Keeping a straight face is an essential ingredient of the practice of child psychiatry and we child psychiatrists get lots of practice. So, with a grave countenance, I asked him, "what's adultery?"

"You know," he replied, giving me one of those how-dumb-can-you-get looks, "filling out income tax forms and all that junk."

Peter's declaration of omnipotence is no more obvious than many I hear. Like most omnipotent children, Peter is minimally aware of the considerable discrepancy between his adult aspirations and his child capacities. But this statement says more about Peter than simply that an omnipotence illusion is alive and well in his psyche. It says something about his self-esteem.

Why is Peter volunteering this grandiose self-appraisal? I believe he is boasting, trying to impress me with his competence, trying to induce me to appreciate and admire his illusory power. However, as such statements usually do, his has an opposite effect; it reveals his uncertainty about himself, tells the perceptive that his self-esteem is fragile.

Problems with self-esteem are characteristic of children caught up in that pattern of adaptive growth failure I call the Omnipotent Child Syndrome. Unlike the other three cardinal characteristics of the Omnipotent Child Syndrome, self-esteem is not an adaptive competence. As we shall see, self-esteem is a product of adaptive growth. When adaptive growth does not proceed well we get adaptive weakness and regularly associated with such weakness is poor self-esteem.

Manifestations of Poor Self-Esteem in the Omnipotent Child

Sometimes the child expresses his dismay about himself directly. He comes slumping in from school one day when the children have been particularly cruel or rejecting. Instead of uttering his usual torrent of vengeful fantasy, he is a picture of woebegone misery, declaring, "I'm dumb. I can't do anything right. Nobody likes me. I'm the weakest kid in the class."

It is on such an occasion that Mother usually first learns her son has a nickname such as Screwy or Stinky or Pampers, or some derogatory perversion of his surname.

Parents are often more distressed about the damaged self-esteem of the omnipotent child than all of his other characteristics. I regularly hear them say things like, "I'd do anything if I could just help him to like himself." But they don't know what to do. They try to find some area of success for him. "If he could just be really good at one thing I'm sure it would do wonders for him." They agonize about how he got this way. "It isn't as though we don't try to find things to praise him for; we try not to make comparisons or run him down."

They feel guilty. For years the child-rearing books have claimed that "all that is necessary to lead a child to value himself is that his parents value him." So, recollecting moments of anger, they wonder if they have valued him enough.

However it is simply not true that parental approval is the principal generator of self-esteem in the child. We shall deal with that later. For the moment let me get back to some other ways in which damaged self-esteem is manifest in the Omnipotent Child.

Rather than declare their poor image of self many children cover their damaged self-esteem by extravagant declarations of worth, such as that made by Peter. To those who do not know the child well, he may seem more in danger of developing a superiority rather than an inferiority complex.

As Peter also illustrated, these children often entertain profoundly unrealistic self-expectations. They aspire to all the competencies of adulthood. Because they have not sacrificed the omnipotent illusion they feel they must be the equal of adults. "I could beat you at chess," they declare, and then prove to have no idea how the pieces move. This discrepancy between their child abilities and their adult declarations aggravates the problem. So long as their omnipotent illusion demands that they compete on an equal basis with adults, they are bound to lose, are they not?*

Another way in which these children's exquisite sensitivity about their worth reveals itself is in their inability ever to take second place whether that means losing a game, taking their place in line, or perhaps even getting the shorter of two pencils or the smaller sheet of drawing paper.

Playing games with these children will often reveal their uncertain self-esteem. They cannot lose, and if this seems likely they change the rules, cheat, or accuse others of cheating. Once losing seems inevitable, they either quit playing or start playing foolishly. One child with whom I used to play checkers would, when he realized it he was about to lose, manage to knock over the board, thus preserving himself from the agony of defeat.

Because these children have not yet moved very far from "magic" forms of thinking, they can come up with some quite ingenious modes of psychological denial of defeat. Faced with losing at checkers, such a child may not take the second last move, the one which allows you to jump his last piece. It is as though by ending the game short of this point he has actually prevented the loss. Another not infrequent gimmick of such a child is to take the second last move but then move your last piece for you, that is, jumping his own man. It is as though, through some psychological alchemy, he has converted himself into the winner by making your last jump for you.

All of this behavior is designed to protect a self-esteem so fragile that even the most minor and reasonable manifestation of second best cannot be tolerated.

As children grow older it becomes increasingly difficult for them to preserve their self-esteem in this fashion. The child cannot always be first; he must lose sometimes. When he does he is forced either to acknowledge his

---

*In their earnest desire to protect the child from feelings of inferiority, it seems to escape the attention of the Adlerian child-rearing experts that the child truly is inferior. To thus participate in his denial of his childhood does not lead to the adaptive growth that will, in time, generate real self-esteem.

limitations and find some way to accept them or to develop even more extensive and unrealistic methods of avoiding that reality.

One not uncommon method children select is to withdraw from competition. The child simply stops trying. He rationalizes that withdrawal in a variety of ways. He may say, for example, "I could get the top mark in reading if I wanted to, but I don't care about that subject." If he tries baseball and can't immediately be one of the best, he decides that baseball is dumb and drops out.

Many such children stop playing with peers and begin to play with younger children where their skills are superior and they win easily. These children also protect themselves by socializing with adults, who will make allowances for them. Either way, they avoid peer comparisons.

There are a number of psychological maneuvers these children use in order to protect their fragile self-esteem. There is the Walter Mitty Solution: withdrawal into fantasies of heroic achievement. There is the Sour Grapes Solution: denying the worth of an accomplishment one fears is beyond his grasp. There is the Sweet Lemon Solution: declaring one's present state to be the chosen one, a variant of the means children use to deny their parent's power. Finally there is the Expert Solution: narrowing the scope of one's effort to some limited area of competence and then regarding that pursuit as the only significant measure of worth. An adult example might be the tennis pro who whittles the senator down to size by declaring, "but he has a lousy backhand."

What has happened to such children is that they have not coped, have not managed to construct an adequate sense of their own worth, and so are driven to defend their fragile self-esteem. Much of their life energy is consumed in these efforts to conceal from themselves and the world the fact of their psychologically crippled state. In time many of them give up, withdraw from competition and settle for truncated lives.

They are the wounded in pride and their numbers are legion.

The Genesis of Self-Esteem

We need now to ask what psychological events in infancy and early childhood lead the child to a comfortable sense of his own worth and confidence in his person. Before laying this out simply, let's define a term and clarify a common misunderstanding.

Let's begin with the definition of the word "pride." Funk and Wagnall's dictionary list six definitions, of which two concern us. These are:

1. An undue sense of one's own superiority; arrogance, conceit.
2. A proper sense of personal dignity and worth.

The first is *false pride*. It has been condemned by the Bible as preceding a fall and seen in literature as the tragic flaw which brings down the hero. What we are talking of here is not real pride. It is vanity. It involves measures designed to impress, to force the world to validate one's pretensions of worth. The worth involved comes from without, not within.*

The second definition, "a proper sense of personal dignity and worth," is *true pride*, an indication of worth coming from within. To esteem oneself is self-esteem. Pride in this second sense is what parents wish for their children. Indeed helping their child to acquire this pride is a major goal for most parents.

Let's us be clear on this, no one wants to turn out haughty and arrogant children; indeed we wish the very opposite. What we wish for our children is that quiet self-assurance that comes from an inner sense of worth. The misunderstanding that needs correcting is that pride is simply generated in children: the notion that all that is necessary is that the parents value the child, and he will come to value himself.

I am forever confronted with guilt-laden mothers and fathers sure that somehow their child's failure to value himself arises from a lack of love or concern on their part. But in most cases these are not unloving parents. They care very much about their child, too much perhaps, and in some cases they have focused so strongly on the child's feelings in a desire to protect him from unpleasures that they have failed him in another area, the area of discipline and training.

The very act of seeking out a child psychiatrist's help is a statement of valuing the child. Any parent concerned enough to come to a professional and lay bare his or her sense of failure and inadequacy is surely valuing the child.

What has confused these parents is that they know there are moments when they do not feel very loving towards the child, moments which stand out as beacons of guilt overshadowing that daily concern and commitment to the child that tells the real story.

My definition of parental love has to do with that commitment to the child that says through actions not words: "I am your person in the world. I am here for you, and no matter how tough the sledding gets, I will be here for you so long as you need me." It isn't always liking the child that counts. It's being committed to him.

Of course the child who is unloved has little chance of developing an adequate self-esteem, but then he has little chance of developing many

*The psychoanalysts, with their penchant for mythology, have called this form of pride narcissism. In so doing they boxed themselves in so that now they are having to posit "healthy narcissism" to take up the slack their semantic confusion created.

other psychological strengths as well. The point for parents who care is that _love is not enough to generate healthy self-esteem in a child._ Love is an essential ingredient, but it is _insufficient_ of itself to produce a child with a proper sense of his own dignity and worth.

How then is self-esteem truly generated?

Self-esteem is "constructed" during early childhood. It is built by the child himself. The building blocks are experiences of mastery, instances of coping with normal growing-up expectations.

All children, when faced with the expectation that they learn to tie their shoes, say, "I can't, you do it for me." And they can't; their fingers cannot manipulate the shoe laces successfully. However, skills develop very quickly in little children, and it takes much less practice for them to acquire a skill than it does us slower adults. So Mother says, "sure you can. Come on. I'll show you." She takes the ends of the laces, pulls them taut across one another. "See, you make an X. See the X?" At this point the child usually becomes interested in seeing the X, so Mother goes on, "now you tuck one end through the bottom of the X." She helps the child to do that. Perhaps the first day she doesn't get much past this point, but that's all right—one step at a time.

The next day when Mother says, "come on, let's tie your shoes," the child says, "I can't, you do it for me." But Mother persists and they have another five-minute shoe-tying session, with him making the X and Mother going on to explain how to make the loop.

So it goes, each morning the child protests a little, but Mother leads him through the task, helping, completing, watching as gradually his fingers handle laces more adeptly. Eventually, perhaps after six or seven such mornings, the child ties his shoes the whole way himself.

Then he will smile with pleasure and jump up and down proclaiming, "I can tie my shoes." Of course his loosely tied shoes may come undone in the process of jumping up and down, but this will have little effect upon his joy. "I can tie my shoes," he will declare to anyone who will listen, and when his father comes home that is the first thing he will hear.

What has happened? The child has encountered an expectation. Because he had never done that particular thing before, he drew back from the challenge, but Mother led him through the task, turning it over to him by degrees. Eventually he did it all by himself. He coped. He experienced _mastery._

Mastery means being able to do something real. It may not be a great something but it is real and he has done it. There is a feeling that accompanies experiences of mastery. Like all feelings it is basically indescribable, but it can be approached obliquely. The feeling is pleasant. It has a component that seems to be a sensation of strength or capability. Indeed it has been called 'joy in being a cause.' I believe this feeling is the core of self-esteem.

Mastery stands in opposition to the omnipotence illusion, for it involves real, not illusory, power. The child manages something real, and he knows he has. There are only a few things children can manage to do, so when they do the victory is sweet.

There are many tasks of development which offer the growing child opportunities for mastery. Some are mechanical: learning to tie his shoes, to feed himself, to cut with scissors. Others are fragments of psychological adaptation: controlling his temper, holding back tears, waiting for his turn, understanding another person's point of view.

Each expectation coped with stretches the child's competence and builds his esteem. After three or four successful copings the child is much less liable to say, "I can't, you do it for me." Inside himself he is remembering, "I coped with the last four things that came my way; I can probably cope with this one too." So it is that self-confidence builds with each experience of mastery. It is in this sense that self-esteem is constructed by the child out of the building blocks of repeated experiences of mastery.

What of the child who has seemed so overwhelmed and woebegone that his sympathetic mother has tied his shoes for him or picked up most of his toys because he said, "I'm tired. You do it for me"? He doesn't cope. He experiences no mastery, builds no self-esteem. Furthermore, after four such expectations evaded, the child's inner statement becomes, "I couldn't cope with the last four things that came my way, and I probably can't cope with this one either." Instead of coming to feel self-confidence, he has come to feel self-doubt.

Expecting to fail, such children don't try hard, which of course leads to the failure anticipated and to more self-doubt. In time the child becomes an avoider. He doesn't want to try new things, and he covers up his apprehension by bad-mouthing the skill: "aw, hockey's dumb. Who wants to play that stupid game?" So it is that non-coping not only fails to build esteem and confidence but also actively builds a poor image of self and undermines self-confidence.

For the child who is desperately trying to preserve his illusion of omnipotence, the situation is further aggravated. Trying to be the equal of adults, the child is setting up impossible standards and aspirations for himself. So long as he compares himself with adults he can only lose. He cannot win at skill games because he is but a child with limited understanding and experience. He cannot equal the physical performance of the stronger adult. In almost all respects he is inferior to the adult: weaker, less experienced, untrained, with as yet undeveloped mental capacities. If he challenges the adult's competence, he is bound to lose.

However, the child who has accepted his childhood is not upset by his parents' superior competence. "When I'm as big as you," he says to his father, "I'll be able to bowl strikes too, won't I, Dad?"

Not so the omnipotent child. He fights fiercely not to acknowledge any form of adult superiority. "Kids are as good as grown-ups," Dewey insists. "Why should I have to go to bed at nine o'clock? You stay up late. Why can't I smoke a cigarette? You do! Why should I have to take math in school? I'm gonna be a hockey player when I grow up. I won't need dumb old math."

There is no way to counter these assertions of Dewey's without challenging his omnipotence illusion. This of course attacks his false pride. He feels he is being defined as weak and worthless, a "child" in a world where adults have all the power he esteems so highly. So long as he clings to the omnipotence illusion he will see childhood as a devalued state. He cannot know that once he accepts his childhood, he will no longer need to judge himself against adult power. Paradoxical as it may sound, the route to true self-regard runs through the foothills of humility. However there is no way Dewey can know this except to experience it.

Measures to Develop Self-Esteem

All four of the adaptive competencies develop in concert with one another. When one fails to develop, the others are impaired also. This is particularly so with respect to self-esteem which, as we have seen, is not an adaptive competence but a byproduct of successful adaptive maturation. Let me remind you of this by recalling a few of our earlier examples.

When Mother set up a program to deal with Terry's temper tantrums, her primary purpose was to wean the child away from his omnipotence illusion. When he began to control his temper prior to removal he was not only beginning to accept his mother's authority, but he was also stretching his self-control and diminishing his egocentricity by accommodating to his mother. All three adaptive competencies were served by the one training program.

Furthermore, when Terry mastered his anger, that is stopped having tantrums, one day he said to his mother, "Mom, have you noticed I don't fuss anymore?" He felt a little real pride in his new growth. He had laid down a brick of self-esteem.

Similarly when Johnny's Second Telling Program had begun to work, he was now tolerating the unpleasure of coming when called, and he was accommodating to his mother as well as accepting her authority. Chances are one day he too said to her, "hey, Mom, you notice I only got two second telling chips all week?" He too has known mastery and built a little self-esteem.

Similarly when Bryan's mother set up a program to get him to dress in the morning, her intention was to stretch his tolerance for tedium. However, when he began to succeed in getting ready on time regularly, he announced to her, "I always get dressed in time in the morning now, don't I, Mom?" This too reflects the the birth of *real* pride, does it not?

So it is that programs designed to promote adaptive growth in the child have some effect on all three adaptive competencies, and, at the same time, generate self-esteem.

The Genesis of Self-Esteem

1. Discipline leads to coping.
2. Coping leads to adaptive growth.
3. Adaptive growth leads to self-esteem.

The time has come to ask what is the precise nature of the discipline that promotes adaptive growth, why has it gone so poorly for the omnipotent child, and how can parents avoid such an outcome for their child? It's time to ask ourselves how Dewey got that way.

6

·

How Dewey Got That Way

"I'm a laying up sin and suffering for us both, I know."

AUNT POLLY TO TOM SAWYER ON AN OCCASION WHEN SHE KNEW
SHE OUGHT TO HAVE PUNISHED HIM BUT LET HIM OFF.

Children like Dewey are heading for sin and suffering if their parents can't find some way to lead them out of their adaptive immaturity. To determine how they are going to do this we first have to get a couple of things clear: we must understand the precise nature of Dewey's problem, and we must ask ourselves how Dewey got that way.

The Nature of the Problem

The Omnipotent Child Syndrome is a constellation of adaptive immaturity; it is a picture of lagged psychological growth. It is *immaturity* because Dewey's behaviors would be acceptable were he four or five years old, but he is far too impatient, self-centered, and willful to cope with what the world reasonably expects of a nine year old. It is *adaptive* because the behaviors we are talking about are those crucial to coping with life in a society with expectations and rules.

Children like Dewey are often labelled neurotic or disturbed. This is done on the basis of their evident unhappiness and emotional distress. But Dewey is not neurotic. He does not have an unconscious conflict buried in his psyche that is creating his difficulties, nor will he be cured by approaches designed to uncover and resolve his Oedipus Complex or his anal fixation. Dewey is trying to cope with the world of a ten year old using the adaptive equipment of a pre-schooler. What Dewey needs is to acquire better adaptive skills. While there is no question these children are un-happy, *their unhappiness is a result of their problem, not its cause.*

Let me illustrate. Dewey is often rejected or teased by his peers. He can't get along with them because he is too self-centered to read and accom-modate to their playtime agenda, too impatient and insensitive to play properly. He offends without realizing how he does so. They tell him to buzz off, that he can't play. Of course, he is unhappy to be rejected like this.

If the child psychiatrist deals with this unhappiness by uncovering its source—peer rejection—and ventilating Dewey's accumulated distress, he will reduce the child's present tension, but this does not solve the prob-lem. Until Dewey acquires the patience to take his turn and moves out of the egocentricity that renders him insensitive in social situations, he will simply offend all over again. And in a couple of weeks his tension will have accumulated all over again. Dewey needs adaptive growth more than he needs emotional relief.

The same kind of social incompetence that undermines Dewey's peer re-lations colors his home life. By the time such children and their parents ar-rive in my office, relationships at home are as strained as those on the play-ground. There is one difference: while the kids at school will blame Dewey for the situation, Mother tends to blame herself.

Though Mother truly cares about Dewey, ninety percent of the ex-changes between them are negative in tone. As a result Dewey feels un-loved, and neither does Mother feel very loving. This is easy to detect, and therapists with shallow understanding leap on it as the cause of the prob-lem. They tell Mother that what Dewey needs is more love. This is not helpful; in fact it is damaging. For months Mother has been trying her hardest to love Dewey despite his difficult ways. To tell her to be more lov-ing is to increase her guilt, mislead her as to the cause of Dewey's problem, and offer her no usable parenting advice.

The simple fact is, if Dewey is ever going to get more 'love' from Mother he is first going to have to become a lot more lovable. So long as he is as impatient and demanding, rude and arrogant as he has been, Mother will, her strongest resolve to the contrary, end angry with him on many, many oc-casions.

To put the horse firmly before the cart, this is the situation: Dewey has few skills to cope with the world, and his non-coping is generating much emotional distress for both him and his family. The question that arises is what happened? What went wrong? Was it something in the child, some-thing in the parenting, or perhaps some combination of each?

How Dewey Got that Way

Whenever a family comes into my office I have to tease out a detailed answer to this question so that I can find a way to lead them out of their dilemma. The first questions that arise are two. What kind of parents are these? What kind of child did God give them to rear?

THE ROLE OF TEMPERAMENT IN CHILD DEVELOPMENT

Let me emphasize: Deweys are made, not born. To be sure, temperament plays a role in determining what kind of an individual the child will become, but in most cases temperament is not the central factor. God, or nature if you will, deals each of us a hand of cards, but it is parenting which gives us the skill to play those given cards well or poorly.

The temperamentally intense and energetic individual may react more vigorously to life, making him a handful as a child, but with good adaptive training this temperament may become an asset in his adult life. To be sure, he may become an adult who feels things more passionately, tackles life more vigorously, suffers more intensely. Such persons may be destined to become movers and shakers who change the world.

On the other hand, some children are mild and accommodative from infancy. As children 'aw, shucks' is their response to major disappointment and 'phooey' their angriest epithet. Ah, but to be blessed with such a child, you say? Well, these docile creatures have their problems too. They may keep things inside which could be dealt with if they were up-front about what was bothering them. As adults they may be too accommodative, too accepting. On the other hand, their style may lead them into contemplative ways, perhaps eventually to wisdom. The world needs its wise men as much as it needs movers and shakers.

Such temperamental differences have a considerable effect on child rearing. I see many a parent who has done a great job with three children, but one, more feisty than the others, has ended in real trouble. In such a case, temperament may be the significant factor.

On the other hand no child, even one in the same family, experiences exactly the same rearing environment. For example parents learn how to parent by practicing on their first child. This usually means a certain amount of overprotection and overcontrol. With the second they relax a little. By the fourth child Mother may have over-relaxed, for one hears her saying things like, "oh, don't worry. He'll be using his knife and fork by the time he's twenty-one."

So, while temperamental differences may make one child harder to rear than another, such differences are only one of a number of factors involved in determining the final outcome. It comes down to this: each Dewey is where he is because there has been some degree of discrepancy between the rearing he, with his particular temperament, needed, and the rearing he received.

THE PARENTING

So we ask the question: given this child's temperament, what has gone wrong? Precisely how has Dewey's parenting not done the job? We are not concerned to fault the parent but to seek the understanding necessary to lead Dewey out of his psychological dead-end and get his adaptive growth in motion again.

The road out of that dead-end is not named "give him more love." Many persons feel it is, feel that all that is necessary to rear children successful is to love them, feel that given enough loving, discipline will be unnecessary. When problem behavior occurs the measures such persons propose always start by urging the parent to appreciate how the child feels and tailor their approach to alleviating his distress. If he's fearful at night, lie down with him. If he kicks a hole in the door, provide him with a kicking board. Even though the behavior is socially unacceptable no hint of disapproval should be permitted to color the mother's response. One parent told me that the teacher of her parenting course advised her thus. In a fit of anger her child had opened the fridge and thrown every item except one out onto the kitchen floor. "Compliment him on that fact that he left one item in the fridge," the instructor advised.

This instructor truly believes that social growth is as inevitable as physical growth, that training children to adulthood is unnecessary, that in a totally loving environment the child will somehow osmose adaptive growth. This is nonsense. From many years of practice I have learned that love, while an essential ingredient for effective parenting, is not the sole ingredient. Nor, with respect to the omnipotent child, is it the missing ingredient.

When one looks deeply into the family life and early development of children like Dewey, one rarely finds real evidence of significant emotional neglect or rejection. Dewey's parents love him, even if they aren't feeling very loving toward him much of the time these days.

Even so, many parents who come for help feel the reason the child is in difficulty is because they do not love him sufficiently. Why do they feel this? Because a thousand magazine articles have been telling them for years. If your child is in any kind of adjustment difficulty, then it follows as the night the day, that he has not been getting enough love.

This is a pat, do-for-every-situation explanation, beloved by the mushy-minded editors of women's magazines. They have been ladling it out like Campbell's Soup for at least three generations of motherhood. The harm it has done to parenting in North America is incalculable.

Add to this the fact that, if you have a child like Dewey, good will tends to erode at a rate equal to if not exceeding that at which the Colorado River carved out the Grand Canyon. Though Mother may be trying her hardest to love her child it soon comes to be that the air in her house is not laden with affection. Then when things fall apart and Dewey declares, as all children do from time to time, "you don't love me anymore," Mother is sure the magazine articles were exactly right.

So it is that when a mother comes to my office with her Dewey in tow, she is usually consumed with guilt, absolutely sure the problem is she doesn't love her child enough. Furthermore she is devastated by disappointment and a deep sense of failure, for this was the woman who, when pregnant, had fantasized her eventual entry in the Guinness Book of World Records as the greatest mother since Eve.

She knows that she's been angry at Dewey. Lots of times. Why? Because he won't do what she expects of him, because he is often rude and disrespectful, because he makes her feel such a failure. She has learned to mistake that anger for not loving him. However, the important component of loving the child is not being sweet and speaking softly on all occasions. It's not hugging him when you feel like wringing his neck. It's both of you knowing *you are going to hang around and do what you can for him until he's full grown, no matter how tough it gets*. It is that deep commitment to the child that is the essence of loving him.

All the parents who come to my office love their child. If they didn't, they wouldn't be there. So no matter what the magazines say, Dewey isn't in trouble because his mother doesn't love him. He's in trouble because she just can't figure out how to grow him up.

Parenting involves two principal activities: *nurturing* the child, and *disciplining* him. In the case of the omnipotent child the problem does not lie with nurturance. It lies with discipline.

Discipline has had a bad press in the last couple of decades. For the love-is-all-it-takes crowd, discipline has become a dirty word. Some have confused discipline with punishment. And punishment itself has been confused with punitiveness. So we need to clarify what discipline and punishment really are. Let's begin with a definition of discipline.

Webster defines discipline as *training which strengthens, molds or perfects*. This is what the term means whenever it is used in this book.

Punishment is one of several methods by which discipline is reinforced, that is rendered impressive enough to communicate its message to the child. Other reinforcers include approval, disapproval, and reward.

Discipline is as essential a component of parenting as *nurturance*. Children need both if they are to mature. A parental attitude which includes both in a balanced way is essential.

In order to clarify this balance let's look at how Diana Baumrind of the Institute of Child Development at the University of California has linked the two and coined the eminently appropriate term 'authoritative love.'

Authoritative love includes both nurturance and discipline and avoids that polarization that seems to say loving the child somehow stands in opposition to disciplining him, when in fact discipline is a major expression of parental love. Despite the women's magazines, *parents don't discipline children to put them down or to demean them or to get even with them; parents discipline children to prepare them to cope with the world, to save them from later sin and suffering.*

Baumrind, working with normal nursery school children, identified three common patterns of child behavior. She was interested to see whether these patterns corresponded to differences in the way the children were being parented. The three patterns were these:

Pattern I children were self-reliant, self-controlled, buoyant, and affiliative, that is to say, they were able to cope with their environment and themselves and were cheerful and outgoing.

Pattern II children were discontented, withdrawn, and distrustful, but they managed to cope with what was expected of them.

Pattern III children showed little self-reliance or self-control. They tended to retreat from new experiences. They were not as discontent as Pattern II children.

When Baumrind and her assistants investigated the related parenting practices through interviews, home visits and structured observations, they were particularly attentive to two aspects of parenting: parental control behavior (discipline in my terms) and parental caretaking, that is warmth and involvement (nurturance in my terms).

They found the parents of Pattern I children, the self-controlled, self-reliant, buoyant and affiliative children, to be highest of the three parent groups in control behavior (discipline). These parents were also high in caretaking behavior (nurturance).

The parents of Pattern II children, the discontented, withdrawn and distrustful children, were high in control behavior but low in caretaking. In my terms these parents offered much discipline, but in a context of insufficient nurturance.

With the Pattern III children, the dependent, uncontrolled, but reasonably contented children, they found the parental caretaking and warmth adequate but the controlling behavior low. These parents loved their children, but they did not discipline them well.

The lesson seems clear. If you love your child but do not discipline him, he may come to be sunny and reasonably affiliative, seeing the world as a friendly place, but he won't learn to cope with it or with himself. He will be a sunny non-coper.

If you offer your child lots of control, but do so coldly without adequate nurturance, without a true concern for his emotional well-being, he may learn to cope with the world, but he is unlikely to enjoy it. He will become a sullen coper.

Finally, if you offer your child firm and effective controls in a context of care and commitment, you have the best chance to produce a child who becomes a sunny coper.

Clearly, the most effective parenting provides a balanced experience of both nurturance and discipline. This is what Baumrind calls authoritative love.

Dr. Millar's Version

Love minus discipline   ▶   sunny non-coper
Discipline minus love   ▶   sour coper
Love plus discipline   ▶   sunny coper

In the case of the omnipotent child, the lack has not been one of love, but of authority, of the effective parental discipline needed to stimulate and guide adaptive growth.

Adaptive growth proceeds when the child is required to cope with a gradually paced program of increasing expectations. This means discipline. Every child must learn to separate, to trust, to wait, to accommodate, to accept adult authority and his childhood. It is discipline which generates these competencies in the child. But how does one discipline effectively? What are the essential ingredients? How can parents provide these?

The Disciplinary Process

The best way to clarify this complicated subject is to deal with specific situations and show how discipline can be effective or fail because one or another of its elements has not been given proper consideration. Discipline involves two principal parental activities: setting limits and communicating expectations. Setting limits means saying *no you can't* and communicating expectations means saying *now you must.*

Setting limits is first undertaken to protect the child from physical dangers. An example might be telling the toddler not to touch the stove or climb on the stair rail. However, once he is on his feet and into things, other forbiddings necessarily arise, such as saying, "no, you can't throw your glass on the floor. I know it makes a pretty sound when it breaks, but you can't go through life breaking things just to hear what they sound like."

Whether Mother's motive be to protect her child or protect her property, setting limits intrudes upon the child's omnipotence illusion. As the child grows older and acquires greater knowledge of reality, there is less need to protect him with limits. However, his capacity for destruction increases so, in the case of the toddler, setting limits is very much the name of the game.

Communicating expectations means saying "now you must." An example might be telling the toddler, "it's time you started helping to dress yourself. Look! I'll lay the shirt out on the bed for you so the arms won't get mixed up. Now, you slip your hands into the sleeves and pull it on, and then I'll help you with the buttons."

Unlike setting limits, it is characteristic of communicating expectations that these increase as the child grows older and more capable of doing things for himself. For the five year old the instruction is "put on your shirt and pants." When he's seven, it becomes "get dressed and don't forget to brush your teeth." As the child grows older and his capacities increase, one expects more of him and leaves more of the detail to his choice.

How easy it would be to discipline children if all that was required was to say "no" or "now you must" and the child smiled sweetly and complied. There are, I understand, children like this. They do not abound in my practice. For most children it is not enough for the parents to express their desires with respect to the child's behavior. They soon find they need to do more if they are to get their child to pay attention to their no's and now you musts.

Discipline with the toddler is much more an action business than a verbal business. Let me illustrate. If Mother says "no" to the average toddler enroute to fiddle with the T.V. knobs he may not break his stride. After a couple of "no's" and ultimate removals, his modus operandi will change. Now he will sidle over toward the set, checking over his shoulder to see whether Mother is observing. If she, seeing him, calls a warning "no", he may back off, but there's a good chance he'll just stand there watching her and, if she does not move, reach his hand toward the knob again, hold it there and wait to see what Mother will do.

This is the moment of truth in discipline. What Mother does now determines what she teaches. If she simply gives him another "no" but "does" nothing, he will move a step closer to the set, extend his arm, and check back again. If she gives him another "no" but still no action, he will take another step closer and repeat his finger action. Soon he is close enough that the next maneuver makes contact. Heretofore patient Mother now removes him and complains, "I told you not to touch the T.V. Didn't you hear me?"

He did. But *he learned what she taught,* that you can safely ignore her "no's" because she doesn't really mean "no" until she moves. The more "no's" he hears before action commences, the more he learns to discount Mother's prohibitions. Action, not words, is what trains small children, and her actions taught him to ignore her words.

Suppose Mother observes him approaching the T.V. and calls out "no, don't touch" and he stops, extends his arm, looks back and checks her out. "Don't touch," she repeats. He takes a step closer, extends his arm and checks her out again. Now she gets up, fetches him and puts him in his playpen for two minutes. He protests, but she holds firm. A few repetitions of this action dialogue and her first "no" will bring his electronic excursions to a prompt halt. Furthermore, future "no's" will begin to carry a little more weight.

So, the first thing to learn about discipline with the small child is that it primarily involves *action dialogue.* It will be some time before Mother's *words* come to carry the power of her actions.

Disciplinary exchanges between parent and child are complicated interpersonal events with more ways to go wrong than to go right. For example, it's easy to be too patient too long, then spill out the accumulated indignations in a soon-regretted over-reaction. This leads to guilt and another effort to be patient too long. Soon you are in a cycle of alternating permissiveness and overcontrol. What does this teach the child? Not what you intended, that's for sure. It is the nature of disciplinary encounters that if you get one detail wrong the whole exercise can come to naught.

Discipline is not only complicated but is also the most unpleasant part of parenting. It's a lot more fun to give to a child than withhold from him. It's much easier to give in and rationalize it as kindness than it is to stand your ground before a woebegone childhood sinner. Even Aunt Polly knew better, but she weakened. Discipline requires patience, understanding and moral courage. All this book can provide is understanding.

While there are no easy recipes there are principles of discipline which can lead a parent to this understanding. The rest of this chapter will be devoted to examining and illustrating those principles one by one.

The Principles of Discipline

There are five steps in planning disciplinary encounters. These are:

1. Set a clear expectation.
2. Set a time limit for the expectation to be met.
3. If the expectation is not met by the time limit, supervise its completion.
4. If you had to supervise, apply a reinforcer.
5. Persist to train.

Let's look at each of these in turn.

SET A CLEAR EXPECTATION

Suppose you have decided that you, your nine year old, and his room would all benefit if he cleaned it regularly on Saturday mornings. You have decided that a little planful firmness is in order, not only because a tidy room would be a considerable asset but also because you have detected in him a certain reluctance to tackle the tedious. You have come to feel a little adaptive growth is overdue.

Your first job is to decide exactly what is reasonable to expect of a nine year old and then consider how to communicate that expectation to the child.

If you were merely to say to him, "I want you to clean your room on Saturdays," it is likely something like this would happen. He will sweep the assorted items cluttering the floor under his bed, push the dirty clothing under the sheets, pull up the spread, punch out the lumps, and announce "hey, Mom, I've cleaned my room."

By his lights he has. It does *look* a lot better, and you can walk clear from the door to the far wall without tripping. What more could a mom expect?

Even so most moms would say, "that room isn't cleaned." So the debate begins.

Unless you enjoy such debating, it is better to introduce the task with a clear expectation. "I want you to clean your room Saturdays, and by cleaning your room I mean the following:

1. Bureau and desk top clear.
2. Toys in their box or the cupboard.
3. Nothing under the bed.
4. Bed made, sheets pulled up, smoothed, tucked in, same for blanket and spread.

He will, of course, protest. "Boys shouldn't have to do housework. You are making me into slave. I think I'm allergic to dust. I'll probably get sick and have to go to the hospital, and you'll probably not even bother to visit me."

Don't let him seduce you into an argument about whether you love him enough to visit him in the hospital. Stick to your disciplinary agenda.

Explain the program to him. "You have until ten a.m. when I'm coming back to check. If those four things aren't done, then I'll supervise you until they are, but if I have to supervise there'll be no cartoons for the rest of the morning."

Keep your task definitions simple. Suppose you had included straightening his drawers, cleaning his cupboard, vacuuming the rug, taking his dirty laundry downstairs, and putting his clean clothes away? Do you think most nine-year-old boys can really cope with so extensive a list? Chances are at least one item will be forgotten, so, of course, you will have to supervise and punish. You will have made the child's chance of coping a remote one, and so the training will not proceed.

It is important to keep in mind that the main purpose of the discipline is not a scrupulously tidy room; it is to promote the child's adaptive growth. This is more liable to happen if your program gives him a reasonable chance of success. You can always up the ante later. So choose your expectations charitably and spell them out in unmistakable terms or else something will be missing and a debate will ensue. "Two sheets! Who needs two sheets on their bed?" Don't let him fudge the expectation, that is do three items and get out of the fourth with a "gee, Mom, I did most of it." If you've detailed your expectation charitably, you should be able to stick to all items of it.

Don't *you* fudge the expectations either. I know it wouldn't hurt him to move his train down to the basement while he's at it, but you should not capriciously add that item to Saturday morning room cleaning. That wasn't part of the deal, and if you do he'll feel put upon. "Boy, give 'em and inch and they'll take a mile."

Not all expectations are equally important. In choosing which things about which to develop disciplinary programs you should think in terms of "you musts" and "I wish you woulds." There are things children *must* do: Get dressed. Brush their teeth. Go to school. There are other things parents *wish* children would do: Come to table when called. Talk politely. Be nice to your sister.

The *musts* are the best areas for disciplinary programming. Children must get up and go to school and programming them to do so is wholly reasonable. Similarly children must come home on time or phone. They must do their school work. They must go to bed on time. These musts are fair game for programmed expectations.

There are things mothers wish children would do, such as wash their faces properly, comb their hair, clean their rooms, hang up their coats when they come in, or help out in the kitchen. While one can expect these things, and perhaps program some of them, it is important to keep one's priorities straight. To insist that a child wash his face properly but let him get away with not finishing his school work is to send the child an unbalanced message.

If one is not going to program some of the *I wishes* what is one to do about them? Such *I wishes* are best handled with a shrug and an, "I'll be glad when you learn to say please . . . to use your fork . . . to stop teasing your sister." Remember, Mother can always choose to escalate an *I wish* to a *you must* when the time is ripe.

Children don't have to do everything they ought to do in order to grow up psychologically. If they do a few *musts*, adaptive growth will proceed. Furthermore, as growth proceeds, many of the *I wishes* come to take care of themselves.

So the first principle of effective discipline is that the parents set clear and reasonable expectations about a few duties, spell these out for the child, and then stick to them, not letting the child vary the requirement. Nor should parents add to or subtract from those requirements so long as the particular training program is underway.

SET A TIME LIMIT

If you don't set a time limit by which an expectation is to be met or a task completed, you know what you will hear when you approach the child about not having taken the garbage out yet? "But Mom, I was just gonna do it." Furthermore, if you don't set a time limit, you will have to nag, and nagging is what teaches the child to ignore your words.

So one details the task and sets a time for it to be completed. The instruction becomes, "Dewey, you are to take the garbage out each afternoon before six p.m. Taking the garbage out means taking this bag from this can, out that door, carrying it to that lane, depositing it in that large green receptacle with the lid, which is to be replaced, and then returning to the house and inserting a new liner in this can."

"Furthermore," the instruction continues, "the operation must be in progress by six p.m. sharp or else I will supervise, that is I will find you, lead you to the trash and walk you through the details. However, since I have better things to do than supervise, that little service will cost you something."

"You mean, even after I take the garbage out, I'm gonna get punished?" he protests, with all the woebegone innocence he can muster.

"Yup," Mother replies, projecting a little Gary Cooper insouciance.

"You mean you're not even gonna remind me when it's getting close to time?"

"Nope."

"But I'll forget the time."

"Probably at first. But soon you'll start keeping an eye on the clock."

And he will. Eventually, at two minutes to six he'll come rocketing into the kitchen, shouting "O.K.! O.K.! I'm on my way."

The time limit is the crucial ingredient that turns *parent discipline* into *self-discipline*. As long as you are willing to find him and get him moving, he will rely upon your fetch rather than his conscience to get him moving.

There are many ways to make sure the child has some way to know how is time is going. Many pre-school children can tell you how long until Sesame Street. The radio can be a useful reminder of an impending duty. As for the clock, one can say, "when the big hand gets to here, I'll be coming up to see if you've finished." Indeed, this kind of thing often so motivates children that learning to tell time proceeds from the imposed necessity.

The goal is that the child come to time himself, that instead of waiting for his mother to tell him to take out the garbage, he learns to tell himself, "it's almost six. I'd better get that garbage out." Without a time limit this internalizing growth will not proceed.

As the child matures, one may make the time limits less rigid. For the eight year old it may be best to say, "it's half past six, time to study your spelling words." However, by the time the child is ten, one hopes to be able to say, "homework is your job; you fit it in before bedtime."

Of course, in the beginning of the school year, before the child has reconciled himself to it having all begun again, he will mismanage his time, and the parent will hear, "I forgot my homework; I've gotta stay up late, and do it." The right answer to this, I have found, is to say, "you can't stay up late. Take the clock and set the alarm for seven a.m. You can do it in the morning." A couple of these occasions and the child learns to compromise, to find some time between the end of school and bedtime into which to fit his homework. And as he learns we have reason to believe an internal debate such as the following is going on.

"I'd sure like to play ball now, but if I do, I'll have to do my homework after supper and then I'll miss *All in the Classroom*. On the other hand, I know what is going to happen, the teacher is pregnant, and the principal is in love with the substitute, so the kids will get another movie. Ah phooey!

I'll play ball and miss tonight's episode." So it is children learn to make the trade-offs, and all because somebody was willing to set a few time limits and stick to them.

The next principle of discipline needs careful planning for it is often mismanaged by parents.

SUPERVISE THE TASK PERFORMANCE

Supposing an expectation that the child take the garbage out had been communicated to him in a clear way and that a time limit of six p.m. had been set for the completion of the task. However, when six p.m. comes the garbage is still sitting there and himself is watching T.V. Now what is Mother to do? She has two options.

Option One: Mother can take the garbage out herself and punish him because she had to. While this may be easier than Option Two—fetching him to the task and enduring a lot of complaint about missing his T.V.—this course of action will never solve the problem. Chances are Mother will still be taking out the garbage when he is twenty-one, after which he will marry and his wife will take over the task.*

The child immersed in some pleasurable activity is much inclined to remain in that blissful state. Faced with the choice of leaving it for a duty or remaining in it and accepting a punishment, most children will opt for the latter. Trading a duty for a punishment is a trade most young children are happy to make.

Option Two: If the child is to be trained Option Two is absolutely necessary. Mother lays this out for him as follows. "Dewey, you are going to take the garbage out every night. You may do so on your own initiative, prior to six p.m., and if you manage this there will be no further consequence. But, if six o'clock comes and you have not taken the garbage out, then I will fetch you to the task, but that will cost you, because it is your job to take the garbage out without reminders from me."

This changes the supervisory situation significantly. The action statement is no longer, "if you don't take the garbage out you will be punished." It has become, "you *will* take the garbage out. If you do it on your own, and by six p.m., fine. If not you will be supervised through it, but supervision is not free; it will cost you something."

Given this action input, Dewey soon realizes that he cannot continue his immersion in pleasure; he must leave it one way or another. Once that be-

---

*While women, particularly those of the liberated persuasion, are much inclined to attribute male chauvinism to the inherent perversity of *that sex*, the fact is male chauvinism needs to be carefully taught, and it is indulgent mothers who teach it.

comes clear to him, the advantage of leaving it prior to punishment rather than after becomes obvious.

Even so, many mothers will select Option One, that is perform the duty for the child and punish him later. They will take out the garbage because it is easier than getting him to do it. They will pick up the child's room or alter their agenda to accommodate to him rather than hold to their expectations. They will complain bitterly of having to do *his* job, but they stop short of finding him, leading him to the task, supervising his performance and then punishing him for *having had to supervise*.

Children will not grow from Option One discipline. Such a program does nothing to stretch the child's tolerance for tedium since he succeeded in avoiding the duty. It does nothing for his egocentricity since he did not accommodate to Mother, she accommodated to him. Finally, such compliance from Mother is not the exercise of rational authority that disillusions omnipotence. In fact it is the opposite, for each time Mother fails to get the child to perform the task she laid down for him, she affirms his view that he does not have to do anything he does not much feel like doing.

Sometimes it is quite difficult to supervise children through tasks. If they decide to do battle, it takes a good deal of parental assurance to stand firm. Fortunately, most children don't carry things this far. They wrangle and complain but, with Mother by their side, they perform. However, some children dig in their heels and refuse. "I am not going to do that and you can't make me." How is Mother to supervise completion of the task then?

There is a very important truth involved here and it is best to be up front about it: NO ONE CAN MAKE A CHILD DO THAT WHICH HE IS ABSOLUTELY DETERMINED NOT TO DO.

This truth needs explanation. Laws in a society and expectations in a home are the rules which makes a particular social organization possible. Members benefit from their membership and they should obey the rules. If they are intelligent and mature, they come to understand this. If they do not understand then it becomes necessary for the society to coerce such compliance. So society invented policemen.

Laws are really for people who need them. Most people don't. They do what is right, not what is lawful. A law cannot force a person to obey. It can jail or otherwise punish the person for not obeying, but it cannot force the person to obey.

A similar situation exists in the family. Rules can be laid down and things expected of children. But children cannot be forced to do the thing required. They can be punished, or expelled, but they cannot be made to conform if they are determined enough not to. Though children do not yet comprehend the social contract, they do know that they have the option of refusing the task and taking the consequence. So one supervises a task, tolerates the child's complaints, waits out his resistances, weathers his stalls, and stands firm. In time most children comply. But suppose he gets to the point he is under the dining room table, clutching the table leg and declaring he is prepared to die under there before he takes any garbage into any lane for anybody.

What do you do now? Do you drag him and out and force him to do the task? Can you? I remember one father whose four year old absolutely refused to pick up his toys. Father was absolutely determined that he do so. Eventually he ended with the boy, off the floor, wedged between his knees, while Father manipulated the boy's arms as one manipulates sugar tongs and picked up each item one by one.

Did the father make the boy pick up his toys? Psychologically speaking, I don't think so. Would it not have been better for him to say to the boy, "alright then, I'll pick up your toys, but tomorrow they stay in the toy box, and the day after we'll see whether you've learned the rule about picking up after play is finished."

When the child absolutely refuses to conform to the supervision, it is time to back off. One makes a statement such as the following: "Of course I can't *make* you take out the garbage, but I may be able to make you *wish* you had." Then one terminates the confrontation by departing the scene.

Once the parent has acknowledged the child's ultimate autonomy and, at the same time, exhibited her sensible determination, the child often capitulates, especially if the parent isn't in the room and the child's loss of face is minimized. He comes out from under the table and bumps about the room a little. Then one hears the clatter of the garbage pail accompanied by an obligatto of minimally acceptable words; "O.K. I'll take your dumb garbage out, Queen of the World!"

Of course, if that does happen he still has a punishment coming because he didn't take the garbage out on time without supervision. Whatever you do, don't rub his nose in it at that minute. Just post the punishment card on the fridge and let him discover it later.

However, if despite this best course, that doesn't happen, Mother will end having to take the garbage out herself. She should do so. In good humor! But now he gets two punishments. One because he didn't take the garbage out without supervision, and one because he didn't take it out with supervision. Again it is best not to draw these to his attention until he has cooled off.

So the third principle of discipline is that, having set a clear-cut and detailed expectation, and having set a time limit for its performance, the parent deals with non-performance by supervising: finding the child, leading him to the task, and directing his performance of it. Although Mother may not succeed in this, the effort to do so will usually prove enough to get things moving and eventually accomplish the disciplinary goal, if not that day, then the next.

So far we have dealt with the first three principles of discipline: the clear expectation, the time limit, and the supervision. It is time now to turn to the subject of the reinforcer: the measure taken to punish, reward, or otherwise induce the child to take one's disciplinary expectations seriously.

IF YOU HAD TO SUPERVISE, APPLY A REINFORCER

This matter of reinforcing one's expectations is an important and complicated subject about which there is much disagreement and confusion. Let's start by being very clear about the necessity for a reinforcer.

If Dewey did not take the garbage out by six p.m. without Mother fetching and supervising him, it is necessary that some consequence ensue. This could be a scolding, a punishment, or a reward withheld. If there is no such consequence, why should he move on the task until his mother arrives to make him? Why should he not just sit enjoying his show, hoping that perhaps this once she will forget or give up and he won't have to do it? He has nothing to lose and a minuscule hope of gain.

If the child is to come to accept an expectation, his failure to do so without supervision has to cost him something. Mother has to lay something like this on the child.

"Dewey! Because you did not take out the garbage by six o'clock, you will not be allowed to ride your bike after school tomorrow, and that's the way it is going to be each day until you learn to watch the clock and get the garbage out by six."

The function of the reinforcer is to lead the child to discipline himself. If one only fetches him to the undone task and supervises his completion of it but does not apply a reinforcer, one will be fetching and supervising forever.

However, if supervision is invariably accompanied by a reinforcer, eventually he will be skittering out before the deadline in order to meet the expectation and avoid the consequence. This does not have to happen very many times before adaptive growth is in motion again.

What exactly is this thing I call a reinforcer? A reinforcer is a parental action undertaken to lend weight to her disciplinary expectations. The reinforcer empowers the disciplinary communication. Children immersed in pleasure do not hear a parental summons or prohibition. However, as was illustrated with the Second Telling Program in Chapter Three, once they realize that if they do not respond some consequence will result, their hearing improves. The consequence has served to *reinforce* the communication.

Reinforcers come in two varieties: those whose power comes from approval and those whose power emanates from disapproval. Approval ranges from smiles and praise to tangible rewards. Disapproval ranges from frowns and scoldings to punishments. Each of these has its place in parenting. Though it is much more pleasant to approve than disapprove, as we shall see later, approval is not always effective, particularly with the toddler who has as yet little awareness of the fact that his mother is not required by God to approve him on all occasions regardless of his behavior.

So, having put things in context, let's now address ourselves to understanding that most essential of reinforcers, punishment.

Punishment as Reinforcer

Punishment is a consequence contrived by the parent to disreward some unacceptable behavior. It is a perfectly respectable part of parenthood. Unfortunately the noun punishment has been confused in some people's minds with the adjective punitive, which means cruel or mean forms of punishing undertaken by sadistic persons for its own sake.

So it has come to be that when one recommends even reasonable punishments, there are those who think you have an unhealthy desire to hurt children.* This nonsense has been popularized to the point that many parents have been frightened away from their disciplinary responsibilities. I believe this has made a substantial contribution to the escalating incidence of omnipotent children in our homes and schools.

Since parents must understand when and how to punish as part of their parenting, let's spend a few minutes making sure we know what the word means. According to Webster, to punish is to "afflict with pain, loss or suffering for a crime or fault: to chasten." Webster lists as synonyms, "chastise, castigate, chasten, discipline, correct."

In psychological terms the process is as follows. SOMEONE (the parent) does SOMETHING (the punishment, unwelcome but not unreasonable) to the OFFENDER (the child) with a view to PENALIZING (that is devaluing and retributing) as well as CORRECTING (altering through psychological means) the unacceptable behavior.

For parents I simplify this as follows: *a punishment is a reasonable consequence, contrived by the parent out of the life materials at hand, and visited*

*Not punishing children because of such a misapprehension is to anchor them in an immaturity that will serve them poorly when they have to leave the protection of their homes. Surely this is the truly cruel thing to do.

upon the child, because he or she did not accept a limit or meet an expectation within the conditions imposed.

The most convenient and easily effective punishment for training children is the removal of a privilege. Here are some examples.

> "Because you did not take out the garbage by seven p.m., without supervision, you will not be allowed to watch T.V. between seven and seven-thirty tonight."
>
> "Because you did not finish dressing by seven-fifty this morning, without supervision, you will not be allowed to ride your bike after school today."
>
> "Because you did not get to bed on time tonight, without supervision, I will not play Yahtzee with you tomorrow night after supper."

The removal of a privilege is a better punishment than the assigning of an extra duty, mostly because the consequence is easier to administer. Telling the child "because you did not take the garbage out, without supervision, you will have to put the dishes away" involves you in supervising the punishment task. If the child is angry and determined, the punishment could turn out to be harder on you than on him.

People sometimes complain that their child has no privileges to remove. In these days of multi-privileged children this is rarely true. I usually discover their definition of privilege is different from mine. They will say, for example, "oh no, I can't take away any of his playtime. Children have a *right* to playtime."

I certainly agree one ought not to remove a child's *rights* as punishment, so his meals (not desserts) should be sacrosanct, as should his home (no child should be turfed out of the house as punishment), and his bed (no child should be made to sleep on the floor). However, I do not believe a bicycle, unlimited playtime, or T.V. cartoons are among the inalienable rights of childhood.

People are sometimes despairing about punishment because it does not "bother the child." They realize that any child can find something reasonably pleasant do when denied T.V. for half an hour. They notice that some days he doesn't bother to ride his bike after school. Obviously losing a half an hour's T.V. or an afternoon's use of his bicycle is not going to cause the child major distress. "So," they say, "what's the use of a punishment that doesn't hurt?" And because they really believe this, they tend to pile on the punishment in the hope that a large enough dose will hurt. This is a losing game. The parent ends up assigning a hopelessly excessive punishment, which they then have to recant while guess-who stands there grinning snidely.

It is very hard to help young parents understand that, in order to be effective, a punishment does not have to "hurt" the child. Indeed, the impact of punishment is ninety percent psychological.

THE PSYCHOLOGY OF PUNISHMENT   Let me begin with an illustration from my practice. Here is a situation that not infrequently develops in my playroom. A six or seven year old begins to see me regularly, usually because his mother is having trouble getting him to mind. I visit with him in my playroom, where we talk, draw pictures and play games. Gradually, as he becomes secure in my setting, he starts acting with me in the way he acts at home. That is to say he messes about a little.

"It's time to pick up the block game," I say, as the clock nears the hour.

"Nope," he says, if he responds at all.

"Come on," I say. "You have to help."

"Too tired," he says.

"There are only a few pieces, and you have to help. That's the rule. If you play with a game, you have to help put it away."

"Not gonna."

Since I have been around this particular maypole a few times before, I simply say, "well, O.K. If you won't pick it up, I will, but that means you can't play with this game next week when you come," and I start picking up the pieces.

He gives me a look, shrugs his shoulders, looks over at my shelf full of games and says, "who cares? I'll play with sumpin' else."

After I finish picking up the pieces, I write a little note on a scrap of paper, saying the words aloud as I write them. "Johnny can't play with this game next week." I stick it to the front of the game box with a piece of scotch tape. As I am doing so, he watches me closely but looks away when he catches my eye.

When he leaves I open my appointment book to next week and write GAME under his name. That's so I won't forget about the punishment I've administered.

The next week when he arrives I see my note and remove the game in question. I deposit it in the secretary's office before I usher him into the playroom.

Although it's been a week, and he's only seven years old, and there's a whole shelf full of other games, I see his eyes searching the playroom. He's looking for that game. It's been a whole week, but he has remembered. Ask yourself why?

I let him look and don't say anything. I know from experience he will eventually ask me about it. But he doesn't want to, because he has already said he doesn't care. But there is something else gnawing at him too; he doesn't want me to get away with punishing him.

Finally he can stand it no longer. "Where's that. . . ah, block game?" he asks in a elaborately casual manner.

"Don't you remember? You're not allowed to play with that because you wouldn't help pick it up last time."

"I don't care! I don't care about the dumb block game!" he says. But it clear from his pursed mouth and angry eyes that he does care. Why?

Miffed, he looks around for something not quite acceptable to do. One such thing most children his age eventually hit on is my children's sink. He walks over, turns the water on, and with a little calculated carelessness spills some water on my rug.

"Turn the water off, you're splashing," I say. But he doesn't, and some more splashes on my rug.

After many years of practice, I have equipped my playroom to handle this kind of thing. The cabinet below my sink unlocks, and I reach in and turn off the water taps from within. Then I close the door and lock it again. Now when he turns the taps, no water comes out.

"Turn the water on," he says.

"No," I reply. "You splash."

"I won't splash."

"You might." I say. "Today we'll play with something else. Next week when you come again, you can try the sink, and we'll see if you've learned not to splash."

At this point he will either have a tantrum or sulk a while. Either way eventually he will settle down. I get him involved in some other game. Now when it comes time to pick up the pieces and put them away he helps.

But you know what they all do? They leave one last piece not picked up. That's to prove to themselves that they really didn't obey. Omnipotence does not give up without a struggle. Since I have no wish to rub his nose in it, I always pick up that last piece and put it in the box for him.

"You missed this one," I say.

There are lots of toys in my playroom. He could have played with something. The real pain of losing the block game was minimal. But the psychological impact was such that he was bothered enough about the loss to remember a whole week and react when reminded of his deprivation. Something was bothering him. If not the pain of losing the game then what?

What bothers a child in such a situation is not that he loses the game, or the half hour T.V., or the bicycle. It's that you had the nerve to punish. It's the definition of roles that you are spelling out for him that he finds offensive. The punishment is a statement of your authority and this shakes up his omnipotence illusion.

THE SWEET LEMON   A common reaction of children to punishment, which I call the Sweet Lemon, further demonstrates how much psychology determines the true nature of the experience. The child deprived of his bicycle after school because he did not dress without supervision says blithely, "as a matter of fact, I wasn't planning to ride my bike after school." When the time comes to suffer the loss he cheerfully finds something else to do.

Had the parent removed a T.V. show, the reaction would have been the same. With the sweet lemon the child is seeking to deny the parent's power to punish him by removing the lost privilege from his catalogue of pleasures. That he goes to the trouble to do this suggests that something is bothering him.

As mentioned before, what bothers him is that the parent has the nerve to punish. This is a parent prerogative the omnipotent child sees as a diminution of his right to be wholly self-determining. With the sweet lemon he is seeking to deny that the disciplinary exchange has significance.

However, if the parent, understanding that the child is simply trying to deny her power to punish, as blithely replies, "well, if you were planning to ride your bike, you wouldn't be allowed," she defuses the sweet lemon. A couple of those and the child changes his tune. He abandons the sweet lemon and opts for a screaming definitions of a child's inalienable right to his bicycle whenever he wishes to exercise that right.

NOT THAT LEMON   There is an opposite, less common reaction which is also an indicator of the psychological nature of punishment. Let me give you a recent example from my practice. A mother, misunderstanding a detail of my punishment cards system, was allowing her child to choose his own card. She laid the cards out, face down, and let him pick one.

The card he picked said, "no cat in with you at bedtime tonight." She was dismayed with the card that had turned up for he hadn't bothered with the cat for the last two weeks. She was sure the punishment would be meaningless to him.

"Not that! Anything but that," her child wailed. "Take T.V.! Take my bike! Anything but my cat!"

If the company of the cat had not become a punishment the child would probably have gone to bed without it and thought nothing of it. But once losing the cat at bedtime was defined as a punishment the loss became psychologically significant, and he reacted to it. True he might have declared that lemon sweet had his mother chosen it, but choosing it himself somehow altered the equation.

A thing is a punishment if the recipient eventually comes to see it as such. Once the parent understands this, punishment is a much easier business. Let me offer another illustration of the degree to which punishment is primarily psychological in nature.

MAKING LEMONADE   Remember when Aunt Polly punished Tom Sawyer by requiring that he whitewash the fence on Saturday morning instead of go fishing? At first Tom was devastated, but then the natural psychologist in him took over. When his friends passed by on their way to fishing he barely noticed them, he was so engrossed in the pleasures of whitewashing. It took them some time to appreciate that Tom was enjoying himself, that the privilege of whitewashing fences was a thing that seldom came his way, and he was going to make the most of it. With studied reluctance he allowed each of them to purchase a fragment of the job with those pocket treasures boys carry. In time he was reclined on the grass, surrounded by his loot, supervising his eager gang of fence artists. Through the alchemy of applied psychology he had converted Aunt Polly's punishment into a coveted reward. That lemon doesn't taste sour. That lemon tastes sweet, and I'll prove it. And he did, except that, in his heart I am sure Tom knew he had been punished.

Most children are not able to shift their ground so handily as Tom did. They are distressed with being punished even when the actual loss is minimal. Why? Because punishment makes a psychological statement they do not want to hear. Punishment says, *I am the parent and you are the child. I have the right and the responsibility to makes some rules concerning your behavior.* It is the omnipotence disillusioning content of this statement that makes a punishment a punishment.

The central *function* of punishment is communication. It is *action dialogue.* It says to the child more clearly and more penetratingly than words that he is a child with a child's prerogatives in a world where many of the decisions are made by adults. Punishment requires the child to accept his childhood at the same time as he accepts his parents' authority.

Since the pain of punishment is less important than its psychological content, a mild punishment has the same communicative value as a severe one. Thus the mild is to be preferred. Why? In the first place it is kinder. In the second it is less productive of parental guilt. Finally, it is more manageable. If you have to punish frequently, as you must when retraining omnipotent children, with mild punishments it is possible do so. However, if one removes the T.V. for a week at a time, one will soon have removed it until he is thirteen or entering high school, whichever comes first, and that is a game no one can play.

In my experience, the best punishments are the removal of privileges since they are easiest supervised. Next comes the assignment of chores or extra duties. The trouble with these is that you have to supervise their completion, and that can lead to more struggle and more punishment. The third and final method is corporal punishment, a euphemism for spanking.

SPANKING   Spanking has a minimal role to play in child rearing. If it is used sparingly in the pre-school child, it retains its dramatic impact. The four year old who runs out on the street and makes a face at the passing cars needs just such an impressive statement of wrongdoing. However, if parents use spanking too much it loses its here and now effectiveness.

For school-age children spanking is not as effective a reinforcer as a planned privilege removal. However there are situations where it is not wholly inappropriate. In my play, *Don't Shoot, I'm Your Mother*, Lydia tolerates a lot more from Dewey than she ought, but when he spits in her face, she decides enough is enough. Though Dewey gives her the "that didn't hurt" version of the sweet lemon, I believe he will be inclined to deal with her more respectfully in the future.

To summarize briefly, because punishment is largely psychological in nature, mild punishments, preferably deprivations of privilege, applied regularly in a context of clear expectations, time limits, and supervision, are the most effective form of reinforcer. This is particularly true when some remedial parenting is in progress, but most children will probably need some mild punishment at one time or another in the course of normal growing up.

Reward as Reinforcer

Reward, providing some good thing for behavior which meets the parent's expectation, seems on the surface to be the converse of punishment. As action dialogue it makes a different statement. Punishment says, "if you don't do this by this time you will be punished." With reward the statement becomes, "if you do this by this time, you will receive a reward." Because the statement is positive in tone, and the contract a "giving" one, many parents find the idea of reward as a reinforcer more palatable than punishment. However, the psychological impact of reward and punishment are significantly different. Before stating these differences let me put the matter into a life context.

Supposing we were to set up the same training program for getting dressed in the morning which was discussed earlier in this book, but instead of using punishment as a reinforcer, we used reward. The communication to the child would go something like this: "Tommy, I want you to get dressed in the morning. That means all your clothes, including underwear and socks, buttons done and shoes tied. You have until eight a.m. I won't remind you, but I will put the clock in your room so you will know when the time is up."

To this point the instructions are identical whether performance is to be rewarded or non-performance punished. However, if reward is to be the mode of reinforcement, Mother now says, "Tommy, if when I come up at eight, you have finished dressing, I will reward you. I will add five cents to your allowance this week" (or some other pleasing thing). "If, however, you are not dressed, I will supervise your dressing, but then there will be no reward."

Since Tommy has been having his troubles getting dressed in the morning, the chances are his limitations in patience and persistence will still let him down when the sock sticks or the buttons get into the wrong holes. So he won't make it those first few mornings, and it will be necessary withhold the reward.

What has happened? Tommy did not dress and he was not rewarded. How has the situation changed? Not at all. He was not dressing before, but then reward was not in the picture. He is not dressing now, so of course, reward is still not in the picture. He does not dress, and there is no apparent change in his reality situation as there would have been had punishment been the chosen reinforcer.

So, what does not receiving a reward say to Tommy? Since nothing different has happened nothing has been communicated; no action dialogue has taken place. The only message Tommy received was the verbal one with which Mother began the program. In essence this came down to, "you may dress on time if you wish, and I would prefer that you do so, and, if you do, you will receive a benefit, but if you do not, I will supervise as before and nothing more will happen."

Whoop de doo!

The fact is non-reward speaks in a very soft voice, such a soft voice that it may not be heard by the immature child.

Consider the same program using punishment as a reinforcer. This time Mother will conclude her instruction as follows, "if you aren't dressed when I come up at eight o'clock, I will supervise you, but since I have better things to do with my time, I will punish you. Every morning that I have to supervise, you will lose your T.V. privileges between seven-thirty and eight p.m. that evening. And that is the way it will be until you have learned to dress yourself on time and without my supervising you."

Now if Tommy fails to perform he receives his punishment and his situation changes. He loses half an hour T.V. that he usually watches. While

he may deny that this concerns him, there is no question that his circumstances have changed as a consequence of his failure to perform without
supervision. Unlike reward, punishment speaks in a voice that a child cannot fail to hear.

As I have said on several occasions throughout this book, punishment
makes a psychological statement that is essential to promoting the child's
adaptive growth. Punishment defines the child as a child and the adult as
an adult. *It challenges the child's omnipotence illusion.* It is this challenge that
the child cannot ignore. It is this challenge of course, that generates adaptive growth.

Reward issues no such challenge. Reward does not say "you must"; it
says, "if you will do you will benefit." It implies that the child does not
have to do as the parent wishes unless he chooses to. So it is that *reward
panders to the omnipotence illusion.* This is the major difference in
psychological import between punishment and reward that makes the latter so much less effective in promoting adaptive growth.

Training programs reinforced by reward tend to be unsuccessful. The
child continues to do as he always has done and quickly reconciles himself
to the loss of the promised reward. And then where can the parent go except to a fresh program, this time utilizing punishment as a reinforcer?

For the sake of further exposition let's consider the unusual case in
which reward works. Perhaps, despite its weak voice, reward does succeed
in inducing some little money grubber to get dressed on time. Each morning he dresses; each evening he is rewarded. After three weeks he is getting
an extra five cents per day added to his allowance.

What now? He is dressing. Is the parent to go on rewarding the child
forever? Parents begin to ask themselves, should I be paying this child to
do what every other child on the street does without getting paid? Eventually the parent will decide to terminate rewarding. Will the child now
regress to not dressing again? If he does, what then? Unlike punishment,
reward as a reinforcer tends to perpetuate itself. Furthermore it teaches
children to greet each fresh parental expectation with "what will you give
me if I do it?"

When punishment is used as a reinforcer, as the child improves, the reinforcer disappears from the child-rearing equation. Soon the child is performing as other children do, that is meeting the expectations normal for
his age without needing to be punished to get him to perform.

Psychologically speaking then, reward is not the converse of punishment. It is something very different. It is best regarded as a concrete form
of approval. Here, in tabular form, is a summary of the differences between
reward and punishment as reinforcer of discipline.

Punishment Compared to Reward in Disciplining Children

Punishment	*Reward*
Communicates loudly	Communicates softly
Disillusions omnipotence	Panders to omnipotence
Disappears with improvement	Remains with improvement

Obviously, punishment is a much more effective method of reinforcing parent expectations and generating adaptive growth in the child.

Other Reinforcers

Many parents would like to avoid the whole disciplinary exchange. As adults dealing with one another they depend upon reason to persuade others to modify their behavior. It is civilized and a lot more pleasant than having to get into all this expecting and reinforcing. So they talk to their children rather than discipline them.

Not infrequently I hear of parents getting into exchanges with toddlers like this. "If you spill that on my rug," Mother explains to her two year old who has somehow gotten hold of a bottle of ink, "it will cause a stain. Stains are hard to get out. Mother will have to work very hard, on her hands and knees, to try to get it out. And if that doesn't work Daddy will have to call the rug cleaners and pay them lots of money, and Daddy has to work hard for the money. Now you don't want Daddy and Mommy to have to work hard do you?"

While the child may be solemnly attentive while Mother goes through this account, his response will often reveal how little of Mother's monologue actually penetrates his awareness. "How did the stains get into the bottle? I'll let them out. Whoopee! Stains all out."

The more "civilized" and educated the parents are, the more liable they are to fall into this error. Because they depend so much on words to choose and govern their behavior, and it is so long since they were a child, they forget how toddlers think. So they explain and expect their explanation to persuade the child.

Talking to two year olds is analogous to talking to the dog. If your dog wet on the rug you wouldn't get down on your hands and knees and explain to him, "you know if you didn't wet on the rug, the room would smell a lot nicer. And I'd like you better. Who knows, you might even like yourself better."

No. What you would do is some variant of the following. Push his nose down to the wet, whap him on the head with a rolled up newspaper, and lead him to his box in the corner. You use some form of action dialogue because words, apart from a few learned commands, have no meaning to dogs. A certain amount of this action dialogue and it will occur to the dog, "if I go directly to the box I can avoid that whap on the head." And he does.

Of course children are not dogs. The toddler has some language. Even so, verbal communication is just entering the the toddler's life. While it is to be hoped that, in time, reason will become the major determinant of the child's behavior choices, for toddlers explanations cut little ice.*

In my example, Mother would have been better to explain less, emit a little emotion, and move fast to intervene. "Hand me that ink bottle this instant or you will find yourself in your bed." If the child gets the message in time, chances are it will be the tone in Mother's voice that impresses him, not the words.

There are two methods of reinforcer which, being verbal in character, become more useful as the child grows older. These are approval and disapproval. Approval—that is communicating pleasure with respect to the child's behavior—is a kind of reward and so has the same shortcomings in remedial parenting as already discussed vis-à-vis reward. Communicating disapproval is a weak kind of punishment that gains strength as the child matures to more awareness and concern for the feelings of others.

For toddlers, approval and/or disapproval are not very effective reinforcers. For a child to want to gain his parents approval, that is please her, he must be able to perceive that his parent is sometimes pleased and other

---

*Communication with toddlers is best accomplished through deeds, not words, but even with older children communication can be an erratic business. Sometimes they ask questions and do not wait for answers, so it always pays to stall a little; you may get off the hook. Here is an instance where one mother was lucky in this way.

Saved by the Bell

One sunny Monday, as it must to all Ma's,
The question of questions came lunging at me.
"Johnny says there's no Santa Claus,
But I said I'd ask you and see."

He stood there, all freckles and trust,
Blinking his eyes and twisting his toe.
While I conjured to answer, as mothers must,
he split: "Ah, What does Johnny know?"

T.P.M., 1979

times displeased. This involves a degree of interpersonal awareness egocentric three year olds have not yet attained. He cannot begin to behave in order to please when he cannot yet comprehend, and care, that others feel pleasure too.

So a degree of adaptive maturity with respect to egocentricity must have been established before approval-disapproval can act as an effective reinforcer. In most cases, the omnipotent child has not yet matured to the point that approval-disapproval can be effective.

The second essential condition for approval-disapproval to modify behavior comes into play after that level of awareness has been reached. Once the child is able to perceive his parent's pleasure or displeasure, *he must come to see that these parental reactions are related in some consistent way to his behavior.* Capricious disapproval, heard only when Mother "has had it up to here," cannot train because the child does not see it as related to his behavior. Similarly, expressions of approval uttered because the mother is feeling badly about her child's self-esteem and wants to praise him only weaken praise as a reinforcer. When approval or disapproval are uttered capriciously, they either confuse the child or train him to discount his parent's utterances.

There is a third condition essential to the effective use of *disapproval* as a reinforcer of discipline. *There must be a reasonable reservoir of good will between parent and child.*

In the case history which began this book Dewey's mother had reached the point that she was crosswise with Dewey a good deal of the time. Good will between them had been steadily eroded, and disapproval was almost constant. For Dewey, being in the psychological soup had become a way of life. He and his mother had become mired in profitless displeasure with one another.

Why would a child modify his behavior to gain his mother's approval when he can barely remember what approval felt like? How can his mother offer approval when most of the time he is so disobedient and provocative that she can barely stand being with him?

While it's possible that approval-disapproval will some day replace punishment as Mother's mode of dealing with Dewey, first some good will has to be restored to their relationship. This can only happen one way. Dewey has to become more lovable and then his mother can come to feel more loving towards him. Punishment can get him there.

Let us recall our program for getting dressed in the morning. We set up the expectation and the time limit. We had supervised if necessary and, if we had to, given Dewey a punishment. Dewey was soon dressing more mornings than not and getting fewer punishments.

Now, since Dewey has been getting ready on time most mornings, he and Mother don't start each day cross at each other. Some mornings are actually pleasant. They have time to visit over breakfast, and they aren't constantly annoyed with each other. *A little good will has re-entered their relationship.*

Supposing one of those mornings Dewey does something to annoy his mother, and Mother shows her annoyance. Perhaps she becomes a little disapproving or scolds. It's possible Dewey, who has been enjoying the good will too, will raise his hands and exclaim, "O.K.! O.K.! I'll do it. Don't get mad."

Because amity has been restored between them, Dewey is now impressed by her disapproval and modifies his behavior to make things right between them. Approval-disapproval is on the way to becoming a useful form of disciplinary reinforcement. In time Mother will have less and less need to resort to punishment as reinforcer.

In summary then, approval-disapproval is an effective mode of disciplinary reinforcement when the child is mature enough to perceive his parent's state of feeling, and when a reasonable reservoir of good will exists between the parent and child. However, for the very young child, or the child in difficulties with his adaptive growth, approval-disapproval tends to be ineffective.

A Pseudo-reinforcer

Before leaving the subject of disciplinary reinforcers, there is a currently popular strategy which ought to be discussed briefly. It is called "natural consequences." Many parents find it a most attractive notion.

It goes something like this. If the child fails to perform some expectation, or ignores some disciplinary limit, the parent does not punish him. The parent allows the "natural consequence" of the child's behavior to develop, and that punishes the child. If the child dawdles over dressing, the parent ignores the dawdling and allows the child to be late, for being late to school is the natural consequence of dawdling over dressing.

While other advantages are sometimes cited, I believe the appeal of natural consequences is that it allows the parent to avoid the painful task of punishing the child. The parent utilizing natural consequences does not have to feel guilty for denying the child some pleasure or visiting some unpleasure upon him. This gets the parent off the disciplinary hook. In the mother's defense it says, "don't blame me. It wasn't I who punished you; it was the world." For the omnipotent child it confirms his omnipotence. "Of course. They aren't the boss of me. They have no right to punish me."

Natural consequences is a pseudo-reinforcer. It does not have the psychological effect of a true reinforcer. It is for the benefit of the parent, not the child. Furthermore it is unrealistic. Consider the following questions and you will readily see what I mean. If the child is too young to perceive the consequence of his action, is it fair to allow him to proceed and suffer that consequence? If the mother allows the child to dawdle and as a consequence be late for school, is she not shifting the responsibility for punishing the child onto the shoulders of the teacher? What if the teacher believes in natural consequences and ignores the child's lateness, saying, "the natural consequence of being late every morning is missing half of math class, the natural consequence of which is eventually to fail math?" Is not this natural consequence so remote from getting dressed in the morning that it has no hope of every modifying that behavior? Are there not many behaviors for which no natural consequence exists? Things like beating up younger brother, being rude to Mother, or stealing cookies? Are there not many natural consequences that are wholly unacceptable and a dereliction of the parent's duty to protect the child, such as getting cavities because one allows the child not to brush his teeth?

The most damaging effect of the natural consequence notion, however, is that it seduces parents into abdicating their duty to disillusion the child's omnipotence and lead him into a reasonable acceptance and comfort in the true limitations of his personal power. Children need to make their peace with authority, to give up their willful desire to make all decisions that even remotely bear upon them, to accept limits, but at the same time not to become so cowed that they cannot stand up for their rights as individuals. They need to find their way to a sense of autonomy, that is a sense of their right and capacity to become self-determining individuals within the structures of society and humanity.

Children achieve such autonomy by working through their relation to authority. This is best accomplished in the protection of the home, in that safe battling between the child and his parents. However, if the parents decline to engage in that battle, if they abdicate their authority and hide behind natural consequences, this working through cannot take place. When it does not the child is not led to surrender his omnipotence illusion and he remains adaptively immature. Now is he in danger of becoming an omnipotent child who must fly in the face of community expectations, protest for the sake of protesting, and reject all rules as personal affronts.

Children are not well-served when parents abdicate their responsibility to discipline. Parenting systems which talk of the parent-child interaction as a "relationship of equals" confuse parents and foster such abdication. Such systems are not part of the solution; they are part of the problem.

Up to now, in our discussion of the principles of discipline we have learned how important it is to define expectations and limits clearly. Further, we have come to understand how the time limit leads the child toward self-supervision. We have seen how supervising the expectation and applying a consequence because supervision was necessary are essential if adaptive growth is to result. It is time now to deal with the fifth and final principle of discipline, the need to persist.

PERSISTENCE TO TRAIN

It is rarely the case that children will modify their behavior promptly and permanently simply because the parent tells them to do so or punishes them once or twice for non-compliance. Even so, parents sometimes think this should happen, and when it doesn't they wonder if the punishment was perhaps not impressive enough. They seek that single dramatic action that will so impress the child that "he will never do that again." They wash his mouth out with soap so that he will never swear. They make him smoke a cigar because they caught him smoking. Mother bites the child, to teach him not to bite others. To be sure, these single dramatic actions sometimes work, but they often don't, and it gets a little primitive for Mother to go on biting her child every day.

Spanking is a dramatic input, which if it is used only on rare occasions can be useful with the pre-school child. If he dumps your aspidastra in the middle of your ivory rug, a whack on the bottom may be the right medicine. If his mother is not in the habit of whacking, this dramatic input may well abolish such decorative impulses.

However, the best training results from persistent application of soundly designed disciplinary inputs. It takes time to change behavior and time for that behavior change to generate growth and change attitudes. The best way to illustrate the role of persistence in discipline is to describe the usual course of events when one undertakes a program of retraining a child who is lagging in some area of adaptive growth.

Supposing Mother has decided to make sure Trevor gets to bed on time, not simply because this is an area of tension between them but also because she wants to promote his adaptive growth. Let's have her apply the principles of discipline.

The first thing she does is *set a clear expectation*. "Trevor," she says, "every night I have to tell you two or three times to get ready for bed. You always say 'inna minute' and I have to get cross and chase you into the bathroom to brush your teeth. I am tired of doing this, so from now on we are going to have a getting-to-bed-on-time program."

"Ya mean you're not gonna nag me anymore? Hooray!"

"That's right. From now on I expect you to get into your pajamas, brush your teeth, wash your face and be ready for me to tuck you in without me reminding or nagging." At this juncture she shows him the timer.

Moving into step two, she now *sets the time limit*. "See this Trevor. This is your timer. At eight p.m. I am setting it for fifteen minutes and that is how long you have to do all the things I expect."

"But that means my bedtime will be eight-fifteen. There isn't a kid on the block has to go to bed at eight-fifteen."

"Eight-thirty," Mother says. "I'm allowing fifteen minutes for me to supervise if I have to. And don't give me that 'too early' garbage. I know you think nine o'clock is early enough, but I don't agree. So, eight-fifteen I expect you to be ready."

"Whattya mean supervise? I know how to put on my pajamas."

Now it's on to step three, *supervision if necessary*. If at eight-fifteen she finds Trevor still watching T.V. or not in his pajamas, or just on his way to the bathroom, she leads him the rest of the way through the routine, standing by while he puts on his pajamas, taking him to the bathroom to brush his teeth.

As she does so she tries her best to keep her cool, not yell or scold, just supervise. And because she has a plan she manages to contain herself. She tucks him in. It may be eight-thirty by now, perhaps even later, but he's in.

Now she moves to step four. *She applies a reinforcer.* "Because I had to supervise you tonight, Trevor, tomorrow night you lose your T.V. privileges from seven-thirty to eight p.m."

"You mean I have to go to bed early?"

"Oh no, bedtime doesn't change. You can do what you like with the half hour, except that you can't watch T.V. That's your punishment."

"Don't you know punishment is mean?"

"Not this one."

"It's not fair. It's your fault I was late. You didn't remind me."

"It's not my job to remind you. It's your job to keep an eye on your timer."

"I don't care about your dumb punishment. As a matter of fact, I wasn't planning to watch T.V. tomorrow night."

"Well, if you were, you wouldn't be allowed to."

Now Mother comes to the final stage. *She persists.* While the occasional child responds to Mother's clear enunciation of expectations and intentions with prompt compliance, it is usually the case that the problem does not immediately disappear.

Typically, for the next three nights Trevor doesn't make it, is supervised, and the reinforcer is applied. The first two days he is blithe about his punishment, but the third he changes his tune. "You're mean. That's my favorite show. Kids got a right to T.V. I'm calling the child abuse line."

The fourth and fifth days he makes it and does not need to be punished. Now, because there have been no consequences for two days, he forgets all about the program, and on day six when Mother comes back after setting his timer, she finds him glued to the box.

Unfortunately, at this point, many parents give up. "The program didn't work," they say, and they decide to try something else. What they should do, of course, is persist, continuing in exactly the same pattern of supervision and punishment. After two more days of punishment, he gets moving again. This time the improvement lasts for four days before he slips back once more.

If one were to graph coping beside punishments administered, one would find the former rising as the latter falls. Even so, it takes a good four weeks for a turnaround to be clearly established. This is why persistence is such an important aspect of discipline.

Parents must understand that they are engaged in teaching the child and that learning depends upon repetition. They must not lose sight of the fact that the goal of the program is not simply behavior change—getting the child to bed on time—but is really to promote the child's adaptive growth. We are trying to stretch the child's tolerance for tedium, require him to become less egocentric, persuade him to accommodate to others, and lead him away from omnipotence. We are more interested in these things than in the amount of sleep he gets.

Once the parent grasps this, it will become clear that learning proceeds not only on those days when he makes it to bed without having to be punished but also on those days when he requires punishment. The learning is different when he makes it from when he doesn't, but it's all part of the adaptive growth we are seeking. When he makes it, he exercises a little patience and persistence and stretches that adaptive competency. Further, he copes, which does something for his self-esteem. When he doesn't make it, is supervised and the reinforcer is applied, his mother has intruded upon his egocentricity, which not only teaches him to accommodate but also challenges his omnipotence illusion.

So when Trevor makes it, Mother wins something, and when he doesn't make it, Mother wins something else. And either way, in the long run, Trevor wins.

One usually finds that in four weeks the child is getting to bed on time without supervision six nights out of seven. Still, one cannot give up the program, for if one does, in another four weeks you'll be back to square one. Indeed, you cannot even be flexible yet. If you alter the bedtime one night, "because there is a special T.V. show he has just got to see," you can be sure the next night he will resist bedtime and wail, "but you let me stay up last night."

Children in difficulty with adaptive growth regard parent flexibility as weakness, not consideration, and they just *have* to try it on the next night. So parents must hold firm, greeting each deviation from the pattern as cause for supervision and reinforcement, remembering that it takes two or even three months for external or parental expectations to become internal or self-expectations.

This is the psychological process one is setting in motion, teaching the child to make his parents' expectations his own, leading him to the point that an inner voice will be telling him what to do rather than still relying on the outer voice of his parents. Persistence provides the time for this process of internalization to take place. Eventually the habit takes and a sense of "ought to" begins to form in the child's mind. He is beginning to accept that it is his obligation to get into bed on time. Soon he is boasting of it. "Hey, Mom. Notice how I'm always ready when is time to tuck me in. How about that, eh?" What you're also hearing in that comment is a building block of self-esteem settling firmly into place.

When one programs discipline, the psychological changes follow in this order. *Behavior* changes first. Then one sees evidence of *adaptive growth*. One sees signs of a little more self-control, a little more consideration, a modicum of humility, a growing tendency to go off grumbling rather than to challenge or defy. Finally, *attitudes* change. He no longer feels so put-down by expectations and is less prideful now that he no longer sees them as an infringement on his right to be wholly self-determining.

Persistence is as crucial a principle of discipline as the others. Unless disciplinary programs are persisted in firmly and without significant variation for at least a month, and be clearly in the wings for use when necessary for the next two months, the training will not accomplish all that it can. There is one comfort in all this; the longer you persist, the easier it gets.

We have now examined the five principles of discipline in detail. Looking back at the problem from this new perspective it all seems quite straightforward, doesn't it? Almost easy. Why then have modern parents had so much trouble with it?

Since I believe there is much to gain by finding the answer to that complex question, I have sought it over many years. My purpose in communicating what I have learned is to help parents understand the history of their problem and perceive the social matrix which plays such a role in influencing their child-rearing decisions.

There are those who prefer recipes to understanding. I have heard from several of them. I have a different view. I believe the more parents understand themselves and their societal role as child rearers, the easier it will be for them to deal with the complexities of the task. However, those of a different persuasion are certainly welcome to skip the next chapter.

7

How Mother Got That Way

"The rules of parenthood are simple enough. Be an adult and enjoy being an adult. Do not permit what you do not soberly approve. Set limits and see that they are kept."

DONALD BARR, *WHO PUSHED HUMPTY DUMPTY?*

"Set limits and see that they are kept." Now there's a brave recipe from an educator who knows what he is talking about. Except that recipes aren't enough. Aunt Polly knew she should have punished Tom, but she let him off. Why? Because she just couldn't summon up the inner strength it would take to go through another hassle, another push-pull encounter.

Successful limit setting involves more than understanding the need for discipline. The attitudes and feelings of the parents play a crucial role in determining how those thorny parent-child encounters will go. Loving children is easy; it's making them mind that frazzles the soul.

Modern Motherhood: A Matter of Guilt

For reasons that we will seek to understand, many modern mothers hold an attitude toward childhood and parenting which undermines them when they have to set limits and expect things of children. Let me illustrate this with a little experiment. Get yourself a little pad of paper and, for one day only, count the number of times you preface each expectation of your child with the phrase, "I'm sorry, but. . . . " "I'm sorry but it's time for supper. I'm sorry, but you can't play with the stereo knobs. I'm sorry, but it's time to pick up your toys."

Why are you saying all these "I'm sorrys"? It isn't your fault that it's supper time. You didn't design stereos or fail to invent toys that pick themselves up. So what are you apologizing for?

Don't know? I'll tell you. You are apologizing for inconveniencing your child, for interrupting his steady stream of gratification. Modern mothers seem to feel the child is entitled to constant pleasure, and if he doesn't receive it, they are somehow failing him.

So add up your score of "I'm sorrys" and ask yourself: What are you apologizing for?

If your score is more than six, it means you have bought the modern fairy tale about childhood. You have been convinced that childhood can and ought to be a golden time, a time of unremitting joy, wholly free of anxiety or disappointment, a never-never land without frustration or anger. And if sometimes it isn't so for your child, then *you* have provided him with less than the best, and you *owe* him an apology.

This is what I call the "fragile child and tread lightly" ethic of child rearing. It is an extremely common attitude among modern mothers. Not only should the child's life be constantly gratifying, and he be never bored, frustrated or afraid, but also he should somehow learn to cope with such feelings even though he has never been suffered to experience them. It is a ludicrous proposition, to demand the strength and deny the exercise that generates such strength.

Grandmother expected nothing like this of herself. If her child came to her for entertainment because he was 'bored', she felt no obligation to drop everything and set up some cut and paste project. No, she waved him away with an, "I'm busy with supper. Find something to do." And he did, with a spool, matchstick and rubber band. Grandmother had no sense of guilt about it at all. And in Grandmother's day the omnipotent child was a rare bird.

The fact is the balance between the nurturant and disciplinary aspects of parenting has shifted markedly in the years since the end of World War II. Parents have come to feel that their main job is to love the child, make sure that he is constantly happy, that he never experiences frustration, anxiety or disappointment. They have come to see the child as a psychologically fragile creature and childhood as a time fraught with developmental dangers. When discipline seems to distress the child, they back off fearful of traumatizing his psyche, and they rationalize the backing off. "Perhaps he isn't ready to tie his shoes," they say as they do it for him. "At least he isn't bottling it all up inside," they say as he enters upon yet another temper tantrum. And, of course, they preface each intrusion upon his self-centered day with an "I'm sorry dear."

What do all these "I'm sorrys" say to the developing child? They confirm his omnipotent and egocentric view of life, to wit, that Mother *is* responsible for life's little unpleasures, that if she really tried harder she could have done better, and so she *ought* to feel sorry. Instead of disillusioning the child's omnipotence, Mother's apologetic approach panders to the illusion. Instead of penetrating his egocentricity, the "I'm sorry" approach accommodates to the child.

Furthermore, such pandering sets the stage for Act II of the guilty-mother-and-demanding-child drama. The conflict tends to escalate along these lines.

Mother can only say a certain number of "I'm sorrys" to no avail before her frustration surfaces. The tenth time Johnny doesn't come for supper when called, Mother, who has had a long day, whose casserole has just burned, and guess who's late for supper again, suddenly erupts.

"Do I have to call you twenty times for supper? Are you deaf? Put those damn toys away this minute, and get out here." Johnny throws a block and swears. Mother yells again. Johnny starts a tantrum. Mother shakes him. He screams. Mother puts him in his room and retreats to the kitchen, by now in tears herself.

After five minutes of psychological flagellation, Mother goes to his room where she finds him slumped on the foot of his bed, eyes red and cheeks stained with tears.

"I'm sorry, Johnny, but you never come for supper when I call you."

"You don't love me anymore," Johnny says, not meeting her eyes.

Now there's a phrase with magical properties. "You don't love me anymore." Not that Johnny knows what the word "love" means—he's too egocentric to comprehend that definition—but he has learned how rapidly the phrase tames Mother.

"It's not that I don't love you," Mother says, kneeling by his bed so that she can look into his face. "It's just that. . . well, I get cross sometimes."

"Nope" Johnny shakes his head, "you don't love me anymore."

"Of course I love you," Mother says. There is a pleading quality to her tone as she tries to convince him. "Didn't I take you to the swimming pool yesterday? Didn't I cook your favorite dinner last night?"

What started out as a discipline problem, getting him to come to supper when called, she now sees as a problem in nurturance, to wit, dealing with Johnny's feeling of being unloved. Because, of course, she has bought his version of their recent encounter. After all, she did say some pretty nasty things to him. Now she collapses. "I'm sorry I yelled, Johnny. Please forgive Mother, won't you?"

She is now firmly in the throes of *maternal guilt.*

Someday, some chemist is going to collect blood samples from seven thousand practicing mothers. He will be seeking to find and isolate the substance that activates the motherhood impulse. He will subject those samples to all modern biochemical analytic techniques, and he *will* find the substance. But I can save him the trouble, for this motherhood generating substance is already known. It has a name. It is called GUILT. Modern motherhood and guilt go together as inevitably as salt and pepper.

Many children come to recognize the clues that reveal that maternal guilt is building; that shaky timbre in Mother's voice, the softening eyes, the breath that catches. Of course they have no more understanding of guilt than they have of love; they just know when she starts sounding and looking like that, it will be only a matter of minutes before she succumbs. Some stumble upon the magic phrases: "you don't love me anymore," "I guess I just can't help being bad," "don't worry about me just because I've got no friends," and use them when they will serve their interests.

Sometimes when mothers get particularly upset, they threaten to leave. "Just don't expect to find me here when you come home from school." Sobered by the threat, Johnny calms down, and when Mother's anger has stilled she is filled with dismay. "No wonder he is difficult and demanding," she tells herself. "What can you expect when he has such a hateful and rejecting mother?"

Mother now tries to make it up to him. She begs his forgiveness and promises to do better, if he will just try too. She tells herself, "what does it matter if he stays up later than he should now and then? What's a little lost sleep compared to having a mother who hates you?"

She gives in. She lets him stay up late or have his way. The more she does, the more he demands, and eventually things wear thin again. Another maternal explosion takes place, and the cycle begins all over again.

Many mothers who come to me for help with omnipotent children have become locked in a cycle of hostile rejection, followed by maternal guilt and earnest attempts at reconciliation involving concessions to the child. In the course of this cycle the child himself gyrates from arrogant willfullness to tearful dependency. It can lead to a situation in which the child tyrannizes the mother.

I see many a mother tyrannized by her child. A method children sometimes happen upon to achieve this end is threatening to harm themselves. I have had a wide variety of such threats reported to me over the years. Here are a few typical ones.

"I'll get a stick and poke my eye out."
"I'll run out on the street and let a truck hit me."
"I'm going outside and let the snow bury me."

Sometimes the threats are accompanied by actions, such as the child grabbing a butcher knife and threatening to stick it in himself if Mother doesn't do as he wishes.

The ultimate such maneuver is the suicide threat. Successful suicide is extremely rare in pre-adolescents. Furthermore, in my experience, the egocentric omnipotent child is the last person who would really do himself injury, unless it be by some impulsive miscalculation. His suicide threats are gestures intended to generate guilt in an offending parent.

Let me illustrate with a true anecdote from my practice. A new patient arrived at our first interview bearing a suicide note her nine-year-old son had left on his bedside table. She had found it when she went up to check on him after a stormy session in which he had been denied television for cause.

This child had been tyrannizing his mother for a long time, and this particular episode had been precipitated by one of Mother's rare excursions into firmness. The note read:

"Dear Mother and mean Dad:
Since nobody in this whole family loves me anymore, I have decided to kill myself. I am doing it now. I am smothering myself to death with my pillow. My life is passing before my eyes. I can feel myself going. Goodbye.

The boy that used to be your son,
Dewey Charles Ransome"

The picture of a child, a pillow clutched firmly to his face and his life ebbing away, except perhaps for an arm projecting out from under the pillow writing the note, was more than I could bear and, I confess, I laughed.

"But it's a cry for help," his mother protested.

"I suppose you might look at it that way," I replied. "But it has a couple of other communicative values I find more persuasive." Once I had managed to convince Mother I wasn't wholly heartless, I reassured her that the risk of her child doing himself serious harm was really quite slight.

Threats to harm himself are one of the most effective mother-taming devices in the omnipotent child's armamentarium; but sometimes they backfire. There was one child, Terry by name, who from time to time threatened to stick his jack knife into his chest if his mother persisted in refusing to meet his demands. Ordinarily Mother was a patsy for this kind of thing, but on this particular day, I guess she had had enough, because she remained unmoved by the threat.

Terry, most unhappy I am sure at this unaccustomed exhibition of strength from his mother, retreated to his room, and things were unusually quiet for a while.

In his room Terry took a small cardboard box, a Jello package I believe, taped one of those small plastic packages of ketchup to it, and inserted the entire construction under his T-shirt in the region of his heart.

Then he took his jack knife and, presumably quite carefully, inserted it through the T-shirt, through the ketchup package, and into the cardboard box, which of course, protected his skin. The knife appeared to penetrate a good half inch into his chest, and a stain of ketchup oozed up around the knife blade and spread into the surrounding cloth in a most convincing manner.

His preparations complete, Terry staggered into the kitchen, holding the knife handle in his right hand. This hand was pulled a bit to the side so that the blood was visible. He groaned and declared weakly, "I did it, I stabbed myself. I'm bleeding from the heart."

His mother shrugged and turned. Then, for the first time in her life, she came close to fainting. She clutched the sink for support. "Migawd Terry, what have you done?"

Terry must have been surprised at the intensity of her response, because he backed off. "I'm O.K. I think the bleeding's stopped. Yes, it's stopped bleeding. I'm gonna be alright."

"Don't jiggle the knife like that," Mother said, running to him. You'll make it bleed more. No! No! Don't take it out. It might be plugging the hole or something."

Terry started moving away from her. "It's just a scratch, Mom. It's nothing much. I'll just go and clean myself up."

"Terry! You sit down this minute." By now Mother had him in her grasp and was trying to examine his wound without disturbing the knife.

Terry tried to squirm away, but Mother pressed on. She then discovered the box. In a second she had the picture. If she had, at that moment, reinserted the knife the full length of the blade, I doubt there is a jury in the world would have convicted her. But she didn't. She may have uttered an unmaternal phrase or two before she called her doctor, who called me. A day later she was giving me a typical history of an omnipotent child and a guilt-laden mother whose discipline had become too erratic to generate adaptive growth.*

*On a recent episode of a T.V. sit-com an incident very similar to this appeared. However, since the image of the mother in that series is of a no-nonsense liberated female, she walked right past the child with an-over-the-shoulder "Nice try, Charlie!" As a playwright I question the validity of this bit. If the mother was really this tough and effective, how was it she had produced a child who would try such a trick?

Omnipotent children appeared in large numbers in our society when young mothers began to perceive their children as vulnerable, fragile creatures who could easily be traumatized by frustration during their infancy years. This led mothers to seek to shelter the child from any emotional distress. But childhood has inevitable stresses, so the task was an impossible one and of course Mother failed at it. Seeing the failure as hers, Mother felt guilty and tried even harder to achieve a golden childhood for her Dewey. The child, taking these efforts as no more than his due, learned to exploit, evade and manipulate, but he did not learn to cope.

What had so drastically altered Mother's view of children and childhood? Let's look at that history.

Recent Times

Listen to Jane, a character in my play *Don't Shoot, I'm Your Mother,* tell us about the children she tried to rear during those confusing years immediately following World War II.

Act 1, Scene 2
Scene: A North American kitchen 9:30 a.m. on a school day. Time the early 1970's.

Jane, a forty-eight-year-old mother of two who has managed to salvage an acid humor from the trauma of child rearing in the fifties, is telling Lydia, who at thirty is currently wrestling with an omnipotent ten year old named Dewey, about those earlier parenting times.

JANE

When it comes to lousy mothering, Lydia, you are looking at the champ, the Olympic Gold Medal, Hall of Fame, lousy mother of the decade . . . and I've got the kids to prove it.

Larry's our Yale man. There hasn't been a student riot or protest march that Larry wasn't right in there waving the Viet Cong flag or somebody's brassiere. Larry was a juvenile delinquent masquerading as a revolutionary, and he changed his causes more often than he changed his socks. When it came to drugs, Larry was a pharmacological garbage disposal. His inner environment was more polluted than the Hudson River. His motto was 'Take one and we'll see what it does.' The only reason the Dean didn't throw him out of college was because he was afraid of the T.V. coverage.

LYDIA

Oh Jane, I'm so sorry.

Don't be. George and I regard Larry as our more successful child.

Susan, my innocent girl child, is now three months into her fourth trial marriage. She wants to be "sure" before she makes a commitment. She has abortions like other people have their teeth filled. Her motto is 'Make love not war,' and no one has made war at the rate she makes love since Alexander The Great conquered the known world. And last Christmas she didn't even send me a card.

LYDIA

(Reaching over and taking Jane's hand.) I had no idea. You never told me.

JANE

George and I don't like to boast about our children.

There has probably never been a time when rearing children has been a more uncertain enterprise than it was in the 1950's. Jane's children, Larry and Susan, are the walking wounded of the era, the first generation of omnipotent children to surface in modern American society. When they did, they did with a bang and more than the occasional whimper.

In the middle and late sixties, the student "activists" appeared on the social scene, disrupting the universities, occupying the dean's office, smoking his cigars, destroying his files, challenging the authorities to remove them, and shouting "pig" and "police brutality" as they did so. They latched onto or, if necessary, fabricated causes to give a facade of legitimacy to doing that which they were psychologically impelled to do, that is impose their retained omnipotent illusion upon community authority.

All the cardinal characteristics of the omnipotent child were rampant in these youths. They were *without restraint*. They did not argue, they abused. They sought instant gratification in pot and promiscuity. They demanded each appetite be promptly satisfied. They were grossly *egocentric*. Their notion of free speech was that they should be free to express their views, but opposing points of view were to be drowned out with shouted obscenities. Their version of justice was wholly concerned with making sure they got their "fair" share, and they were quite unable to perceive how this might sometimes infringe upon the rights of others. Their *omnipotence* would allow no authority, however rational, to impose limits upon or expect things of them. And observing these youth for any length of time one could not fail to suspect that beneath their vociferous braggadocio there lurked a deep and abiding *conviction of childish incompetence.**

Because these student activists seemed very much like omnipotent children grown large, I made it my business to learn all I could about them. I missed no opportunity to see them in action, and I kept *au courant* with their exploits as these were reported in the media.

As my data accumulated, I became increasingly convinced that these youths were suffering from the Omnipotent Child Syndrome. It became clear that the issues they espoused were much less central to their behavior than was their need to protest, to defy, to articulate their life thesis, to wit: "You're not the boss of me. I don't have to do what you say."

These were omnipotent children. I wondered what had produced them. I wondered if the ineffective parental discipline which I was seeing associated with the Omnipotent Child Syndrome could have been responsible for the emergence of these student activist youths. I considered ways to find out.

I decided that perhaps the popular child-rearing literature their mothers had been reading when these children were pre-schoolers might give me a clue concerning their upbringing, so I obtained the *Index to Periodical Literature* for four relevant years in the 1950's and checked out the titles of the child-rearing articles that appeared in the major women's magazines at the time.

There were articles which focused upon the child and others which which focused upon the parents. The articles which focused on the children all painted a picture of the developing child as vulnerable, fragile, at considerable psychological risk. Consider the following typical titles:

Baby's Fears
Can They Take It?
Children in Distress
Children's Right to Emotional Security
Fifty Frightened Children

Remember, most mothers of pre-schoolers are young women not many years out of high school, and the idea that they are now wholly responsible for a helpless new human can be overwhelming. When one adds to that mix a steady diet of parenting articles focused on the negatives—on fear, anxiety, insecurity, and the many ways in which child rearing can go wrong—it is hardly surprising that these uncertain young parents learned

*For an update on these children see Appendix B, my review of the movie *The Big Chill.*

to greet each sign of distress in their toddler as evidence that something was going awry.

This was the child-rearing climate of the early fifties. Young mothers were being hammered with the twin notions that their children were immensely vulnerable, psychologically fragile creatures, *and* that growing up could and ought to be a wholly painless process, free of anxiety and insecurity.

These mothers were under immense pressure to accept this view of the situation. Consider now this next set of article titles. These articles focused on the parents, and in wholly negative terms.

What's Wrong With American Moms?
Are American Moms a Menace?
Report Cards for Parents
The Real Delinquent, the Parent
By Their Parents Ye Shall Know Them

Clearly, if the child was not doing well, the villain was Mother. She was the "menace," the "real delinquent."

So mothers backed off, and the result was the first North American appearance of the omnipotent child. These soon acquired names. They became known as the 'now' generation, the 'me' generation, the "revolution for the hell of it gang."

It is clear the editors of the women's magazines in the early fifties have much to answer for. But despite their claims to significance, magazine editors don't create trends, they report them. They popularize the current fads and they vilify ideas no longer popular. In the last ten years, for example, can anyone remember reading an article in a woman's magazine that mentioned the word punishment in anything but condemnatory terms?

Though women's magazine editors think of themselves as experts on child rearing, they have no true expertise. What they have is an ear to the ground for what is currently the 'correct' view. Well, in the fifties the professionals were smoking the love-is-all-it-takes weed too.

·It is now fashionable to blame it all on Dr. Spock, but that is not getting to the heart of the matter. Dr. Spock was just the most prominent disseminator of the "fragile child and tread carefully" ethic. He did not invent the notion. He heard about it, found that it appealed to his liberal nature, and so he touted it.

It is interesting to note that Dr. Spock himself has been uttering some "mea culpas" these days. However, he does not apologize for giving bad advice! He apologizes for giving advice at all, claiming this led parents to turn their child-rearing responsibilities over to the experts rather than use their own judgment. It sounds as though Dr. Spock is saying that since his book had results other than those he had intended, and since the advice he gave was sound, writing books on child rearing is a mistake.

I cannot accept this as an accurate appreciation of the situation. What happened was that Dr. Spock's *advice* inhibited parents, was so at variance with those maternal attitudes which lead to discipline that parents backed off and their children then suffered from a lack of training.

We cannot stop our search for answers with Dr. Spock. We need to penetrate the matter more deeply. The next step takes us to Sigmund Freud and a tad closer to the heart of things.

Childhood as Trauma

Dr. Freud told us about the unconscious. He told us that conflicts in the unconscious are responsible for neurotic behavior in adults. He said that those conflicts arose in the course of early child development. He invented the Libido Theory to account for the variety of such conflicts he encountered in his adult patients.

According to the Libido Theory, the child passes through stages in which his sexual energy is attached to various erogenous zones: his mouth, his anus, his genitalia. If, in the course of navigating any one of these stages, the child encounters real difficulty, excessive amounts of libido, or sexual energy, remain attached to that stage, becoming the basis for later neurotic conflicts of an oral, anal or genital nature.

While most young parents of the fifties and sixties probably knew very little about the Libido Theory, the professionals bought it hook, line, and sinker. The social workers, the psychologists, the nurses and the educators all went dancing after the psychoanalytic Pied Piper. Soon the twin notions of instinctual conflict and libido stages provided the whole basis for their advice to parents.

Everywhere parents were advised to avoid frustrating the instincts of their developing infant and toddler lest they generate some conflict which might fester in his psyche and become the basis for a later neurosis. 'Don't give him a trauma' became the *leitmotiv* of motherhood.

A thousand articles urged parents to be sensitive to their child's inner state and warned of the dangers if they were not. Permissive measures to avoid frustration were recommended. These included breast feeding with unlimited opportunity to suck, gradual weaning, demand feeding—all measures intended to avoid 'oral' conflicts and later neurosis. Gentle and late induction of bladder and bowel training were advocated in order to forestall later 'anal' hangups. Toleration of masturbation and sexual curiosity was recommended in order that the 'genital' phase might be navigated successfully.

The common element in all this advice was *permitting,* not expecting or frustrating, but *permitting.* Implied, and sometimes stated, was the notion that growth was somehow *in the child,* and as long as the parent did not frustrate him, all would come out right in the end.

Nowhere was attention paid to the necessity of *expecting* function, to the *inevitability* of frustration, to the *universality* of conflict as part of normal child development. No! The parents were assured that all they had to do was be sensitive, kind, and patient and eventually the child would master his own growth.

We have seen what that approach leads to. The failure of psychoanalytic approaches to child rearing has been thoroughly documented, and the analysts have backed off a great deal.* But still nobody's admitting anything. The analysts aren't coming out and saying "we were wrong and we're sorry." All they do is change the emphasis and continue pontificating.

Well, that's not really good enough, so let me say it right out. While I don't think the Libido Theory has been wholly responsible for the present state of child rearing, it has certainly, on balance, done more harm than good. Although its oral, anal and genital phases have been proven irrelevant by direct observation of developing children, these notions continue to be bruited about the land. It's time we called a spade a spade and put a stop to the nonsense.

The fact is, the Libido Theory, and its handmaiden, the Instinctual Conflict Theory of Neurosis, have simply not stood up to rigorous examination, and it's past time these theoretical structures were abandoned.

Freud was a creature of his times, and I am sure if he had never come along we would still have found ourselves in our current social dilemma, a society peopled by increasing numbers of defectively socialized individuals. Like Spock, Freud was as much a means as he was a cause, and he was even more surprised at the outcome of his theory than the rest of us. William Sergeant, a psychiatric colleague, reports that Freud said to him somewhat ruefully, not long before his death, that he hadn't 'meant it all to happen.'

Freud's theory crystallized a view of man that had been building for couple of centuries. The parenting practices which burgeoned as out-

---

*For a current appreciation of the validity of psychoanalysis see my paper "The Sterile Couch," which appeared in *Perspectives in Biology and Medicine,* 32, No. 2 (Winter 1989): 272-80.

growths of his theory merely accelerated a process already in vigorous motion.

Values and Parenting

The principal determinant of how parents rear their children is the values they hold, their sense of what is fitting and what is not. Let me illustrate.

"He can't act like that," Mother says. "Who does he think is?" This is a statement of indignation, a sure sign that the parent is reacting to some behavior which contravenes her values.

In times of social stability, values become consensual, that is to say there is a wide agreement with respect to what is 'good' behavior and what is 'bad' behavior. In general, this agreement extends also to what one should do about unacceptable behaviors when they arise.

There was a time when it was generally agreed that work was good. This value was evident in statements, now old fashioned, such as "work is its own reward." This view was widely held in America prior to World War II. Today we refer to this notion as the *puritan work ethic,* and the term *workaholic* has entered the language. Suddenly a heretofore consensual value is no longer consensual and a generation gap is building.

There was a not yet distant time when premarital chastity was considered mandatory for *decent* girls. However, in the fifties we began to hear a lot of talk about frigidity, sexual hangups and the need for a less rigid approach to this natural function, and today there is considerable evidence to suggest that premarital chastity is not a widespread value anymore.

There was a time when swearing was vulgar, when pornography was depraved, and children who indulged in the former or showed interest in the latter were disapproved of in no uncertain terms. Both of these behaviors, while still not approved by parents these days, are much less disapproved than used to be the case. Indeed the surest route to improving one's thesaurus of epithets these days is to spend a couple of recesses on an elementary school playground.

When values are consensual they tend to shore up the discipline of uncertain parents. When everybody agrees the child ought to finish his school work whether he likes it or not, his parents send him a strong message to this effect. Similarly, when premarital intercourse is unthinkable, daughters are left in no doubt as to what is expected of them in this arena of behavior. But what if things are being said like "you don't want him to grow up to be a workaholic, do you?" Is not the message Mother sends *vis à vis* finishing school work liable to be stated less forcefully and have less impact? Similarly, when daughter shows signs of sexual interest, if part of

Mother's mind is saying "Go slow now, you don't want her to become a frigid old maid," is not the message the child receives liable to have more the quality of a night letter than an urgent telegram?

The point is that a small change of parental attitude with respect to a value can have a profound effect on the disciplinary message sent to the child and, of course, on his training. Perhaps the parent would merely like the child to have a more relaxed attitude about work, not to grow up a 'workaholic' or to have a 'Sunday neurosis.' However, first thing you know, parent and teacher are wrestling with a child who won't finish his school work and regards homework as an invention of the devil designed to spoil his television. Perhaps the parents merely intended that their sons and daughters not grow up to be uptight about sex, but again, a little disinhibition tends to go a long way, and 'make love not war,' became the behavioral guideline of the most sexually enthusiastic generation to hit this globe since the declining days of the Roman empire.

Each generation of parents, by the way in which it rears the children, reconstructs society afresh. We are each of us architects of the society that follows.

We are not conscious of these reconstructive efforts. Parents simply do what seems right to them. In times of little cultural change, generation after generation is reared to the same values. Such is an easy time to be a parent.

But in times of cultural turmoil, parenting becomes a more uncertain business and change tends to build upon change. As parents deal with their children differently from how their parents dealt with them when they were children, they often generate a greater effect than they intended. Their doubts about the wisdom of chastity become their daughter's convictions. Their reservations about the work ethic become their son's *modus vivendi*. And when *these* children raise *their* children, the message is diluted one more time. So does the process of value change accelerate, until in the final phases of cultural decay, it proceeds at such breakneck speed that each generation is alienated from the one that follows it.

This is what is happening to our culture. We are in the final phase of a process which began over two centuries ago. The magazine editors, Spock, Freud, all of us have been unknowingly immersed in that process. The omnipotent child is a late product of such decline. He is a product of parenting grown ineffectual owing to decaying, or changing, values. He has appeared before in the history of the world. Each time his presence has been associated with cultural decline.

So, thoughtful people must concern themselves with understanding the values that underlie our parenting efforts. We need to tease them out; make them explicit. We need, each of us, to ask ourselves how we perceive man's nature. We need to ask ourselves what we feel is best for our children. Is it better to produce a semi-psychopath who will be able to scrabble through life unimpeded by concern for those he exploits, or ought we to equip our child with a conscience and hope it will not turn him into a loser?

The best way to get a handle on where we as a society stand on this is to examine the historical process. By looking back and seeing the road we have travelled, perhaps we can guess at the road ahead.

From the Age of Reason to the Age of Passion

In the early 1700's, prior to the Romantic Rebellion, it was widely believed that man had a dual nature, part animal or brute and part man.

In this the Age of Reason, it was believed that brute was where man came from, and becoming human was a progression initiated by parenting and continued by man's own efforts. It was believed, however, that the progression was not inevitable. A man could remain a brute if he were not nurtured or did not persist in his strivings to become man.

The author of *The Accomplished Rake* (1717), Mrs. Mary Davys, put it quite succinctly for the style of her times: "It requires a pretty deal of pains to distinguish ourselves from brute. We must have a share of probity, honor, gratitude, good sense... so that all who are designed for men are not rightly called so till acquired advantages confirm their title."

The first of these acquired advantages was control of appetites by reason. The brute was led by his sexual hunger or aggressive instincts. Man sought to control this side of his nature by the exercise of reason. Samuel Johnson expressed this view of his times when he said, "whatever withdraws us from the power of our senses... advances us in the dignity of human beings." Jonathan Swift, in his portrayal of the Yahoos, told his time what a brute man could become if he allowed his senses to dominate his reason.

With the Romantic Rebellion this view came under attack. Creative persons, feeling stifled by the suppression of what they felt to be natural emotion, declared war on reason and moderation. They sought to rehabilitate sensuality and promote its spontaneous expression. A mighty poet undertook to change our view of mankind. William Blake, seeing reason and restraint to be but suppression of a vital part of man's nature, declared, "the road of excess leads to the palace of wisdom." The philosopher Søren Aabye Kierkegaard administered the *coup de grâce* to reason when he stated "the conclusions of passion are the only reliable ones."

One wonders if Blake and Kierkegaard would hold the same views if they could spend a month or so immersed in our times. Many have travelled far down the road of excess, but somehow the palace of reason seems to have escaped them. The conclusions of passion, it would appear, are those which underlie the actions of our mass murderers.

However, in Blake's time these ends were not foreseen. The Romantic Rebellion gave promise of freedom for the sensual part of man's nature. The led to a new view of man's nature. This view reached full flower in Jean Jacques Rousseau's concept of the "Noble Savage." Rousseau held that the most noble man is the uncivilized man, the savage unspoiled by society's molding influence. This is a far cry from man as brute with appetites to be tamed; it is man as naturally human, needing only to be left alone to perfect his nature. The implications for child rearing of these contrasting view of man's nature are profound. If you hold the view that man must tame the tiger in him, then you will feel it essential to discipline the child, to "mold, strengthen and perfect him." If you hold the 'noble savage' view, you will shy away from such discipline, fearful of destroying the unspoiled child's unique humanity.

Most people hold one or the other of these views, whether they are aware of it or not. In order to discover which of these views a person holds I ask this question: "If you were to put a seven-year-old child in a room where there is a large table loaded with all kinds of edibles—steak, hamburgers, peanut butter, sandwiches, carrots, peas, french fries, milk, coke, coffee, ice cream, pies, nuts, cotton candy, chocolate bars—all varieties of food, sweet and sour, nourishing and junk, and you were to leave him there for mealtimes each day, which foods would he eat?"

Take a moment to ask yourselves this question. Write down your answer and read on.

I get two different answers to this question. The first is that the child would gorge himself on candy, ice cream and pop until he threw up. The second is that he would eat a balanced diet.

The first person sees man's nature in Age of Reason terms: until persons are trained to restraint and wisdom they will be victims of their impulses, brutes who will indulge themselves even against their interests. The second person believes children have a natural or body sense which will lead them to behave with restraint and wisdom. This view says, "do not suppress your instincts, they are wiser than you are." As the hero of Star Wars puts it, "the force is with you. Trust it."

A parent of the first persuasion will see discipline as an essential ingredient of parenting, see training the child to restraint as crucial as loving him. The second parent, believing that psychological growth is within the child as naturally as physical growth, will see parenting as protecting and nurturing the child but will be loathe to train him, seeing this as Rousseau saw civilization, a spoiling of the savage.*

There is more to be learned about the omnipotent child and how he got that way by taking a hard look at the Age of Reason and comparing its rearing goals with our own. What kind of a person was the society of Blake, Pope and Dryden striving to produce?

The ideal man of the Age of Reason had three prominent characteristics. First, he was a man of *moderation.* Secondly he was a man of *decorum,* that is he believed behavior should stay within certain social guidelines. Finally he was a man at peace with his social order, a man who *accepted external authority as rational and inevitable.* So it is reasonably assumed that the concerned parent of those times approached child rearing with these goals in mind.

The opposite of moderation is a lack of restraint and poor self-control. The opposite of decorum is egocentric dealings with others. The opposite of accepting authority is rejecting it in favor of maintaining one's omnipotence illusion. But these three characteristics are those of the omnipotent child.

Consider! *The principal characteristics of the ideal man of the Age of Reason are precisely opposite to the cardinal characteristics of the Omnipotent Child Syndrome.*

The Age of Reason saw moderation, that is restraint of the senses as an essential ingredient of manhood. Today we see man as most authentically man when he is "letting it all hang out." Samuel Johnson said, "whatever withdraws us from the power of our senses . . . advances us in the dignity of human beings." Norman Mailer tells us, "if it feels good, do it."

Decorum was the second quality the Age of Reason prized in men. Manners are but the codification of concern for others. They are rooted in taking regard for the situation of the other. One must learn to perceive situation and adjust his behavior if he not to injure others. Only the man who has grown out of his infantile egocentricity can read others and be sensitive to their situation, for he has acquired the capacity for consideration. So it is that good manners and egocentricity are incompatible.

Today we have in our midst the 'me' generation, persons so concerned for self that they honor no commitment to others. Marriages fail for a lack of concern and consideration one for the partner. Our society is widely populated with egocentric, mannerless persons who lack the smallest ca-

*For a modern exposition of the latter point of view, the reader's attention is drawn to the film *One Flew Over the Cuckoo's Nest* which literally contains a 'noble savage.' My review of this film is included herein as Appendix C.

pacity for accommodation to others. They are, to use C.S. Lewis's felicitous phrase, Trousered Apes, barred from any real participation in society by their truncated perception of others. While these persons are often so immersed in self they are oblivious to their social ineptitude, as time goes on they come to sense their isolation, their outsider status. Then, not understanding its source, they strike back at the society that has no place for them. Mindless crime, so characteristic of our times, is rooted in such rage.

The third characteristic of the Age of Reason man was his acceptance of societal authority as rational and inevitable. He was a man at peace with his world. Perhaps there were wrongs in society, changes that needed making, but he did not feel these to be of such magnitude as to invalidate the social order. Nor did he see rebellion as the reasonable route to changing things. Finally he was humble in the face of God's authority. Today we have amongst us a generation who tolerate no authority, be it that of the college dean, the police, the draft board. Indeed, they have even declared God to be dead. Humility is a word that does not appear in their dictionary.

From pride in obedience we have come to pride in disobedience. Anti-authoritarianism has seeded, grown and flowered in these two centuries. Edmund Burke, commenting on the rising anti-authoritarianism of his times, stated the Age of Reason position most clearly when he said, "men are qualified for civil liberty in exact proportion to their disposition to put moral chains upon their own appetites... society cannot exist unless a controlling power upon will and appetite be placed somewhere, and the less of it within, the more is without. It is ordained in the eternal constitution of things that men of intemperate minds cannot be free. Their passions forge their fetters."

His words were unable to stem the tide.

In the arts the anti-hero began to show his face. He presented as an amoral, mannerless, but always 'noble' creature who was merely taking up arms against an oppressive authority. From those humble beginnings the anti-hero has become a common character in movies, books and plays. He has largely supplanted the hero.

Political anti-authoritarianism was on the rise too. It first surfaced in the New World when America thumbed its nose at George III, and from that moment it became a cherished portion of the American birthright. A decade later the French Revolution dethroned Louis XVI and a wave of chaos and civil disorder engulfed France until Napoleon, by force of arms, restored order and, incidentally, illustrated the truth of Burke's comment.

Religious anti-authoritarianism began as a reaction to the despotic authority of a centralized church, and dethroned that authority handily. Who could foresee that what began by freeing the individual to worship by his own lights would end by dethroning God?

Perhaps political authority in the Age of Reason was excessive. Perhaps religious control was despotic. Perhaps literature was too coldly classical, needed a breath of sensuality to make it human. Perhaps the rejection of such authority was understandable. It certainly occurred.

Slowly, over the past two centuries, man's values have changed. The values of the Age of Reason, moderation and restraint, manners and decorum, respect for constituted authority, have been questioned, modified, and ultimately dissipated. We have come to an age with very different values.

I have christened this age the Age of Passion. I do so because passion, that is feeling and desire, plays as large a part in our decision making as reason did for men of that age. And the omnipotent child, though he not be the 'ideal' of our times, is the embodiment of our age. He is the Age of Passion man.

In this chapter we have sought to understand how two generations of normally intelligent and concerned young women have had such a difficult time rearing their children. We have rejected the neurotic mother explanation the analysts have attempted to thrust upon us. We do not accept that Mother is simply having trouble working out her ambivalent dependency upon her own mother. Nor do we accept the vilifying labels of the popular press. To call Mother a menace or label her delinquent is both untrue and unfair.

What we have discovered is that parenthood in this trough of culture has become a terribly confused task, that today's mother picked the worst of times to rear children: values, which give direction to child rearing, have become hopelessly confused; traditional and personal supports have all but evaporated; parenting has become the playground of instant experts who stridently perpetuate child-rearing recipes as shallow as their understanding. The result has been widespread uncertainty and guilt.

Donald Barr's advice, "set limits and see that they are kept," remains the best advice we can offer. Even so I feel that we have not traced Mother's troubles back to their historical roots in vain. When Mother comes to realize how she got where she is, she is in a better position to think clearly about the parenting task. When she understands where she is trying to lead her child and why, she becomes a better judge of how to get there.

8

A Little Remedial Parenting

"To rear the infant is a demanding joy; to rerear the child is a mighty but still possible task; as for the adolescent, what else is there to do but freeze him in nitrogen and bring him back when we've found a cure?"

ST. MECONIUM OF THE AUGEAN STABLES

Up to now we have concerned ourselves with the fundamentals of adaptive growth in children. It's time now to see how these fundamentals are converted into specific parenting techniques to help a child whose growth isn't going all that well. The best approach to that, I believe, is to tell you how I would have advised Lydia and Frank to deal with Dewey. In Chapter One, you'll remember, I had taken the history and interviewed Dewey. Now, after I have had a chance to pull my thoughts together, I normally make an appointment to see the parents. Dewey is not invited, of course.

"When I told him we were coming," Frank said, holding Lydia's chair for her, "he wanted to know when he was coming back." Frank raised his eyebrows. "Kinda surprised me. The way he barreled out of here I was sure this was the last place he'd ever want to come back to."

"I hope he wasn't too difficult," Lydia said, starting to mangle her gloves again.

"Oh no. We had a lively time. He's a sharp boy."

"He didn't say a thing about what went on in here," Lydia observed, a note of inquiry in her voice.

"They never do," I replied, taking my seat and opening my file to the dictation of my interview with Dewey. "So we'll all have the same information, let me read you my notes about my interview with Dewey." I do so, and it comes out pretty much like I described the interview earlier in this book.

Lydia is shocked that Dewey was so rude and challenging. Frank is surprised that he was so communicative.

"His last words to me," Frank said, "were 'I'll go but I'm not talking to no dumb shrink.'"

"They all say that." I turned to my summary formulation. "What I've done to date is this. I've taken all the information I have gathered about Dewey, the story you told me, what I got from Miss Grant, what I learned from talking to Dewey myself, and I've pulled it together and formulated an understanding of him. It is that understanding I'd like to give you now. Then I want to design a program to deal with the situation. Today it's my turn to talk."

The sooner one gets into this the better. It is not an easy thing for parents, this coming back for the answer. They have a lot of unhappy questions in mind. How sick is he? How big a mess have we made of things? Is it too late to straighten him out? I know the questions, so I don't need to wait for them to be asked.

Frank and Lydia settled back, relieved that for the time being they were not required to participate.

"Let me say right away," I began, "that Dewey's problems don't stem from any deep-seated emotional conflict. He is not neurotic. Dewey's troubles, his symptoms, arise because he doesn't *cope* as well as he should for his years. Many of the ways he behaves would be normal if he were four or five, but for a nine year old these are just not adequate. Dewey is adaptively immature. He's lagged in three important areas. Let me tell you about these one by one."

They nodded in uncertain agreement.

"When Dewey wants something he wants it now, he just can't wait. If he's mad, he explodes. If he's disappointed he cries. If he has something tedious to do he drifts from the task. The first area in which Dewey's development has lagged is with respect to patience, persistence and self-control. I call this developing tolerance for life's normal unpleasure. Dewey hasn't developed much."

I like to tie my explanations to concrete symptoms. There is nothing worse for parents than high-sounding dynamic explanations they cannot follow.

"Let me describe how this particular aspect of adaptive growth usually proceeds. Nobody expects a baby to wait. When you bring a baby home from the hospital you don't say to him, 'Now listen Charlie, here's the way we do things around here. After supper we go to bed and that's it till breakfast, which is seven-thirty a.m.'"

They smiled.

"Of course you can say that if you like, but I doubt that he's going to pay any attention. No, what you are going to do is get up and feed him at two a.m. as every other parent does, whether you feel like it or not. We don't expect babies to wait. Not yet. But we expect toddlers to. Not a whole lot maybe, but a bit. We begin to expect the child to tolerate a little bit of life's unpleasure, to wait a little. Measured doses of such minimal waiting stretch the child's capacity for unpleasure. It's a little bit like weight lifting, four pounds today, five pounds next week and in a month yesterday's challenges have become today's cinch."

Frank nodded. It was an image he could relate to.

"Dewey has lagged in this respect. He has remained intolerant of even minor degrees of unpleasure. The first bit of trouble with school work and he quits. A page of math looks like a mountain to him. If he can't find the shoe when he's dressing he gives up and grinds to a halt. This is why, unless you nag or stand over him, tedious tasks just don't get done."

"I'll say they don't," Frank said.

Lydia nodded.

"But there are other kinds of unpleasure besides tedium. There's anxiety, anger, disappointment. Dewey handles all of these unpleasures poorly. Take minor anxiety for example. Sure he wants to turn out for baseball, but when try-out time draws near, he starts wondering if he will drop the ball. Suddenly he loses interest. Though he won't admit it, he's afraid. He deals with this unpleasure by not dealing with it. He finds a way to avoid."

"I guess we should have just made him go," Frank said.

"But he was really worried," Lydia said uncertainly.

I nodded. "So are many boys, but most of them tough it out. It's a matter of degree. Dewey has developed less tolerance for anxiety than he needs to cope with normal childhood apprehensions. Dewey can't handle disappointment either. Though he's nine he still cries when things don't work out. The same with anger. When Dewey's mad he ought to grumble or complain. He's too old to be throwing tantrums."

I paused a moment then summarized. "Dewey is impatient and impulsive, he lacks persistence and self-control, and all of these qualities are manifestations of the first area of adaptive weakness, his intolerance for normal degrees of unpleasure.

"You got that right," Frank said, "that's just the way he is. But why did he stay that way? Why didn't he grow like he should?"

"If I may I'd like to come back to the how and why a little later,"·I replied. "You see Dewey has three adaptive weaknesses that underlie his symptoms, and I want to tell you about all three of them before we come back to asking ourselves how it all came about and what we can do about it."

Frank accepts that but I give him just a little about cause because I can see he needs it.

"For now, just let me say two things. I don't think Dewey has suffered from any lack of love or nurturance. Oh, I know, you don't feel very loving towards him at times, that you've said things you've regretted, maybe over-punished too, but those troubles *arise* from Dewey's problems, they do not *cause* them. Furthermore, if you are ever going to feel more consistently loving towards Dewey, he's first going to have to become a whole lot more lovable."

I was pleased to see that Lydia was beginning to relax a little. I needed her undivided attention.

"The second thing I'd like to say," I continued, "is that it's discipline, setting limits and expecting things of children, that stretches their tolerance for tedium. Somehow, the way you have disciplined Dewey hasn't worked as well as it should. It needs to be done again and better. The how of that is what we are going to have to come back to, after I've finished telling you the other ways in which I see Dewey."

I noted, as is always the case, how intensely attentive they were. Parents really want to understand.

"The second area of adaptive delay is Dewey's self-centeredness. Dewey sees the world as if he were the sun and everybody else a planet in orbit about him."

"I'll say," Frank muttered.

"Family life has to revolve around him," I continued. "He doesn't realize that others have things they want to do, at least until they make a large noise about them. Which most mothers are not inclined to do. 'Oh! I didn't really care about watching that show,' Mother will say as she lets him change the channel."

Lydia smiled ruefully.

"But kids won't defer to Dewey in the way that Mother will. If he expects them to fit the play around him, they'll tell him to bug off. First thing you know he's playing with the little kids or the other rejects."

Frank nodded.

"The problem is Dewey is still as self-centered as the four year old who thinks daytime starts the moment he opens his eyes in the morning. All three year olds are like that and so long as parents will go on accommodating to them, they'll stay that way. It's discipline again, setting limits and expecting things that intrudes on this normal self-centeredness."

Frank shrugged. "We just wanted to make sure he was happy, but I can see we overshot a little."

"It's natural for parents to put themselves second. After all, that's where you start from with the baby," I explained. "But, there comes a time when parents naturally begin to change, to expect him to accommodate a little. It helps if you have a second child when he's two or three. There is no mother who can make two children each the sole focus of her life. Something has to give."

"How could I have managed another child?" Lydia said. "Just trying to cope with Dewey's demands took all my time and attention."

"Precisely! You were trying so hard to be sensitive to Dewey's needs that instead of teaching him to accommodate to the world, you accommodated the world to him," I said. "That's why he remained so self-centered."

Lydia nodded in glum agreement.

"The third adaptive delay I want to talk about has to do with accepting authority. Dewey has not made his peace with authority. He hasn't accepted his childhood. It isn't just that he minds being made to do things he doesn't enjoy, all kids complain about that. No, Dewey is offended by your assuming the prerogative of requiring him to do things. He doesn't concede you the right. He feels put down by adult authority. 'You're not the boss of me' is the thought that passes through his mind."

"Comes out of his mouth," Frank corrected. "If I've heard that phrase once I've heard it a dozen times. 'You're not the boss of me. I don't have to do what you say.' It's his catechism."

"We didn't want to come on strong," Lydia said. "We tried to *ask* instead of *tell*."

"But if you ask," Frank interjected, "he just says no, and then you have to tell."

"And then he starts acting as though we were the meanest parents on the block," Lydia replied. " 'Johnny doesn't have to take out the garbage. Sean doesn't have to check in right after school.' "

"It isn't taking out the garbage or coming home that offends Dewey," I said. "It's that you are telling him what he must or must not do. You're bossing him and he finds that offensive. That's why he protests so strongly over trivia, why he always has to wrest some tiny concession from the expectation."

"To prove he didn't do as we ordered him to," Frank crowed. "That's what I said."

"Precisely. It truly upsets Dewey to encounter the realistic limitations of his power. You see, he's still defending his omnipotence illusion."

"His what?" Frank asked.

"Let me explain. Babies have no idea of cause and effect, of power. When they holler and the bottle comes, they believe their hollering made it come, that the world is under their control. It's an illusion. It preserves their security. If they really understood their helplessness, they'd be flooded with anxiety every time the mother left the room. But they don't understand. They have this illusion, the illusion that the world is under their control."

"It's his security," Lydia said. "Knowing his mother will come when he calls."

"That's where all children start; believing their mother must come when they call—that she is on a string and they can jerk the string. And with babies we parents go along with this. We come when he calls, fetch when he says fetch. At least until he stops napping and gets on his feet, when, if Mother doesn't want to become his slave, she's going to have to deny his authority now and again."

"Or be his slave," Lydia echoed from the plains of despair.

"That's when battles-of-wills first start. When Mother won't do what he says, it scares him; it hints at his true helplessness, his realistic dependency. He gets anxious. We call it separation anxiety. So he sets out to prove she is his robot, that she must do as he says. He throws his spoon to the floor and orders Mother to pick it up. If Mother obeys, he wins the battle-of-wills and his omnipotence illusion is sustained; at least until the next battle. But if Mother doesn't obey, if she sticks to her guns, he gets a big dose of the reality of his powerless state. 'If she doesn't have to do what I say, what if she left me? Where is she? Get her here this minute.' He experiences separation anxiety. This makes him fight harder to prove his omnipotence."

"Then it's a no-win situation," Lydia exclaimed.

"Not really," I said. "Suppose he doesn't win the battle-of-wills? He fears separation, fears that his needs will not be met. *But they are met!* Eventually Mother returns. Not necessarily with what he wants but surely with what he needs. So he begins to get a new appreciation of the situation. Perhaps his fears were groundless? Mother will come back. He will get fed and looked after. A new solution to his problem occurs. Perhaps I am not omnipotent, but perhaps I don't have to be. Maybe I'm not the king but I'm a close friend of the king's and I'm going to be alright. So it is that children begin learning to trust."

"So by losing he really wins," Frank said thoughtfully.

"Right. For children really to win they need to lose a few battles-of-wills. Some children don't lose any. Or enough to grow. When this happens they get hung up in the omnipotence-devaluation phase."

"Like Dewey," Frank said.

"He's hung up on authority. Omnipotent children just can't accept authority. It isn't the task that distresses them, it's the parent or teacher assuming the right to make rules that bothers them. That's why its so important for them to win or at least maintain a facade of winning. These children don't believe parents have more competence than they. This is part of the reason they don't trust adults. They don't believe a thing simply because an adult said it."

I could see the explanation was coming together for Frank and Lydia.

"These are the three adaptive weaknesses behind Dewey's symptoms. He lacks tolerance for life's normal unpleasures. He has remained egocentric. He is reflexly willful as he struggles to maintain his illusion of omnipotence. And there is one other characteristic I need to discuss. Dewey lacks self-esteem."

"I thought that was the whole problem." Lydia said.

I explained that though the omnipotent child may sound arrogant, he almost always has a poor sense of his own worth. It is a realistic self-appraisal. Every time he has a temper tantrum afterwards, in his heart, he knows his behavior was infantile. Every time he succeeds in avoiding some life task that other kids cope with, the price he pays is to feel a little weaker. Self-esteem is built from coping, and the omnipotent child has not coped much so he has not built much self-esteem.

That's Dewey," Frank said. "The whole schmear. But what are we going to do about it?"

"We're going to have to re-rear him; take him through the adaptive growth he missed first time around. Primarily this means disciplining him more effectively."

"I guess I thought loving him would be enough," Lydia said a little sadly.

"Loving a child doesn't intrude upon his omnipotence; it panders to it. It's saying 'no' or 'you must' that raises a question as to who is in charge."

"We may have raised the question," Frank said ruefully. "But he answered it."

"Not only does discipline deal with the omnipotence business, but it also stretch the child's tolerance for tedium and intrudes upon his egocentricity."

"So what we have to do is find ways to discipline Dewey that work," Frank said. "What I can't understand is why we didn't manage it better. "We have standards. We don't think kids should make the rules. We just didn't seem to be able to convince him of that, but we sure tried. Believe me there have been plenty of storms over Dewey in our house."

"I have no doubt that you tried hard to discipline Dewey, and I have an idea why things didn't go well enough. I suspect it was a combination of circumstances. Dewey is a first child. It was first time around for you and child rearing. You know what some people say: the first child, like the first waffle, should be thrown away. You learn on first children, and the natural inclination is to overparent, to hover a little, to be a bit oversensitive. Many mothers are inclined to run when the baby cries just to see he is alright. A more experienced mother might saunter in to see if the problem is serious. First mothers tend to start out a little overprotective. Lydia, you impress me as the kind of person who might well go that route."

Frank smiled at Lydia, who shrugged in a noncommittal manner.

"Furthermore, some children are placid little creatures. If they don't get something they want they wail a little, then they turn their attention elsewhere. Some, like Dewey, are energetic and intense. When they feel even a little distress they let you know loud and clear. Put together a mother a little too anxious to do right by her child with a demanding little fireball, and it's not hard to get into some developmental trouble."

I could see by Lydia's face that I'd hit pay dirt so I carried on.

"It's easy to slip into ineffective overcontrol?"

"Ineffective overcontrol?" Frank asked.

"That's shrink talk for nagging. It's overcontrol because you have to stand right beside Dewey to get him to do things. If it's getting dressed there you are, 'come on Dewey, put on your socks, find your shoes.' If it's room cleaning it's 'under your bed too; no, don't put clean clothes back in the hamper.' Unless you stand right there supervising, the job just doesn't get done. It's ineffective because while it gets Dewey dressed or his room cleaned, things get no better. You can expect to be standing over him again the next morning."

"Exactly," Lydia said. "That is exactly what happens. And I end up yelling at him, sending him to school in tears without a proper breakfast and feeling like the worst mother in the world."

"Ineffective overcontrol doesn't generate adaptive growth. As you stand there supervising, it's your patience that is being exercised, not his; it's you doing the accommodating, not him, and he is not learning to do what he is supposed to do. He is only responding to the force of your presence."

"But how do we manage it then?" Frank asked. "If we don't stand over him, he just won't do it."

When parents ask this question I know we are ready to move into treatment planning.

"What we do is program it. That is, we set up a pattern of behavior control designed to grow him up. We get all the details of that pattern clear in our own minds, then tell it to Dewey. Then we do it, regularly and without deviation for the time it takes to get growth going again. I call this remedial parenting."

"Remedial parenting?" Lydia said. "Oh, I see, sort of like remedial reading only done at home for socially illiterate kids."

I laughed. "Exactly. Just a moment while I write that down for my book." And I did, and here it is.

Planning the Remedial Program

Before I bring the parents back for this meeting, I block out in broad outline the program I am going to try to set up with them. Through years of practice I have learned what the essential elements of such reparenting are so I have a little table to guide me. Here it is.

Remedial Parenting: The Overall Program

1. Select areas for programmed retraining
   A. The bottom line
   B. Routines and who does them
   C. General behavior: e.g. second telling
   D. Specials: e.g. school work finishing
2. Select areas for judicious neglect: the 'I'll sure be glad when' approach
3. Make out punishment cards
4. Arrange for continuing supervision

SELECTING AREAS FOR PROGRAMMED RETRAINING

I begin by choosing which areas to work on and which areas to ignore for the present. Obviously, if one tried to set up a program of discipline to correct everything Dewey was doing wrong, poor Dewey would be getting punished from dawn to dusk and no growth would result from that.

The criteria for selecting areas are practical. I like to deal with behaviors that come up daily, for the more frequent the disciplinary encounter, the faster the learning proceeds. Getting dressed in the morning or going to bed on time at night may not be the worst of Dewey's offenses, but they might be the best place to start retraining. I like to select expectations that are naturally clear-cut, so that there can be no question of whether the job has been done or not. There can be little argument about whether Dewey is dressed or whether he is in bed, but if the expectation was that he be polite, one might get into a debate whether or not making faces is rude.

It is useful if the areas for retraining are adapted to time limits, as getting dressed and going to bed are, for these lend themselves to clear-cut disciplinary encounters.

There is one exception to these criteria. Some behaviors must be dealt with. If the child is stealing or refusing to go to school, one cannot ignore these symptoms while he works on something easier or more convenient. There is a special instance of this which always takes priority.

The Bottom Line

When a child is firmly required to meet a parental expectation he will usually protest. In the case of the omnipotent child this protest frequently escalates to out-of-control behavior. The granddaddy of out-of-control behaviors is the *temper tantrum*. There are other forms of bottom line such as *the terminal woebegones, interminal arguing* and *rude defiance*.

The management of temper tantrums has been dealt with at length in Chapter Four. The management of other bottom line behavior follows the same pattern. The important thing is that the child realizes that when you give him the bottom line signal, he can expect program A to follow. Here in tabular form are the steps of this program recapitulated.

Temper Tantrum Control Program
1. The Signal
2. The Silent Seven
3. The Removal
4. The Punishment
5. Persistence

Until you have a bottom line program, all the other programs can come to naught. This is true even of older children, except it is a little harder to make the program work. For example, after the Silent Seven is complete, what if the child refuses to go to his room. What do you do? Though the father might manage to remove the child, the mother might not. All she can do is this. Tell him, "you have one minute to go to your room for your timed stay. If you don't go, then you will earn a punishment card." She then removes herself from the scene. In time this usually results in the child stomping off for his four minute seclusion, yelling obscenities perhaps, but going.

Routines and Who Does Them

Routines are the easiest behavior to program. That is why I see some omnipotent children whose routines are under quite good control despite their willfulness in other areas of family life.

Suppose we decide to deal with two areas of routine retraining: getting dressed the morning, and going to bed at night. "Who's going to handle getting him dressed in the morning?" I ask.

I like to involve both parents in the retraining, but I have learned it is best to assign separate tasks. It is hard for two people not to interfere with each other if they are both trying to handle the same piece of behavior. Invariably, one is a lot more fed up with the behavior than the other. The *spectator* parent's eye is on the child's distress, and the *disciplining* parent's eye is on the offense. Parents tend to get crosswise and undermine each other's resolve.

"Aren't you being a little hard on him?" the spectator parent asks.

"I think you might give me a little support instead of criticism," the disciplining parent says.

Once that debate starts the child may be forgotten, and what happens to discipline then?

The answer is for one parent to take care of a particular area of discipline without interference. If Mother is there in the morning, let her handle the dawdling over dressing. If Father is there in the evening, let him handle bedtime. Neither is to comment on the other's performance. If Father is messing up the bedtime routine Mother should bite her tongue and retreat to the kitchen. She is off duty.

We decided Lydia will handle getting dressed in the morning and Frank will put Dewey to bed at night. Since we have handled the getting dressed routine in Chapter Four, let's talk about Father settling him at night.

We are guided in designing our approach by the principles of programming discipline which I have enumerated before in this book and will (over the objections of my editor) do again now.

> Principles of Programming Discipline
> 1. A clear expectancy
> 2. A time limit
> 3. Supervision if necessary
> 4. Punishment if supervision required
> 5. Persist to communicate

In designing any program the first thing we have to do is to define for the child exactly what is expected. So we agree that Dewey is to have his pajamas on and teeth brushed by a certain time. This is a timed task and either a clock or a timer ought to be involved. Father must not nag or remind but, when the time is up, he will come up to tuck Dewey in. If Dewey is not ready as prescribed, then Father is to supervise him and tuck him in. However supervision is not free. It always costs. So Dewey gets a punishment card. Suppose in this case the punishment selected is that Dewey cannot ride his bike after school the next day. Father is to lock it up himself prior to going to work. (It is not reasonable that mothers have to enforce punishments assigned by fathers.)

I warned Lydia and Frank that things are liable to go a little differently when Father disciplines, that Dewey might, being a little less aware of his father's psychology than his mother's, begin by benign compliance. "As a matter of fact I think eight-thirty is a good time for me to go to bed; I need the sleep." And in bed he'll be. On time and everything cozy as a Walton family spelling bee.

Addressing Lydia, I completed my little story. "You can expect Frank to arrive in the kitchen and flex his child-rearing muscles for the next hour: 'You see dear, all you have to do is be firm, no pleading, no threats, just a no-nonsense statement with a smile.' "

For some reason mothers find this account of mine more amusing than fathers.

"Bear with it," I said to Lydia. "It isn't going to last. A couple of nights of this and Dewey will start testing the limits. At first when his father arrives he will be in the middle of doing his teeth. If Father fails to punish, the next night Dewey will have his pajama top on but still have his shoes and pants to go. If Father cops out again things will get steadily worse. If Father doesn't cop out, there'll be some static from Dewey and fewer claims to child-rearing expertise from Father."

They both laughed.

"However," I carried on, "three weeks of no-slip parenting and you can expect Dewey to be watching the clock and skinning off to get ready on time. More important of course is that he is coping with a little unpleasure, accommodating some, and accepting his father's authority."

What I am doing is tutoring the parents in discipline, starting out with a concrete situation, making sure the principles of discipline are obeyed in the design of the intervention, and hinting at these principles as we work out the design. As treatment progresses further parental guidance will lead them through this and other exercises of effective parenting. The goal of course is not just getting Dewey growing but also teaching the parents how to discipline effectively and eventually changing the attitudes of guilt and uncertainty which have played such a part in undermining their prior effectiveness.

General Behavior Management

There are a number of behaviors that, coming up at various times of the day in a variety of contexts, do not so easily lend themselves to planful intervention. For example many mothers complain of it taking six tellings and a yelling to get Dewey to move to anything, be it come for supper, come in the house, go wash his hands, and so on. For these we use the Second Telling Program detailed in Chapter Three.

'Jar' systems, or 'keep-score' books in school, are designed to deal with intermittent mild behaviors that need remediation. Suffice it to say that, with a little ingenuity, the jar system can be adapted to many such. I have had parents implement swear jars, hit your sister jars, lie jars, rude jars, stay at the dining room table jars. But don't line your window shelf with jars. Two at a time is plenty. However, as soon as improvement throws one into disuse you can start another.

Special Situations

If the principal referral symptom was 'not finishing his school work,' then the program outlined in the chapter on schools would have to be part of the initial training approach. Similarly if 'refusal to attend school' was the major referral symptom that too would need to be programmed. And, even though both of these matters were approached as symptoms requiring relief, their proper management turns them into vehicles for adaptive growth.

SELECT AREAS FOR JUDICIOUS NEGLECT

Now, having selected a few areas for programmed retraining and having assigned the task to one or another parent, we are ready to move on. So I advised Frank and Lydia to let other things go. "If he has been a little rude, tell him 'that's no way to talk' and forget it. If he doesn't hang up his coat when he comes in, either do it yourself or get him to, and tell him, 'I'll sure be glad when you remember to hang up your coat without being told.'"

Many parents are concerned with the advice to ignore some of the unacceptable behavior. They want him to be a model child, and tomorrow if not sooner. But this is impossible. Growth is a process and it takes time. If they try to correct everything at once they will lose it all.

This is not to say they should not disapprove of unacceptable behaviors. I think they should, but in terms like this: "I'll be glad when you can sit through a meal without leaving the table," as they bring him back but do not punish him. "I'll sure be glad when you stop picking on your sister," as they terminate the behavior but do not punish him. "I'll sure be glad when you stop asking the same question over and over when I'm on the telephone," but not punish him.

Later, if the growth obtained from the initial programs has not improved their authority to the point that disapproval itself is enough to correct these other behaviors, then they can use a newly freed jar to program one of them.

It is important to let some behavior go, offering nothing but disapproval. You see, Dewey thinks there are two classes of people in the world: kings and slaves. This is part of his omnipotent concern. We are telling him, through our *action dialogue,* that it isn't that way. By making him do some things and letting him not do others we are introducing the notion of autonomy, moving away from his boss-or-be-bossed version of family life. This makes surrendering one's omnipotence illusion a much more tolerable thing.

I have found that once the parent succeeds in one retraining, the next goes easier. One says to Dewey, "you remember how we handled getting to bed on time? Well I'm going to invent a program just like that to deal with your coming straight home after school. You have one week to clean up your act or that program goes into effect."

"I'm sure you are right," Lydia said. "But sometimes when he gives me that arrogant stare and says, 'I don't have to do what you say,' it makes me so mad I want to prove to him, then and there, who is the parent and who is the child." Just thinking about it Lydia was getting worked up.

What Lydia is talking about is attitude. She can't stand Dewey's nasty contempt for authority and his arrogant self centeredness. She would like to reach in his head, turn his attitude control all the way over to 'respect your parent' and leave it there. I know how she feels. If I believed such a thing were possible, I'd remuster to neurosurgery tomorrow.

"I know his attitude is hard to take, but with adaptive growth, behavior has to change before attitudes will. When parents are firm and don't let the child evade his responsibilities in the areas they have chosen to focus on, first the child learns to do what he is supposed to do. Later he comes to respect the parent's authority. It takes a while but it is the only way to get there from here."

Parents tend to approach attitude problems head on, to lecture the child on respecting their authority or punish him for not doing so. At best this teaches the child to build a facade of respect, that is to say "Yessir" and go off blithely, ignoring the chores he is supposed to do. At worst it can have no impact at all, such that neither performance nor attitude improves.

"So behavior first, attitude second. If he is a little rude, disapprove and forget for now. But if he doesn't get dressed on time, or whatever you have programmed, within the time assigned, and without supervision, make it happen and give him a consequence. A month of this and you will have generated a little real respect for your authority. Then, if the rudeness disappears, it is probably a sign of his changing attitude.

"The way to retrain Dewey, I summarized, is to select a couple of areas, set up clear programs to deal with the selected symptoms, and get off his back over the less important things. Then follow the principles: a clear expectancy, a time limit, supervision if necessary, and now the hardest part, punish him because you had to supervise."

"I'll say it's the hard part," Frank said. "How can you punish him when nothing bothers him?"

As it happens, I have a program for this.

MAKE OUT PUNISHMENT CARDS

All disciplinary roads lead to step four, punish the child if he fails to meet the expectation on time without supervision. This is a nettle parents are reluctant to grasp. But they must for not to do is to lay up sin and suffering for all concerned.

The best form of punishment is the removal of a privilege. What privilege? Here's a suggested list:

Lose half an hour of prime-time T.V.
Lose bike for one day
Lose half an hour outside play
Lose Lego for one day
Lose transformers for one day
Lose Cabbage Patch for one day
No game with Mom today
No story from Dad today
No computer time today
No video movie this weekend
No skiing this weekend
Lose telephone privileges for a week

Every family will have its own set of privileges. Notice that none of these amounts to a serious deprivation. They don't touch his rights, just his privileges. We aren't going to deny him his meal if he doesn't come to dinner, as our 'kindly' magazine editor recommends. None of these measures is punitive. In fact, any imaginative child can shrug them off with ease. Who couldn't find something else to do when denied his Lego for an afternoon?

It is customary for children to point this out to you. "As a matter of fact," he will say with ultimate *sang froid,* "I wasn't planning to watch T.V. this evening." and he will go off and blithely read a comic book.

This is what was getting to Frank when he said 'how can you punish him when nothing bothers him.' Frank is buying Dewey's 'sweet lemon' ploy. He shouldn't. It's probably the oldest trick in the child's book of how to deal with parents.

One of the hardest things for parents to grasp is that it's not the pain of the punishment that bothers the child, it's that you have the nerve to punish. To the omnipotent child this is *lese majeste*. The best way to deal with the 'sweet lemon' is to ignore it. Say, "if you were going to watch T.V. you wouldn't be allowed" and leave it there. He'll change his tune.*

Since Dewey's parents are going to have to punish Dewey from time to time they should prepare for this by making out punishment cards, that is choosing eight or ten chunks of privilege to remove as punishments and writing them on cards which are then stored in a little box on the top of the fridge.

"Dewey," Father explains. "These are your punishment cards. If you earn a punishment, you'll get a card. It will be posted on the fridge until it has been served and then it will go back in the box."

Punishment cards have a number of advantages. They keep you from overpunishing. They are something to show *now* when the message needs to be sent, but which you can deliver later when it's convenient. They are concrete. Children come to believe in them. Their psychological value becomes apparent when you see the child become more upset when he receives the card than later, when he serves the punishment. Punishment cards are valuable. Guard them or they will disappear.

Now we have discussed all the elements of the retraining program. All that remains now is for Frank and Lydia to go home and do it. Sometimes in my practice it is actually that easy. Usually it isn't. What I have laid out for the parents is a complicated restructuring of their parenthood. Though I have tried to limit the programs to three or four areas, assigned the task and set up the punishment cards it is a lot to remember and not easy to do. Furthermore there are sometimes parental habits to break.

Let me tell you a story about that. There is a delightful Irish lady of my acquaintance whose lifetime habit in any situation where conversation is possible is to begin talking, secure in the knowledge she will soon stumble on to something to say. This had led her into some difficulty disciplining her three children.

As children will do they would squabble in the adjoining room. When the decibels reached a certain level, Mother would go in to settle things. Conversationally speaking, these were certainly Mother's children. Each

*For a more complete exposition of this subject see Chapter Six and Appendix A.

had an explanation for the problem. Each explanation exonerated its author and vilified the nasty siblings. Each was delivered simultaneously. At the same time Mother was asking questions, not waiting for answers, and offering various homilies about brotherly love and family unity. Soon enough words to fill a good-size dictionary had been uttered and nothing settled.

I designed a program to deal with this. I now call it the Referee Program. It is becoming quite popular. Here's how it was to work. When the shrieking began, Mother was to call from the kitchen, "do you want me to come and referee?" If things did not settle down to an acceptable level within ten seconds Mother was to go in and referee.

I defined refereeing for Mother thusly. "Go in. Say nothing except 'each of you go to your rooms.' Take no history and pay no attention to any that might be volunteered. After five minutes fetch them back. 'Now! See if you can play together without fighting.'"

Poor Mother! She tried. God how she tried. But silent refereeing was not a talent vouchsafed to her. One child would, on some pretext such as having children, accuse her, the mother, of responsibility for the problem. Mother would defend herself. Another child would chime in. First thing you know it was Webster's dictionary all over again.

"I know what I'm supposed to do," Mother said. "But I forget to do it."

Her husband found the solution. He bought her a referee's whistle, fixed it upon an wide and garish band of ribbon. Then each morning when leaving for work he slung it around her neck and told her not to take it off until he returned home. The bloody thing swung and banged about her head and shoulders all day long, reminding her of her refereeing duties.

"It's working," she explained when she came in for her next visit. " 'You want me to come and referee' I call and a hush you could butter on bread falls on the place. The darling thing is working."

Next visit I got some more details. "I've expanded a little," she said. "If one of them comes out to tell, I say to him, or her, 'you want me to come and referee?'" She laughed. "He looks at me a moment then says, 'Welllll! I don't think so.'" She laughed again. "The other day after I called out my referee bit, I sneaked over to hear what was being said. 'Why don't we give Carly a turn,' himself is saying. 'Then she won't fuss and Mother won't come in and referee.'"

The serious point is that parents have to learn new habits. They have to train themselves if they are to retrain their children. This is why I spell out my programs so explicitly. So parents have something specific to keep them on track while they learn to parent better. But oftimes more is needed.

ARRANGE FOR CONTINUING SUPERVISION

The final step in my overall program is to arrange for continuing involvement until I am assured adaptive growth is back on track. There are many degrees of involvement, and the question becomes how much professional intervention from my office will it take to get Dewey's adaptive growth going again? Will the insight I have given Frank and Lydia about Dewey be sufficient, or do we need some regular guidance? Should Dewey be involved regularly too?

Sometimes a great deal of intervention is necessary; sometimes very little. Some families need little more than an explanation of the problem and some direct advice such as I have been offering Lydia and Frank. This seems to change their understanding of the child, allow them to see him through my eyes, and that simple alteration in perspective coupled with a few concrete programs does the trick. The parents call me back a month later to tell me the symptoms are practically gone. "I don't know what on earth had me so confused about that child that I let him get away with the things I did, but those times are passed, and thank you very much for your help."

Other families need regular guidance if things are to change. In this connection I have formulated a policy: the least professional intervention that will do the trick is the best. When in doubt about how much help is needed, I say to parents, "why don't you have a go on your own? I have given you an idea of the nature of the problem, and we have discussed some programs. Why don't you give those a try and come back in a couple of weeks and we'll see how things are going."

When they return I go over the situation with them. If they haven't seen some reasonable indication that they are on the right track—if the symptoms aren't diminishing with fewer tantrums or if there isn't some sign of resumed adaptive growth—then it is necessary to increase the professional input, to undertake some regular child-guidance work.

Continuing Parental Guidance

In my practice treatment means seeing the parent, or parents, once a week and also seeing the child once a week. I am not too happy to use the word "treatment" when referring to this parent-guidance work. The word implies that Mother has some "neurosis" of her own which is clouding her perception of her child and causing her to parent poorly. To be sure there are "neurotic" mothers. Adaptively incompetent children grow up to become adults with inadequate coping styles, who defend against the world rather than cope with it, and some of these become mothers. They cope with parenting as poorly as they do other aspects of their adult life. But these are a minority.

Most mothers I see are reasonably competent persons who have slid into ineffective modes of parenting. While I do believe many of these women feel guilty about their parenting, I don't think this guilt is neurotic in origin. As I have said, maternal guilt is all but universal these days. It arises because mothers have been posed the impossible task of training the child to patience, reasonable awareness of and accommodation to others, and acceptance of rational authority, and at the same time are besieged with the notion they must never traumatize the child by subjecting him to the pain of anxiety, disappointment or anger.

Since the guilt is situational, not neurotic, it does not have to be probed and analyzed. There is no deeply rooted unconscious conflict behind it. Alter the situation by smoothing out the stormy disciplinary interaction between mother and child and the guilt melts away.

There is another reason I don't like to use the term "treatment" to refer to parent guidance. Treatment has implications for many psychiatrists, psychologists and social workers which distort the guidance process. If the "therapist" thinks he is treating the mother, he may respond to her pleas for help in the management of her child's behavior with a provocatively irrelevant remark such as, "I wonder why Pammy's throwing porridge on the walls seems to bother you so much?"

Psychiatry has a rich tradition of responding to patient questions with doctor questions, usually of the "I wonder why" type. The reason given for doing this is "because Mother must find her own answers if they are to be of value to her." Somehow, leaving her to fumble herself is supposed to bring her up against her own resistances, so she can "work things through."

What it does, of course, is suggest to her that somehow her concern about porridge on the wall is abnormal, another manifestation of her inadequate capacity for motherhood. It nurtures her maternal guilt.

While the *therapist* says he responds to Mother's questions with questions for reasons of treatment, I strongly suspect there is another reason: *he has no answer to her question.* He doesn't know what to tell Mother to do about Pammy's target practice with porridge, and he ducks the issue with a neat gambit that makes a virtue of his evasive necessity.

So let's not call continuing parental guidance "treatment of the mother." Let's call it what it truly is, a collaborative effort to tailor a parenting program that will dislodge this particular child from his particular developmental dead-end. *In child-guidance work, the psychiatrist would more properly be called a child-rearing consultant than a therapist.*

To get back to our case, Frank, Lydia and I arranged to collaborate on Dewey's management. Together we set up a retraining program, choosing a couple of areas to focus on. We work out the details of the expectation, the time limit, the supervision and the reinforcement. We decided how to deal with non-programmed items. I explained the usual outcome and armed the parents to deal with Dewey's likely responses. We agreed to meet weekly, at least until we have things going well.

When we meet a week later we discuss how things went I anticipate a couple of different responses: horrible battles or sudden compliance. Dewey chose the latter. Perhaps he detected a note of assurance in his mother's voice and, not wanting to risk his omnipotence illusion in a confrontation he might lose, he chose to comply. He "fled into health," as my dynamic colleagues would put it.

"I don't understand," Lydia said. "I've been telling him that I want him up and dressed by eight a.m. and no nonsense for a year. He paid no attention before. Now, suddenly, for no reason I can see, he responds, 'as a matter of fact, Mom, I had been planning to get an early start in the mornings for some time.' And you know he hasn't missed a morning all week."

Lydia cannot understand why Dewey obeyed. To her mind she said nothing she hadn't said a thousand times before. Well, it came out differently. Lydia had the program clear in her mind and when she told Dewey about it he realized this wasn't just another stars on the chart bit he can safely ignore. He sensed the assurance in her voice and, not knowing what to make of it, decided to comply, at least until he figured out what was going on.

"It won't last," I told Lydia. "His lack of persistence will let him down once his sense of urgency fades. But that's alright. You're ready for him. Just supervise and punish when that happens."

Parents feel that unless the child copes progress is not being made, but I am as content to have the child fail and be punished as have him cope. True, in the latter case his tolerance for tedium is exercised a mite, but when he doesn't make it and is punished, he is learning something about authority, and his egocentricity is being breached.

Either way, the parent's purpose is served: either way, at least one adaptive competence is being trained.

But it isn't always that simple. Many a child doesn't make it for three mornings, has to be supervised and punished. The first two punishments he greets with an "I couldn't care less" insouciance: the third activates a tantrum. However, as I have detailed in Chapter Four, an intermittent but steady trend towards compliance is usually observed.

If, on a follow-up visit, I find the program isn't working, then I review it in detail with the parents. I usually find that some principle of discipline has not been adhered to. Perhaps, instead of telling him once and coming back when his time is up, Mother, hoping to avoid having to punish him, has checked up a couple of times and kept him moving. This doesn't teach him to worry about the time himself . . . he continues to rely upon her reminders. Indeed, the morning she doesn't remind him and he doesn't make it, he will complain, "but you didn't remind me. You always remind me a couple of times."

Perhaps Mother compromised on the consequence. "O.K. you nearly made it. I'll accept that for today, but tomorrow right on time or else you do get punished." You can be sure tomorrow he will be even further from completion when the time is up.

This is the way continuing guidance works. Through trouble-shooting, explaining, and supporting, one conducts a kind of tutorial practicum, all the time inculcating the principles of discipline and helping the parents to ventilate their concerns and clarify their prerogatives as persons. In time the parental guilt dissipates and eventually one hears some *turned the corner* phrase such as *"who's the parent around here anyway?"* or *"I don't know why I let that child bully me."*

Complications can occur and the training can get sidetracked; Deweys don't give up their omnipotence without a struggle. Sometimes they demonstrate a capacity for shrewd manipulation which, if it could ever be tempered with a little compassion, might serve them well in the adult world.

One child, who chose to comply suddenly and completely, startled his mother by not only doing all the items on his morning list promptly and on time but also adding an item. He not only washed his face, brushed his teeth and got dressed by eight a.m., but he also made his bed, and that wasn't on the list.

For four days he did this. Then the fifth day, he didn't make his bed. His mother, confused by this gambit, told him he would be punished that night.

"That's not fair," he wailed. "Making my bed wasn't on the list. Boy, are you mean. I try to be really good, and all I get is punished."

Confused and guilty his mother apologized, but he withheld his forgiveness. And the next morning he didn't brush his teeth, which *was* on the list. Still, to make up for yesterday's unfairness, Mother didn't punish him. In three days he was back to square one, and I had a busy hour helping her understand what had happened to her.

Once one has guided the parents to reasonable success with a couple of areas of retraining, signs of adaptive growth begin to appear. There is a pattern to improvement.

First there is usually a noticeable change in the frequency and amplitude of emotional outbursts. Sometimes instead of blowing up when told to do something, he goes off grumbling. "I can see he is making an effort to control himself," Mother will report. "He doesn't always succeed, but at least it seems to have dawned on him that he ought to try."

Quite frequently mothers tell me, soft amazement in their tone, "do you know what he did? He offered to set the table for me! I mean, I didn't think he realized tables had to be set, that he somehow believed the necessary implements appeared by magic when needed."

Such episodes of helpful or considerate behavior not infrequently follow upon some particularly vociferous "knock down, drag out" exchange. It is as though the child had, for the first time, realized that his mother was truly upset with him. This time his mother's state of mind seems to have dawned upon him. I'm not so much convinced he is making amends as he is trying to get back in her good graces but, at least on this occasion, his egocentricity has yielded to the point that he has been able to concern himself with the mental state of another than himself.

When he grumbles instead of defies, when he wheedles instead of insists, when he pleads instead of demands, he's beginning to surrender the omnipotence illusion.

These signs of adaptive growth are often accompanied by a change in mood, a perhaps subtle lifting of the spirit. "He seems almost happy sometimes," Mother reports. "Some of the tension seems to have gone out of him."

Some of this change may be in her. Most mothers are surprised, and pleased, to find that they can discipline him effectively, that they aren't a totally incompetent mother after all. Further, they are relieved to find that punishment does not make him hate her, and that the next day he has gotten over his anger, indeed, seems almost happier, more at peace with himself.

Now things start unwinding. Now that Dewey is getting dressed in the morning most of the time, Lydia is not so uptight, and mornings are no longer dreaded occasions. Lydia has stopped asking herself, "what is going on up there? Time is running out. I do hope he's going to have time for some breakfast."

·Now that Dewey is making it most mornings, Lydia is not only less worried, but she is also pleased with him for doing it and with herself for parenting effectively. In the mornings now there is time for breakfast, and since nobody's cross the meal has become a pleasant occasion. *Good will between mother and child has begun to be restored to family life.* With the return of good will we can start looking forward to the day when punishment will no longer be the only effective reinforcer.

Parental guidance is the most important of the three levers of change available to the child-rearing consultant. In my experience, when the program fails, it is usually because parental guidance fails.

It is not easy to face one's failures and do something about them, and despite the psychiatrist's efforts to be non-judgmental and supportive, some mothers find it too threatening to do so. They slide away from the remedial task.

Sometimes they find comfort in the notion that "food additives" are responsible for the child's tantrums and report instant success with some diet program. Perhaps they read an article about "dyslexia" and decide that their child's learning problems have nothing to do with his immaturity and limited persistence, but are owing to a hitherto unrecognized learning disability. A few decide the problem is not ineffective discipline, it is too much discipline, that Dewey ought to be treated as an equal not a child, that "natural consequence" is the royal road to raising super children. They feel they are being human and sensitive and I am inhuman and overbearing, and they depart, freed from the nitty gritty of parenting, the tough role of discipline.

However, such are a minority and by and large the results are good. Many parents get the problem under control with simply a diagnosis and a follow-up visit or two. Some require continuing guidance but three or four months usually gets adaptive growth going to the point that only intermittent consultation is needed.

Sometimes just parental guidance isn't enough. Sometimes the other lever, direct treatment of the child, needs to be added to the mix. This means bringing the child into regular office "treatment," seeing him on a weekly basis too.

Treating the Child

Children who are brought to a child psychiatrist rarely have much idea either why they are there or what is to happen. Since most of them are television sophisticated about "shrinks," they have an idea someone is trying to say something is wrong with them, if not that they are crazy, then that the family problems are their fault. So they are frequently guarded and often a little resentful, at least initially.

This is really no problem, for children are quick to change their minds given a little contrary evidence, and if the psychiatrist is willing to do more than his share of the initial communicating, one gets past this soon enough. Even so, one never gets to the point, at least with pre-adolescents, where adults begin: the "I am here because I need help—here's what's been happening to me—and this is the way I feel about it—what am I doing wrong?" posture.

So the child psychiatrist cannot lie back and wait for the child to bring the content of his life to the interview.

The child experiences this relationship as a new and independent one with an adult with as yet undefined authority, undefined instructional or helping functions, and a remotely companionate potential. Once he feels reasonably secure in the situation, he starts testing these issues.

Chances are his parents have tried to clarify this for him with declarations such as, "he will be a special friend," or "he is going to teach you how to get along with kids." But children, wherever they are born, are all from Missouri. They prefer to find out for themselves just exactly what kind of creature this "shrink" is, and what he is up to.

The best way for the parents to prepare the child for the initial interview is to focus on a concrete problem the child cannot deny he has, such as "you and I get cross with each other a lot" or "you have this trouble going to sleep at nights," and then say, "this is a doctor for that kind of problem. I've seen him and told him of the problem in our family. Now he wants to meet you, to learn more, and to find out what kind of boy you are."

In the first few minutes of the initial interview most children can sum up the situation, at least to the point that they are no longer anxious about it, providing the doctor is forthcoming and reasonably amiable.

As the child tests the dimensions of the new relationship, he does so in terms of *his* way of coping, his adaptive style. Soon the adaptive incompetencies which comprise the Omnipotent Child Syndrome are being expressed in here and now situations. It is this that provides opportunity for the doctor to generate growth in the child.

The child may have, even the previous day, got into a peer conflict situation arising, perhaps, out of his self-centered bossiness. However, if one, knowing about the situation from his mother, decides to explore it with the child, hoping to clarify for him how his egocentricity caused the difficulty, he is unlikely to succeed. This is not the way egocentricity is disillusioned in children.

In the first place, if one brings up the situation, the child will be defensive about it. "It wasn't me; it was those mean kids. They hate me." If, despite this, one persists in trying to bring out the details that will demonstrate the child's role in generating the problem, he will feel you are just trying to put him down. Then he will act on this negative understanding in some provocative way that you will have to deal with, which of course completely closes off the pursuit of insight.

Forget insight. The way to deal with egocentricity in children is not to discuss yesterday's manifestations at home or school but to deal with it as it arises in the playroom, in the here and now. If the child interacts in a self-centered way such as taking your pencil from your hand because he has decided to draw, you take the pencil back saying, "don't take mine; go get one from the pencil box on the window sill." If the child is grossly egocentric, such opportunities will arise frequently.

As one continuously requires the child to take *you* into account, one intrudes on his egocentricity, gradually teaching the child to check you out before he deals with you. This of course is the first step toward social decentering and the giving up of the egocentric posture.

Furthermore, when one will not surrender one's pencil, the omnipotent child may turn this into a cause célèbre. He insists on having your pencil. "It's got a better point." Or he may fetch another but insist on trading. He is trying not to accept your authority, your right to control him in *any* respect. If the doctor holds firm, this situation may escalate into a battle-of-wills. Now the doctor has an opportunity to deal with another area of adaptive incompetency, the child's retention of the omnipotence illusion.

Office battles-of-wills with omnipotent children are an inevitable aspect of direct *treatment* by the child psychiatrist. He learns to expect these, resigns himself to the inevitability, and assembles an armamentarium of techniques to deal with them. Success here means winning the battle and not losing one's temper.

Winning the battle means making the limits stick or, if that is impossible, giving the child a consequence for his failure to accept reasonable authority. Oftentimes, if one handles such situations lightly but firmly, allowing the child to save a little face yet communicating to him your determination and not letting him win, the child will give up. For example, in the pencil bit, I in my style might say to him, "you can't have my pencil because it was given to me by the Six Million Dollar Man because I helped him out once when he wasn't strong enough to win a battle with some crooks."

"That pencil wasn't given to you by the Six Million Dollar Man," the child says, grinning. "You just made that up."

"It sure was, and that one over there came from Superman, that one with the green kryptonite lead."

"That's not green kryptonite," he says, looking in the pencil box. "Besides, green kryptonite causes you to lose power."

"It does? I thought that was red kryptonite."

So he comes back, pencil in hand, and forgets the battle. Maybe I didn't rub his nose in it, but I won, and deep inside he knows it.

Supposing a child sets up an omnipotent challenge and keeps at it. For example, my office has a divider separating the children's area from the adult's area. There is an open passage between the two, but children are not allowed to go into the adult's area unless I take them. Some omnipotent children decide they are going to go down there anyway. I tell them no, but they ignore. I move my chair to block the passageway. They try to climb the divider. I seize them by the trousers and pull them back. All the time I am making light conversation about the necessity to remain in the child's area. The child, although he's mad, is also laughing at my nonsense.

In most cases somewhere along this progression, the child concedes. Sometimes the struggle continues. I remain firm. He may continue. Then I speak sharply to him, telling him that we've had enough nonsense, that he cannot go into the adult area. I give him a few minutes to calm down. If he returns to the struggle I tell him I am tired of restraining him and if he goes down the other end, I will punish him. "He won't get to work on his model the next time he comes in," or some such office activity which can be deemed a privilege. He may run down to the adult end anyway, but he will lose the model. It wasn't the ideal solution but a degree of omnipotence disillusionment has taken place. The next time such a thing happens he often backs off en route.

I appreciate that, if I were a pediatrician and wanted to listen to his chest, the first time he cut up I would look at him sternly, speak gruffly and probably get prompt cooperation. But I am not a pediatrician. I am a child psychiatrist. I want this child to show me himself, and I must help him to do so. I cannot make him bury his willfulness if I want to help him surrender his omnipotence illusion.

So one treads the narrow line, neither over-reacting to the child's omnipotence nor allowing him to bully, threaten or otherwise impress that unreality on this relationship. Through *action dialogue* one says to the child *you are not omnipotent.* This of course can generate stormy times, temper tantrums and battles-of-wills, but by continuing to accept the child at the same time as one limits his behavior, the doctor demonstrates to him that it is not necessary to control the world to be safe in it.

The child psychiatrist has a number of advantages over the parent in this retraining task. Since it is not *his* child, his approach is not contaminated by a sense of guilt. He does not feel *it's my fault he's this way so how can I get after him for being what I made him.* Further, the doctor sees lots of children like this. They may tell him he's a *rotten* doctor, but he's heard this lots before and he knows next visit it will all be forgotten. He's reasonably confident he can cope with this one, and the confidence helps. Finally, he sees the child for an hour only. He doesn't have to live with the problem. It's a lot easier to be firm with a child when you know if you just hang on time will rescue you.

So, when working with the child directly, the child psychiatrist deals with the adaptive incompetencies of the child as these manifest themselves in the playroom. If the child can surrender his omnipotence illusion in this relationship, if he can deal with the doctor in a less egocentric fashion, if he can develop some self-control and tolerance for unpleasure in this relationship, he can take these strengths home with him.

Direct "treatment" of the child does not uncover and interpret; it interacts and retrains. While it can supplement parental guidance it cannot replace it. It is too dilute an input for this.

The final lever the child psychiatrist can utilize is consultation with others who have a significant input in the child's life. By and large this means his teacher, but I have had occasion to consult with "nannies," grandparents, and playground supervisors.

When Deweys surface in the primary grades, they become problems to the teacher. Often they are too impatient to persist at the learning tasks, even for the brief period expected of the first grader. They are often too egocentric to perceive and accommodate to the classroom rules. They are out of their seats without permission, they talk out, daydream or disrupt. They are unimpressed with the teacher's right to require things of them, and if she insists, some of them will reveal that their omnipotence illusion is alive and well-nourished.

One principal told me of a seven-year-old child who was sent to his office from the cafeteria to be scolded for throwing food across the table. This particular child had not been there before so, when he sauntered in and started examining objects on the principal's desk, the principal was a bit taken back. First visitors to his office tend to be on the uptight side.

However, before the principal could say anything, Frankie put both hands on the edge of the desk, leaned forward, and said in a explanatory tone, "the trouble, you know, is that you don't run your cafeteria right. If you were to bring the second graders in first and let them all sit at the corner table, and have the cafeteria lady stand at the end of the food line to make sure those pesky first graders go straight to the end table, you'd probably have a lot less trouble. Of course you'd have to make sure they all go there but . . . "

Frankie gave the principal a three-minute cafeteria consultation then, with a shrug, turned. "Well, I gotta be going or I'll be late for my class." And he left.

The startled principal, fascinated by Frankie's aplomb, wasn't too sure what had happened to him, until he talked with the teacher after school.

"But that's the problem," she said, "he's so damn plausible and self-assured the first thing you know you're buying his schtick, talking to him like the adult he seems to think he is."

Classroom omnipotence is not always amusing. It can easily escalate to defiance and disrespect for the teacher's authority. Also the child's egocentricity soon alienates the group, and his impatience means he not only fails to do enough work to learn, but he also often behaves so impulsively that he disrupts the learning of others.

Parents report symptoms such as these, and when the child psychiatrist talks to the teacher she will often fill in the details, sometimes with considerable heat.

At this point a question arises. Is there some way the child psychiatrist can help the teacher teach this difficult child more successfully? Clearly, if there is, this constitutes an important opportunity to promote adaptive growth, for the teacher has the child for six hours a day. Furthermore, if things go badly in the classroom with respect to work, peers and teachers, there is a very real danger that adaptive growth will be further distorted, delayed or halted.

So consultation with the teacher has the potential of being an important lever to promote adaptive growth in children. Unfortunately this potential is infrequently realized. The reasons for this are several.

As teachers try to teach these difficult children, they try to be patient and planful, but like the parents they become frustrated and in time become angry and sometimes say or do things they know in their hearts aren't helpful. This generates guilt and not infrequently restitutive measures. So it is teachers can slip into a cycle of unproductive disciplinary relationships with omnipotent children.

Further, these days teacher guilt, while not quite so universal as maternal guilt, is still quite common. It doesn't help. By the time a teacher has had a Dewey for four months, she has exhausted her repertoire of techniques. She is beginning to feel a failure, not only because she hasn't been able to teach him, but also because she isn't too sure she likes him.

A child psychiatrist who ventures into this tense arena is liable to encounter a somewhat defensive teacher. Indeed, in some cases he may never get past the telephone.

Consultation sometimes doesn't get off the ground, but if it does, there are three things I try to do. I try to help the teacher understand how Dewey's symptoms are primarily owing to adaptive immaturity, that emotional conflict is secondary. I try to tell her that she is not required to treat him, and show her how sticking to her instructional focus offers her the best chance to promote his adaptive growth. Finally I try to help her devise methods to deal with selected problems: perhaps finishing his work, staying in his seat, or not punching kids.

Finally, I try to repair home-school communication to the point that it serves the child's interest.

While it is not the school's responsibility to rear children, and I believe they should be discouraged from incorporating such a role into their professional identity, the teacher does promote adaptive growth of all the children when she teaches well. With help she can do this for the omnipotent child too.

In our next chapter we shall deal at length with some particular symptoms and situations about which parents and teachers have a mutual concern. My goal is to help parents understand what is going on in schools these days, help them to appreciate the teacher's situation so that they can communicate successfully for the child's sake.

However improving the parenting is the most important lever for change available to the child psychiatrist. When, for one reason or another, this fails, remediation fails. When this happens the omnipotent child remains omnipotent. He grows larger, but he does not grow more patient, does not come to perceive and accommodate to the rights of others, continues to defend his omnipotence illusion against increasing odds, and can salvage little pride from his increasingly evident incompetence. He suffers, and so does the world that must find a place for him.

9

Parents, Teachers and the Omnipotent Child

"Success has a thousand fathers, but failure is an orphan."

PRESIDENT JOHN F. KENNEDY
FOLLOWING THE BAY OF PIGS CRISIS, 1961.

In this chapter I am going to discuss the cause and management of some common school-based symptoms of children. In order not to become seduced into euphemistic and abstract discussions of these tender subjects, I shall focus upon concrete situations. Let's begin with the first and most common of these school-based symptoms: learning difficulty.

Learning Difficulty

It is variously estimated that twenty to thirty percent of public school children are in significant difficulties with their learning. Doing poorly at school is probably the most common complaint that brings parents to my office.

There is no question that this symptom is one where home and school need to communicate and cooperate if the child is to be served. To do this each needs to know where the other is coming from. Let's take a look at how differently parents and educators sometimes define the role of the school.

For most parents, instruction is the primary function of the school. Parents see knowledge and skill as the way to a better life for their child, so when instruction is not going well they become concerned.

While most educators still place learning high upon the list of the school's tasks in society, some have come to see the school in quite other terms. Some see the school as the principal community social agency for children, and they feel it should love, treat, feed, and provide medical and dental care if, in their opinion, these things need doing.

As we shall see, these different perceptions of the school's task complicate dealing with the problem of the child who is learning poorly.

When an individual child is learning poorly the question becomes whether he *can't* learn, he *won't* learn, or whether he is being *poorly instructed*.

This is a difficult thing for the involved parties to determine. Since *won't* implies negatives about their parenting, Mother and Father are inclined to give first thought to other alternatives. *Poorly instructed* does not sit well with teachers so they are prone to favor other labels also.

The beauty of *can't* is that it takes them both off the hook. So, it is that Learning Disability has become such a popular diagnosis, so let's deal with *can't learn* first.

THE CHILD WHO CAN'T LEARN

Today, if a child having the mildest difficulty learning to read so much as sneezes in a fashion that seems to favor his left nostril he risks being diagnosed dyslexic. The label has become a wastebasket term. Nevertheless, true disability exists.

Disability means what is says; the child is not *able* to learn what he ought to be able to learn. *Can't* does not mean that he lacks the patience and persistence to learn; those are aspects of his adaptive maturity. Nor does *can't* mean that he has been slackly instructed. *Can't* means something is wrong with his ability to know, with his cognitive not his adaptive maturity.

Before we get in over our heads, let's define cognitive. The mind has several faculties. Chief among these is its power to *feel* and its power to *know*, that is to think and understand. Think, in this connection, means to acquire knowledge by perceiving and understanding what one perceives. It is this mental power to know that is called cognition.

So when we say *can't* we are saying that the child cannot yet manage some of the mental operations necessary for learning to proceed. In the case of reading the mental operations involve perception, that is being able to see and discriminate one letter from another, and conception, in this case being able to understand letters as symbols standing for meaning. It means also practicing and perfecting these operations so that, in time, one can decode a line of print, that is turn it into meaning. These cognitive abilities are not themselves learned: they are innate, emerging in the course of normal neurological development in the pre-school child exposed to language in his home.

For the baby the letter on the page and a fly are different only because the fly moves. But soon he sees that O is different from X. One is fat and funny and the other is squiggley and cross. In three short years he can discriminate most letters from one another. The last to come are the horizontally reversible letters, d↔b, p↔q. To discriminate these he needs to have his sides sorted out. In cognitively sophisticated circles this is known as *laterality.*

There are stages to sorting out one's laterality. Most first-grade children still reverse some letters and numbers, but by second grade almost all children know left from right and have formed the habit of beginning on the left and moving to the right. This is called sequencing.

Understand, the capacity is neurological and developed, but the conventions are man-made and learned. In China, for example, they read up and down, and Hebrew is read right to left.

There are a couple of ways the child can convert his perceptions into meaning. He can recognize a letter, know the sound it makes, sound the letters in a word out one by one, say the whole word, and then recognize it as part of the speaking vocabulary Mom and Dad have been using with him for the past six years. This is phonetic decoding.

The other method, called look and say, involves recognizing words visually, for example the word COW. Maybe in the child's mind those are the horns on the left, the belly in the middle and the haunches on the back. It does not matter how he first associates the visual pattern COW with the the four-legged, horned animal that gives milk, in time as soon as he sees COW this picture comes to mind. This the way most children eventually do most of their reading.

The important point is that when the normal maturation of the nervous system for one reason or another does not proceed at the usual pace, these important cognitive capacities are not available to the child when his schooling requires that he use them.

This is what is meant by *can't.* The child is not cognitively ready to accomplish the learning most children his age are ready to accomplish. Such a child is not just poorly motivated, he is over his depth with the schoolwork.

However, to use the term learning disability, as some school-based psychologists do, as a wastebasket category for any child in trouble learning is to degrade diagnosis to the point that remediation becomes indiscriminate and prognostication impossible.

Readiness to learn to read is a consequence of normal neurological maturation, and the usual family experience is sufficient input to serve this growth in neurologically normal children. Parents cannot accelerate this maturational process in their child, nor should they try. The 'flash cards in the crib' syndrome which has been appearing lately is just another form of trendy nonsense.

If one were to graph readiness to learn to read against age, the bell-shaped curve characteristic of normal development would appear. It would look something like Figure One. The shaded extension on the right indicates that there are a few children for whom readiness to learn to read develops outside of the normal developmental pattern.

READINESS   TO   READ

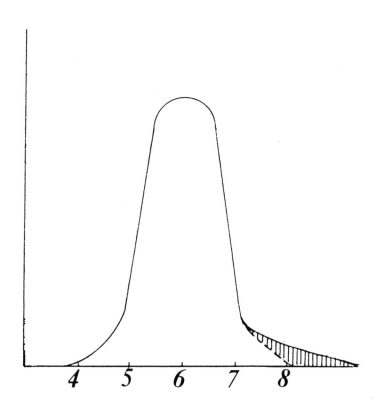

age

As this graph demonstrates, most children are ready to learn to read somewhere between the ages of five and six-and-a-half. There are a few ready at four-and-a-half, and very few ready at four. On the other side of the graph, it is apparent that some children are not ready until seven and an even smaller number not until seven-and-a-half.

These are the normal children, for neurological maturation proceeds at varying rates. None of these is learning disabled, though some on the right extremity of the bell-shaped curve may be mistakenly diagnosed as such.

The bell-shaped curve I have illustrated is distorted on its right end. This is because some children are not neurologically normal with respect to this cognitive development. These are truly disabled for reading.

Suppose you have a seven year old who is still reversing letters and whose reading is way behind most of his classmates. He could be truly disabled or he could simply be a normal child on the right side of the bell-shaped curve. In the second case, in another six months his cognitive readiness will be in place and he will proceed to learn to read. In the former case he won't improve and eventually will surface as a truly disabled child.

Leon Eisenberg, Professor of Child Psychiatry at Harvard University, says two to four percent of children in American schools are truly disabled. This means that, in a class of twenty-five second-grade children *one* at most is truly disabled for reading. However, these days many more children than that are having the label 'learning disability' attached to them by a wide variety of semi-professionals with limited understanding of the true situation.

Parents don't care about statistics. They care about their child. If you have a seven year old as I described, how can you tell if he is truly disabled or is simply a late normal who will be fine in another year? If the educational professionals have trouble differentiating these, where are parents to turn for sound guidance?

True reading disability is not easy to diagnose. But it can be done. Family history, the precise learning picture, a detailed developmental story, an extended neurological examination, and special psychological tests all contribute to making this diagnosis. Any parent whose child is labelled learning disabled ought to seek out such a proper evaluation before agreeing to special education designed to remediate his 'dyslexia.'*

Even though only two to four percent of children in trouble learning to

---

*It is not germane to this book to detail the clinical picture of either dyslexia or reading retardation secondary to minimal brain damage. Suffice it to say, dyslexia is a known disorder with a classical clinical picture and typical history. It can be diagnosed. So can reading retardation secondary to brain damage.

read are truly disabled, it is regularly estimated that twenty to thirty percent of school children are in significant difficulty with learning.* What of these others then? What is responsible for their trouble?

Well, what's left? Only two things, *won't* and *poorly instructed*. Since, in my opinion, *won't* is the common problem, let's deal with it first.

THE CHILD WHO WON'T LEARN

In the vast majority of cases, this is the child who needed supervision to get dressed in the morning, to clean his room, or to go to bed at night. He is no better at meeting the expectations of the classroom than those of home. He is not so much defiant as he is feckless. He drifts from unpleasure without knowing he has drifted. Often he also shows the other aspects of adaptive immaturity that comprise the Omnipotent Child Syndrome.

When parents bring such a child to me we will embark upon a program of remedial parenting designed to get his adaptive growth back on track. This will include measures designed to increase his tolerance for tedium. When the program starts to succeed and adaptive growth begins it often spills over into his school life and teachers report that he is working better.**

However, such improvement does not always generalize to school, and there are many children whose failure to finish their schoolwork continues to be a major problem. In such cases the symptom itself needs remedial attention. Setting this up requires cooperation between home and school. This is not always easy to arrange.

Tensions between home and school focusing upon 'whose job is it to get him to do his schoolwork' may have arisen. Though never so directly expressed, the essence of the two party's respective positions often comes down to this.

The teacher feels, "I have done my best to get him to do his work, but unless I stand right over him, nothing gets done. It's not my job to grow him up." So, when keeping him after school doesn't work, she begins

---

*There is a rare mathematical disability that is caused by neurological factors, but this accounts for very little of the overall problem.

**Sometimes the teacher does not know the family are coming to me; without permission from the parents I cannot contact her. Sometimes, not always, Teacher says to Mother, "I don't know what you are doing at home but keep it up. He's getting his work finished most of the time now." Other teachers attribute the improvement to their having moved his seat in the class, or some new method of instruction they have recently instituted. As I mentioned, *success has a thousand fathers*.

sending the unfinished work home every day. "Let Mother try and see how hard it is to get anything out of him."

The parent now struggles ineffectually on a nightly basis. Soon she begins to get frustrated too. "I'm not his teacher. I don't know what he's supposed to do. I can't explain it to him. It's her job to teach him, not mine."

Both versions contain some truth. Though the child's problem is manifesting itself in school, he did bring it from home with him. Somehow his parents failed to generate sufficient adaptive growth in this child to equip him to meet the normal expectations of the classroom. On the other hand, while it is reasonable to expect parents to get him to cope with things wholly within their purview, such as cleaning his room or getting dressed in the morning, is it to fair to expect them to enforce an expectation emanating from elsewhere?

Is it possible? Parents tend to run into this kind of resistance. "We only had to do every other problem," he says. Or, "I don't know how to carry numbers, the teacher never showed me." Or "I left my book at school." Though the parent may suspect these are just avoidance techniques, it is difficult for her to deal with them.

As we shall discuss later, communication between home and school is, at best, a shaky business. When tensions like these arise the situation often deteriorates into mutual blaming. Parents blame teachers and teachers blame parents, and the child psychiatrist who ventures into this no man's land may end taking flak from both trenches.

Getting the child to finish his schoolwork is such a common problem that I have constructed a program to deal with it. When I am able to secure the cooperation of both parties this program works well. However, when the teacher will not cooperate, which is the more common problem, the program fails.

The fact that teachers are the ones who sink the program is not because teachers are more contrary than parents; it is because I have no leverage with them, no way to get past their normal resistance to having an outsider come and tell them how to teach.

With parents I have leverage. My treatment role gives me a mandate. Parents come to me for help. They hope I will tell them what to do about their child. When I do, they are disposed to cooperate. This puts me in a position to short circuit their 'blame the teacher' defense; to move them past blaming into remedial planning.

In most cases I have no such 'mandate' with teachers. They didn't ask for my help, and when I arrive on the scene they wonder if I am those mindless twits whose only prescription is 'give him more love.' Or perhaps that I am going to 'analyze' them! Or perhaps that I am there as the parent's 'lawyer' to put all the blame on them! Regardless of reason, many teachers are not disposed to give me much opportunity to explain my program. .

If the teacher does not understand the program or is unwilling to implement it, the program will fail. Similarly, if the parents do not do their part, the program will fail. But if both work at it, pay attention to its details, and persist, in many cases we see a distinct improvement in the child's work-finishing behavior within a couple of months.

The program is based on the principles of discipline framework I enunciated earlier in this book. Let me first repeat those principles, then describe the program, explain the reasoning behind its several details, and finally answer the common questions teachers and parents raise concerning it.

Principles of Discipline

1. A clear expectation
2. A time limit
3. Supervision if necessary
4. Punish if supervision required
5. Persist

*Program For Parental Reinforcement of Schoolwork Expectations**

INDICATION   The program is being instituted because of the following considerations:

1. The child is capable of doing the work.
2. The child is not *completing* his regularly assigned work.
3. The teacher has exhausted her normal remedies.

Under these circumstances it is reasonable that the parents support the teacher's expectation that the child complete his work.

GOAL   The goal of the program is the *completion* of classwork. It is assumed that if a child of reasonable intelligence completes all his classwork he will absorb sufficient information and acquire adequate facility with the subjects involved.

Initially the quality of the work is not a prime consideration. While this is not a matter of indifference it is felt that the first goal should be limited to completion. Later a dimension of quality may be added to the program.

METHOD   In order to modify the child's perception of his responsibility in the learning process it is necessary that he experience *clear-cut ex-*

*This program was first published in *Children Today*. It was reprinted in the *1981 Yearbook of Educational Psychology*.

pectations and *predictable consequences* if he fails to meet those expectations. This involves assignments, time limits for their completion, prompt detection of failure to complete, and reinforcing action consequent on that failure.

Assignments: The teacher assigns work. The child fails to do it. The teacher applies her normal reinforcer: miss the movie, stay in at recess, or remain after school. He still doesn't do the work. Now what? We institute the program. If the parent is to offer effective support to the teacher's expectations she needs to know precisely what was assigned and what was not done if she is to play her part in the program. So the teacher has to accumulate this data and send it home Friday. (We are speaking here of regular seat work, not long-range assignments.)

Communication: A foolproof method of communication between teacher and parent must be set up. Here's my version. All the work that was not completed that week is *sealed* in a large manila envelope and sent home Friday. If all the work has been completed a note stating this should be placed in the envelope and the envelope sent anyway.

Trusting the child to bring the envelope home is like asking the fox to guard the chickens, but since this is the principal method of communication between parent and teacher we have to try our best to make it work. Children have been known to *lose* such envelopes. When this happens mothers have been known to misinterpret the situation. "Wonderful," she says. "He's finished all his work this week." By the time the truth outs a week later both parent and teacher are inclined to fault the other for the communication breakdown. Meanwhile the child has learned what nobody wanted to teach him, to wit: with a little ingenuity he can work the system and continue on his effortless path through life.

However, if Mother begins the program by handing the teacher ten dated manila envelopes on day one and explains the need for regular communication even if everything has been done, this situation can be minimized. Then if no envelope arrives and he declares, "I guess the teacher forget to make me one," Mother should post haste to the school, himself in tow, roust out the custodian, and search her child's desk. In many cases, en route to the school, the story will change. "Oh yes! I remember now. She gave me an envelope. I musta left it in my desk." But he won't try that again.

Communication failure can sink the program, and some children can find chinks in any system. One child of my acquaintance showed marvelous ingenuity in this respect. Every week he came up with a new envelope-disappearing gimmick. His mother finally rose to the occasion. She arranged for a courier to pick up the envelope at three-fifteen every

Friday afternoon. After five Fridays of proving she really meant business, she added another dimension. If she had to continue using the courier, she would but it would cost him, either that week's video movie rental or his next ski day. Would he like to try bringing the envelope home himself? That was the end of the communication problem.

Reinforcement: Once the parents have the unfinished work, they now have to set up the *expectation* that he do it. Here's the best way to do that. Though chances are he won't listen, begin with an explanation of the program.

"It's your job to do your schoolwork. In the class! When Miss Farrell expects you to! There's no way she can teach you if you don't do your work. She has tried her best to get you to do it but by the end of the week there's a lot not done. So now your Dad and I are going to take a hand. Here's the deal. Miss Farrell is going to send the unfinished work home in a sealed envelope every Friday, and you are going to get another chance to finish the work. You are going to have another half-day school per week: starting at nine a.m. Saturday and finishing at noon Saturday, or when the work is finished, whichever comes first."

It doesn't have to be Saturday morning if another time suits Mother best, but it should be the same time each week. A place should be arranged with a table and materials, but no toys, comic books or other distractions should be available. Mother can give him a ten-minute recess if she wants to but there he is to be until the work is finished or noon arrives, which ever comes first.

·The parent is cautioned not to extend the time if he hasn't finished. When noon comes, check what he's done, put it back in the envelope with a note to his teacher saying, "as you can see he didn't finish it, but he did lose his Saturday. Hang in!"

There is no way a parent can make a child do schoolwork he is determined not to do. And if you try, say by keeping him in that room all weekend, after two weekends you're bound to weaken. All you can do is what is reasonable to do, so just persist in that.

You could sit beside him for the three hours and keep him moving, but this merely exercises *your* persistence. It does nothing for your child's, and it is exactly what we are trying to get out of having to do, supervise him all the time.

The teacher gets the envelope back on Monday. Seeing so little done, she may become discouraged. "What's the use, he didn't do the work?" she says to herself. She has lost sight of the fact that we are more interested in *training* the child to do his work without supervision than we are with the actual work itself. She is reminded of the following realities:

1. He wasn't completing his work anyway, so while we still haven't yet gained anything, workwise, neither have we lost ground.
2. Not doing the work has cost him his Saturday morning and promises to do so again next week.
3. Home and school have communicated and presented a united front which serves notice to him of a new order of things.

COURSE OF THE PROGRAM   The first Saturday the child twiddles his thumbs. "You can't make me do that dumb work you know." And he whistles and sings and variously conveys the information that he is not suffering in that work area you have arranged for him.

The next week he tries to foul up the communication, but we are ready for him and the envelope gets where it is supposed to be. Again he refuses to work. Some will try bargaining: "tell you what. You let me watch cartoons this morning and I guarantee to do the work Sunday night." The right answer, of course, is "no way, José!" To this he will probably reply, "O.K. then, I won't do the work." And he won't. Even so, when the time's up, let him go. Pack up the unfinished work and send it back to school Monday.

The third Saturday one of two things happens. He may throw a royal tantrum including this type of monologue: "Boy! Who do you think you are trying to make a slave out of me? It's dumb work. I'm not doing it. As soon as I'm sixteen I'm dropping out of school," etc., etc., etc.

Go away and ignore.

The other thing he may do is dash off the work Friday night and say, "you can't give me your dumb old extra half day school. I've already done the work. Ha! Ha!"

There are a couple of ways to handle this. You might say, "oh, phooey" and look as if he's ruined your fun with his improvement. Or you might say, "fine. Enjoy your cartoons. But I've got an even better idea—do your work during the week, and you won't have to do it Friday night."

The fourth week there is half as much unfinished work in the envelope. What has happened? Some variant of this. Sometimes when he gets stuck on a piece of seatwork during class and is about to quit on it he thinks, "Migawd! I'll see that Saturday," so he takes another run at it. Sometimes, when he is sitting in after school with Wednesday's work in front of him, (the teacher should continue her normal reinforcers) instead of whiling the time away daydreaming, he does some of the work, again to lighten his Saturday.

The important thing to note here is that the voice which now gets him moving is not his teacher's or his mother's; it's his own. He is beginning to build an inner policeman with views about finishing schoolwork. From then on he does more and more at school, either in class or afterwards, and soon there is little coming home in his Friday envelope. After eight weeks most of his work is being finished in class. Even so, the program must remain in place for at least the ten weeks for which we prepared envelopes, and longer is there's any sign of slipping.

CONCLUSION   The purpose of the program was to lead the child to police himself vis à vis his schoolwork. He can think it's dumb work if he wants to. That is his opinion, but the other kids do it and so should he. Self-expectations begin as external expectations. If these are communicated through well-planned and consistent action-dialogue such as the program I have just described internalization of these expectations takes place. And with this comes adaptive growth.

By the time the child finishes elementary school he should have internalized his work expectations. He should feel "it is my work and I have to do it." With this attitude he is ready for the independent learning upon which success in high school depends. If he has not developed such a sense of responsibility for his work, then he is unready for high school and will sink when he gets there. More of this situation later.

Problems and Questions About the Work Finishing Program

The biggest problem I encounter with this program is getting teachers to go along with it. There are a variety of reasons for this. In the first place, it puts an extra burden on them. Some are willing to go this extra mile, but some are not. Others are convinced it will not work. They have tried sending an assignment book home, usually *daily*. They have seen the *communication* break down because the child loses the book either on the way home or on the way back. Sometimes, by sending the book daily, they pull Mother into nightly supervision of the child's work, which gets it done but does nothing for his work habits. Furthermore some now complain that "Mother does all his work for him."

Another reason teachers reject the program is that it makes demands on the child. "Children should want to learn," they say. They should indeed, and some do. Those children don't need a work finishing program. However we are talking about the sixteen to twenty-six percent of children who are not disabled and are learning poorly. Most of these children's desire to learn is not strong enough to keep them moving. Nor is their sense of obligation to the task.

There is a program many teachers prefer. It is called the contract system. This is the way it works. The teacher and the child sit down and decide how much work he is to do that day. A contract is drawn up and both sign it.

The trouble with the contract system is that, while it may extract agreement from the child, it does not guarantee performance. If the child ignores the contract, as many do, how then is the teacher to get him to do the work?

Why is the contract system so attractive to the educators? Because of this notion that the child should want to do his work. Many teachers will say, "so long as I make him do the work, he will never learn to make himself do it." This is wrong thinking. The real question is, unless somebody makes such children do the work, can they ever learn to make themselves do it? Furthermore, as we have just seen, a well-designed program to make him do the work eventually ends with the child policing himself.

Another reason teachers are attracted to the contract system is that it allows them to rationalize reducing their expectation of the child. This often stems from their concern for the child's self-esteem. "If I lower my sights a bit; give him a lesser task at which he can succeed, I'll give him a taste of success, and that will help his damaged self-esteem."

Though children who are not finishing their work usually have self-esteem problems, I do not think the contract system will help with these. In the first place, since it cannot guarantee performance and these children are automatic evaders of unpleasure, the child may not complete even the lowered expectation. In the second place, even when he does complete the work his self-esteem is often not served. Let me give you a little example from my practice.

A child told me about his *contract.* "I don't have to do the regular amount of work. Each morning Miss Gillis and I write down how much I agree to do that day."

"Agree?"

"Yep! I have to sign and everything."

"How much do you usually agree to do?"

"Not much," he replied, giving me a sidelong look.

"What if you don't finish everything? Do you have to stay after?"

"Nope. Miss Gillis doesn't believe in detentions."

"What does she do then?"

"She spazzes a little then tells me to take it home and do it. But next day she mostly forgets to ask for it."

"Tell me, are you the only kid in the class on a contract?"

"Nope! Ryan's on one. He's dumb too."

'He's dumb too!' Where the self-esteem in that statement? With my program, teachers frequently object to sending the envelope weekly. It's too infrequent they say. He'll get way behind. However, the fact is he already is way behind. The program does not create that situation; it just does not correct it immediately.

The teacher does not always appreciate that the goal of adaptive matura-tional programs is not merely to *control* the involved behavior but to *train* the child out of it. Too little supervision does not alter the behavior; too much does not train. By using a weekly envelope we leave room for the child to improve. To be sure, at first when improvement begins, most of the work that gets done will be done at or near the weekend, but in time, increasing amounts of it are being finished in the class. And with no super-vision except that now emanating from his inner policeman.

Some teachers, as soon as work finishing improves, start to complain about the quality of the work, so they put completed work in the envelope for him to "do over because it's so untidy." Though this may not be the teacher's intention, such will sabotage the program.

Look at it from the child's point of view. "I finished almost everything and I still got a full envelope. What's the use of doing the dumb work; nothing satisfies old Gillis." The program has had its natural reward re-moved from it. If I were the child I wouldn't do her 'dumb work' either.

Once the program has been running well for twelve weeks, it is now rea-sonable to add a dimension of quality to it. But the teacher shouldn't sneak it in. She should announce it. In terms such as the following:

"Johnny, since we started the envelopes you have got a whole lot better. You finish almost everything in class time now, and that's eight hundred percent better than things used to be around here. Some of the work was not too tidy, but I told myself, never mind, Johnny's getting it done and that's a whole big improvement. But some of it's still pretty untidy, so I'm going to have to change the program a little. Sometimes when a piece of work is really untidy I'm gonna have to ask you to do it over and hand it in again. And if you don't find time to do that by Friday, then it will be in your envelope.'

Johnny may protest what he will see as moving the goalposts in the middle of the game, but the teacher should hold firm. "Listen Johnny, you really coped with finishing your work, and in only ten weeks. You can cope with this too. I know you can."

Most teachers are not so defensive that they cannot change their tune when they see things are beginning to work. But some are. For others the program is just too much work. Without the teacher's whole-hearted cooperation the program will not work. When teachers are not prepared to extend themselves for the child, I cannot design a program that will work.

The same is true of parents. If they are too lazy, or too disorganized, or too soft-hearted to stick to their guns, the program will fail. When parents are not prepared to extend themselves for their child, I cannot design a program that will work.

When the child 'won't' learn, and nothing effective is done about his condition, he fumbles along grade to grade, scraping through. Very often the question of passing him to the next grade or retaining him in this arises. Parents must participate in that decision, and they need to understand the pros and cons.

Should the Child Pass or Fail His Grade?

To pass or not to pass is a difficult situation for educators. If the school elects to fail normally intelligent children people begin to wonder how well they are doing their job. If the educators pass children who have not learned what they were supposed to have learned the schools get into another kind of trouble. This is called social passing, and schools have been arousing considerable community ire by indulging in it. Some American states such as Florida have outlawed social passing. Others have been passing minimal competency laws, that is requiring a 'minimal competency' for high-school graduation. Even so, decisions to pass or fail must be made and parent as well as teachers have to be involved in that decision.

The specific situation I want to deal with here concerns the parents who are told in late spring that the school is considering retaining their child in his present grade, and what do they think of the plan? Many come to me with this problem. Over the years I have had to learn how to advise them about it.

Again the issues come down to *can't* or *won't*. Let's deal with the first. Can the child cope with the learning task that will be required of him in the next grade? It is now more than a matter of intelligence or disability.

Of course children of limited intelligence will peak somewhere and passing him beyond this level is cosmetic. Similarly, dyslexic children will eventually be unable to succeed when learning has become wholly dependent upon reading; some special educational method will be necessary if their learning is to proceed.

However, for the cognitively normal child another factor has come into the equation. *Won't* has had a little piece of *can't* added to it. This is a thing I call Learning Deficit. An avoidant child who never does his work soon accumulates such a deficit. Though he is normally intelligent he hasn't done enough work to learn what he is supposed to have learned. A simple example might be the sixth grader who still hasn't learned his times tables. The measure of Learning Deficit is not the report card; it is achievement testing.

All children are given standardized tests in each school subject. In Canada the commonest such test is the Canada Test of Basic Skills. Most psychologists have more sensitive achievement instruments in their testing armamentarium. The child receives a grade level score which tells us his situation with respect to the major subjects; for example he may score fifth month of fourth grade in math, eighth month of fourth grade in reading. Now the question arises, if he is just completing fifth grade should he go on to sixth, when his achievement testing tells us he may be over his head if he does so?

This is the kind of picture one is liable to encounter in a child with normal intelligence but poor work habits. In the case illustrated the decision to retain is fairly obvious. However, a child of superior intelligence and poor work habits may, despite his lazy ways, score above grade level on his achievement testing. He's bright enough to pick up the information despite doing little class work. Such a child will not be overwhelmed by passing, and retaining him is questionable thing to do. However his report card has been a symphony of 'D's' 'E's' and 'Incompletes' with the odd 'A' thrown in for a subject that turns him on. The problem in such a case is that, though he certainly doesn't deserve to pass, surely failing him is lowering the sights for him and pandering to his laziness.

In my view the *first consideration with respect to the decision to pass or fail is to determine where the child's achievement levels say he ought to be.* If this information is not available to me from the school, I get testing done. I want to know his I.Q. and his achievement levels, so that I can help the parents think their way through the decision.

The second consideration is the crucial one. If he's managed to slop along the whole of fifth grade doing little or no work, how will another year of the same help him? So the second consideration is, regardless of which grade is decided to be best for the child, *how is he to be trained out of his ineffective work habits this time around?*

If he is not so trained in another year the question will arise again. And again the year after. In time the ultimate question arises, is he ready for high school? Because if he isn't, he is on the brink of losing his education entirely.

Before turning to this subject let me comment on one aspect of failing the child that looms large in the minds of most parents and teachers. What will failing do to a child whose self-esteem is already shaky? The answer is that it will be a blow to him. But not an overwhelming one. All year he has scraped along. He already sees himself as a poor learner. Failing does not create that situation; it confirms it. However, we have determined he will be over his head if he passes, else we would not retain him. What would being low man on the totem pole all next year do for his self-esteem?

In my experience I have found that children who are retained soon get over the blow. Indeed those who felt retaining the child would shake him up and make him work harder next year are often distressed to see how little effect retention has had on his work habits. If he is teased, and he probably will be for the first week of the year, it will not be by the children in his new class, it will be by those who have left him behind. However these soon lose interest in him now that he is no longer a member of their group. So if all the factors point to retention as being the wise course, then it should happen and the child supported through the distress it causes him.

But Is He Ready for High School?

Many children these days come to the end of seventh grade unready for independent learning, which means of course unready for high school. How so? In my opinion by the time children finish seventh grade they ought to have the following three things well in hand:

1. They should have learned to work independently, without teacher supervision.
2. They should have developed a sense of obligation toward their learning: "It's my work; I ought to do it."
3. They should have experienced enough success so that, should they stumble, they will first look inside themselves for the correction, not immediately seek out the teacher for advice.

If the elementary school has taught them well and *required* them wisely, they will possess these qualities and be able to cope with high school. However many children now arrive at high school not having acquired the capacity for independent learning. The problem soon surfaces. The high-school teachers don't feel responsible for the situation. "He came up from elementary that way. What do they expect me to do? I've four classes and a hundred kids. If he's prepared to learn, I'm prepared to teach him. Otherwise, send him to the counselor."

What happens to these unready children? They drift along completing some assignments, copping out on others. The child's minimal tolerance for the unpleasure of classwork regularly lets him down. Soon he is way behind. He discovers most teachers rarely take attendance, and since he's liable to get in the soup if he shows up to class, he begins spending his time in the 'smoke hole,' commiserating with others of like persuasion. Soon he's in the counselor's office wanting to drop French and never mind if he is forever closing off some of his college options by doing so.

It is Christmas before the computer spits out the truth about their minimal performance and the parents receive their first warning notices. "Nobody told me he was skipping classes," Father complains. "He's in high school now," the counselor responds, "we can't stand over him you know." And he goes on to raise the question, since eighty percent of the children are coping with the system, why not this one?

This child is about to board what I have called the Blackboard Express.

This is a railroad that departs from the high school three or four times a year. It provides a one-way trip to educational oblivion. Let's take a short look at the itinerary of that journey.

The first hamlet on that journey involves a layover of uncertain duration. It is called the LEARNING ASSISTANCE CENTER. Most of its inhabitants are more disinclined to learn than unable. From here the children are routed to a variety of way stations. These include such whistle stops as STUDENT TUTORING, CONSUMER MATH, FUNCTIONAL ENGLISH, or COMMUNITY STUDIES (a euphemism for afternoons checking out such service organizations as the beach, the recreation center and McDonald's). Soon the child is on the rails again heading for the twin cities of PARTIAL PASS and DOUBLE PROGRAMMING. Now he is coming to the border that separates school and community where is located that ambivalent city known as WORK STUDY PROGRAM. Leaving here he arrives at a covey of villages collectively known as ALTERNIA. They bear such names as SWAT, SWET, and SWAP. Now does he approach the end of his journey, the tar paper shacks of DROP-OUT.

What a waste! Children who might have gone to college pumping gas. What a loss to themselves, and to society! In these times we cannot afford to waste minds in this fashion. No parents want this for their child, and when sixth or seventh grade makes it clear this outcome is almost upon them, they become desperate. Sometimes they blame the school for teaching the child poorly and passing him along from grade to grade despite his poor achievement.

If they are knowledgeable about such matters they martial the evidence. They point to the fact that twenty percent of college freshman are so defective in language skills that they have to take a remedial English course before they can cope with college-level learning. It has been widely publicized that, in the United States, Scholastic Aptitude Test scores have begun falling for the first time in over a hundred years.

These days many are questioning how well the schools are instructing children, and there has been a strong move for more accountability in education. It has increasingly been recognized that throwing money at the problem does not solve it. There is a growing move toward private education and a demand for tax arrangements to support this option for parents who choose it. More and more parents of primary grade children are opting for home instruction. There is a feeling public education has lost its way and it's time for real change.

Earlier I said the child who is not learning well either *can't* learn, *won't* learn, or is being *poorly instructed*. I have dealt with the first two of these. It is time to consider the third.

POOR INSTRUCTION IN THE SCHOOL

In order to instruct a child properly his teacher must provide him with information and show him how to perform certain mental operations. Then she must *require* him to absorb this information and develop his skills through practice. Instruction has two parts then: *informing* and *requiring*.

I do not believe that most public schools are instructing children well these days. The problem is not usually with *informing*, although fad teaching methods come and go. The problem is with *requiring*. A number of factors have contributed to undermining quality of instruction with respect to its *requiring* aspect.

One of the major factors is that many educators are no longer serious about instruction. These feel the school has more important tasks to perform for the community. Such have swung the school away from instruction into other societal roles. While many school people claim it is society that is foisting these roles upon them, I am not persuaded that this is so.

What roles? Here is a short list of these educator-assumed roles, which of course, always trickle down to the classroom teacher for implementation. How would you like to have such a job description as this?

"Be's" for Today's Teacher

1. Be provider of love for unloved children
2. Be psychotherapist to the child with psychological symptoms
3. Be sex educator to the child
4. Be abuse educator to the child
5. Be drugs educator to the child
6. Be AIDS educator to the child
7. Be values educator to the child
8. Be social reformer especially with respect to:
   Abortion
   Racism
   Nuclear war
9. Be detective to find and report sexual and physical abuse of children
10. Be policeman of children's behavior in class and on the playground
11. Be the child's instructor
    (if there is any time left)

How did all this come about? Let's examine the recent history of this redefinition of education. In 1962, Eli Bower, an American educator, defined the function of the school thus: "today public education has found itself facing the task of providing the intellectual, social and affective nutrients to children."

I don't know exactly what Bower means by social nutrients, probably having the school provide health care, clothing and lunches. However I can figure out what affective nutrient means. Since affect means feeling, and nutrient has supply connotations, it means providing love. Bower has decided, albeit he implies the task was thrust upon the school, that schools should take over the parents' function of loving the child.

In the first place, how dare he!

In the second, how silly! The teacher has twenty-five children for a maximum of six hours a day. That's three hundred and sixty minutes. Divide that amongst twenty-five children and you get a little less than fifteen minutes per child, per day. During this fifteen minutes the teacher is supposed to fill all those other roles assigned her, teach the child to read and write, and at the same time provide the child with his missing *affective nutrients?* Woe to the child whose chief source of affective nutrient is his teacher.

But the story continues. Shortly after Bower's pronouncement a fellow called Earl Kelly decided to run with this ball. He invented a thing he called 'affective education.' This meant education primarily concerned with feeling, not with cognition. Kelly said so. He declared, "how a person feels is more important than what he knows." He went on to define the teacher as a "conditioner of emotional responses."

Suddenly the teacher as instructor had become pretty small potatoes compared to the teacher as therapist, don't you think?

What was happening then and has burgeoned since was that education was being skewed away from instruction into a primary concern for the child's emotional well-being. The teacher was being told that her job was to make sure the child was happy. Like the mother of the fifties, the teacher was having her function redefined for her. She was to be child's nurturer not his trainer.

Instruction has two parts, *informing* and *requiring*. *Requiring* is expecting the child to do the work necessary to learn. It is a form of discipline. If the teacher is led away from *requiring* the child by some excessive concern for his affective well-being, he will neither learn nor will he grow adaptively in the classroom.

Perhaps parents have sent children to school with less adaptive maturity than they ought to have, but teachers have dropped this ball too. In trying to be all things to the child, they have stopped providing the one thing he has most right to expect from them, that is good informing *coupled with firm requiring*.

It is in this sense then that some children fail to learn because they are being *poorly instructed*. This need not be so. Teachers can bring the same understanding to their methods of *requiring* as I have suggested parents bring to their *discipline*. At the end of this chapter I shall explore this with an example. For the moment I would like to describe a couple of ways principals could, if they have a mind to, set up programs to *require* the work-avoidant child more effectively by simply redefining the boundaries of the school a mite.

The question is, can I persuade some elementary school principal that he could do a good deal to prevent children buying a ticket on the Blackboard Express if he implemented the following program? Are the principals prepared to swim against the tide and give the program a try? Here's the program. It's called Academic Detention and I stole it from a private school in Connecticut.

The children in a particular grade, perhaps fifth, are told that they are required to complete all their seat work by Friday. If any seat work is unfinished the child is assigned to Academic Detention. His parents are called and told that they are to bring the child to school Saturday and deposit him in the study hall at nine a.m. The classroom teacher then makes sure all the unfinished seat work gets into the duty teacher's hands Friday afternoon.

Saturday morning the child is given his seat work and told to do it. The duty teacher helps if necessary, maintains order but leaves him to do it. When noon comes, whether the work is done or not, she dismisses him. The program continues as long as the child needs it.

If this program is instituted in late September there will probably be enough children in need to warrant starting it. By October the study hall will be full. Usually, by mid-November, there are very few children on Academic Detention. And later, when the children know Academic Detention is a regular part of the instructional methodology of their school, it's mere existence will have an effect.

If some daring public school principal were to institute this program he would receive three benefits. The local high schools receiving his children would begin to remark upon how most children from his school came to them ready for independent learning, and they would wonder what his secret was. The second benefit he would receive is that the parents in his district would think he was one fine educator going to so much trouble for their children. Finally he would like himself for doing his job wisely and well. With all these potential benefits, how is it no principal seems interested in implementing Academic Detention in his school?

Since so many elementary school teachers are requiring poorly these days, and Academic Detention is not being implemented, many children are arriving at high school unready for independent learning. What is to be done about them?

As it happens, I have a program. It's called Night Prep. Again I have had no success interesting high school principals in my program. However, should one of them implement it, I think some of the same benefits might accrue to him as that elementary principal.

The way it works is this. For the first month of high school the work of the new eighth graders is monitored carefully; it is not supervised, but close track is kept of who is doing it and who isn't. What we are trying to do is flush out the non-independent learners.

Once we have done so, all the flushees are placed on Night Prep. This means their parents are to bring them to school at seven p.m. The children will then do their homework in the study hall, under the supervision of the duty teacher, until nine p.m. when they will be dismissed. This will occur Monday to Thursday nights inclusive.

Children are assigned to Night Prep for two-week periods, at the end of which their situation will be reviewed. If there is indication of improved classroom performance they will be relieved of Night Prep, pro tem. This means they are still being monitored and if Night Prep again becomes indicated they will be re-assigned to it.

Though the children may not work that diligently during Night Prep they should not be stood over. Improvement shows up in not needing Night Prep, not in using it efficiently. Again, once the children believe it is there waiting for them, fewer will need it. I believe such a program would soon turn a significant number of non-independent learners into independent learners and so cancel a number of tickets on the Blackboard Express.

But I fear that educators have more important fish to fry than these wee herrings. If the choice is between education to reform society and simple old-fashioned instruction of children, which course will the educational heavy thinkers opt for? I fear it will not be my wee herrings.

Before turning to the subject of home-school communication I would like to discuss a common syndrome that surfaces in schools. This is the problem of the child who suddenly refuses to attend school, the misnamed School Phobia child.

The Child Who Refuses to Attend School

Up until 1961, when I first drew attention to the 'refusal' nature of the pattern,* these children were believed to have developed a phobia: that is,

---

*"The Child Who Refuses to Attend School," The American Journal of Psychiatry, 18, No. 5 (November 1961).

it was believed they were displacing some inner anxiety onto the school and then avoiding the now phobic object. Since then it has become generally recognized that the dynamics of phobia do not apply to this clinical syndrome. One of the reasons this is important is because it means forcing the child to attend school is not going to precipitate a panic attack, and this is the case. The refusing child does not get panicky when forced to go to school; he gets hopping mad.

The school refusing child is usually an omnipotent child strongly attached to his mother. Like Japan's *ochi benki* or angel lion, outside of home his omnipotence illusion is concealed. But it is within him and it is strong. Oftimes his school refusal is precipitated by a threat to this illusion. His teacher may have made it clear who is in charge of the class, presented him with the realization that if he continues with her sooner or later he is going to lose a battle-of-wills. It is to preserve his omnipotence illusion that he declines to enter her arena any more.

The first step in treating this disorder is to get the child back into regular school attendance. This is not just because we are dealing with a battle-of-wills and omnipotence devaluation depends upon the child losing such battles. We must do so for the refusal symptom is progressive. The longer a child is out of school, the harder it is to get him back, so the sooner one grasps this nettle the better.

The matter then comes down to the logistics of return. Somebody has to escort the child to school and somebody has to receive and retain him when he gets there. This can be a stormy business and mothers need a lot of support to accomplish it.

There is one asset here that is sometimes overlooked. Since these children often 'have their mother's number' and fathers are more likely to tough out battles-of-wills, involving the father in the conveying process may be necessary, at least initially. It may be enough simply to separate the mother from the child in the mornings, and actual escort to school may not be necessary. This may be accomplished by sending Mother to the neighbor's right after breakfast and have Father dispatch the child out the door twenty minutes later. If this method is used, don't tell the child where Mother is or, instead of going to school, he will join her there. Or someone may have to escort the child to school.

In this case it is sometimes necessary for someone to receive the child at school and keep him there for the few minutes it takes for his inner turmoil to settle. This task usually falls to the principal. Smiling firmness and a tight grip are the essential ingredients of this management. But don't let him go home for lunch or you'll have to do it all again the same day.

With the use of such methods most school-refusing children are usually brought back into attendance quite quickly. If, at the same time, the parents are being guided toward making up some of the missing adaptive growth, the fundamental problem of failed omnipotence devaluation may ultimately be solved.

If return to school fails the child should be admitted to hospital, preferably a children's psychiatric ward where the child can be kept for a week, to be dispatched from there to school on a daily basis. When attendance is under control, then return home can be considered.

The psychological impact of such hospitalization is twofold. It 'separates' the child, and it 'wins the battle-of-wills.' If such hospitalization is not undertaken and the child does not return to school the problem will become chronic, adaptive growth will cease and the child will join the myriad walking wounded of our society.

Home-School Communication

Before closing this chapter with a discussion of classroom management, I'd like to spend a short time on a subject of considerable importance to children. Though the parent and the teacher have a mutual concern for the well-being of the child, they often communicate poorly with each other. When this happens it is the child who suffers most.

The schools have formalized communication with home with two devices. These are the parent-teacher conference and the report card. As communication devices they function adequately only so long as there is nothing significant to communicate. They are lightning rods that work perfectly except during electrical storms. Let me begin by discussing the parent-teacher conference.

THE PARENT-TEACHER CONFERENCE

There was a mother once who found herself unexpectedly pregnant. Since her youngest child was nearing the end of elementary school, she was not altogether delighted by this fresh excursion into motherhood. When her friends commiserated with her she responded, "it isn't the night feedings you know. Or even the diapers." She paused and sighed deeply. "I'm just not sure I can cope with parent-teacher conferences again."

Let me tell you, teachers don't find the encounters exhilarating either.

The parent-teacher conference has become a kind of verbal *pas-de-deux* that meticulously avoids areas of possible strain. Mothers are motivated for this by their fear that their parenting failure is about to be laid out before all the world in bitter detail. At the same time teachers are much inclined to avoid alarming the parents, "at least yet." However, the teacher's motive may not be so kindly as it sounds; often it stems from her suspicion that eventually responsibility for the problem will be laid on her doorstep. So first time out, both parties smile and exchange a lot of small talk.

However, a month later, unable to take it any more, the teacher calls up the mother and tells her of the latest outrage she has had to endure from 'that' child. "Furthermore," she concludes, "he's been doing that kind of thing all year." At this point the parent utters an anguished "why didn't you tell me before?" And that, as Bridget O'Leary was wont to say, is how the fight started.

What has happened is that the child, for one reason or another, hasn't coped with the normal expectations of the classroom. That is no big deal. Lots of kids are like that. It isn't necessarily that they have been badly parented. This child may have been one of those any parent would have had trouble rearing. Further, the teacher always has to work more teaching some children to accommodate to and accept the expectations of the classroom. That he is one doesn't necessarily reflect upon the teacher's competence either.

The thing to be emphasized is that there is no place for the assignation of blame in such communications. Blame harvests no apples. What is needed is for parent and teacher to share their understanding of the child and coordinate their efforts to grow him up, despite himself.

THE REPORT CARD

The report card is another formalized communication device that oftimes conceals as much as it communicates. By changing the marking system from letter grades, to checks, then to euphemisms such as 'needs strengthening' and then back again a few years later, the educators make sure it stays that way. Since some parents see the report card more as a measure of how well their child is being taught than how well he is learning, guess who they think is concealing what?

Again the problem is one of who's to blame. However, the purpose of the report card is to share information about how well learning is proceeding. This sharing is undertaken in the child's interest. When that learning isn't going well the concerned parties get upset. While the first reaction of both parties may be critical, this soon settles down to "what can we each do to repair the damage?" Then planning begins. For example, my work-finishing program is an instance where the parent, recognizing that the teacher has done all she can reasonably do to get the child to do his work, comes in to back-stop the teacher's expectation with some home input.

There is a need to have report cards. I think they should be realistic, up-front documents and parents and teachers need to learn not to get defensive about them. As with parent-teacher conferences, true communication won't occur so long as the parties dance around the hard facts instead of dealing with them.

Designing Behavioral Management Programs in the Classroom

This chapter on education was written to help parents understand what is needed to deal with adaptive problems which surface in the school. It was not intended to lay out programs for teachers to manage classroom behavior. However, the same principles of discipline that I have laid out for parents to use in designing their management strategies can be applied by teachers attempting to *require* difficult children wisely. Let me reiterate those principles.

The Principles of Discipline
1. The clear expectation
2. The time limit
3. The supervision
4. The reinforcer
5. Persistence for training instead of control

Here's a simple example chosen because it gives me a chance to cover all the bases. Let's say we are talking about a primary grade child who is moderately disruptive. Suppose he does four variously unacceptable things. He gets out of his seat, bothers his neighbor, 'borrows' stuff and calls out.

Now let's apply our principle of discipline. The first is to set a clear expectation. To do that we must first decide which if these four behaviors we are going to work on first. (If we try to work on all four at once we will be up to our elbows in punishment cards.) Suppose we select 'out of your seat' for our first project.

Now we define the expectation, which isn't really too hard. "Johnny," we say quietly after school. "I have a plan. I don't want you getting out of your seat anymore. Getting out of your seat means moving your trousers outside the circle made by this arm of your desk on the right and the aisle on the left." And you show him.

"Is it O.K. if my arms go out?" he may ask if he's a lively character.

"Just so long as they don't make contact with any thing or person," you, being ready for his smart-ass gambits, reply. "And here's the rest of the deal, Johnny. If you get out of the circle I'll come over and put you back. But that will cost you."

"Cost me? I got no money."

"You see this little book? This is my keep-score book. If I have to put you back in your seat, I will put a letter 'T' here on this page below your name."

"T?"

"For trousers where they shouldn't be. And when you get three 'T's' you get a punishment. (If I had punishment cards, I would say this instead. And I don't see why teachers shouldn't have a set of punishment cards for use in the classroom, but more of this later.)

Let's go back now and see where we are with respect to the principles of discipline. We set the clear expectation. What about the time limit? Because our goal is stay in his seat, and he is out before the program starts running we need immediate compliance. So the time limit is zero.* What about supervision? Well we return him to his seat, that's the supervision. But we punish. He gets a 'T' in the book, and when he gets three of those he gets a punishment. Maybe he loses his turn at the play table, or has to stay in after school. So we have complied with that principle also. Now we persist.

After nine 'T's' and three punishments we begin to notice it is taking longer for Johnny to accumulate his three 'T's'. Some of the time when his trousers lift from his seat, he, mindful of his 'T' accumulation, sets them down again. As he does this he gradually becomes increasingly aware of the present location of his trouser bottoms, and so he gets better at restraining himself. This is adaptive growth. Before long he rarely leaves his seat without permission.

But we have four problems we are concerned with. What do we do about the other three? While we are working on 'getting out of his seat', we just *control* the other problems but we do not *program* them. The teacher does this by saying, "I'll sure be glad when you . . . don't call out . . . leave other people's things alone . . . don't bother your neighbor," whichever is appropriate. Then she terminates the behavior. And that is all she does.

Until the trousers problem is solved. Then one day she sits Johnny down after school and says, "Johnny, I have a plan. I don't want you calling out the way you do. So, each time you do I am going to shush you, but then I am going to put a little 'C' here in my book. Right where I used to put the 'T's'.

"C for calling out," Johnny observes. He is a quick learner.

"And when you get three 'C's' guess what?"

"A punishment?"

---

*Time limits are useful because they give kids a chance to get better. But some behaviors, usually those involving *stopping* doing something, would be poorly served by a time limit. For example if Mother were to say, "you have three minutes to stop beating on your sister," she would be making a tactical disciplinary error.

"You guessed her, Chester."

Now we go through another training exercise, but because we have been over the ground once, it goes quicker this time. Soon we can move to item three.

By now another thing is beginning to show. Johnny seems to have a little better self-control, to be a little more respectful of his teacher's authority, and occasionally he even demonstrates a dawning awareness of other people's rights. His adaptive growth is proceeding.

What I have tried to illustrate here is how, using the principles of discipline, the teacher can design her own classroom management strategies.

The simple truth is, this is all I have to offer her. I am not a teacher. I have never tried to run an elementary school classroom. I know I couldn't. But I do have enough sense to stay out of the situation. The fact is I cannot tell teachers, chapter and verse, what to do. I am from another discipline.

Disciplines can and ought to talk to one another. And listen to one another. What I have to offer, from what I know of children, is an understanding of the psychological base upon which sound discipline has to be constructed, whether at home or in the classroom. The teacher, seeing things from the perspective of her discipline, will have to take what she can from this and use it in her own way.

Before closing this chapter on parents and the school I would like to say two more things about punishment. The first of these has to do with punishment cards.* I don't see why a teacher could not have a box of punishment cards to draw on when she needs them and so bring their advantages to bear on her disciplinary efforts. At the risk of getting in over my head, let me start a little list for her:

Punishment Cards
1. Lose library corner
2. Lose play table
3. Lose field trip
4. Lose recess
5. Stay after
6. A.N. Other
7. etc.
And don't forget the sweet lemon

The other thing I wanted to talk about is this. Quite often parents come to me with a teacher complaint. There is some classroom misbehavior that is not responding to the teacher's usual remedies.

*See Appendix A.

I suggest parents propose to the teachers that she zero in on the behavior with a 'keep-score' book. When the child earns three marks the teacher gives him a detention. And when he gets four marks Mother gets a call. Let the teacher explain the program to Charlie.

"Charlie," the agreeing teacher explains. "Your mother and I have made a deal. If you get three marks for bugging other kids, I'll give you a detention, and if you get four marks I give her a phone call, and when you get home, she'll give you one of your punishment cards."

"What if I get five marks?"

"Good question!" the teacher should reply with studied insouciance. "Why don't we just wait and see?"

The thing I like about this program is that it brings the teacher and the parent together in dealing with the child. This is the kind of home-school cooperation that best serves to promote the adaptive growth of children.

It is time now to leave the subject of children in school and talk about prevention.

Publications Related to Education by Dr. T.P. Millar

PROFESSIONAL ARTICLES

"Program Development in A School For Delinquent Boys," *Social Casework* (November 1960): 472-90.

"Reading Retardation," *Northwest Medicine* (November 1960) 1385-90.

"The Child Who Refuses to Attend School," *The American Journal of Psychiatry* (November 1961): 398-404.

"The School and the Mental Health of Children," *Northwest Medicine* (July 1962): 585-87.

"The School and the Mental Health of Children, Part II," *Northwest Medicine* (August 1962): 666-69.

"The School and the Mental Health of Children Part III," *Northwest Medicine* (September 1962): 758-61.

"Home-School Communication Concerning Nonadjusting Children," *Journal of the American Academy of Child Psychiatry* (April 1965): 320-24.

"Psychiatric Consultation With Classroom Teachers," *Journal of the American Academy of Child Psychiatry* (January 1966): 134-44.

"The Child Who Does Not Finish His Work," *Archives of General Psychiatry* (July 1967): 9-15.

"Schools Should Not Be Community Mental Health Centers," *American Journal of Psychiatry* (July 1968): Letters.

"When Parents Talk to Teachers, The Elementary School Journal (May 1969): 393-401.

"Some Observations Concerning Reading Retardation and Delinquency," *Connecticut Medicine* (July 1969): 457-63.

"Reading, Writing and Portnoy's Complaint," *Current Medical Dialogue* (July 1971): 580-94.

"A Physician's Guide to the Report Card," *British Columbia Medical Journal* (August 1978): 219-20.

"The Reluctant Learner," *Children Today* (September-October 1980): 13-15. (Reprinted various places.)

"School Phobia, An Alternative Hypothesis," *Annals of the Royal College of Physicians and Surgeons of Canada* (September 1983): 549-54.

NEWSPAPER AND MAGAZINE ARTICLES

"The Child Who Won't Try," *Parents* (February 1969).

"Schools Should Not be for Love and Therapy," *The Vancouver Sun* (7 September 1976): Page 6.

"Learning Disability, The Latest Cop-out Diagnosis," *The Vancouver Sun* (23 February 1980): Page 6.

"Values for Students," *The Vancouver Sun* (9 October 1980): Page 5A.

"The Crisis in Canadian Education," *The Vancouver Sun* (2 February 1981): Page 5A. (Reprinted various places.)

10

A Little Preventive Parenting

*"Ten thousand times I've done my best
and all's to do again."*

A.E. HOUSMAN, "YONDER SEE THE MORNING BLINK."

Introduction

The Omnipotent Child Syndrome is a particular pattern of failed adaptive growth. It is the result of training that for one reason or another has failed to promote adaptive growth during the pre-school years. This book found its beginnings in my effort to understand the syndrome as it was manifest in elementary school children and my attempt to find a way to remediate it. It was written to guide parents with children in such difficulty. While it traced the beginnings of the problem to the pre-school years it was not written as a manual for child rearing during this stage of growth.

However many parents and physicians saw it as such. Parents dealing with the normal omnipotence-devaluation phase in childhood sought to deal with their child by applying the primarily remedial methods I had described. But these were not written with four year olds in mind.

However things change. Physicians began sending pre-school children. In general child psychiatrists do not receive many referrals of pre-school children. The role of child-rearing consultant is not one many are privileged to fill. However, soon over fifty percent of my practice consisted of pre-school children. The opportunity to do prevention had arisen. I soon discovered prevention is a lot easier and more effective than remediation.

When mothers of three- and four-year-old children come to me for help, they do not bring full-fledged Deweys. To be sure these children are incipient Deweys, but impatience, omnipotent ways and egocentricity are normal characteristics of energetic toddlers. These children turned out to be lively toddlers, heavily involved in the normal process of omnipotence-devaluation. They may become Deweys if they do not make their way through this normal phase, and since the parents were confused about managing them, there was certainly a need for parent guidance.

In writing about these children, I am not dealing with a specific and already formed syndrome such as the Omnipotent Child Syndrome. I am dealing with all children in a specific phase of adaptive growth. Because of this I must broaden my canvas, begin at the beginning.

Children normally come into the omnipotence-devaluation phase of adaptive growth somewhere between eighteen months and two years. The "terrible two's" are a common sign that this phase is beginning. However, prior to this, important psychological growth has already taken place. Or ought to have. Sometimes it has not, which means the child is unready for omnipotence devaluation. It would be irresponsible of me to offer blanket guidance for this phase of development without first making sure parents understand how this readiness comes about.

When children enter the omnipotence-devaluation phase, two major pieces of development have already been accomplished. The *instinctual* infant as become an *emotional* creature. Secondly the child has become *attached* to its mother. These two changes render the child ready to begin the process of becoming a *rational* being, the first significant step of which involves omnipotence devaluation. So let me now review these developmental events and discuss, briefly, the picture when they go wrong.

Child Development: Birth to Attachment

When a mother brings her baby home from the hospital it is not as a stranger. For months Mother has lived many hours of every day conscious of the child within her. While the physical attachment of mother to child ends with birth, the mother's psychological attachment is not diminished. Indeed a kind of psychological union of the mother with her newborn tends to persist into late infancy. This maternal union serves to provide the vulnerable infant with a person in the world with the capacity to protect and nurture him, and bonded by love to do so. This is a crucial need of the newborn, and if it is not reasonably met, the psychological damage can be extensive and permanent.

In most cases the need is met. Indeed, for the first year of life nurturance is the major part of parenting. One does not discipline an infant; one serves it. To be sure, one does not have to pick up the infant every time he cries, but discipline as an essential ingredient of parenting is minimal in that first year.

This is not merely a matter of sentimental choice; it is a biological reality. That portion of the human brain which *learns* through discipline, the neocortex, is not yet functioning during infancy. Many essential pathways have not yet developed the coating of insulation necessary for them to begin conducting nerve impulses.

So it is that the newborn is not a rational creature. He is an innately regulated creature, an instinctive organism who cries when hungry, sleeps when sated, evacuates reflexly, and is more aware of pain, heat and cold than of sound and sight.

However, brain growth proceeds rapidly and soon the becoming child is ready for some reflex learning. Without necessarily realizing she is doing so Mother now begins that first *training*. "He's not an infant anymore," she reasons. "It won't kill him to wait while I heat the bottle."

It certainly won't kill him, but it will begin to train him. Here's how it works. When the mother responds to her baby's need, say hunger, she reinforces his awareness of that need. However when she delays satisfaction, as she now must from time to time, the child's attention is directed out of himself. He uses his distance senses to search the environment from whence the expected supply has yet to come. While satisfaction placates the inner, instinctual child, delayed satisfaction promotes outer attention and stimulates the child's awareness of the world about him.

Gradually the child comes to attend more to seeing and hearing and less to his inner sensations. The eyes and ears he has been given for this purpose now begin to play a large part in his waking life. As the child becomes increasingly capable of seeing, he finds there are classes of objects to see: his crib that is always there and doesn't move, his hand that is always there and moves when he wills it to do so, and that round-topped mobile object that isn't always present but always comes when he yells.

The perceptual capacity of the child soon increases to the point that he is capable of recognizing familiar objects. Furthermore, as the limbic system of his brain begins to function, he becomes capable of experiencing a range of emotions. These emotions are soon linked to his various sensory inputs. His cries contain these emotions, and mothers soon learn to distinguish between the cry of rage, the cry of distress, and the plea for company.

The child has become ready to realize what is perhaps the most crucial step in human psychological development, the capacity for attachment. Two developments have set the stage for this. First, the interaction of maternal care and perceptual maturation has brought him to the point that he can now *recognize* his mother as a constant in his environment. The functional activation of the limbic part of his brain has given him the capacity to experience *emotion*. These two developments render him capable of fashioning an emotionally significant bond to another person.

Most mothers are bonded to the infant from birth, but the infant has yet to acquire the capacity to bond. Given normal neurological maturation and reasonable care from an constant care-giver, this capacity will usually develop. A common sign that the infant is on this road is the phenomenon known as *making strange*. The child, now capable of recognizing and preferring his mother's face, reacts with tears and unpleasure to the approach of a stranger.

This first attachment is the relationship which opens the door to becoming human. However this emergent capacity has a down side; to be able to feel secure means one has also become able to feel insecure. So it that a normal concomitant of attachment is separation anxiety.

Separation anxiety, that is distress when the mother is not present, is normal in the life of the developing infant. There is no way to be human and not to feel such anxiety. The role of parenting is not to seek to avoid the unavoidable, but to protect the child from overwhelming degrees of separation anxiety at the same time as one allows him to experience manageable doses of the unpleasure and so become able to cope with it.

Separation anxiety in infant and toddler is not a sign that the child is being insufficiently nurtured. It is a positive sign, a sign of forming attachment.

The Pathology of Attachment

There is a pathology which results from a lack of nurturance in early childhood, a pathology which may be on the increase. We must explore that here, for when it exists the child is unable to grow into the omnipotence-devaluation phase normally. What happens to the child who experiences such inadequate nurturance during infancy that the capacity for attachment is not developed?

Not all mothers are capable of loving their infant. Some are physically sick, some too depressed to address the task, some schizophrenic, some too narcissistic to love anybody but themselves. The infants of such mothers may easily end without enough infantile nurturance to proceed to normal attachment.

Furthermore, these days in America, more and more infants are going to day care for their primary rearing. While such day care may provide enough nurturance for this growth, it may not. The emerging fact is some day care infants do not receive sufficient nurturance to ensure the development of normal attachment.

Then too, some infants have no mothers. Adopted children have been showing up in Canada who have spent an undetermined number of infancy months in some Vietnamese or Columbian infant hostel. There one or two women have been trying to spread their care over thirty cribs, sometimes with two or even three children in each. Despite the concern and good will of these women, these children, some of whose very birthdates are unknown, receive almost no individual care.

What happens to such children? In the worst case their neurological capacity for attachment, meeting no environmental activation and reinforcement from one-to-one nurturance, is not exercised. In time the capacity for attachment withers and is lost. Once this happens, no amount of remedial nurturance provided later will reawaken it.

Such children become psychopathic. These psychopathic children have some cardinal characteristics. They are indifferent to human relatedness. They lack the capacity for normal feeling. They have no social anxiety and no guilt, so they lie, steal and exploit others without feeling the justification of vengeance. While such persons may in time become perceptive of the psychology that drives others, this perception does not involve any feeling for these persons. The understanding of psychopaths is not informed by compassion. They simply accumulate such information because they have learned it may be useful to guide them to their exploitative ends.

Many professionals are reluctant to diagnose children as psychopathic. Some find the pathology so distasteful that they deny its existence or, if not its existence, the profound and permanent nature of the damage. Some prescribe intensive psychotherapy in the hope that this will cure the condition. It will not. Sometimes adoptions into loving homes are arranged. This can bring ruin to the lives of caring people who simply wanted a child to love and be loved by.

When these children were infants and the need for one-to-one nurturance arose within them, the environment did not respond. In time the unmet nurturant need became extinguished, and so these failed children wandered irretrievably from the path to human becoming. It is in this sense that the psychopath can be considered truly sub-human.

There are other children in devastating infancy situations who seem to have received enough nurturance for attachment and emotional need to develop, but not enough to satisfy that need and allow psychological growth to proceed normally.

These children do not display the cardinal characteristics of the psychopathic child. They have no moral understanding but they do attach.

Insatiable is the word I use for such children. They are so pervasively hungry for infantile gratification that, despite later love and care, there is simply no filling them up.

Their adoptive parents sometimes bring them to me and the picture they present is similar in certain particulars. As mentioned, they are insatiably greedy. They raid the fridge so incorrigibly that it is not unusual to hear that the parents have installed a padlock. They hoard food, under their beds and in their cupboards. They steal like magpies, collecting and hiding supplies of everything. They exploit other children shamelessly and rarely have any friends.

There is a peculiar behavior they sometimes demonstrate in my office. I call it searching. They simply must look behind every door, in every drawer, explore every cupboard. I am not sure what they are looking for, but I suspect is has something to do with the mother that was not there when they needed her to be.

Such children have grown past psychopathy. They have some capacity for attachment, enough to need and reach for human care. However, in their infancy they received too little nurturance to grow past infantile wanting. When age brings them to the training, or adaptive growth stage, they have little psychological energy left to apply to such learning. Soon their picture is complicated by immaturity laid on top of insatiable need. In a way such children are worse off than the psychopathic child for they themselves suffer, while with the psychopathic child and adult, it is those about him who suffer.

There is much to suggest that the population of psychopaths and psychological insatiables is on the increase. If so, is this a result of the progressive weakening of family rearing in America? Is this a generational problem? Could it be that Big Chill parents, still immersed in self, have brought too little to the nurturing of their children? (For more on this, see Appendix B.)

There is no remedy for true psychopathy.* The only answer for such sorrow and human wastage is prevention. The purpose in including a discussion of these matters here is to make it clear that while training is the principal parenting task during omnipotence devaluation, it takes adequate early nurturance to set the stage for this to begin. It is also to urge

---

*Because of his egocentrism the omnipotent child can look and act like a psychopath at times. He can be inconsiderate, exploitative and remorseless and people wonder, "has he no sense of guilt?" However even a brief history reveals that he is strongly attached. He is what Levy called an "indulged psychopath," who is not really a psychopath at all. The important point is that the omnipotent child, with training, can outgrow his amorality; the true psychopath cannot.

parents to make sure their infant receives adequate one-to-one nurturance during the crucial first eighteen months of life.

Fortunately most Canadian and American families still succeed in bringing their children into attachment and so making them ready for the adaptive growth to come. Their reward is the "terrible twos."

The Omnipotence-Devaluation Phase

Let me begin by reviewing the situation of the child when omnipotence devaluation begins. This has been discussed earlier but since it is particularly germane to what needs to be said now it will not hurt to recap things briefly.

Once the child has identified his mother as a separate individual and has developed an attachment to her, he is on the road to appreciating how dependent and vulnerable he is. The first time she does not obey as promptly as he thinks she ought, this unwelcome information comes to his attention.

"Wow," he thinks. "If she does not come when I call, who will feed and look after me?"

He has received a hint of his powerless condition and he rejects the input. "No way," he declares. "She *has* to come when I call, and I'll just prove it." He hollers! She comes! He has proven it.

She certainly isn't like his hand that comes the moment he summons it. But she comes! She is separate, perhaps, but still subject to his will. Now he begins to see her as separate, but now as his robot. Maybe not on a string but still subject to his magical control.

This, of course, is the omnipotence illusion. This is the essential, first position from which the infant begins the lifelong journey towards understanding the nature of power in the world. It is an illusion which serves to protect the infant from an appreciation of his totally dependent state when such understanding would be overwhelming to him.

The toddler still believes that his mother is his to command, partly because his need for security impels him to, but also because he is naive. When it comes to his bottle, he knows nothing of relevant factors such as cows and milkmen, stoves and mother love. All he knows is he yells, and she fetches, and that the sequence keeps happening.

About now mothers normally begin not to fetch so promptly as before. "It won't hurt him to wait a moment while I heat the bottle," they think.

"Where's the bottle?" her infant wonders. He yells louder. Soon Mother arrives. "That's more like it," he concedes, as that uneasy feeling settles in his breast.

What uneasy feeling? When he's older he'll recognize it as anxiety. For the moment let's call it the vague presentiment that his omnipotence might not be quite so absolute as he thought. He has received a hint of the truth of his situation, that he is wholly unable to fend for himself, that he is totally dependent upon his mother's care, which *she might just withhold if she chose to.*

But the second call fetches her, and the presentiment fades. Except that tomorrow it happens again. And again the next day. He begins to wonder if perhaps she is not his to command. This is bad news indeed. He needs her to fetch and carry! Then it occurs to him: "what if she doesn't come at all? Who will feed me? *Where is she?*"

So it that as omnipotence is challenged, separation anxiety, the consequence of attachment, is mobilized.

The normal two year old does not take this kind of thing lying down. He fights back. And this is what the *terrible twos* are all about.

Not every mother experiences a terrible twos with her toddler. Some children are so mild-tempered, and the situation so low key, that omnipotence devaluation proceeds without much ruffling of the surface waters. Sometimes, if it is her first child and she has nothing else to do but serve him, Mother continues to obey her child's orders: sometimes to the point that his omnipotence remains unchallenged. Hitler's mother was such a one.

However, in the usual case, around the age of two, the heretofore sunny child becomes provocative and demanding. "I don't want Wheaties, I want Corn Flakes." Then, when Mother brings Corn Flakes it's Rice Krispies he wants. Or back to Wheaties again. The point is there is no satisfying him because his agenda is to set up a battle-of-wills, win it, and preserve his tattered omnipotence illusion.

That may be his agenda, but it cannot be his parents' for his psychological growth depends upon surrendering the omnipotence illusion and learning to trust.

The sequence of events in lively, up-front children begins with a battle-of-wills and escalates to a temper tantrum if Mother does not defer to him. Dealt with properly the sequence is soon worked through. However, if not dealt with properly, the terrible twos can persist and become the terrible threes, fours, fives, forties, or fifties.

In Chapter Two I dealt with the the omnipotence-devaluation sequence at length, and there is no need to repeat that in detail here. Suffice it to say that battles-of-wills arise naturally and that some must be won by the mother if adaptive growth is to proceed.

These days I see many parents in difficulty with normal omnipotence devaluation. I see many three or four year olds who have their parents climbing the walls with their demanding ways. Temper tantrums, willful contrariness, refusal to go to bed at night are common symptoms with these lively children.

To my practiced eye it is clear we have an omnipotent child on the way if something isn't done soon. However, preventive intervention is much easier than repair work, and it often takes but a few visits to get things moving in the right direction.

Managing Difficult Omnipotence Devaluation: A Typical Case

"I don't know what happened," the young mother said. "He was an angel until he hit two."

"Comparatively speaking," her husband demurred.

"Well maybe he was a little lively," Mother agreed, "But there were no temper tantrums until last November. Remember when he threw his cereal and tried to kick me?"

Her husband remembered. And it had been the same since. Every time he couldn't get his own way Simon opened his mouth and turned up the decibels. They had tried spanking but that made him worse. They had tried putting him in his room; he screamed for an hour. They were expecting the child abuse people to knock on the door any minute. It had gotten so they were afraid to cross him and had begun to walk on eggs whenever he was on the scene.

"A funny thing," Father said. "He can go through one of his wing dings and twenty minutes later is happy and wants to play, while we're still jangled the rest of the day."

"Tell him about bedtime," Mother prompted.

"We have to lay down with him," Father said. "Otherwise it's six stories, three snacks, two trips to the bathroom and, if we protest, it's 'I'm scared. Lay down with me.' If we don't then it's a temper tantrum."

"The pediatrician told us to let him cry it out," Mother said.

"What happened?"

"He cried until he had absolutely exhausted himself," Father reported. "He was all red and sweating. I was really worried about him. And still he didn't go to sleep. We had to lay down with him."

"And you've been doing it nightly since?"

"He just won't go to sleep unless we're in there with him," Mother said. "And some mornings he absolutely refuses to go to play school. I've tried to drag him in. It's so embarrassing."

This is the typical picture, a hitherto amiable albeit lively and intense child who suddenly becomes willful and demanding and escalates to temper tantrums when he can't have his way. Sometimes the parents attribute the situation to some recent event, such as the death of a relative or the arrival of a new sibling, but unless the event involves a significant amount of separation from Mother—a hospitalization perhaps—the connection rarely pans out.

In almost all cases what we are dealing with here is the onset of the omnipotence-devaluation phase of adaptive growth. The child, beginning to sense that his power is limited, sets out to prove that this is not the case by setting up battles-of-wills. If the parents resist, he escalates to his bottom line, which is in most cases the temper tantrum. Because, despite his efforts to assure himself with demonstrations of power, the child senses his mother's independence of his will, he worries about whether she will be there for him when he needs her; separation anxiety develops. This is usually expressed during the day by clinging behavior or sudden refusals to separate to nursery school or the neighbor's. Night-time settling problems are frequently a part of this separation picture.

In order to help parents deal with their child I begin by explaining normal omnipotence devaluation to them and the necessity for mother to win some of the battles-of-wills that enable this growth.

If the child is to lose then the mother must win. However, the child's ultimate weapon in these struggles is his bottom line, the temper tantrum. So the first thing parents need to get Simon back on track is a way to deal with his temper tantrums. So, we begin with one program only, a temper tantrum control program.

In Chapter Two I detailed my temper tantrum control program and its rationalization. Here it is in summary.

Temper Tantrum Control Program
1. The Signal
2. The Silent Seven
3. The Removal
4. The Timing
5. Persistence

Let me review the important elements.

THE SIGNAL

Mother stands over the screaming child, points her finger at him and says, "you're having a temper tantrum." She points her finger because small children, like express trains on tracks, need simple signals if they are to grasp the essential information, and because the yelling child is often making so much noise he may not hear the accompanying word. The word doesn't have to be 'temper tantrum'. It could be 'fuss', or 'whoop de doo,' even 'splotch.' It doesn't matter so long as it always the same word.

THE SILENT SEVEN

Once the signal has been sent Mother crosses her arms, looks down at her child and counts to seven. Soon the child realizes that when Mother's arms are crossed some kind of a timing process is underway. The purpose of the silent seven is to give the child time to stop his tantrum before removal takes place.

THE REMOVAL

If, when Mother has finished her silent counting, the child is still crying, she escorts him to his room, puts him inside, locks the door ajar with a big hook and eye on her side, sets a timer down by the crack where he can see it, and retreats to the kitchen.

THE TIMING

Four minutes is the right length of time. Any longer and you can't repeat the program four times in a row if you need to, and destruction is liable to flower. When the dinger sounds, Mother unlatches and opens the door. "Your time is up" she announces, standing aside to avoid being trampled.

PERSISTENCE

Simon exits his bedroom still tantruming. Mother allows him ten seconds to get into position then gives him the Signal again. This is followed by the Silent Seven and the Removal for another four minutes.

After another Timing, she opens his door and we go through the whole sequence again. The fourth time Mother gives him the Signal and begins the Silent Seven, Simon stops hollering. "Migawd," he thinks, "she's on with the crossed arms bit again. I know where that leads." So he goes off muttering but he has stopped his tantrum.

Four times four minutes, plus four silent sevens, plus three ten-second get-into-position times adds up to sixteen minutes and fifty-eight seconds. Better than a hour screaming in his room! And he has had not one but four lessons. What's more, it worked. He eventually stopped his tantrum at his mother's behest.

Of course, an hour later he will go through the whole sequence again.

And the next day a couple of times. However, the second of these times he only goes through two complete sequences, eight minutes and twenty-four seconds of bedlam. The next day only one sequence is necessary. And sometimes he stops his tantrum during the first Silent Seven and doesn't have to go to his room at all. Soon all it takes is the word and crossed arms to stop the noise.

Now that Simon has stopped having temper tantrums, Mother is no longer fearful of crossing him. So she can set a few limits, win a few battles-of-wills. It is through losing battles-of-wills that the child navigates omnipotence devaluation. Soon Simon has made his peace with his childhood, discovered that while he is not the king he is a close friend of the king and is going to be all right. Furthermore, he has discovered that though his mother is free to leave him, she always comes back, and his separation anxiety diminishes. In most cases the night-time settling improves. Sometimes this requires a program too, but more of that later.

There is another, less common bottom-line some children escalate to. I call it the *terminal woebegones*. Instead of having a temper tantrum the child dissolves into pitiful sobbing that goes on, and on, and on.

The remedy is simple. One approaches the child, points a finger and gives her the Signal. "You are into the woebegones." The one crosses one's arms and begins the Silent Seven. In other words, the same program is slightly modified to suit the behavior in question. In time the signal terminates the woebegones just as it came to terminate Simon's tantrums.

Let me return now to the problem of Simon's night-time settling. Most children, as they make their way through omnipotence-devaluation, begin to experience less separation anxiety as trust of their mother develops. But some get into the habit of minimally traumatic night-time settling and won't settle for less than Mother laying down with them until they go to sleep, forever, and forever, and forever.

There are those who believe in the 'family bedroom' and would deal with this problem by moving his cot into their room. I think this is naive and growth avoidant, more liable to produce an adult who is agoraphobic than a coper with life. I do not recommend it.

When a child first comes to me with the twin symptoms of temper tantrums and night-time settling problems, I tell parents to forget trying to retrain his settling at night for a while, just to go along as they have been doing while we concentrate on his temper problem. When the tantrums have finished, the child has learned something about Mother's determination and night-time settling may be easier to manage. Also, since we have worked out his omnipotence devaluation to some extent, his separation anxiety will probably have reduced in intensity. In fact the problem may have solved itself.

But not always. What then is Mother to do with Simon if, despite his daytime improvement, he still will not settle for less than one parent lying on his bed with him until he goes to sleep? As it happens, I have a program for dealing with such problems. Here it is.

THE THREE YEAR OLD:
GOING TO BED AND STAYING THERE*

To begin with, let's understand that Simon shows no signs of *pathological* anxiety. He is not particularly tense. He has no nightmares. The only time he claims to be frightened is when he is required to go to bed without company. Though he may worry a little about the separation of bedtime, his anxiety is not of such magnitude that he cannot reasonably be required to cope with it. And since he will grow from doing so, the wise course for his parents is to find a way to put it on him.

"Simon," Mother says. "Here's the deal. I'm gonna help you into your P.J.s. Get you your snack. Take you to the bathroom. Read you one story. Leave your night light on and your door open. But I'm not laying down with you. What I will do is come back in fifteen minutes to check on you, but you are not to come out of your room. That's the deal."

The promise to return in fifteen minutes is an important ingredient of the program. The reason for this is that the child, lying in his bed, is probably experiencing some separation anxiety. Mild as this may be, it is harder to deal with if he thinks he is not going to see his mother again until morning. He may not be able to tough that notion out, but fifteen minutes is another matter entirely. What we are doing is lowering the psychological sights a little for him at the same time as we are raising our reality expectations.

What will the child do? One of two things. He will lay there and tough it out, perhaps calling out a couple of times but staying there, or he will appear on the parent's scene with an excuse. Though this is probably not the course Simon would follow, let's deal with the least of these situations first.

The child who stays in his bed, perhaps feeling a little anxious about where his mother is and concerned whether she will return as promised, is coping with a little anxiety. Coping with anxiety is like weight-lifting in that today's challenge becomes tomorrow's cinch. So he gets stronger. The first night Mother may have to go through two fifteen-minute returns. But,

---

*My paper with the same title was published in the *Journal of the Canadian Medical Association* 134 (January 1986).

each time Mother returns as promised, trust accumulates. The next night waiting is easier and the next night easier yet. In time the child's anxiety diminishes to the point that he gets drowsy waiting for her to come. And, when the program has been in place a while, Mother returns to find him asleep.

Now let's look at the other case. Simon is not going to stay in his bed for fifteen minutes. He is not going to stay in his bed for one minute. When Mother looks back, there he will be on her heels. What is she to do?

"Simon," she says as she 'escorts' him back to his room. "I said I would come back in fifteen minutes and to stay in your bed. I'm taking you back. If you come out again I shall have to latch your door."

Simon gets out of control and Mother has to latch his door. Mother should then set her timer for eight minutes; when the time is up, she should go into the room, pick him from the floor, comfort him, tuck him in again and repeat her spiel.

"Simon. I am going back out to the kitchen. I shall leave your door ajar and I will return in fifteen minutes. If you come out I shall bring you back, but then I will latch your door again." Then she kisses him and departs.

As with the temper tantrum control, the short period of confined time is preferable. It is more tolerable to both parent and child, can be repeated and so offers greater opportunity for training.

If Simon comes out again, the same sequence is repeated. However, if Mother has already proved herself with her daytime tantrum control system, Simon is more liable to believe he is not going to be able to bend the situation to his will. Regardless, Mother goes through as many eight-minute segments as she can stand. Even though she fails that first night, that is weakens and ends lying down with him, she has begun a process, and a couple of nights down the road she won't fail.

What happens now? Simon stays in his room with the door open until fifteen minutes later Mother comes as promised. Of course he may call out a few times but soon we are dealing with the lesser situation we discussed first.

One time soon Simon will boast to his mother, "I don't fuss at night anymore, do I, Mom?" Actually the victory is really Mother's for it takes real courage to cope with disciplining an up-front three year old. This kind of parental coping is what the naive sentimentalists find so unpalatable. They avoid the task by defining it as unnecessary. However, disciplining the child is as important a part of parenting as nurturing him, and the mother who comes up to the task deserves our earnest admiration and respect.

Disciplinary No Nos

There are two areas of pre-school child functioning that should never be used as adaptive training grounds. These are eating and bowel training. The child is in charge of both of these orifices and there is no way a parent can win a battle-of-wills on these playing fields.

EATING

Many parents come to me concerned about their child's eating habits. Usually they are worried that he is not eating enough. Though their family doctor has assured them that the child is staying on his normal growth gradient, they worry about his caloric intake. So they nag. And they demand: "you're not leaving the table until you've cleaned your plate"; or they get involved in some heavy actions like saving last night's dinner and threatening to keep serving it to him until he does eat it. Sometimes they even end spoon feeding a six year old.

All of this goes nowhere, and in some cases mealtimes become a horror story. It is very difficult to get such parents to back off. Some are merely stubborn. "If I go to the trouble to cook it for him, then he can damn well eat it." Most of them are just concerned. "He doesn't eat enough to keep a bird alive," they say about their robust toddler. I rarely scold parents, but when I do it is usually because I have tried everything to make them believe what I have learned from long experience. *If they leave the child alone at mealtimes, he will eat more than if they nag and bug him.*

By leave him alone I don't mean there should be no dinner table rules. What I mean is the rules are there and they won't change to suit him, but he will not be forced to conform to them. Civil disobedience at the dinner table will be tolerated so long as he is willing to accept the consequence.

What rules? How about "you have to come to table for supper, and stay there for twenty minutes. If you don't want to eat you don't have to, but you can't leave until the time is up." And, "I have given you small portions of the usual things. You don't have to finish them but if you don't you don't get dessert." "You get one glass of milk and one slice of bread." "If you dawdle, I'll set the timer when there's ten minutes left, and when the dinger goes, that's it until your usual bedtime snack."

These are reasonable rules, and if they are not harped upon, but calmly enforced, in time the child makes his peace with them. And, as I said, even if he doesn't get dessert, he'll probably eat more this way than if he is nagged. Furthermore, mealtime stops being the family shouting arena.

Despite the popular literature, anorexia and bulimia are uncommon conditions, but pre-school kids winning battles-of-wills about food are numerous as dandelions in spring. Since battles-of-wills are inevitable, why not choose to fight them on ground where you have a chance of winning?

THE BOWEL AS BATTLE GROUND

I see quite a few three year olds in the midst of omnipotence devaluation where the bowel has become the battle ground. Mother takes him to the potty. He smiles and produces nothing. Ten minutes later he does it in the corner of his bedroom.

She tries approving him. "Big boys do it in the potty." He is unimpressed. She tries threatening him, "You'd better or you'll be sorry." He shrugs. She tries reward. "If you do it in the potty for three days in a row, I'll buy you a toy." He doesn't do it one day in a row. She punishes him. "O.K. then. You miss Sesame Street tomorrow." Tomorrow he does it behind the T.V.

A major element of my training programs is making the expectation happen by supervising, and then punishing because you had to supervise. However, *you can't make a child have a bowel movement, much less make him have it when and where it suits you.*

It takes two to set up a battle-of-wills, and if you won't battle, then he simply has to take his omnipotence-proving agenda to some other arena. This is what I arrange to have happen when a mother of a pre-school child who is having such difficulties with bowel training comes to me.

Invariably these children are in the midst of an unresolved omnipotence-devaluation phase. Very often the mother has slipped into ineffective overcontrol, nagging until she can stand it no more, then standing right over him until she makes it happen or doing it for him. When such is going on children soon go past task avoidance into the *contrarys*. If she says black, he'll say white, and no is his favorite word.

What Mother needs to do with discipline is back off and make a new start. And not on a no-win issue like bowel control. I tell Mother, "forget the bowel for the next four weeks. Just clean him up, express the hope that he will eventually manage things better, and leave it at that."

However, he probably needs to have a battle-of-wills, for that's where he is in his adaptive growth. So Mother and I choose the best turf for that encounter to take place. By best turf I mean where the odds are in her favor. There are a variety of things going on in children's growth that are better battle grounds than bowel training; doing his share of getting dressed, perhaps, or picking up his toys.

Suppose this mother decides to work on getting him to come when called. She sets up a variant of my Second Telling Program (see Chapter Three). If he doesn't come on second telling he gets fetched, but that costs him. We don't use a chip jar because he's too young. We organize some simple punishments to use if necessary, maybe no story, no Sesame Street, or loss of a favorite toy for a morning. We arrange a tantrum control plan as a back-up in case we need it. Now we are ready for him.

Here's what happens. He doesn't come on second telling, Mother fetches him and gives him a consequence. He has a bowel movement under the dining room table. She clean him up and expresses the benign hope that one day he'll be past that sort of thing. The next time he doesn't come on second telling and Mother gives him a consequence, the same thing happens. The third time he gets fetched after a failed second telling, he has a temper tantrum and has to go to his room for four minutes. He may have a bowel movement there, which receives the same benign management.

Within a week the battle ground has become second telling, with occasional rounds played on the temper tantrum wicket. But no fusses about the bowel. This is because Mother declines to play on that pitch. The bowel is slowly becoming psychologically neutral the way it ought to be. Furthermore second telling is beginning to work, tantrums are becoming rare, and the mother-child climate is becoming sunnier.

In another week, the bowel problem may have solved itself. I have seen this happen, to the utter amazement of Mother, Grandmother and assorted relatives. If not, then a gentle return to encouraging expectation of toilet function, or mild disapproval will have an effect. If not, we stay neutral and start another training program about, perhaps, doing his share of getting dressed in the morning.

With pre-school children this kind of approach to hung-up bowel training works quickly and easily. However bowel problems can become chronic and there is a stool retention syndrome in the school-age child called encopresis which can be exceedingly difficult to treat.

ETCETERA

There are many little circumstances of early childhood which worry parents. For example, five year olds discover lying as naturally as they discover mud puddles. While the behavior has little moral content, the time to deal with it is right away. All that is required is a planned approach to detecting and disrewarding the behavior and it is nipped in the bud before it can become a moral problem. For such a program see my paper "What Cherry Tree?" in Appendix D.

Throughout this book a number of disciplinary programs are spelled out. Most of these were devised for school-age children and are not necessarily effective with the pre-school child. For example chips in the jar usually aren't immediate enough to communicate with the three year old, but some fours and most fives can figure out the system. Punishment cards are most effective with the elementary age child, but one woman of my acquaintance, a graphic artist, adapted them for use with her pre-schooler by painting tiny pictures of her Big Bird and Cabbage Patch toys and a story book and posting these on her fridge when the occasion arose. Many parents, once they have grasped the principles of discipline, tailor their own programs out of the materials of their household and so deal with the little problems that are the soil from which adaptive growth proceeds.

Planful firmness with children is the effective way to train them. With the pre-school child it takes but two or three weeks for an unacceptable behavior to disappear. Parents are sometimes amazed at how rapidly behavior changes when it is dealt with in a planful way. Even so, it is not possible to exaggerate the long-term benefit that accrues to the child from this early adaptive training.

The price to our society of massive adaptive growth failure has become increasingly clear in these declining decades of the twentieth century. In our last chapter I am going to take a hard look what this failure has meant for our culture. Those who wish may skip this chapter, but I cannot end without closing the circle in this fashion.

11

The Age of Passion Man

*"The heart never takes the place of the head,
but it can and should obey it."*

C.S. LEWIS, *THE ABOLITION OF MAN*

I began this book saying that many parents these days were dismayed that their child was growing to become a very different kind of person than they had intended or hoped him to be. I was referring, of course, to the Deweys, to the omnipotent children that have become so common these days.

In the course of this book I have made it clear that this outcome is by no means inevitable, that it can be prevented by wise parenting, parenting which not only nurtures the child but also disciplines him, parenting which leads his head to take precedence over his heart. However, in this Age of Passion when the notion that feelings should take precedence over reason is so widely espoused, it is swimming against a strong tide to seek to teach your child restraint, decorum, and the acceptance of rational authority.

The sad fact is, many parents are not successful in this aspect of parenting. Many a Dewey is not salvaged. What then becomes of him? He grows older, and bigger, in time assumes the physical stature of the adult human. But psychologically he remains immature. He becomes an "omnipotent" adult, the creature I call the Age of Passion Man. I chose this label because passion is as much the essence of life in this age as moderation characterized the Age of Reason.

The Age of Passion man believes his feelings are the best guide to action and regards reason as an inadequate instrument for coping with the pace of modern life. The Age of Passion man espouses a vague anti-intellectualism which makes him distrust learned men. He rejects restraint for he feels to deny an impulse expression is to deny his self. The Age of Passion man has little use for the forms of social order. He has a need to fly in the face of convention. With mindless charges of hypocrisy he expresses his contempt for a decorum he grants no license to interfere with his head-long pursuit of self-expression. The Age of Passion man insists on making his own rules and will not acknowledge the rational authority of society when the exercise of that authority interferes with his right to be wholly self-determining.

If one examines these characteristics in terms of the adaptive growth of the child the psychological core of the Age of Passion man is easily discerned. He is the omnipotent child become cultural prototype.

Too impulsive to wait for satisfaction, he has become an unrestrained hedonist, a pleasure-bound member of the 'now' generation who seeks instant gratification in violence, drug euphoria and promiscuity.

Too egocentric to read and accommodate to his fellow humans he has remained incapable of significant involvement with others. So he drifts from one shallow relationship to another, in and out of marriages and common-law relationships, making no commitments along the way. Too egocentric to mature beyond his weak *rules* morality, he behaves psychopathically, insensitively fulfilling his transient desires without recognition of, or regard for, the rights and needs of others.

Caught up in a continuing need to preserve his omnipotence illusion, he involves himself in mindless anti-authoritarianism and provocative defiance. Then, feeling the need, he latches onto some current guru, some Charles Manson or Reverend Moon. Rejecting religion, he embraces the mysticism of I Ching or Astrology. When one considers these contradictory actions their essence becomes clear: this human has made little or no progress on the road to accepting the realities of man's limited power to affect his own destiny.

Despite his arrogance the Age of Passion man has no real sense of worth, no feeling of dignity or manhood. Mostly he hides from this awareness, but moments come when he perceives this deep lack in self. Then he reacts with rage, striking at the society which deprived him of his humanity and taught him to hate himself. Surely this is the dynamic which underlies the modern vandal, the spectacular criminality of the terrorist, the senseless murders of assassins who choose their victims not for the magnitude of their political faults but for the extent of their fame.

The Age of Passion man reflects our times. He is the omnipotent child, floribunda.

Many persons have detected the growing presence of the Age of Passion man in our world. They have named him various names. They have ascribed his origin to different causes, but reading their accounts it is soon clear that all are talking about the same impulse-ridden hedonist, the same anti-authoritarian, semi-psychopathic personality we are here concerned with.

It was the poets and literary men who first drew attention to the presence of this new man among us. W.B. Yeats asked, "why are these strange souls born everywhere today?" In his classic little book, *The Abolition of Man,* C.S. Lewis warned us that, by our failure to teach the proper relationship between heart and head, we were creating "trousered apes... men without chests." Herman Hesse first perceived the relationship between this creature and his times when he created the Steppenwolf, his animal man, and described our condition thus: "There are times when a whole generation is caught between two ages... and thus loses the feeling for itself, for all morals, for being safe and innocent."

Many have written about the rise of this form of psychopathic individual during these last few decades. In his famous essay *The White Negro,* Norman Mailer estimates that "ten million Americans are more or less psychopathic." Christopher Lasch sees the Age of Passion man as a new form of narcissistic neurotic. Robert J. Lifton sees him as a new personality mutant, a later sequela of Hiroshima whom he calls Protean man.

It was Robert Lindner, a distinguished psychologist who devoted a great deal of his life to the study of psychopathic behavior, who put the matter in its true perspective. He says, "I am convinced the end stages of any civilization are marked by the appearance of a new breed of man. This man is always psychopathic, dedicated to action, violence rather than contemplation and compassion."

Lindner is right. The Age of Passion man is a harbinger of cultural decay. Because humanity is acquired in early childhood the Age of Passion man is a failed human. Children are born with the *capacity* to become human beings, but this potential must be nurtured in them else it will wither. Parenting is the matrix in which the child is guided to his human becoming, and in the declining phases of any culture, parenting loses its way, becomes ineffectual, and allows many persons to reach their adult years unreared, their humanity only partially realized.

Not everyone shares this point of view. Mailer for example, sees the psychopath as the hope of the world, as a kind of twentieth-century Indian scout who will open up some new cultural frontier. Lifton seemed to regard his Protean man as a progressive mutant rather than a degenerative phenomenon, but he presents little evidence to support such an optimistic view. Perhaps he is one of those who see man and his culture on a progressively rising curve. Such optimists seem unaware that greater cultures than ours have come and gone in the history of mankind. For such men change is always progress.

Perhaps some are just enamored of the Age of Passion man as cultural hero, for this he has become. Perversely labelled anti-hero, he has been celebrated in a thousand modern films, novels and plays. Dr. Michael Glen, writing in the *Village Voice,* put the James Bond phenomenon in focus when he said, "the hero of our age is the psychopath. Free from responsibility, free from anxiety, he pursues his interests without compunction, manipulating others to reach his goals."

The Age of Passion Man has become a common 'human' variant in these two decades. What does this say about the health of our civilization?

It took Pitirim Sorokin's great intellect to make it clear how the human acquisition of the capacity for moral behavior and the life and death of cultures are intimately linked one with another. In his monumental work, *Social and Cultural Dynamics,* Sorokin traced the rise and fall of cultures throughout the history of man. He perceived a pattern to their decline, a pattern whose phases he labelled "crisis, catharsis, charisma and resurrection."

In his 1932 study, Sorokin carefully delineated the four-hundred year decline of our culture from the Age of Reason to this present Age of Passion. In his final chapter, "The Twilight of Our Sensate Culture," Sorokin predicted the terminal phase our society would be going through. That was over forty years ago, and the passage of time has shown how chillingly prescient his description was.

Sorokin predicted, "values will become still more relative until they are devoid of any universal recognition and binding power. The boundary lines between the true and the false, the right and the wrong, the beautiful and the ugly... will be obliterated... until mental, moral, aesthetic and social anarchy reign supreme."

He went on to detail the process of disintegration. The "world's conscience will disappear," he said. "Contracts will lose their binding power—force and fraud will lead to wars, revolutions, revolts and brutality—freedom will become a myth for the majority and turn into unbridled licentiousness for the minority—governments will become fraudulent and unstable—the family will disintegrate—divorce and separation will increase until any profound difference between socially sanctioned marriage and illicit sex relationship will disappear—artistic creativity will decay into vulgarity—peace of mind and happiness will disappear—suicide, mental disease and crime will grow—and in this way will our sensate culture decline to bankruptcy and destruction."

All of these things have been happening at a steadily increasing pace ever since the end of World War II. The final crisis is very nearly upon us.

During these forty years parents have been bearing and raising children, performing their task as architects of the renewable society. Is it surprising that a "new breed" has emerged? Need we ask why these "strange souls" are among us?

The omnipotent child is a creature of cultural decline. He is a failed human. He has not experienced that steady environmental input necessary to develop crucial psychological competencies. So he remains unformed and deals with the world in the only way he can. Though he is essentially incompetent, he survives because the protective society tolerates and supports him and will until, like some virulent bacterium, he finally kills his nurturing host.

But there may still be hope. As Sorokin points out, other forces may come into play. In the widespread suffering that accompanies such societal crisis as ours sometimes a catharsis is experienced. From this catharsis emerge new St. Pauls and St. Augustines who, with their charisma, guide the world to a moral rebirth and set in motion a great new socializing impetus. So is man led into a new becoming.

There is now widespread recognition of the urgent need for this moral rebirth. The historian Christopher Dawson underlined the urgency of our situation when he said, "the recovery of moral control and the return of spiritual order have now become the indispensable conditions of human survival." Herman Kahn sees a counter reformation in the making, a movement for ideological renewal whose strivings are already detectable. Julian Huxley sees as large an opportunity for moral growth in our present crisis as a danger of human extinction. John Garcia, in his book *The Moral Society,* calls for the construction of the "ethical" state.

But it is Richard Means in his book *The Ethical Imperative* who opens up the heart of the matter. He speaks of man progressing from Homo Sapiens to Homo Ethicus, and suggests that in these latter centuries of cultural genesis and decay, man's fundamental nature has been evolving, that he has been moving toward a being more characterized by his moral than his cognitive capacity, by his ability to discern and choose the "good" than by his scientific accomplishments.

Perhaps it takes the crucible of cultural crisis to alter the alloy of man's nature. Perhaps these four centuries of cultural decay have been but a gathering wave sucking back the shallow water before breaking into a great new surge of becoming.

How can we as citizens and parents align ourselves with the direction of that change, go with the flow of that crucial becoming? Only by addressing ourselves to ensuring the moral growth of the child, concerning ourselves with such unfashionable notions as virtue and sin, can we play our part in the coming moral reformation.

Morality is born of the need for humans to live together in some kind of social harmony. Virtues are virtues because they promote that harmony, and sins are sins because they disrupt it. It is no coincidence that immorality and social anarchy go hand in hand, for morality is the cement that holds society together.

What then are these virtues we would promote, these sins we would prevent? The chief natural virtues are prudence, justice, temperance and fortitude. The seven deadly sins are pride, covetousness, lust, anger, gluttony, envy and sloth—deadly because they bar the way to man's spiritual becoming.

How can parents ensure that their children acquire these virtues? By promoting their adaptive growth. What is temperance but the control of appetite by the child learning to wait for satisfaction, stretching his tolerance for unpleasure in response to his parent's expectation or prohibition? What is fortitude but the same tolerance applied to situations of disappointment and discouragement? What is prudence but self-control combined with the capacity to appreciate the effects of one's actions on others? Is it not the core of justice to see another's human prerogatives as clearly as one sees one's own, coupled with the humility to accept that society has rights which sometimes take precedence over self?

The three adaptive competencies—tolerance for unpleasure, the capacity for social decentering, and the acceptance of rational authority—must be present in the individual if he is to behave in a moral fashion. If he has not these competencies, even though he has learned to perceive the good, he will not be able to choose it and sustain that choice.

Instead he will fall into moral error, into sin. Are not lust, anger, gluttony and sloth all clearly related to the inability to tolerate unpleasure, be it sexual tension, angry frustration, oral pleasure or duty? Does not pride, the false pride of hubris, arise because the adaptively incompetent individual has not constructed a sound sense of his own worth, has no true pride? Does the mature man need to covet another's possessions? Is he not armed by temperance and his sense of justice to rise above such error?

There is no way for man to acquire the moral capacity so essential to his species survival if his childhood does not equip him with the three adaptive competencies that have been our focus throughout this book. There is no way Homo Sapiens can progress to Homo Ethicus except that he tread this childhood path.

There seems little doubt we humans have lost our way in these latter years, but we can find it again. We have more than hope and fond expectation going for us. We have the obstetrics of culture on our side. For this is the way it happens, Sorokin tells us. Similar crisis in the history of man have regularly led to the replacement of sensate cultures such as our

waning one with cultures that are ideational or idealistic in nature, cultures based on consensual values such as "The Absolute, God, love, duty, sacrifice, grace and justice."

Robert Lindner underlined the importance of this generation's task when he said, "one of the highest missions a man of our culture can have is to identify the psychopathic antagonist, and struggle against the conditions which have produced him."

The omnipotent child is always with us. It is parenting which leads him to his humanity, so it is as parents we may yet salvage this sorely troubled world and, in time, construct a new society, one where the best man can be will flourish.

Appendix A

A Card a Day Keeps the Social Worker Away

This paper originally appeared in the B.C. Medical Journal 29, No. 11 (November 1987). Permission to republish it here is gratefully acknowledged.

The family physician is on the child-abuse firing line, but detection, important as it is, is not where the family physician's contribution is most needed. What parents need is help with discipline and effective ways to deal with the resisting child. Many parents say or do something they regret because they simply have no better idea how to approach the disciplinary task. The thorniest aspect of that task is punishing the child. What follows is the kind of guidance I offer to parents needing help with discipline, but such guidance doesn't require the skills of a child psychiatrist. If the family physician can take the time to offer such help, the benefit to children and their parents could be considerable.

The Nature of Discipline

Wouldn't it be wonderful if all one had to do was say to the child, "I wish you would, dear," and the reply would be, "sure thing, Mom, right away"?

However, most children, sometime or another, don't want to dress themselves, go to bed, clean their room, turn off the T.V., start their homework, come to supper now, or cope with one of the normal unpleasures of childhood. No! They procrastinate with "inna minute," argue like lawyers, or resist with passive techniques that would have done Gandhi proud.

If one nags, eventually the task gets done, but then the child never learns to do it without seven reminders. If one avoids nagging by setting a time limit, and the child doesn't make it, one ends by having to supervise. Unless one arranges to have it cost the child something, supervision then becomes a continuing ingredient of the task performance.

"Costing" means getting a consequence, which is nothing but a fancy way of saying punishment. These days, punishment has become a dirty word. This is partly because a lot of naive do-gooders who have never been in the child-rearing trenches think that simple approval can do the job by itself, and partly because people have confused the noun punishment with the adjective punitive. The former means a contrived consequence designed to disreward undesirable or unacceptable behavior. The latter denotes mean or cruel techniques of punishment.

Punishment is the fourth ingredient of discipline, the limit-setting process that promotes the adaptive growth of children. Here are the other ingredients:

A *clear expectation:* "I want you to get dressed, which means underwear, two socks, preferably matching, pants and belt, shirt on and buttoned, and I'll help you with your shoe laces when you get there."

A *time limit:* "You have fourteen minutes to do the job. I am setting your timer. When the dinger goes I'll be up. And don't fool with the handle because I have another timer on my stove and that's the one that counts."

A *supervision to completion:* If when you come up, "himself" isn't dressed, you supervise him through the job until it is complete, dressing him if necessary. Unless you are prepared to supervise forever, it is now necessary to punish the child.

None of these ingredients may be scamped if the discipline is to do its job. If you don't spell out the task in detail, he'll say, "I'm dressed," and you will say, "half-dressed," and away the argument goes. If you don't set a time limit, you'll have to nag, which drives everybody crazy and sometimes leads parents into saying or doing something they later regret. If you don't supervise, he'll be late for school. If you do supervise and it doesn't cost him, why shouldn't he just wait every morning until Mother or Father arrives to drive him over the bumpy course?

Fair, Effective Punishment

All roads lead to step four, that is, providing the contrived consequence that disrewards the unacceptable behavior—in this case, the need for supervision. There is no way to duck this most unpleasant of parenting duties. Don't be seduced by the silly notion of natural consequences, or letting life punish him. "If he doesn't brush his teeth he'll get cavities and that'll teach him." Too late it will. "If he doesn't get dressed on time, he'll be late for school and the teacher will punish him." What's natural about that consequence? That's just fobbing the role of heavy off on the teacher.

Since punishment is an essential ingredient of training children, parents need to learn all they can about its characteristics. Let's bring some of these into focus.

The best punishment, in my opinion, is the removal of a privilege, such as:

Lose half an hour prime-time T.V.
Lose bike privilege for one day.
Lose half an hour outside play time.
Lose Lego for one day.
Lose Transformers for one day.
Lose Cabbage Patch for one day.
No friend over this week.
No visit to friend's house this week.
Lose telephone privileges for one day.
No game with Mom or Dad today.
No story after supper.
Lose half on hour Saturday cartoons.

Each family will have its own special privilege activities suitable for use as punishments. Notice that none of these amounts to a serious deprivation, for the child's rights are not involved, only his or her privileges. These losses do not hurt the child; any imaginative child can find something else to do when T.V. or Lego is withdrawn.

Chances are he or she will tell you so. "As a matter of fact I wasn't planning to watch that T.V. show today." "I'm really getting kinda tired of bike riding." "Who wants to play old Lego anyway? I prefer reading comics." And he will get one and read it, laughing uproariously as he does so (within parental earshot, of course).

What's going on here? The parent is being given the 'sweet lemon,' the oldest ploy of childhood. "You're not bothering me, you know. That lemon doesn't taste sour. That lemon tastes sweet."

The hardest thing is to convince parents that punishment does not have to 'hurt' to be effective. Punishment derives its effect from its psychological impact, not its pain. What really bothers the child is the psychological statement punishment makes. Punishment says in a way words can't, "I am the parent and you are the child. I have the right and responsibility to set limits on your behavior, and you must accept those limits."

The immature child has not yet made peace with this reality but must eventually come to see his parents as his pair of caring adults, not equals; he must learn that the world is a place that can be trusted, and childhood a protected state. When the child gives you the sweet lemon he or she is clinging to the illusion of omnipotence, trying to deny this encroaching reality.

The best answer to the sweet lemon is simply to say, "well, if you *were* going to watch T.V. (or whatever) you wouldn't be allowed to," and leave it at that. Soon the sweet lemon will stop working and the child will abandon it, moving oftimes to a statement of protest rather than denial. "That's not fair! That's my very favorite show. All kids got a right to T.V. I'm calling the child abuse line."

So far we have learned four things about punishment:

There are ways to punish that are not punitive.
Punishment does not have to 'hurt' to be effective.
Punishment communicates the message, "I am the parent. You are the child. I have the right and responsibility to set limits for you."
The sweet lemon seeks to deny this reality but is really an indication the message is being received, even if not yet accepted.

Since parents *are* going to have to punish the child as part of his adaptive training, it is a good idea to be ready to do so. If you aren't prepared it is easy to overshoot the mark, like taking away T.V. for a week and then having to recant, or to let the punishment go because you're just too tired to think of anything right now and later on you forget about it. What does that teach the child?

One must be prepared to punish when the necessity arises. The best way to do this is to make out punishment cards. Mother and Father sit down and review the child's privilege activities. They write down the items on little cards, much like the list above. They'll end with ten or twelve cards that they put in a box on top of the fridge.

Though most children, who are terrible realists, won't believe it until it has happened a few times, it's not a bad idea to tell them about the system. "See these. These are your punishment cards. If you earn a punishment for something you did or didn't do, I will choose one of these cards and post it on the fridge where it will stay until the punishment is served, and then it will go back in the box for future use."

"Punish for what?"

"Well, dressing for one thing. If you don't make it by your time limit and I have to supervise, it will cost you one of these cards. Maybe rudeness for another. I'll let you know which things will earn you cards."

"Cards on the fridge! Big deal!"

Pay no attention. He'll find out.

Now, when some situation arises such that he deserves a punishment, say he didn't get dressed within the time limit and you had to supervise, you simply say, "you'll get a card."

"Which one?"

"I'll post it when I get around to it. Watch the fridge for coming attractions."

Cards relieve the parent of the necessity to think up a punishment at the troubled moment when anger might lead one to overpunish. This takes the urgency and frustration out of giving the child a deserved consequence, so it's easier to keep one's cool and not utter a lot of nasties.

In time the cards come to "stand for" the punishment and initiate the psychological communication themselves. Soon one finds the child protesting the card when it is announced, even though not yet chosen and posted, more than he later protests the punishment when it is served. And here's a bonus: punishment cards almost never generate the sweet lemon response.

Another advantage is that for little children of five, six, and seven, cards are a lot more real than words. "You'll get a punishment" is vague; "you'll get a card from your box" initiates a sequence the child soon comes to understand and believe in.

Programming a routine like getting dressed in the morning is easy with a box of cards from which to select a consequence if the child doesn't make it on time without supervision. Once this, the heaviest aspect of discipline, is organized, the process becomes a piece of cake.

Punishment Versus Reward

Some people ask, "why not reward instead of punish?" For several reasons, the most important of which is that reward does not communicate what needs to be communicated. Reward does not say, "I am the parent and you are the child. I have the right and responsibility to set limits for you." Reward says, "I wish you would do this and if you do I shall give you something." This message does not clarify the difference between parents and children and does not lead the child to a comfortable surrendering of the illusion of omnipotence and acceptance of his or her childhood.

Furthermore, reward tends to be ineffective. It speaks in a soft voice that children often do not hear. When the parent faces the child with some new expectation he or she will likely hear from the child, "If I do what you want, what will you give me?" Eventually it dawns on even the most solicitous of parents that maybe they shouldn't be rewarding the child for doing something every other child on the block does as a matter of course.

Reward is sometimes sufficient to train the child, but most children will require programmed expectations reinforced by punishments to lead them through some parts of their growing up.

Punishment and Child Abuse

There is much concern these days that parents are becoming more punitive with children, and there are those who would prescribe disciplinary limits for parents. Seeking to outlaw spanking is not going to solve the problem. What parents need is real help with the thorny task of discipline, not magazines filled with terrifying articles about rampant child abuse or sloppy sentiment about 'love' being all good parents need provide to promote the adaptive growth of children. Certainly, true abuse must be vigorously uncovered and children protected, but the current hysteria has done serious damage to normal child discipline. For example, how many children these days have learned to threaten their parent with the "Help" line? I wish some social worker would release statistics on what percentage of help line calls arise from trivial situations. Their subsequent effect on family life is not trivial.

Behaving to Please

Wouldn't it be wonderful if all children responded to parental requests with, "sure thing, Mom" and bustled off intent on pleasing their parent? How much more pleasant parenting becomes when the child behaves not to avoid a consequence, but to please the parent.

Most children eventually get there, but it is discipline that fuels that journey. Until the child has accepted childhood, received and become comfortable with the disciplinary message, "I am your parent; I have the right and responsibility to set limits for you," he or she will not come to trust. The child who has learned to trust is the child who, in time, wants to please. Not until this has happened can parents throw away their box of punishment cards.

Appendix B

The Big Chill: A Review

This motion picture review was first published in *The Medical Post*, December 27, 1983. Permission to republish it here is gratefully acknowledged.

If there was one thing the college revolutionaries of the '60s were good at, it was dramatizing their existential despair. Remember the march on Washington when each of them carried an accusatory card bearing the name of a Vietnam casualty? Remember when Columbia University planned to build a gym on a site of which they disapproved, so they occupied the dean's office, smoked his cigars and burned his files? Remember how they would set up "nonnegotiable demands," bait the police, call them pigs and hog the TV cameras? But what I remember most is their rallying cry, "Never trust anyone over 30."

Well, it's twenty years later and they are over 30. The question arises, what has life done to them; have they changed? Mellowed? Matured? Now that they are over 30 do they trust themselves?

A movie has appeared addressing itself to the question, what have the years done to the '60s revolutionaries? The movie is called *The Big Chill*.

Death, for which "The Big Chill" is a dramatic euphemism, has claimed one of the members of a '60s group from the University of Michigan. Now the others have assembled from across the nation to attend the suicide's funeral. As the story develops it becomes clear few of them have had any contact with him for five years, and none has any idea why he committed suicide. So why do they come? Because, it would seem, they have felt the big chill. "The Big Chill" now refers not only to the corpse's condition but also to the pericardial coldness the survivors feel as intimations of mortality knock at the door of their awareness.

The seven of them, plus the girl friend of the man who committed suicide, spend a weekend together. They raise eyebrows at the girl friend's superficial response to her loss, then go on to demonstrate their own. En passant, four of them renew old sexual acquaintance. When they are not assuring each how much they love the other, they are jiving to rock music, conducting self-interviews on a TV monitor, smoking pot or popping pills. They are still cool, it would appear.

The '60s youth have been commented upon by many observers of society. Three particular qualities have been commonly noted in them.

The first was their impulsive desire for immediate satisfaction, a quality that earned them the label the 'now' generation.

The second was their immersion in self, the egocentricity that caused them to become known as the 'me' generation.

The third was their spectacular need to become involved in protest against constituted authority.

The 'now' quality was expressed in their immediacy, their inability to wait, to tolerate even a brief hiatus between the desire and its gratification. The quick fix was their bag, whether that meant sex with strangers, a high from pot, pills, or acid, or gleeful vandalism.

Patience, the ability to postpone pleasure, is an acquired capacity, trained into children by parents as they begin to expect things of them. It is discipline that gives children the strength to wait. These youths had not received the discipline they needed, so they grew up expecting life to be constantly pleasurable and felt cheated when it proved not to be. 'Boring' was their ultimate condemnation.

How have the passing years affected this 'now' quality? In the movie they squabble over trivia, flare up and fight with one another. Although some admit they can't handle being stoned as well as they once could they still go for the instant fix with pot and pills. In their behavior, excess is still more evident than restraint, uncensored expression still more prevalent than tact in their social intercourse. Perhaps they no longer let it "all" hang out, but they are still letting ninety percent of it blow in the wind.

Time called these kids the 'me' generation, commenting on their self-centered lives and their inability to recognize and accommodate to the needs of others. I perceive this as egocentricity, a self-immersed state of being normal for the four year old who truly believes the sun gets up when he does, follows him around all day, and goes to bed when he does. But soon he is not four any more and his parents refuse to continue organizing life around his expectations. So do they teach him that he is not the sun but one of the rotating planets. Slowly he gives up his egocentricity for an awareness of the rights and desires of others, and he develops a willingness to accommodate.

Not so the Big Chill generation. The '60s revolutionaries had remained as egocentric as four year olds. Their idea of free speech was "me having my say while you listen," then "me shouting you down when you try to feed us that establishment garbage." Their idea of justice was getting what they perceived to be their fair share, but they were unable to see when fairness to them would involve unfairness to others, and that justice would imply some accommodation from both parties. Because they heard only themselves, there was no way to hold a dialogue with them. Indeed, in their relationships to one another there was more talking than listening, little real awareness and accommodation one to another.

Has this changed in twenty years? In the movie the lady lawyer tells that she has been dating men for these twenty years. Now, she tells us that within fifteen minutes she is able to see exactly how "this guy" is going to turn out. Can it be that all men in the world are shallow, or is it possible this lady still lacks some capacity to perceive the internal reality of others?

And this same lady, since all men fail her fifteen-minute test, has concluded she'll never marry and has decided to become a bachelor mother. She wants one of the old gang to lend her the semen, and deliver it of course. It seems not to occur to her, or the other women present, that she is sentencing an unborn child to a family without a father, or indeed that some men might consider that they had a vested interest in the offspring too.

It seems to me her charter membership in the 'me' generation isn't about to lapse.

Another instance. One of the women is married to a man she chose because he was stable and would make a good father and good provider, and he has done so. He accompanies her to the funeral, and the others meet him. Without so much as two words exchanged with the man, they conclude he is a square, and when they encounter him in the kitchen late at night, and he confesses to chronic insomnia and a little unhappiness, they show no sign of hearing or caring. Later, after he has left, his wife sets up a sexual liaison with one of the old gang. Discussing her husband, she labels his fidelity a "fear of herpes." And the film leaves us with these shallow judgments. Sounds a whole lot like '60s 'me' stuff, doesn't it?

And listen to them talk. A lot of wry one-liners but little communication. True, they sometimes laugh at themselves, at their little foibles, but they laugh at the warts and seem not to recognize they have no chests. One says something like this: "We're all alone out there, and when this weekend's over, we'll have to go back out there." My impression is that no matter where that particular man places himself, he'll always be all alone, for he's imprisoned in his own egocentricity. If he ever figures that out, maybe his suicide will afford the occasion for the next get together.

The '60s kids were omnipotent. The clarion call of many a five year old is, "you're not the boss of me, I don't have to do what you say." But with reasonable training he makes his peace with the authority of his parents. Not so the '60s crowd. The phrase remained their battle cry, the litany that gave oppositional significance to their rudderless lives. That they were caught up in this struggle was everywhere apparent as they flew in the face of their parents' expectations and standards. The issue was spelled out by one of their peer gurus who exhorted them to "kill their parents!"

So they ignored the social decencies, defied the dean and the police, made demands and, when these were met, escalated them because they were more concerned to battle authority than change the world.

In my terms they were struggling to retain the omnipotence illusion normal to infancy. Because they had been uncertainly disciplined, they managed to evade this aspect of adaptive growth and the need to control the world to feel safe in it dominated their striving.

Have these '60s revolutionaries, revisited twenty years later, given up their omnipotence? "Since when did you become a friend of the police?" one snaps at the other when he becomes involved in a scrape with the law. Plainly he still sees our finest as his enemies.

The hostess, hassling with her young daughter on the telephone, finally declares, "do it because I tell you to." As she hangs up she apologizes to her listening friend: "I never thought I would end up saying things like that."

Why is she apologizing? It is part of a parent's duty to make the rules, and you can't get into endless explanations on the telephone. Indeed, in lots of situations you can't explain and you shouldn't argue. So one ends up saying, "do it because I tell you to." It is an inevitable phrase in any parent's vocabulary.

While this mother is still uncomfortable exercising her own reasonable authority, she is miles ahead of many '60s revolutionaries turned parent. Many just abdicate their responsibility to discipline their children and see some kind of anti-authoritarian virtue in so doing.

These weekending Bill Chillies mildly deplore how they have abandoned the altruistic values they held in college. The lady lawyer, who was going to defend the poor, has defected to the rich. "But," she offers, "the poor were such crooks." The host is about to become a millionaire. A major company is about to take over his business. Although stock exchange rules strictly forbid that he tell anybody of the pending deal, he tells some of his revisiting buddies so they can buy stock and become rich. It isn't just the wealth he is trying to distribute; it is the vague guilt he feels over sell-ing out that he'd like to assuage. The crusading college journalist has become an opportunistic muck raker, but he doesn't seem to be particularly disturbed about it. One man only seems to have remained true to his professional ideals: he is still a drug dealer, and he drives a Porsche.

These film characters are models of a tragic generation. Of course they feel a chill when a member of their group commits suicide, but it is a concern for self, not for the other, that generates the ominous shiver.

We might ask ourselves why did their brother commit suicide? Could it be that, in a dark moment, he caught a glimpse of self and perceived his psychological crippledom? Could it be that he looked down the bleak corridor of his blighted humanity and decided to terminate the adventure? Perhaps the others have come close to similar glimpses of self. Perhaps they too have felt vague intention such as that he exercised?

Whatever his motive, for the group one of their members has died. Why should this be so upsetting? Remember this is the group that marched on Washington carrying those names of war dead. Is it possible they could do this and not really perceive the reality of death? What about all those laments about living in the shadow of the atomic bomb? Was that just self-dramatization, a modern version of that old Harvard student song, "we are poor little lambs who have lost their way?" Can it be that this is the first time the big chill has really touched their awareness? Like wow, man! Suddenly death is real; it truly happens.

Can it be that for the first time they have perceived the ultimate disillusionment of omnipotence, and it chills them?

The Big Chill is a good movie. The characters seems very real to me. There are a whole lot of such persons around. Their condition is a sad state of being. They deserve our kind concern. But we mustn't forget what they are, and we musn't expect too much of them, for when the crunch comes, they won't be there.

The motto they authored for the '60s has taken an ironic twist. It has become "Never Trust Anyone Nearing 40."

Appendix C

The Trousered Ape Goes to Hollywood

Modern movies and plays reflect our times, and nowhere are the trends that signal the decay of our civilization more evident than on our screen and stage. Here is a review of the movie which was voted best picture of 1975, an accolade which surely tells us something of how deeply corrupt we have become.

One Flew Over the Cuckoo's Nest is a movie that celebrates the psychopath as the man of our times in the person of J. Patrick MacMurphy, a man with six convictions: five for assaultive behavior, the sixth for statutory rape. MacMurphy is escaping the rigors of the work farm by playing crazy. He has conned his way into a mental hospital. Once he gets on the ward and sizes up the situation, it's "us" against "them," the "kids" against the "teacher."

Before it is over, the picture manages to suggest that patients are not in the mental hospital because they are sick, but they are sick because they are in the mental hospital. It demonstrates that the doctors are foolish, the ward attendants venal or sadistic, and the nurses petty tyrants. It mocks all forms of treatment. Group discussions and drugs are silly. Shock treatment and lobotomy are portrayed as vengeful attacks on uncooperative patients.

It also manages to suggest that all these pitifully overwhelmed souls need is a few more psychopaths like MacMurphy to teach them how to "bird dog chicks" and trap "beaver" and they will be restored to mental health.

What makes this film worth reviewing is its classic anti-authoritarian formula. It is as blunt an advocacy of disobedience to institutional authority as I have ever seen.

This is the source of its appeal. Everyone who has ever felt oppressed by an arrogant policeman, a picayune civil servant, or a disapproving librarian will get a vicarious tingle from J. Patrick MacMurphy's fearless disdain for Head Nurse Ratchett. It isn't until this disdain erupts in violence that one appreciates how deeply uncivilized a man J. Patrick MacMurphy really is.

Anti-authoritarianism is the solvent that may yet dissolve this fragile civilization. While Hollywood has been re-exporting it for years, it was originally a European creation that fermented throughout the middle eighteenth century.

While political anti-authoritarianism arose as a reaction to the despotic authority of Europe's kings, it first surfaced in the New World when the Americans thumbed their nose at George III. From that moment it became a cherished part of the American birthright. A scant decade later it claimed its first European victory in the French Revolution, when Louis XVI was dethroned. Since then the pendulum has continued its inexorable swing to the point that thoughtful people have begun to ask themselves if individualism is not as capable of excess as monarchy ever was.

Religious anti-authoritarianism began as a reaction to the despotic authority of a centralized church. It dethroned that authority handily. Who could imagine that it would begin by freeing the individual to worship by his own lights and end by dethroning God?

Anti-authoritarianism in literature began as a reaction to the classical view of man, a view that enthroned reason, stifled imagination and restrained emotion. The romantics declared war on this conception and asserted that emotion was the truest and most authentic guide to action. Rousseau expanded upon this revolutionary theme with his concept of the Noble Savage, the notion that primitive man guided by instinct was both nobler and wiser than civilized man. Kierkegaard, the father of existential thought, administered the *coup de grâce* to reason when he declared, "the conclusions of passion are the only reliable ones."

If these seem academic concerns, let me assure you they are not, for they have given birth to the model upon which present hedonism is founded, the anti-hero, the amoral man who seeks authenticity by denying expression to no impulse, however asocial. So it is that today sadism and pornography dominate popular art.

J. Patrick MacMurphy is the perfect anti-hero. He is without manners, except when he is mocking the decency they reflect. He is graceless, unshaven, sloppy. He lurches, slouches, scratches and leers lasciviously. He exults in his animalism while denying that anyone is better than he. He cheats, cons, manipulates and exploits his fellow patients as well as the staff. He is incapable of understanding that others, more imaginative and sensitive than he, might find life overwhelming. That some of these are voluntary patients is beyond his comprehension. When the mute Indian finally speaks, J. Patrick MacMurphy concludes, gleefully, that that 'noble' savage has been conning the staff all these years.

J. Patrick MacMurphy is a twentieth-century vandal. Shut off from truth and beauty by his truncated soul, he can only lash out at a society he can barely comprehend, let alone join. He is, to use C.S. Lewis's felicitous phrase, a "trousered ape."

In a thousand films Hollywood has extolled the mannerless lout with a heart of gold. They have created a monster. In seeking to con us, they have finally conned themselves. J. Patrick MacMurphy has taken charge. How else could *One Flew Over the Cuckoo's Nest* be voted Best Picture of 1975!

Appendix D

What Cherry Tree?

This article was first published in *Children Today* (November-December 1985). Permission to republish it here is gratefully acknowledged.

"Guess what, Mom," five-year-old Johnny whoops as he bustles in from kindergarten. "Miss Fraser put two of my colorings up on the wall."

"Wow!" Mom says, and wow she means, the way he colors.

The fact is, Miss Fraser did no such thing. Jennifer's two colorings were put on the wall, and ambling home it occurred to him how pleased his mother would be if those had been his. So? Simple! He made them his.

Mom gives him a popsicle instead of an apple for a snack, and he begins to realize what a gold mine he has stumbled upon. Soon some freshly fabricated triumph is reported every day.

Four- and five-year-old children discover lying as naturally as they discover mud puddles. Heretofore it never occurred to them not to tell Mother the truth when she asks where he got that little car, or why he wasn't at the playground where he was supposed to be. But one inspired day it crosses his mind to tell Mother something different from what really happened. Lo and behold! It works. Johnny doesn't fall into the soup as usual!

Like Columbus discovering America, he realizes he has stumbled onto a whole new dimension of social function. It isn't necessary when interrogated to recite what happened; he has an option. He can invent a something, and it isn't long before he discovers that the something he created may serve not only to keep him out of the soup but can also embroider his day in exciting and parent-pleasing ways.

Soon he finds ways to extend the practice. "Mom," he calls, "Mrs. Reynolds asked if I could come over and play with Jeff this afternoon. Is it O.K.?"

Twenty minutes later he is on the Reynolds' doorstep. "My mom's got a headache. She wants to know if I can stay at your house this afternoon and play with Jeff."

Plausible he may be, but he lacks foresight. It does not occur to him that Mrs. Reynolds may inquire about Mother's headache next time she runs into her shopping.

The point is, sooner or later Mother finds out she been had, and the knowledge distresses her. After all, she is trying to raise a decent human being, not a liar—a George Washington who owns up, not a Benedict Arnold who innocently intones, "what cherry tree?"

So she applies her usual remedy for unacceptable behavior, which I am sure, works in many cases. When it doesn't is when I may enter the picture.

First, one must determine that the lying is not part of a larger picture of trouble. Most often it's just one of those pitfalls of growing up which, properly handled, will quickly come under control. Here, then, is my program for getting nascent prevaricators back on track.

Step One: Catch Him

To train a child not to choose a lie over truth, we have to derogate that choice. To do this, we have to catch him or her making it. So the first thing is to develop a high index of suspicion. Don't take his word for things. Ask him "now did that really happen? Did Mrs. Reynolds really ask you over to play?"

Don't fall for that woebegone "you don't trust me. Your very own son!" Of course you don't. Trust isn't something you turn on or off at will. And if you're going to trust him again, he'll first have to prove to be telling the truth on several consecutive occasions. You can try explaining that to him if you want, but you'll probably be wasting your breath, and you may also run a serious risk of being out-lawyered. Best let your actions speak for you.

The second half of catching him is checking up on him. And let him know you're going to do it. "I think I'll just check with Mrs. Reynolds." If he gives you an "actually, I think their phone is broken," you're dealing with a bright one, so you'd better be bright yourself. Do check on him, and if he proves not to be telling the truth, implement step two.

Step Two: Keep Score

Suppose you catch him or her lying. You need now to take some action to penalize the behavior—in psychological terms to devalue and retribute it. This is a lot easier to do than many parents think. Here's an effective method.

Get a small jar and some chips. Anything will do: buttons, tokens, pieces of Lego. Label the jar the LIE JAR. Show it to him and explain your program in these terms.

"Johnny. You see this? This is your LIE JAR. Every time you tell me a lie, that is, something not the way it really happened, I am going to ask you if that's the truth. If you say it is, I am going to check up, and if it turns out you were lying, I'm going to put a chip in your jar. When you get three chips in the jar, you are going to get a punishment. Then I will take those three chips out of the jar, and we'll start over. And that's the way it is going to be, until when I ask you if that's the truth, you own up. If you do, no chip. If you don't, I'll find out, and you'll get your chip."

Responses vary, from "good idea, Mom!" through "chips in a jar," enunciated with oceans of contempt, to a cagey, "what's the punishment going to be?"

It doesn't have to be a jar. One parent I know posted a picture of Pinocchio on the refrigerator. She made a movable nose that lengthened by a third with each lie. Another used magnetic letters on the refrigerator—L.I.E.—and when the word was spelled out, guess what?

Chips in a jar is simply a way to substitute a "now" symbol for a "later" punishment. Also, it avoids excessive punishment when the behavior is minor and its occurrence frequent. Furthermore, it works. Soon children are much more indignant over receiving a chip than they ever were about losing half an hour of T.V.

Step Three: Punish

By this I do not mean beat the child, but why use some silly euphemism to hide from the fact that an inevitable part of parenting is to disapprove behavior in action terms? An essential ingredient of "molding, strengthening and perfecting the child" is applying negative consequences when those are necessary.

Nor is this the place to debate punishment versus reward in training children. Suffice it to say here that one should not reward normal behavior, except in the natural way of being pleased with it, and reward is a weak device for retraining unacceptable behavior such as we are talking about here.

So one punishes the child for lying, saying something like this: "if you get three chips in your LIE JAR, you will miss half an hour of your prime time television." Or "no bike after school this afternoon"; "you lose half an hour outside playtime"; or "you can't have a friend over this afternoon."

One penalizes a child by taking from him or her a moderate amount of some privilege. But remember, the thing that hurts about punishment is not the loss of some T.V. or playtime; any imaginative kid can take that in his stride. ("I don't care. I wasn't planning to watch T.V.") No, what bothers kids is that you had the nerve to punish.

Step Four: Persist

It will take three full jars and three punishments served before the child really believes you are going to persist with your "chip nonsense." When he does, this is what usually happens. He tells you something that arouses your suspicion, so you go into your spiel: "Is that the truth?"

"Actually," he says, digging a hole in the rug with his toe, "that's not quite the way it happened." Or, as improvement proceeds, "Gee, Mom, don't you know when I'm kidding?"

Finally, we see him open his mouth, then change his mind about reporting the item burbling around his imagination, or else he reports it in "I wish" terms, rather than as fact. He has discovered the imperative nature of truth. He may never become President, but the neighborhood cherry trees are now a little safer for his growing up. Which is a beginning.

Index